CAMPFIRES

A NOVEL

DC RIVERA

RUNNING WILD

CONTENT WARNING

Campfires is a new adult/dark drama novel set in 1969-1971 and uses language and events from that period. While Campfires aims at historical accuracy, it may contain elements that may not be suitable for some readers. Mentioned cases: drug/alcohol use, premarital sex, gun activity, abortion, physical violence, and rape. For audiences who are sensitive to these variables, please take note.

"All the glory goes to God/Christ Jesus. Love to my family for your support."

"To all the girls who were told not to tell, may your voices be heard."

CHAPTER ONE

MAY 1969

K aylen heaved the box up the thirteen steps to her new lair. The portent number committed to memory by the tenth trip, huffing profanities by the fortieth climb, her muscles twitching, electrolyte-depleted thighs, and biceps screaming *no more*. Boxes were multiplying like amorous rabbits. Aww, bunnies. Cute. Cardboard cartons, not. She deposited the container into the neat stack with the others. It would've been great to enlist her dad's help lugging stuff, but his work had summoned him. Again. She was used to jockeying by herself.

The sky had swirled pewter and pepper, the temperature a low boil when they'd first arrived that morning at their closed-in-escrow waterfront house. Within hours, the heat licked up over the azure lake, like a shot from a flamethrower, the air conditioner sputtering awake from a six-year coma. Its sonance, like children taunting the new kid, the bullying beast spewing air funky as a wet Labrador. Kaylen wrinkled her celestial nose, attacking the stench with Clorox and patchouli incense. Sweat gleamed upon her *Seventeen* magazine face as the A/C puffed out wind hot as a politician's bloviate, and she added the

1

problem to her growing list of repairs. She'd love to ditch the unpacking in favor of a swim, but her need for order wouldn't tolerate it—perfectionism—a blessing and a curse.

Kaylen's therapist, who had only seen her once, called her compulsion a coping mechanism for trauma. Her dad banked on the counseling to alleviate Kaylen's anxiety and sadness. Who wouldn't be messed up after what had happened to her mom, then her brother? But when the therapist hinted that Kaylen's problems stemmed from broader psychopathologies (of course, requiring extensive, expensive treatment), her father had marched her right back out the door. No, he insisted, time and a change of scenery were the tricks for healing Kaylen. Their rhythm spun, hopping from one town to another, wherever her father's job sent them.

Having to change schools every year was social harakiri, killing Kaylen's fit-in. By 11th grade, she halted guys in their tracks with her Anita Ekberg looks. The girl-packs dive-bombed, glowering, and hissing by their lockers. Kaylen's name bled in Magic Marker in their slam books, their cat claws flexed and waiting to pounce. With her textbooks pressed to her chest and her blue irises hooded, she ignored the male double-takes, the girl's assassinating squints, biding her time until her father's next transfer.

Despite the uprooting, she graduated high school last year. But the umpteen relocations, coupled with her family tragedies, banged Kaylen down. Her father purchased the lake house with hopes of assuaging his guilt over his demanding job, of assigning Kaylen permanency, stability. He'd still be on the road, but she could stay put. Growing up as a latchkey kid with a workaholic father taught Kaylen self-sufficiency, but she wouldn't leave her dad. Ever.

The peaceful lake home, a place eighteen-year-old Kaylen could thrive. Beyond the cyclorama and portico, her balm awaited—the swash of speckled perch rippling the sun-tipped water, a punch of flora and brambles beneath slash, spruce, and loblolly, like nature's Pine-Sol skooshing the warm air, its tasseled tang the secret referred to in a Dora Sigerson Shorter's poem.

Upstairs, she unpacked belongings, moving in a systematic grid, like a cop working a crime scene. She tackled bedrooms, bathrooms, everything demanding structure. Clothes had to be categorized by color; toiletries grouped by size, content, or similarity. She couldn't permit herself a breather until she was satisfied with the arrangement. She itched to finish all chores, but later she could face the chaos downstairs. Ready to escape the suffocating house and bask in the glittering lake, Kaylen slipped on a white bikini—skimpier than Honey Ryder's in the James Bond movie *Dr. No*, more like a slather of Elmer's Glue drying on her skin. Outside, she fiddled with the AM/FM, finding a Top 40 station and placing the transistor radio beside a can of Tab on her towel.

She went boneless in the cool water, then recharging and swimming laps in a cocoon of gold sunbeams and Spanish moss, its tinsel bedizening cypress boughs, The Who belting out Pinball Wizard. Kaylen, toweling off and intent on nailing the chorus with Roger Daltrey, never saw the strangers until they were close enough to touch.

CHAPTER TWO

"It's hotter than a three-balled tomcat," Bran grumbled to his cousin, wrestling the rotting stave out of the way.

Tony popped a wooden plank in its place as they repaired the commercial swim raft, their work assignment for the day. "Now, is that one of those Southern sayings? Or just another weird Florida thing?" Southernisms about the hot weather abounded in the Sunshine State, as did its urban tales and oddities—from sightings of Skunk Apes to pink tutu wearing gators, wrestled and garbed by drunken swamp hillbillies.

"Yes. We have plenty of 'em. And no. We got our fill of Florida crazies and lore, but I can't say I've ever seen a kitty with three testes. But I *have* kept company with a triple-nippled country girl."

"No doubt." Tony's cousin's escapades were legendary. With Bran's corn-silk hair and the green-gold eyes of a night prowling Florida panther, he had no trouble collecting girls. His harem in constant flux—baubles, he fancied, discarding them once they'd lost their sparkle. Tony might not crush Bran's numbers but he did okay for a guy with a nose like a tumor and a buckshot blast of stubble and pocks across his chin and jaw.

The lake lapped around the men as they labored, the humidity a death grip around a larynx. It choked out their talk, with only their visual synchrony—a slanted glance or a jerk of the head, dictating their rhythm. Bran nattered because he liked the sound of his own voice.

"You know, as many times as we've repaired this raft, don't you think we could just get a new one? I mean, it's a waste of time." Bran swayed, balanced straddle-legged as a boater zoomed by, blasting bubbles beneath the floating deck.

Accustomed to Bran's frequent but harmless rantings, Tony's mouth curved, easing the Clint Eastwood squint scored around his eyes, dark as fresh tar. "Hmmm, maybe. But why bellyache to me about it? Run it past Luke." Luke, Tony's best friend, and the cousins' employer. He unfurled a crumbled pack of Marlboros from his shirt sleeve, tapping one out. His brand of cigarettes, a badge among men's men, the rugged Alphas and wranglers. Not a cowpoke, but virility oozed from his pores.

"I will. And if kids would hang out on it instead of abusing it, we wouldn't have to fix the stupid thing all the time."

Tony nodded, smoke mantling his dark hair like a sombrero. "I know, but what kid can resist fooling around, playing King of the Mountain on it? Anyway, we do it too, right?"

Bran snorted. "That's different. We don't wreck things when we're out here! Not like some of these little brats, who'll crack planks on purpose. And don't forget the time that kid tried to unlatch the drums." Two rows of buoyant 30-gallon drums built beneath the wooden platform. No drums, no flotation. "You gotta be like a freakin' hall monitor watching 'em, especially when they showoff, like doing backflips off the deck." He motioned for Tony to bestow him a drag. "Someday, someone's gonna get hurt out here. Maybe split their head open, drown or something, and sue us! And I got better things to do with my bread than to hand it over in a lawsuit." As usual, Bran's concern only for those events affecting Bran.

"Yeah, well, that's why we're all covered under liability insurance, so little chance of that happening, right?" Tony retrieved his cigarette from his cousin, sucking down one last puff before flicking it into the lake.

Bran shrugged—a gesture he repeated three dozen times a day. His friends and family found it both endearing and irritating. "Oh, the tedium of it all! If I have to fix this thing one more time, I will go insane!" He Tarzan bellowed his exasperation.

Tony jumped at the jungle cry. "Next time, give a guy a warning, you ditz! Either you've been in the sun too long, or all the drugs you've taken have burned out your brain cells. Which, by the way, you didn't have that many, to begin with."

"That's hysterical. Listen, I'm bored! Let's do something."

"We are." Tony waved the hammer.

"Big thrill of my life. Come on, humor me."

"I'm constantly humoring you. I promised Luke we'd get this done today. People have been complaining. We repair it; people stop griping. Bada Bing, problem solved."

"You know, you're turning into a frigging fuddy-duddy old lady. You're starting to act the age people *think* you are!" Sporting an Elvis snarl and a tease of silver at his temples, most people misinterpreted the nineteen-year-old Tony's chronological age. "Even older. Like the elderly, like an antique! You're getting to be a fogey, worse than goody-boy Lane." Lane, Luke's younger, priggish brother.

"Watch it! You better never compare me to that square Lanesy. You step it up, and we'll get finished in no time. Then I'll do whatever it is you want, even kiss up to you, okay, flake?" Tony said.

"Promise? Plant that pucker right here, then you geriatric." Bran pointed at his "plumber's crack."

"I'll show you who's a geriatric!" If Bran wanted a distraction from boredom, Tony jubilated to oblige him. Bran scuttled across the wet deck, evading his cousin's deadly fists. Tony nabbed the band on Bran's BVDs, tugging skyward. The wedgie sent Bran screaming like a little girl, Tony busting a gut and the two going at it. They grappled, the decaying raft creaking under their weight.

"Hey, you're crushing my neck!" Bran, locked in Tony's full nelson.

"Better that than the family jewels!" His cousin's lofting height impressed, but Tony ducked doorways daily. He had no problem maneuvering Bran to the edge of the platform.

The forewarning of crumping wood got muffled in the cacophony of the men's laughter. The fissure wriggled under their feet like a provoked viper, they teetering into the lake.

"Oh, seriously? All that work for nothing!" Bran bemoaned.

"As usual, all trouble starts with you, crap-for-brains."

"Very untrue. If anyone looks like trouble, it's you! I got the face of a choirboy, and you're like a throwback 50s greaser."

Tony couldn't dispute the claim. "I know it wasn't the plan, but the swim feels good." He moaned in relief, paddling his feet.

"Well, we finally done did it with the dickin' off." Bran wiggled his hand between two gaping boards sagging down the middle of the raft. "We can't fix her anymore. Big Bertha, you served us well." He wiped away a fake tear.

"Yeah, you're broken up about it, I can tell. Now we'll have to get a new one."

"I know. It's sad."

"You know what's sad? This." Tony removed the mushy

pack from his pocket. "That was a waste of smokes. You owe me, idiot. You gonna buy me a new pack?"

"Hey, you started it! But, yep, yep, else you won't shut up about—whoa, fox alert!" Bran, a beagle, picking up a scent, tracking his quarry. Tony shielded his eyes, the sun glancing off the tranquil water like Fourth of July sparklers as he brought the object of interest into view.

The woman trod water on the other side of the lake, her butterscotch hair fanning behind her like a wedding mantilla as she alternated between a doggy paddle and a frog kick.

"Think she needs help with her breaststroke?" Bran leered.

Unaware of her admirers, she stirred from her swimming spot. She snapped a peppermint-hued towel, its stripes unreeling against the bright blue windless sky, and she proceeded to blot her mane and to dab at her breasts and between her thighs.

"That's a lucky towel." Bran sighed.

"Are you thinking what I'm thinking, kid?"

Bran's smile burst at the "kid" reference. Even though Tony's age defied him, and he looked fifteen years Bran's senior, a scant two years separated them. "I think we should show some Southern hospitality and take a little ride over there to welcome our new neighbor."

Tony's dirty old man chuckle was a spot-on impersonation of Arte Johnson's character Tyrone F. Horneigh from *Rowan and Martin's Laugh-In*, Bran's favorite television show.

They scrambled, unhitching the canoe from the gurgling raft and stroking toward the young woman. "That house has been for sale forever, but I didn't know old man Tompson had finally gotten rid of the place." The air thick with unspoken words of what occurred there, how it changed everything.

Bran shrugged. "What's it been? Five, six years?" A time gap of non-activity at the vacant house, spat with sporadic flurries of bustling landscaping crews, the whish of mowers and trimmers as realtors readied the property for showing. But interest diminished in sprint time for the overpriced, poorly-maintained, isolated home, falling victim to weeds and neglect. The guys paid no attention to the random maintenance worker or yard crew, foretelling the house would remain unoccupied. Until now...

"How ya' doing?" Tony called, the woman girding the towel around her upper torso in reaction to the stranger-danger startle.

They grounded, Bran, leaping out, rocking the canoe. Tony, with one leg in and one leg out, flapped his arms to keep from toppling. "Smooth move, Einstein!" Tony yelled at his cousin.

The girl stifled a giggle.

"Like what's happening?" Bran swanked a peace sign along with his smile. He relied on his looks and wasn't opposed to promoting them.

"Not much." She drank him in—white-blond hair bright as a halo and those devastating cat eyes. The stunner might have gotten away with upstaging his aesthetically challenged companion–if not for that companion's Herculean body, hewed as a rocky cliff and topping at least six feet ten inches.

"We work at the campground across the lake," the giant explained. "You just move in?" Rhetorical since he knew the answer. The house and its secrets, locked up snug for a dog's age.

"Yes. We closed on the place Tuesday, got the utilities turned on yesterday. My dad and I got here super early this morning. I was unpacking, but it's so hot I decided to take a dip."

"Definitely a scorcher today. Not even summer yet, and we're already sweltering. I'm Tony, and this is my cousin, Bran."

The woman spired a brow. Tony, dark as a walnut burl slab and the face of a B movie character actor, and Bran, glossy like a magazine cover with his platinum hair and buffed golden-as-a-biscuit arms. Nothing in their features trumpeted "we're related." Maybe they were pulling her leg with their cousin's claim. "Hi. I'm Kaylen."

"Kaylen?" Bran tested the moniker on his tongue. "Is 'Kaylen' one word, like Jacqueline? Or is it two words: 'Kay Lynn?'"

"One. It is 'Kay' and 'Lynn,' and since I'm from the South, you'd think it'd be a classic double name, you know—Sue Ann, Mary Jo, Betty Lou. It's not. You gotta run the 'Kay Lynn' together."

"Got it. Kaylen. Far-out, I like it." Tony gave the thumbs up.

"From the South? Where?" Bran asked.

"Born and raised in Florida," Kaylen said.

"Yeah? Me, too," Bran said. Sparkling smiles at each other, bonded by their roots.

"Are you a native too, Tony?" Kaylen asked.

"I am. But I was raised in New York. That's where I met my best friend Luke and his family. We all moved down here together. They're the ones who own the campground."

"Our friendly campground crew—Luke, his folks, his brother, me and Tony, my brother and parents," Bran added.

"A real family affair, huh?" Kaylen's knuckles relaxed, her towel dipping, her cleavage on display.

A moment of pure male delectation. "Yep. Nepotism alive and well," Tony said, grinning at his cousin's frown and knowing he'd have to explain the word "nepotism" to him later.

Kaylen half-smiled, puzzling why they were dripping wet in their company logo tee shirts, shorts, and tennis shoes, yet didn't explain. Barring this oddity, she liked the pair, guessing

Bran to be close to her own age, and Tony, add a decade and a half.

A high-pitched crackling. Bran explained: "I think we're getting paged; my fans can't leave me alone."

"I know, I got the same problem," Kaylen murmured, prompting his cackle.

"I got a problem too. I call him Bran."

They chatted, and several minutes later, the loudspeaker boomed. "Give it a rest," Bran groaned.

"Apparently, you're missed. Two pages in less than ten minutes? Someone's anxious to see you," Kaylen said.

"Well, obviously, who wouldn't be?" Bran said.

"Or could it be that we left chores undone, and they want us to wrap it up?" Tony said.

"Work. It gets in the way of important stuff, like talking to pretty girls," Bran said.

"Yeah, work. The thing you try to avoid, you goof-off. Listen, we gotta split right now, but we'll catch you later." Tony propelled his cousin along.

"Okay. Nice meeting y'all."

"Hey, how about grubbing with us? Wanna come to dinner tonight?" Bran asked.

"Uh, I don't know. I still got a lot to do."

"Take it from me; work will always be there. All that mess and having to unpack—you don't wanna fool with having to cook too, now do you?" Bran asked.

"Well, no," Kaylen answered.

"And you gotta eat, right?" Bran asked.

"Yeah, but I could just make a sandwich, you know?" Kaylen shrugged at Bran, mock dramatically. In the brief interim she'd known him, had picked up on his quirk, and he grinned in appreciation.

"Sandwich? Who wants a stinking sandwich when they can have a home-cooked meal?"

"It does sound better your way, Tony."

"Fine. It's settled then. And your old man, will he be joining us?" Tony asked.

"Huh? No, my dad's not even here."

"See? Then you'd have to eat alone. We're rescuing you," Tony said.

"We'll be chowing over at the campground owner's house. The Vincuzzi's are great people! And they've always got room for an extra guest—especially the beautiful ones," Bran said.

"Good deal. Thanks for inviting me."

"No problem. After all, you're our closest neighbor now, so we're just doing the neighborly thing," Tony said, and the men hopped into the canoe, shoving from the shoreline.

"I'll do something for her that would be really nice and neighborly, know-what-I-mean?" Bran said in an undertone.

"Oh, wait!" Kaylen waved her hands. "I don't even know where to meet y'all."

"You see that green building? That's the pavilion. Follow the path beside it. It'll take you directly to the campground owner's pad. White house, grey door. Can't miss it," Bran said.

"Alright. What time?"

"Eightish. I know it's kinda late for dinner, but we usually get a few campers checking in right before nightfall," Tony said.

"It's fine."

"By the way, stems, water, or wheels?" Bran megaphoned his hands to his mouth.

"Excuse me?"

"Are you walking over, boating, or driving your car?" Bran inquired.

"I've got a kayak."

"That'll work. Tie it off at the dry dock," Bran suggested.

"Okay. See you then."

The cousins retrieved their tools from the dying floating raft, half-submerged on one end.

Bran crossed himself, intoning the last rites, his cousin snorting in amusement.

Kaylen scanned the horizon as they drifted away. She skipped up the embankment, wondering what she'd gotten herself into.

* * *

"Listen, this chick is prime," Bran said to his kith. "Right, Tone?"

"Yep. True stone fox."

They gathered in the campground's game room—their daily meeting place post-work. Attached to the office and snack mart, it housed commercial amusement equipment—billiards, ping-pong, air hockey, foosball tables, and pinball machines. They seized any opportunity to pool shark and perfect trick shots or demonstrate their wizardry at Alligator and Royal Guard.

Today, they were too distracted by juicy man gossip to concentrate on their cutthroat matches, even though they had been showing off their Z-shots, flick and chop, and pump fake.

Bran and Tony lolled side by side on a pool table. Tony's best friend, Luke, slumped across a pinball machine, and Luke's younger brother, Lane, perched on an air hockey table. Bran's older brother, Schaffer, hovered nearby. Campfire-orange signs with friendly warnings—'By Order of Management'—banned customers from sitting on the equipment, lest wear it down. It didn't mean the rule applied to employees.

A patron plinked a few coins in the jukebox, punching out some songs. Dizzy by Tommy Roe vibrated the room.

"Hey, cuz, they're playing your theme song." Tony ribbed Bran.

"Yeah? Too bad it's not The Fool on the Hill." Bran referenced The Beatles song. "Then it would be *your* theme."

Tony clutched his heart as if someone had stabbed him.

"This Kaylen is choice, huh?" Schaffer protracted his six-foot five-inch frame across the pool table. His peace sign necklace shifted from his throat to his collar bone as he pillowed his right arm under his head, caching the dragons, skulls, and menagerie inked from his wrist to his shoulder. He draped his left arm across the pool table, his bicep a billboard advertising Crystal Lake Campground and an image depicting it.

"Totally. We saw her in her bikini. Smokin' hot." Tony whistled.

"Yep. She's definitely shag-worthy. When she came out of the lake, she was like a goddess rising up out of the water," Bran said.

"Like Bolbe."

The others blank stared Lane. "Bolbe, the Greek goddess of the lake. Kaylen would be like Bolbe. Or even Nerthus—the mistress of sacred lakes and springs."

"Yeah? Who's the goddess of Lake-Who-Gives-A-Flying-Frig?" Bran javelined a you-are-so-lame look, and Lane's mouth clapped shut.

"Never mind him. Does this Kaylen have what counts?" Luke slicked a black ringlet out of his coal-colored eyes.

"You mean hooters, right? Hmm, not exactly the biggest." Bran shrugged, swinging his foot to the beat of The Fifth Dimension's Aquarius/Let the Sunshine In.

"Yeah, but not too shabby either." Tony rushed to Kaylen's defense when Luke grunted his disappointment.

"Yep. She's got a bounce to those babies." Bran executed juggling motions under his chest.

"Anyway, she makes up for it with her face, figure, and *culata* (butt)," Tony said. The men routinely peppered their conversations with Italian—the female anatomy and getting lucky their root topics.

"Well, three out of four ain't bad, I guess. Anyway, I was never good with arithmetic. My specialty is languages—the language of love!"

Luke's friends whooped. Tony dug in the pocket of the pool table, launching the ball at his best friend, it whizzing by Luke's ear. "I would have smothered you in your sleep if it had popped me."

Tony relaxed, in no way worried by Luke's threat.

"Bazooms or not, that Kaylen is a knockout! She woke up the troops, know what I mean?" Bran cupped his groin.

The others guffawed, and Luke tilted, his elbows skidding across the pinball machine and a millimeter from a face plant as he tottered to the side, his friends erupting in fresh laughter.

Even Lane, who was usually chastised for being uptight, chuckled at his brother's epic stumble. The cutting up alongside the men, a rare moment of camaraderie—as opposed to their usual bullying and disdain. The daily onslaughts reflected in his wearied drooped gaze, his sotto voce, slouch-shouldered and a tentative step despite his commanding height. Lane, the "runt" of the group at six feet three, his older brother and friends towered like NBA players. A mop of black Slinkys framed his milky face, his glistering irises like a clash of the sky over crystal waters.Luke's friends recuperated from laughing themselves sick. "What did my mom say when you told her you had invited this chick to dinner tonight?" Luke bummed a cigarette from Tony.

"You know Rosa, always accepting. A typical Italian mother; wants to feed everyone. *Mangia.* And your dad was all about it."

Luke and his brother crowed. "Pop slays me. Sill a player at his age."

"Yeah, that's a trip. He'll have to live vicariously and admire my moves, how I operate with Kaylen."

"No way!" Bran filliped his finger in Tony's face. "*Nei tuoi sogni* (in your dreams). Remember? She obviously liked me better."

The cousins sallied insults at each other.

"Children, children, we must learn to share our toys!" Schaffer clapped like a teacher calling a class to order.

"Ridiculous. Fighting over her like she's a Tonka truck." They glared, Lane sighing, spinning the air hockey puck with his thumbnail.

"Hey, who asked you? Get lost. Anyway, maybe this chick won't be interested in either one of you wussies. What she needs—if you'll pardon the expression—is a *real* man." Luke preened his dark hair.

His friends booed, he dodging a speeding eight ball fast-pitched by Bran. "That's it; now I have to off the both of you," Luke told Bran and Tony.

"Of course, that goes without saying. But that's only if you can catch us." Tony shot Bran a side-shufti, both pelting Luke with a ball. He yelped, then a mad scramble as he tore off after them, all three slamming out the door and the cousins turning on him to subject more pain and torture. Schaffer filed behind them, leashing back his tawny, middle-of-the-back length hair, horseplay-ready.

Lane sighed. Clowning as usual, but Luke was thinking ahead, checking his track record and trying to make time with yet another girl. Some things never changed.

CHAPTER THREE

"Well," Bran shrugged, passing the joint to his cousin, "what do y'all think?"

"Dunno," Tony gasped, his lips tight, not about to waste the hit.

"It's cool with me." Schaffer reached for the doobie.

"Maybe things are fine like they are. I mean, why all this commotion about Kaylen? She's just a chick! Chicks pass through here all the time," Tony grunted.

"Exactly. We enjoy them for a short time and then shine 'em on. Kaylen isn't temporary. She's home-grown, and she's here to stay. Plus, we really like her." Schaffer toked. Kaylen had visited them daily at the campground by the men's request since she moved in a week ago. They clicked. Fast friends. But inserting a girl into their all-bros alliance and workplace merited debate.

"Yeah, yeah. Still, why all the interest?" Tony said.

"Because I want her around," Luke said, toking.

"Listen, I ain't got nothing against her. I mean, I like her. A lot. Hey, I introduced her to you! But when you start letting

17

chicks mess in your business, things happen, know what I mean? Like they try to rearrange things. They like to change things. Hey, they're great for eyeballing and doing the deed with, but most of the time, they're a real pain to be around!" Tony said.

"True," Bran agreed. "And they cry a lot! Don't forget those waterworks."

"Yeah, but Kaylen strikes me as being solid, you know?" Schaffer said. "A chick who can handle things, dig?"

"Strong women tend to be bossy women," Tony pointed out.

"Who needs that?" Bran scoffed, inhaling.

They hung out at Schaffer, Bran, and Tony's house. Luke and Lane Vincuzzi's parents owned the place, annexed as campground property, but resided in by the Mancuso family. Cousin Tony, brothers Schaffer and Bran, and their parents lived there rent-free in exchange for working at the campground—a deal brokered when the Vincuzzis purchased the campground. The Mancusos expansive house angled on the west side of the lake, the Vincuzzi home mounted east side. The houses, like bookends, with the campground office, game room/snack mart, hutches, camping cabins, bathhouses/comfort stations, and pavilions stuck between them.

At the Vincuzzi home, the parents lived downstairs. Luke and Lane resided upstairs. They each had a master bedroom/bathroom at opposite ends of the tier. Luke's side reeked of cigarettes and Brut aftershave, and the floor was strewn with piles of Crystal Lake Campground T-shirts, his failed dunk toward the dirty clothes hamper. At Lane's end, the bathroom sparkled, a batch of sunshine-scented towels racked each day, and his crisp hospital corners made bed, an exemplar of barracks. Luke ignored Lane's supplication to not smoke in or traipse his dirty shoes across their common area and kitchen, the offenses flaming their roomie/sibling wars.

At the Mancuso residence, Bran, Schaffer, and Tony occupied the second floor—3000 square feet boasting a private outside access entrance, kitchen, bathroom, living room, and bedroom. Although the men shared one bedroom, its master-grand suite proportions accommodated three California king beds and bureaus. The cave's cathedral ceilings spared the Willis Reed-sized Tony from stooping. Bran and Schaffer, raised on the lake's canals, marshes, and outlets in the backwoods, bragged they'd gone from "living country" to becoming "redneck royalty." While the men resided in their own bachelor pad and the parents inhabited the first floor, the risk loomed they'd venture upstairs. It diluted the thrill of getting high there but didn't deter them from indulging. Anyway, the Mancuso parents weren't home at that moment.

Schaffer popped a record on the turntable. One of his favorite albums: IN-A-GADDA-DA-VIDDA by Iron Butterfly —great music to get stoned to.

Luke eyed the others. "It's gotta be a consensus. We've always stuck together, right?"

"Let's say we let her in," Tony presented. "How much are we planning to let her know? And what about your cousin?" Luke's cousin lived out of state but played an integral part in their group and friendship.

"If she's in, it's like us, okay? She works here; she hangs out with us, we count on her, dig? Old business, old history—we don't tell her nothin' we don't want to. Anything new, well, we'll have to wait and see where she fits in. And as far as my cousin Raymo goes, he's in New York. I still call the shots around here," Luke said.

"But is he gonna be down with having a chick in the group?" Bran asked.

"He'll be okay with anything we decide—especially when it involves a beautiful girl," Luke said.

"Kaylen, is that," Bran said.

"But what about Lane?" Schaffer pinched the doobie between his fingers.

"What about him?" Luke asked.

"You know," Schaffer reminded him.

"Oh, *that*. I don't think there's anything to worry about," Luke said.

"Do you think he thinks we're gonna spill our guts about him?" Tony asked.

"You bet your sweet bippy!" Bran uttered the catchphrase from the TV show *Laugh-In*. "Didn't y'all check him out? He digs her! He'll have an aneurysm if we even hint at saying something to Kaylen! He doesn't want anything to screw up their buddy-buddy friendship."

"Yeah. We're gonna have fun with this. Feed him little prompts about what we want from him," Tony said.

"Subtly, of course." Luke matched Tony's sadistic sneer.

"And gently," Tony snarled, extending his long legs out in front of him.

"Actually, this is epic!" Bran opened a bag of Doritos with his teeth. "Kaylen is perfect for keeping Lanesy in line."

"We don't want Kaylen to ever find out anything." Tony crunched a mouthful of chips. "We want Lane to think Kaylen is gonna find out!"

"Ingenious!" Bran breathed.

"One more way to make him do what we want." Tony munched.

"Because we love him and don't want him to make another mistake, now do we?" Luke sneered, biting into a chip.

"So what about Kaylen's initiation into our circle? What are we gonna have her do?" Schaffer asked.

"Let's see if she'll give us all a good time!" Bran brightened, swiping Doritos crumbs from his mouth.

"Think she'll go for that?" Schaffer asked.

"Never hurts to ask," Bran said.

"That's off the table." Luke clamped the joint in the roach clip.

"What?! Why not?" Bran asked.

"Because he wants her for himself." Tony bent down inside the refrigerator, tossing a can of R.C. Cola to each of the men.

"Whoa! Is this like official? When did this happen?" Bran tipped his head back and guttled.

"The first night she came to dinner. Pay attention, nimrod. Luke is hung on her." Tony slid his drink next to the bag of Doritos. "First, he wants her in the group; then he wants to hog her. What gives?"

"What's the big deal?" Luke snarled, dropping the roach into the Crystal Lake Campground ashtray. "I dig her, that's all."

"Yeah? I dig her too. And so does Rover!" The name Bran dubbed his penis.

"Well, Kaylen is way too refined for a mutt like Rover," Schaffer snorted, and Tony added: "No one cares about your little pud. We're more interested in why Luke's crushing on Kaylen."

"Stop busting my onions already," Luke said.

"This ain't fair! Me and Tony were the first ones to see Kaylen. The decision about who gets her should be between us."

"My cousin is absolutely right!"

"It's us who should decide. And we'll be real classy about it too. Maybe a duel to the death, right, Tone?" Bran asked.

"Yep. Maybe we'll even do it gunslinger style. Stand back to back, pistol in hand, then pace off, huh?" Tony said.

"Except Bran doesn't know how to count," Schaffer deadpanned.

"No woman is worth fighting over. Or is she?" Tony asked.

"No doubt Kaylen is special. But what is it about her that *you* want so bad?" Schaffer asked.

"Will you give me a break? She's different, that's all," Luke said.

"Explain, pretty please," Bran said.

Luke took his time kindling his cigarette. More than lust or infatuation for Kaylen. Her beauty, that body, those lips—she got to him, like her decked in that furry bathing suit. Man, she rocked it—much like Raquel Welch in her deer-skin bikini in the movie *One Million Years B.C.* "Dunno. Stop asking."

"They're all the same under the covers, buddy." Tony elbowed his friend.

"I checked her out to the max. T's and A, just like the rest of 'em." Schaffer detangled a strand of his long blonde-brown hair from his dangling gold earring.

"Well then, maybe it truly is LOVE!" Bran lilted little chirping noises, clasping his heart.

The others joined in, sparrows and robins trilling, grinning like idiots.

"Suck mine," Luke muttered, beaning Bran with a throw pillow from the couch.

"There's not enough money in the world, dude," Bran said, wedging the pillow behind his head.

"I got it figured out," Tony said. "She's different because she's a virgin. She's not our usual campground groupies and skanks."

"How do we know she's a virgin?" Bran asked.

"Ask Lanesy. He'd know. She'd tell him." Schaffer devoured the last few chips in the bag.

"*Va bene* (okay)," Tony said. "Luke wants the virgin, fine he gets her. But he'll owe us big time for this."

"Then what are we gonna do for an initiation?" Bran blew into the empty Doritos bag, converting it into a balloon, clasping the top of the bag with one hand and punching it with his other. Three tries before it popped.

"We'll think of something," Schaffer said, always chill and not worried about what comes next.

"Yeah, maybe. But Rover is disappointed now," Bran said.

"Then maybe Rover will have to make a date with Mr. Hand." Tony demonstrated a dirty gesture.

"I don't have to resort to that since I have no trouble finding girls to accommodate me. However... I'm sure some of us are very familiar with hand-dating!" Bran directed this comment to the man easing up the stairwell.

The others cackled, the man stepping in, glaring, cerulean ice-cubes.

"Hey, Lanesy. We've decided to let Kaylen in the group. How do you like that?" Bran scooped up the burst bag, eating chip crumbs off the avocado-colored tiled floor. "Five-second rule. Don't judge."

Lane's baby blues narrowed in disgust. "I like the idea of Kaylen joining us. I don't like what was said about her, though. I heard what you were saying."

"Exactly what do you do, Lane? Hide in the air-conditioning vent and eavesdrop? One minute he's not there, then all of a sudden, he materializes. Like a specter. Like a spy extraordinaire. Like James Bond. Got your spy gear, Lanesy?" Tony asked.

"He thinks he's Bazooka Joe. Got your decoder ring there?" Bran asked.

"Maybe he thinks he's an agent from *Get Smart*. What's up Lanesy? You work for CONTROL? You got a shoe phone there? Maybe we should get a Cone of Silence so he can't hear our conversation," Tony said.

"I think he transports like Captain Kirk on *Star Trek*. Beam 'em up, Scotty. How much did you hear?" Schaffer asked Lane.

"Enough," he flared. Lane only caught the tail end of the conversation, but he could piece together what was said based on his prior knowledge of how the group's minds worked. "I don't like the way you guys talk about Kaylen. I don't like this plotting behind her back."

"Who's plotting? We were discussing," Luke corrected.

"You're gonna use her, just like every girl you get," Lane said.

"MYOB, baby brother," Luke said.

"It's not right, Luke," Lane said.

"Yeah? You're the moralist when it suits you, Lane," Tony accused. "Or do we have to remind you of–"

"All right!" Lane never free from the truth, his friends' flinging it in his face.

"Cool-out, Lane," Schaffer said. "This is an important day in history; Kaylen is gonna be our first official female member."

"You could even say it's our contribution to the Women's Movement," Luke smirked.

"Alert Gloria Steinem and Betty Friedan," Bran said.

"Hey, no one can say we're male chauvinists!" Tony chuckled.

"No way, we love women here!" Luke said.

"Yeah, I think every man should own one!" Bran simpered.

Lane refused to crack a smile among the men's backchat.

"What's wrong, Lanesy? Can't take a little joke?" Bran asked.

"You weren't kidding. And I didn't find it amusing."

"Well, then maybe you'll find this to be funny, and it ain't no joke. Kaylen invited us to dinner tonight. At her house. How do you like that?" Luke asked.

"But I haven't been in that house, in the Tompson's house, since, since..." His companions, reveling in perverse delight.

"Aww, whatsa' matter, Lane? Afraid of old ghosts?" Luke clucked.

"I can decline her invitation." Lane's chin hitched, but his eyes ticced. The prospect of setting foot in that house... his heart hammered, his lips twitching. No, not after what happened there.

"You gonna avoid Kaylen's house? Are you not going to socialize with her over there? How will you explain it?" Bran asked him.

"Don't you think she'll wanna know why? I mean, aren't you and her getting to be palsy-walsy now?" Schaffer asked.

"Gee, that's a shame, Lanesy, especially when Kaylen wants to be hospitable. Maybe we'll have to tell her why you won't go over there." Tony pretended to pick his fingernail.

"Maybe we gotta drop dimes," Luke said.

"I'll go!" he snarled, hating their blackmail and powerless to stop it.

Luke's mean smirk crept up. Lane glared, haltered. Love or hate, the brothers, bound for life, their secrets the glue—as tacky and toxic as flypaper.

CHAPTER FOUR

"Yowza, this is great!" Bran heaped another helping of homemade spaghetti sauce.

"Right on." Schaffer agreed.

"The pasta might not be from scratch like my mom's, but the sauce is phenomenal!" Luke smacked his lips.

"Not many cooks could duplicate Rosa's to-die-for homemade bucatini. But thanks anyway for the compliment. Lane, what about you? Enjoying it?"

"Very much."

Kaylen nodded, relieved. The group arrived at the back door via the kitchen. Lulled by the delicious smells and homey atmosphere, they settled in at the table for conversation as Kaylen hustled up dinner. Lane's initial squirreliness was baffling. But those nasty little grins the men unleashed at him bothered Kaylen more.

"Mamma mia, you maka' me proud." Tony delivered the accent, squeezing his eyes shut, kissing his fingertips, and becoming ultra-Italian.

"Where did you learn to cook like this?" Bran mumbled, his mouth full. "So good!"

"Oh, you know, here and there. Experimenting. Trial and error."

"Well, you got this recipe down."

"We should make you an honorary. You cook traditional like a true one. I dub you *bella principessa italiana*." Tony placed a pretend crown on Kaylen's head, bowing.

"I will accept the title, but I hate to disillusion everyone since you think we're eating an authentic Italian dish. Spaghetti is not Italian; it's Chinese."

"Blasphemy!" Bran flailed his arm, knocking the pretend crown from Kaylen's noggin.

"No. *Sei pazzo* (you're crazy)." A protest, Luke as he blotted his mouth with the napkin.

"You're thinking of chop suey, honey." Tony pointed his fork at her.

"No, she's correct," Lane said. "Historians credit Marco Polo with discovering it in his travels to China."

"Isn't Marco Polo a game you play in the water?" Bran asked.

"You have water on the brain." Schaffer tapped his brother on the forehead.

"The Chinese supposedly invented the noodle—pasta, including spaghetti," Lane continued, "but of course, we Italians can take credit for introducing marinara."

"Well, I still say it's bogus."

"Bran, why won't you believe me? Several top researchers have documented it."

"Yeah? Document this!" Bran flipped him off.

Lane sighed, returning to his meal.

Kaylen blinked, perplexed as to why the others resented Lane.

"This trivia is all very interesting I'm sure, but what's important is, can you cook Southern-style?"

"Schaffer, bless my honeysuckle mouth if Ah don't cook the best chitlins and hog jowls y'all will ever eat, sugar." Kaylen exaggerated her normal Southern lilt.

Bran and Schaffer cheered, but Tony shuddered. "Gross. I'd rather die than eat that disgusting mess."

"Listen, you eat bacon, right?"

"Oh, yeah. My favorite man-snack."

"All hog jowls are, is simply thick, crunchy bacon," Kaylen pointed out.

"I could live with that. It's the chitlin thing I object to. Pig intestines, no can do."

"Kaylen, can you cook mustard greens, grits, and corn-bread?" Schaffer asked.

"How about collards and hush puppies?" Bran added.

"Yep. All of that and cracklins, too," Kaylen said.

"This is my dream girl." Bran placed his hand over his heart.

"Cracklins and collards—Southern fare I could never grow a taste for," Luke said.

"Your loss. Hey, lady, about more wine?" Bran tapped his empty stemware.

She leaned across the table to retrieve the bottle. Her denim shorts rode up her derriere, inches from Luke's eyeballs. He pinched in the air near Kaylen's rear end, a hair from brushing his fingertips as she returned to her seat. Luke's cherubic expression, the other's puckering mouths, cluing her in. "What's going on?"

"Nothing."

"Were you trying to touch my butt?!"

"No, definitely not. Fondle maybe. Molest, absolutely," Luke said.

The men howled. Lane sighed in disapproval.

Tony seized the bottle of wine, replenishing. Schaffer slid his glass over, Tony pouring him a thimble-sized full.

"Give him more. He needs it, my brother, the lush," Bran pleaded.

"Hey, shuddup. You'll give the lady the wrong impression of me," Schaffer said.

"You've done a fine job of that already," Bran said.

"Hardy-har. A million comedians out of work, and we're stuck with you," Schaffer said.

"You mean you have to put up with that verbal abuse all the time?" Kaylen feigned shock.

"Hey, I only have to share a room with him. But we're not joined at the hip, you know," Schaffer said.

"Thankfully." Bran pretended relief, but the brothers' gaze locked. Heart and soul bonded, unable to hide their affection for each other.

Kaylen compared brothers to brothers. Bran and Schaffer, finishing each other's sentences, playful punches to the shoulders, tousling each other's hair. Lane and Luke, cutting one another off in conversation, cold staring at each other, and barely civil working next to each other at the campground. The glaring contrast wrenched Kaylen's heart.

"Don't hold back on the wine," Bran said.

"Yep. Cough that bottle up," Luke said.

"I can't cough a bottle up, but I can cough a hairball up."

"Or you could *cough up* a hairball," Lane corrected Bran.

"Did I not say that?!"

"English usage. Correct grammatical order. Etcetera," Lane said.

"Bran, you are a man of many gifts. But I don't wanna know why you would be hocking up a hairball." Tony teased, topping his wine glass to the brim.

"Well, I made that up to impress Kaylen."

"I am so wowed."

"Hey, show her *your real* trick!" Schaffer bunted his brother.

"Oh, now this will blow you away," Luke promised.

"I call this talent 'now you see it, and now you don't.'" Bran rose to deliver.

"We call it disgusting. But it's a beautiful display of Bran being a freak of nature," Schaffer said.

"Here goes, for your viewing pleasure." He extracted a long strand of spaghetti, slurped it, burped, and sniffled rapidly, his orbs rolling back.

"Is he okay?" Kaylen asked.

"Wait for it." Tony pounded the table. "Wait for it!"

The spaghetti noodle emerged from Bran's nostril like a tiny curious worm, and he tugged it out. "Hoo-rah!"

"That was gaggy," Kaylen giggled.

"No, now this is gaggy." Bran slung the noodle on Schaffer's plate.

"Hey! I was eating there!" Schaffer cried.

"Who's stopping you now?" Bran asked.

The others chanting: "Dare, dare, dare! Dare you to eat it!"

"I'd rather see Lane eat it."

A lifetime of their bullying, he stiffened at Bran's proposal.

"Don't get your butthole in a pucker, Lane. This dare goes out to someone who has the balls to do it. What's it gonna be, Shay?" Tony said.

"If you eat half."

"Let's do it."

Schaffer sliced the strand. "On the count of three, we down it."

Tony and Schaffer took their respective halves, slurping the noodle that had tickled Bran's nostrils seconds earlier.

"I think I wanna throw up!"

"Listen, it's not that bad, Kaylen. We three share the same blood, right? What are cooties among brothers and a cousin?" Schaffer clasped the men's shoulders.

"I need lots of alcohol after viewing that grossness," Luke said.

"I still have a couple more bottles," Kaylen informed Luke.

"I love you." Tony blew her a kiss.

"Actually, you should love my dad. He's the one supplying the booze."

"How'd you manage that?" Luke asked.

"I told him I was having friends over; could he buy a few bottles."

"Let me get this straight. Your old man bought you hooch, you—a minor. And he was okay with you drinking with a couple of guys?" Tony's dark brows sloped up.

"First of all, I'm not a minor. Wow, do I look that young?! And secondly, my dad spent time in Europe where teens are allowed to drink in the home. He always said he'd rather I do it at our house instead of out somewhere like a common drunk."

"Common drunks. Like Bran?" Tony said.

"Sir, I may be a drunk, but I am certainly not common!"

"Your dad's line of thinking is very cosmopolitan," Lane pointed out. "But I'm surprised he'd be okay with you drinking with five men he hasn't even met yet."

"Well, I didn't exactly tell him you were guys."

"Ahh! So you lied? Not even hanging around with us a full two weeks and she's already learning!"

"I did not lie, Bran. I said I was having new friends over for drinks and dinner. He never asked, 'what friends?'"

"You implied that it was female friends?" Bran asked.

"Sort of."

"Kaylen, you're awesome!"

"No, Bran, you misunderstand."

"No, your dad misunderstood. You misrepresented. Two distinct differences."

"Well, it seemed easier that way. Do you know what I mean?"

"Oh, believe us, Kaylen; we know exactly what you mean. Not all truths can be told." Tony cut a glance at Lane.

"Still, it is never right to lie. I don't want you to think that I make a habit of that."

"Oh, we could never think less of you, Kaylen," Schaffer said.

"We only think less of Bran," Tony said. "Clueless. Brainless. Branless."

"Yep. His head is empty. Like this bottle." Luke turned it upside down.

"I'll fetch another." Schaffer volunteered, scooting back from the table.

Bran plunged his finger into the pot of sauce, slurping and licking it clean.

"I do have perfectly good utensils. Can I interest you in a spoon?" Kaylen asked.

"Get your mitts out of it, dummy—no telling where that finger has been," Tony, the straight man for the setup.

"Well, if you really want to know..." Bran delivered, the banana man for the joke. The others hooted, Schaffer returning with a Merlot, asking: "Under the skirt of a camper-skank named Ann?"

"Jan," Bran corrected, tossing a piece of garlic bread at his brother.

He snatched it midair, biting off the corner. "Who cares? By next week it'll be a Penny or a Linda or Sue."

"I've never had a Kaylen." Bran twinkled.

"And you never will." She fluttered her lashes, the men splitting their sides.

"She's too smart for your lines. You gotta be more debonair. Like Cary Grant," Tony said.

"What would you know about being debonair? Says the guy who has the mug and the height to have played Lurch on *The Addams Family*." Bran razzed his cousin. "I'm completely debonair! I'm all suave and swagger."

"As well as being a pillock."

"Pill lick? Huh?"

Lane spelled it out.

"Like pill lock? What is that? That better be a compliment, Lanesy."

"Of course." Bran eyed Lane but said nothing more. Lane winked at Kaylen, who did know the definition of 'pillock.'

"Pill lock. That's a good idea. To lock up our pills." Schaffer swirled the wine in his glass.

"Like, who's gonna take them?" Bran asked.

"You never know," Schaffer said.

"What pills?" Kaylen crinkled her forehead.

"You know. Amps, bennies, ludes, Valium." Schaffer ticked them off his fingers. "To name a few."

"You take all those?" Kaylen asked.

"Yeah. We all do, from time to time. Except for Lane."

"That's what you brought with you?" Tony asked.

"No. Ganja, mon."

"Schaffer is one of our go-to persons," Tony explained.

"For drugs?" Kaylen guessed.

"Yes. Is that going to be a problem?" Tony asked.

They all peered over. A half a beat went by. "No." Changing subjects, Kaylen asked: "Are we all finished eating?"

"Not quite. I want more spaghetti. And salad. And bread."

"He's demanding, huh? Bran's dedicated to his food, stomach, appetite. And of course, doing the wild thing with willing wenches," Tony pointed out.

"What more do you need in life?" Bran shrugged, twisting a forkful of spaghetti.

"Natch," Kaylen said. "Hey, I wanna know something. I know Luke and Lane are Italian. And Tony. But what about Schaffer and Bran? I mean, I know Tony is your cousin. But there's no way you guys could be Italian too."

"Why wouldn't they be?" Tony asked.

"Are you sure that they weren't adopted?"

"What's that supposed to mean?" Bran asked.

"No offense," Kaylen said.

"Well, Bran and I may be Italian, but our first claim is that we're Southern-bred."

"In other words, Sicily may be in your blood, but Dixie is in your heart?"

"You know it," Schaffer said.

"Yeah. Bubbas and bumpkins all around me," Tony said.

"Watch it. Some of us have kin who are Bubbas and bumpkins. That's what you get here, you fake-native-Floridian-city-boy."

Everyone hooted at Kaylen's barb. "I've adapted. Luke and I missed the hustle-bustle of New York City when we first moved here. It was a culture shock. Down here, Miami's foremost to the action of the city life we were used to in the Big Apple," Tony said.

"Yep. But now I like the laid-back pace—and the beautiful Southern women," Luke added.

"Flattery, flattery. But listen, getting back to the Italian thing, I don't get it. I do realize that there are light-haired, light-eyed Italians. Case in point: Lane with those impossibly blue, blue eyes. But Bran and Schaffer just don't look Italian! *At all.* Look at Bran with that towhead!" Kaylen said.

"Jealous?" Bran smoothed a palm over his shimmering white-blond mop.

"I am. It's perfection. And especially Schaffer! All that luxurious hair! You should show it off in a television commercial. Maybe get an endorsement from Breck shampoo, right? Like Cybill Shepherd?" Kaylen said.

"Okay, this is what happened. My uncle Mario—a dark Italian—came to Florida on vacation and met a beautiful green-eyed Southern blonde bombshell down in West Palm. A little co-mingling and hence the byproducts, Schaffer and Bran." Tony double-pointed at them.

"Ahhh, I see. But where do you fit into the picture, Tony? Aren't you the oldest cousin?"

"Okay, here's the backstory: My father Sal and Uncle Mario—the brothers Mancuso—originally came over from Italy and settled in New York. You know, off the boat and Ellis Island? Fast forward a few years to when my mom and dad met in New York City and then married. Shortly afterward, my uncle Mario heads down to Florida. He hooks up with my aunt, who by the way is a native Floridian, but believe or not, is of Italian descent."

"Soon after, my father and mother came down here for the big event—the marriage of Mario and his intended," Tony continued. "My mother was hugely pregnant with me. Well, all the excitement must have gotten to her because she went into labor a month early. I wasn't even supposed to be born here! Everything was planned, bassinet and nursery waiting back in New York City."

"He came early then, and he still does."

"Funny. No, Luke, that would be you. I was born in Palm Beach, but we eventually made our way back to New York. A few months later, my aunt announces she's expecting, quickly expanding the handsome Mancuso bloodline."

"Me. The number one son." Schaffer's choppers bedazzled.

"Thirteen months later, baby number two," Tony added.

"The lovely blond dude." Bran ruffled his own hair.

"Technically, the brothers are quarter Italian?" Kaylen asked.

"But 100% imbeciles." Tony made the cuckoo sign.

"You do the math. My mom's dad—full Italian, last name *Camella*," Schaffer explained. "My dad–full Italian. I guess if you put all the halves and quarters together in the genes, that has to make a whole, right? Not to mention that we're all fluent in Italian."

"Totally bilingual." Tony puffed out his chest.

"Not to start something, guys, but what gives with the names? I mean, 'Tony' is a good old-fashioned Italian name. But what type of heritage name is 'Bran and Schaffer?'"

"Excuse me, ma'am, 'Bran' is a very distinguished name!"

"It sounds like roughage you gotta have in your diet," Tony said. "Get more oats, fiber, and Bran so that you can crap a lot. You know, KYBO?"

"Well, isn't a 'Tony' a home hair permanent?" Schaffer shot back in defense of his brother.

"It's Toni. Girl's spelling. The home hair permanent. Not Tony, male spelling."

"Thanks, Lanesy. I wouldn't have been able to sleep tonight if you hadn't cleared that up," Schaffer snorted.

"Actually, Kaylen, my name *is* Italian. It's Brando-Belvedere."

Kaylen giggled until her sides ached. "Sorry."

"Hey, now that was just mean! Did you see me making fun of *your* weird name Kaylen Katina?"

"Even worse, his name is hyphenated!" Tony snickered. "I mean, come on!"

"My brother's name does seem wack at first, but then you

realize it's very appropriate. In Italian, Brando means 'fiery torch,' and Belvedere means 'beautiful to see; beautiful structure.' He's definitely those things."

"So his name doesn't come from 'Brandon,' as I figured," Kaylen said.

"Nope. And he wasn't named after the actor Marlon Brando either, another misperception," Tony said.

"Brando. Shortened to 'Bran.' Now I get it. Honestly, 'Bran' suits you," Kaylen said.

"True. But what exactly is a 'Schaffer' anyway?"

"Don't screw with me, Luke. It means 'shepherd,' and for some reason, my mom liked the cadence of it. And if that's not Italian enough for you, my middle name is Mario."

"I can't believe Uncle Mario would let his wife name a kid 'Schaffer.'"

"Well, I like my name. It's novel. It's different."

"Yeah, different but not in a good way," Luke snickered.

"Dude, who are you to judge me? What kind of Italian name is 'Luke?'"

"Listen, you burn out. Did you forget my real name is Luciano? Some say Lu *chee* ano. Others, pronounce it Lu *cee* ano."

"Yeah? Then why didn't they call you 'Lucy?'"

"I'll give you five good reasons why." He splayed his fingers, clenching them into a fist under Schaffer's chin. His friend remained Zen, not at all fearful. "That was my mom's idea of Americanizing an Italian name," Luke continued. "She wanted to remember the motherland she immigrated from but also pay honor to the first generation in her family to be born in the U.S., and 'Luke' actually comes from Luca—another Italian name."

"Let's not forget about you, Lanesy. What kind of Italian name is that?"

"Tony, you know my legal name is Lanario."

"And Ma again, trying to Americanize a name. Lanario became Lane-nar-io, then the nickname Lane."

"What's with the names anyway? Mario, Brando, Luciano, Lanario—what's the deal with ending everything in an 'O?'" Kaylen asked.

"Everyone wants the Big O." Tony shimmied his eyebrows.

"And my dad Al, his real name is Alphonso," Lane pointed out.

"See? That's what I mean!" Kaylen cried.

"Then I guess we shouldn't tell you about Raymo. Raimondo Vincuzzi, a.k.a. Raymo—Luke and Lane's cousin."

"Oh, seriously?! Both his nickname and his legal name have a suffix with an 'O?'" Kaylen spouted.

"Suffix." Bran tested it on his lips. "Sounds like something dirty, doesn't it?"

"Do you even know what a suffix is?" Lane asked.

"No, but I do know when someone is talking down to me."

"I'm not trying to be condescending, Bran."

"Tell me about Raymo." Kaylen steered the focus from Lane.

"He's an Italian wooer and loves the babes," Tony said.

"Is this Raymo dishy?" Kaylen asked.

"He thinks he is!" Tony said.

"Hey, give him some credit. He's *almost* as good-looking as me." Luke winked, and the men laughed, their inside joke.

"He's always got a woman," Schaffer said. "He must have something. Call it handsome if you want."

"Call it a big schlong." Bran slid his hands wide like a fisherman describing his catch. "Good looks always run second to being endowed!"

"That's what you think, huh?" Kaylen slanted her pupils toward the heavens.

"Yep. My mind is always in motion."

"Which explains why he can't hold a thought," Schaffer said.

"My cousin and I are spitting images," Luke said, "blessed with the Vincuzzi style and charm."

"Another gorgeous hunk, huh? I don't think I can take it; too many studly men already surround me." They sashayed, puffing out their chest at Kaylen's compliment. "Okay, stop. But for real? You and your cousin are identical?"

"Yeah. People swear we're twins. He's six months older than me, though. We've even been mistaken for each other too, especially if you would see us from a distance. With us having the same coloring, height, mannerisms—it's easy to mix us up," Luke said.

"Well, when I meet him, I guess I better make sure that I'm with the right one, huh?"

"Oh, you'll be with the right one, baby." Luke leaned back, crossing one leg over the other.

"Can we move this shindig into the living room?" Lane scowled. As they chatted, Lane's attention kept drifting toward Luke and the lady of the house he was flirting with. Despite only having known her for little more than a week, Luke seemed to be laying it on pretty thick. It reminded Lane of Bran's brief and shallow relationships with girls, and he couldn't shake the feeling that Luke was less than ideal boyfriend material. Lane knew from experience that Luke tended to move from one romantic interest to another without much thought or commitment. He worried that this girl might become another one of Luke's casualties, and the thought made him uneasy. He decided to keep an eye on the situation and be there for her if she ever needed him.

"Wow, you changed up the place." Bran flopped into the oversized dark green beanbag chair.

"Oh? I didn't realize that you'd ever been here before," Kaylen said.

"Exactly how did you get a hold of this house?" Luke probed, disregarding his brother's twitching face.

"Well, my dad's job involves traveling, but he still needs to be able to check in regularly with the home office. We started searching for a place within range." She squeezed between Luke and Tony on the couch. Lane chose the Barcalounger, and Schaffer settled next to the stereo, sorting through Kaylen's record collection. His eyes widened in awe—of how many she owned and the way she alphabetized the albums by either band name or genre. He selected Days of Future Passed by the Moody Blues.

"My dad remembered this property from when he passed by on his way to his corporate office, a 40-minute drive from here. He would see realty signs, but when they disappeared, he assumed the property was off the market. However, he asked our agent, who said it was still vacant and waiting for the right owner. Although it needed cleaning, airing out, and lots of minor repairs, the house was still in pretty good shape. I wondered why the seller had let it get so run down in the first place."

"Who can figure people?" Tony posed, the haunting strains of Nights in White Satin in the background.

"Did you know him? The owner? I think he was a councilman," Kaylen asked.

"No, not really," Luke answered. "Talked to him a coupla' times. He was a weekender, a summer resident. But I think my brother did yard work for the guy's wife."

Lane faded, translucent as a premature baby, the veins pulsing along his jawline like the slither of blue coral snakes.

Bran slipped out, returning with more wine. "I'm stoked that you have an endless supply of booze."

"Well, it's not exactly infinite. I think there's one more bottle left after this one."

Bran quaffed straight from the bottle, offering it to his brother, who gulped and handed it to his cousin.

"Uuhh, you know, I have these cylinder things. They're called 'glasses.' Would you like one? Much easier than everyone sharing," Kaylen offered.

"You saw that whole spaghetti deal. You think we're afraid of each other's germs?" Tony sipped, passing it to his best friend. "Three of us share the same blood, same DNA. And we've been friends with Luke since preschool. All of us have snotted on each other or sprayed with each other's pee and vomit."

"I don't even wanna know." Kaylen's tapered brow shot up.

"Anyway, I only backwash a little bit." Bran swished another mouthful.

"You scared to swap spit with me?" Luke chugged.

Big smiles, everybody waiting. "Not at all."

Those black irises danced. "Prove it."

Kaylen swigged, leaning in and pressing her lips to Luke's. "Happy?"

"Very."

"Here's to your old man." Bran lifted the bottle skyward. "For buying the booze. Here's to... Whatzhisname?"

"Ross."

"Here's to a great man, Ross. Father to the beautiful Kaylen."

"Where is he?" Lane asked, color pumping into his pale cheeks.

Kaylen wondered if she had imagined his distress earlier.

Lane waved the bottle away when his friends proffered it.

"My dad? He's one of his company's top salesman. He's

probably in Atlanta right now, Florida and Georgia being his normal territories."

"He's on the road all the time? He leaves you by yourself a lot?" Tony asked.

"Yes. Weeks and weeks. Even longer."

"All by yourself, little girl?" Tony's maniacal boom of Mwahahaha.

"Yes, evil one, but don't get any ideas because I can handle myself quite well."

"But don't you worry about being alone?" Bran wiggled deeper into the bean bag chair. "Don't you get scared?"

"No, I've been doing this for many years. I'm used to it."

"But then it's just you and your dad here? Where's ya' mother?" Schaffer asked.

"Gone."

"Your parents are divorced?" Schaffer asked.

"No, mom died when I was young."

"Sorry. How did it happen?" Schaffer said.

"Boating accident. We lived in South Florida. My mom liked to sail, to go off by herself in her little catamaran. My dad cautioned her many times not to. Y'all know the weather in Florida. Beautiful one moment and storming the next. That day had been clear, sunny, hot. A squall came up, and the water got choppy. They found her boat capsized in the bay. They never found her body."

"Supreme bummer. My sympathies."

"Thanks, Schaffer. But you know, for the longest time, I didn't think she was dead. I believed she was coming back." She guzzled from the bottle, circulating it.

"Children often think that. The concept of finality is too abstract," Lane told her.

"I know. But that wasn't it. I didn't think she was dead

because I believed she had run off with another man and might miss us enough to come back again."

"No way! What made you think that?" Bran asked.

"Because of... Listen, I have never told anyone this before."

"Well, we're your best friends now, so you've saved this reveal for the right people. The time is ripe. Do tell. We love secrets." Tony rubbed his hands together.

"And after you tell your story, maybe Lane's got a few secrets he'd like to share too. Right, Lanesy?" Bran said, Lane, going rigid.

"Do y'all wanna hear this or what?" Kaylen attempted to scotch the brewing tension.

"Go ahead. Dish your dirt. *Dire tutto* (tell everything)," Tony urged her.

"The investigators were positive my mom drowned, that maybe sharks got her body. My dad couldn't handle it; he wanted out of South Florida. When he got a job offer in Tampa, we started packing up, getting rid of stuff. He told me to clean out mom's closet. I found a stack of old love letters she had hidden. Some were from my dad when he was still in the service. But then I found this one letter; the handwriting was different. A guy named 'Gary.' It wasn't old; it'd been postmarked a few months before the accident. I began to wonder: Did my mom leave us to be with him?"

"Were your folks having problems?" Lane asked, adjusting the recliner to upright.

"I heard them arguing sometimes. It didn't appear to be anything major. They always made up right away."

"What about the content of the letter, the context?" Lane asked.

"Well, I was seven years old, so there were things I didn't understand about the nuances between a man and woman. But I did understand that Gary and my mom were close and had a relationship. Now whether it was extramarital or a friendship, who knows?"

"You still got the letter? Let's read it!" Bran cried.

"It's long gone. I trashed it. My dad was devastated by the loss of my mom. I knew it would kill him if he suspected she'd been having an affair."

"Listen, with all due respect, I think that was ballsy of your old lady to hoard that sort of evidence," Schaffer said. "I mean, your dad could have discovered that letter instead of you."

"Maybe he did," Luke muttered.

"What do you mean?"

"Maybe your dad did find it. Maybe he decided to end the Gary/Mommy thing for good. It wouldn't be that hard to sabotage a boat, you know. Think about it. A little creative tinkering with the boom, the mast, the mainsail. Well, that could make the boat less than seaworthy. Add in strong winds and killer waves..."

"What? My father could never do that! He loved my mother."

"There's a fine line between love and hate, Kay." Luke's dark eyes, wise. "And it forces you to make choices."

"Choices," Bran echoed, peering at Lane.

"Who's this guy?" Schaffer pointed at a picture hanging in the hallway.

"Huh? Oh, that's my brother."

"We've never seen him! Does he live here?" Schaffer asked.

"My brother was killed in Vietnam a couple of years ago. My father isn't over that either. I miss him like mad too."

"Give me the booze," Tony said. "Kaylen's family history is bumming me out. I think I'm getting severely depressed."

"Another life taken because of this freaking war." Schaffer's hot-button topic. "It's a farce! DuPont and Dow Chemicals are making money off killing our soldiers. Bureaucracy is bullcrap!

What if my number comes up? Am I gonna be in the next draft lottery?"

The Selective Service System's upcoming drawing in December, when a colossal glass jar would determine the men's fate, hundreds of blue capsules inside containing slips of paper with the days of the year. A number assigned to the selected birth dates. Eligible men called up if allotted the fated number. The Mancuso and Vincuzzi boys fell within the 18-26 draft age.

"My brother wanted to serve his country. But I wouldn't blame anyone who didn't want to. Will you go if you get drafted?"

"No way. I'll try to get a deferment," Schaffer said.

"Then you'd be a draft dodger," Lane pointed out.

"So?! I'd rather be a live draft dodger than a dead war hero! No insult to your brother, Kaylen. And you're going to judge me, Lanesy, about *my* character? *You*, of all people?"

"You guys have been pretty lucky, considering that you're all in the draft pool," Kaylen said.

"Hey, the government wouldn't dare split up this daycare. Going to make sure," Bran said.

"Bran's plan if the military calls him up?" Luke said. "Act like a flaming homosexual! Scare the crap out of the dress blues down at the draft office."

"Will that work?" Kaylen asked.

"Dunno, don't care, but I'm willing to try it. For added effect, I might even grab the worm of the guy standing next to me in line!" Bran said.

"I don't know, man, that's either gonna get you a date or a beat-down!" Tony's peepers crinkled.

"I'm not into boys, nor do I wanna disfigure my beautiful face. But wouldn't my gay act stir up those good ol' manly, homophobic recruiters? Give those Hawks what they deserve and blow their mind. The powers-to-be certainly don't want their soldiers diddling with other soldiers in the foxholes! No attractions to dudes and certainly no distractions on the front line."

"No, indeedy, don't want our soldiers distracted from fulfilling their patriotic duty of sweating in the jungles of Asia, smoking pot, wiping out commies, killing babies, and raping women." Schaffer's lips pursed.

"That's what you think goes on over there?"

"You read the papers, Kaylen. You listen to the news reports. You got a TV. You've seen the reels! And that's the details they actually air. You can imagine what they're *not* showing you! Do you think your government cares? You think our military even knows which Charlie they're supposed to save and which ones they're supposed to annihilate?!"

"Don't even get him started on conspiracy theories," Tony warned. "Next, we'll have to hear about dead Kennedys and LBJ ordering the assassination of Martin Luther King Jr."

"Screw off." Schaffer's tone soft, no scathe in his words.

"So what happened to your brother?" Luke patted Kaylen's leg.

"It was a firefight. Two years ago in Binh Doung, South Vietnam. My brother Ken's unit moved into enemy machine gun emplacement. Ken and another guy were the only ones in their platoon who didn't make it out. It was the end of his first tour. Three more weeks, and he would've made it home. So close, yet so far away."

"Stinkin' unfair. Sucks majorly." Bran sighed.

"Yeah, I mean first your mom, then your brother, and your dad being away all the time. You must get lonely sometimes," Schaffer clucked.

"Well, my mom's been gone a long time, and I've always been independent. My dad was constantly away on business, and even when Ken was there, he had his own life. Five years older than me, hung with his friends most of the time."

"Listen, you never have to worry about being alone again. You're going to get real tight with us. Even more so than you have already," Tony said. The men had bonded with Kaylen from the start. They were ready to bring her in closer.

"Yeah, Kay," Luke said, prompted by his best friend's declaration. "Me and the guys have been talking. We want you to be part of our inner circle, you know? We wanna count you in."

"Count me in?"

"With us. Our clan. Our family," Luke said.

"What do you mean? Like a club?"

"Yeah. Only the most beautiful people get invited." Bran fluttered his lashes.

"Of course. Am I ever special? How many people are in this?"

"All of us here," Bran said.

"That's not a club. That's a group," Kaylen argued.

"Whatever. You want in or what?" Luke asked.

"Depends. What's in it for me?"

"Oh, ain't she all business-like," Tony said, amused.

"We're always there for each other, dig? All for one and one for all," Schaffer said.

"After your initiation," Tony said.

"Initiation?" Kaylen asked.

"It's a friendly test." Bran shrugged.

"Don't scowl at us like that. It's nothing. We've all done it."

"Tony, I've heard stories about initiation fiascoes. These frat boys at Tallahassee State took one of their pledges and chained him naked outside of their dorm. Left him gagged, bound, and nude for the whole world to see."

"Oh, yes! That's the ticket."

"That is *so* not gonna happen, Bran!"

"Our initiation will be a lot milder than that," Tony said.

"Speaking of mild, where's that doobie, Shay?" Luke asked.

"Oh, right. Here, Kaylen, from me to you, a house-warming gift." Schaffer removed the joint hidden in his headband.

"Thank you. I think."

"You do smoke weed, right?" Schaffer asked.

"Oh, is this the friendly test part? If I do it, then I've passed?"

"No, this is us having a good time." Bran pumped his arms, a little dance. "Normal stuff."

"Does the lady wanna do the honors?" Schaffer extended the lighter to Kaylen.

"Go ahead. I trust you to get things started."

"She trusts me. Biiiig mistake on her part." Schaffer deep toked, offering it to the others.

Kaylen's turn, five faces scrutinizing. Despite the men's casual attitude regarding getting high with her, she understood they were putting her through the paces. Her one-time experience of smoking dope with a casual acquaintance in 10th grade had taught her to avoid making the newbie mistake of erupting into a coughing fit.

"This blend doesn't get you super stoned. Just makes you kick back, nice and mellow." Schaffer swapped out the album, fed the needle to Tommy James and The Shondells.

Lane refused the joint as it circulated, Kaylen not surprised.

"Take a toke. Don't be a spoilsport." Tony blew a pall in Lane's direction.

"Yeah, Lanesy. You'll offend Kaylen if you don't party with us."

"It's okay if he doesn't want to."

"Lane, do it." Bran paid no heed to Kaylen.

"Why are y'all trying to make him do something he doesn't want to do?" Kaylen asked.

"Hey, Lanesy, why don't you tell her what it's like to push someone to do something they didn't ask for?" Luke asked.

Lane shot to his feet. "Kaylen, I have to leave."

"What? Why? Don't go yet, Lane."

"I can't stay here."

"Because of what Luke said?"

"Stay put," Tony ordered Lane.

"I don't understand. Please don't leave," Kaylen begged him.

"Stay. Go. I don't care. But quit being a buzz kill." Schaffer pinched the joint between his thumb and index finger.

"Kaylen, great dinner. But this is not my scene right now."

"Yeah? What *is* your scene, Lanesy?" Bran cocked his head. "Right. We know what scenes *you're* into."

"Lanesy doesn't like this scene because he only makes scenes," Tony said.

"We'll talk later," Lane told Kaylen, ignoring the others. "You're awesome. But if you'll excuse me, the rest of the company sucks."

"Yeah, and likewise," Bran carped as Lane hustled away.

"Good riddance," Luke said.

"You don't like him, do you?"

"Did I ever say that Kay?" Luke's cool squinch as he lit a cigarette.

"It's obvious. Why?" Kaylen said.

"Lane is weak," Luke said.

"You mean he's sensitive."

"No, I mean weak. Plain and simple. I don't mince words, Kay. And whether I like him or not has got nothing to do with it. Blood is still thicker than water, baby. No matter what. At all times. To the bitter end. Remember that," Luke said.

"But what was he talking about? Why was he upset?"

"Don't rack your brain over things, Kaylen. It's sibling squabbles," Schaffer said.

"Yeah. Sibling squabbles. My brother and I argue like thirty times a day. It don't mean nothing," Bran said.

"Forget about it." Tony pulled a cigarette from Luke's pack. "Lane's got issues, you know? We're your friends. Your family now. That's all you need to know."

"Yeah, Lane's got problems—mental, physical, emotional, spiritual, neurological, psychological. All those other ones that end with 'al.'" Bran related.

"Takes one to know one," Schaffer muttered.

"Listen, you never did show us the rest of your pad, Kaylen. How about giving us the layout?" Tony unfurled to his full height.

"Sure. I'll show you the upstairs."

"Like your bedroom? Where the magic happens?" Luke brightened.

"Afraid not. I fly low here. You only get magic when you watch *The Magic World of Allakazam*. You'll have to ditch if you want those kinds of kicks. Do I gotta rescind my offer of a tour?"

Schaffer sounded a sad trombone—womp-womp-womp.

"Don't worry, Kaylen. We will protect you from the clutches of this villain." Bran struck a superhero pose.

"Get lost," Luke snarled without malice, doling a soft push to Bran.

"No way," Tony nickered.

"And don't think that I don't know that y'all are staring at my butt."

They all cackled from behind Kaylen in the stairway. "Don't flatter yourself. Actually, I was staring at my own."

"Now, that would be a trick, Bran. Better than the spaghetti noodle thing." Schaffer poked him in the back.

"Hey, it's difficult to do but well worth the view," he japed.

"Here we go." Kaylen's bedroom, the walls splashed peach and tangerine, a smack of lemon and citrus in the air, hues, and scents like a bite of fruity sherbet. The nectarine comforter billowed, a mainsail across her bed, a dressing table loaded with hair clips, make-up, bottles of Faberge', Chantilly, and Jean Nate' lined up with military precision. The room was a reflection of Kaylen's personality, of her generation's influences. A fluorescent Peter Max tacked to the wall, and Jim Morrison and Janis Joplin posters hanging above the bed. The sign over the doorway read 'War is not healthy for children and other living things,' and a plaque on the opposite wall vowed: 'There shall never be another season of silence until women have the same rights men have on this green earth—Susan B. Anthony, 1868.'

"Rad setup. I like the pro-peace vibe. And your feminist stance is cool," Schaffer said.

"Righteous. Who wouldn't like to stare at a groovy psychedelic poster? Especially when you're stoned!" Bran inspected a bottle of perfume, spraying his crotch. He aimed at his cousin, but Bran halted when Tony's King Kong-sized hand splayed next to his ear. Instead, he set the bottle on the table, millimeters from its original spot. At Kaylen's sigh of pain, Bran maneuvered it back into its perfect row.

Schaffer examined the framed photo on Kaylen's bureau. "Wow. This is your mom? She was beautiful! You're just a younger version of her."

Kaylen's face softened. "Thanks. You know she had dark blue eyes, and my dad has light blue. Because of their combination, I have this odd thing: when I get mad, my eyes go indigo. But when I'm anxious, they're more turquoise. Then there's my normal—sorta a hue in between the dark and light."

"Well, obviously, you got the best from both parents," Tony said.

"Like you," she returned the compliment kindly, though no one would describe Tony as handsome. But when his brooding mask eased, he bloomed attractive. Even sexy. "Remember when you told me you moved down here with Luke and Lane and their parents when they relocated? You came to live with your aunt, uncle, and cousins, right? But weren't you quite young when you moved down, Tony? Your folks let you go, just like that?"

"My parents were having problems, were stressed. And I was a lot to handle; big for my age, a bully, and getting into trouble. Since I was a toddler, I'd spent every summer here with my cousins. I've always been close to my aunt and uncle. My folks trusted them. They lived on a canal off from the lake, not far from the campground.

"They began inviting the Vincuzzis to come with me on my summer visits, knowing Luke was my best friend up in New York. When my uncle heard that the campground was up for sale, he told the Vincuzzis, knowing they wanted to move to Florida and were scouting for a business to run. My aunt and uncle told them they'd help out if they decided to buy it. When the Vincuzzis signed the papers and got ready to relocate, I told my parents I wanted to move with my best friend; I wanted to live with my cousins. They didn't fight me on it. My folks felt it would be more stable here than being with them."

"I get that. But to let your child move away from you? I mean, you were just a kid!"

"A *kid*? Check out this middle-aged face, Kaylen. Gander my giant body. I was already 5' 11 and 180 pounds by the time I was eight years old! I don't think anyone ever thought of me as being a kid."

"Yeah, Tony had a full beard when he was like ten years old, no lie." Schaffer rubbed his cousin's chin.

"He's not exaggerating. Then you factor in my height, my muscles... well, people always thought I was putting them on when I told them my *true* age."

"You got cheated out of your childhood then, didn't you?"

"Didn't you? Losing your mom at such an early age? Being forced to be the woman of the house?"

"Yeah. I guess you could say that. We got something in common—even if our circumstances are much different."

Tony nodded at Kaylen, his mind drifting to how she had been forced to grow up too quickly. But he knew all too well the feeling of being thrust into adult-sized problems as an adolescent. He had faced having to make man-sized decisions, ones with life-changing consequences. And it all circled back to one person—the one they had blackmailed, bullied, and hounded. As the men regarded Tony, each of them couldn't help but think of Lane.

Kaylen apperceived the shift. But the moment was wiped away as Bran cantered: "So Kaylen, this is your room. Where you sleep and clean and walk around in your little shorty nightgowns."

"Except I don't wear shorty nightgowns."

"No? What then? Negligees? Shorts and t-shirts?" Bran asked.

"Nope. Birthday suit."

"Oh, be still my heart!" Bran cried.

"You honestly sleep in the buff?" Schaffer asked.

"No. Gotcha."

"Quit messing with me. Okay, this has been real," Bran yawned, "but I gotta get some shut-eye. Tomorrow comes early for the working class."

"Yeah? How would you know this?" his brother bantered. "The only thing you work at is getting out of work."

"But Bran, aren't you going to stay and help me do the dishes?"

"Gee, I'd love to, but my ol' arthritis is acting up." His fingers were retracting, a claw in its place.

"Always an excuse." Tony coaxed Bran to straighten his fingers by rapping his knuckles.

"I'll stay and help you," Luke offered. "Okay, you guys shove off already. I'll catch up to you."

The men kissed Kaylen's cheek in goodbye.

"Now, are you really going to help me clean up, or you're here because you think there's gonna be an after-dinner dessert?"

"Is there?"

"A clean-up? Absolutely. The other? Not a chance."

"Wouldn't take us that long to whip something up in the kitchen." Luke's winky wink.

"Cooking is an art, don't you know? Special dishes need crafting, attention to detail, slow-cooked to bring out all the juices."

"Juices, huh?"

"You like that, do ya'?"

"Oh, yeah. You got those juicy lips, and I'm heating up."

"Savor the slow-cooking process, Luke. The marination. Got me?"

"Well, I'm sort of a quick-grill guy, myself."

"Hmmm. Noted."

Since he was getting nowhere on the subject, he said: "I have another proposition instead."

"Do I dare ask what?"

"We—the guys and me—would like you to work at the campground."

"Yeah?"

"You said you wanted a job, right? And we need an extra hand. Besides my parents and the guys, we got Schaffer and Bran's folks and a part-time dude, but we could use someone else full-time. My mom said you'd add a nice womanly touch."

"Well, when you put it that way." Visiting the men every day at the campground, showed her what the job entailed. She'd observed Luke's mom and dad checking campers in and out, the list of chores the employees carved out daily, read their marketing pamphlets spotlighting the campground's amenities. No shortage of work.

"Anyway, I like having you around."

"And do you always get what you want?"

"It's always the goal."

"When do I start?"

"Right now. A little on-the-job training." Luke pulled her to him, his lips kneading hers.

"Do you always go one-on-one with your recruits?"

"Well, I'm making a special exception in this case."

"Oh, you're such a good boss."

"Yeah, this is employee appreciation week. Let me show you again how much I care." He kissed her deeper and longer.

Kaylen felt a surge of bliss with the fooling around. But it was moving at racetrack speed, and traffic snarl pace was more to her liking. "You have to beat feet now."

"You sure?"

"Yeah" she sighed. "You gotta go."

"I'd rather come."

"I got it. Bran-style joke."

"Kay, what you did tonight? You taking up for Lane? I understand. But if you're gonna hang with us, you better get used to how we talk to him. I know you won't believe me, but he deserves it. Especially when he acts all goody-goody."

Luke's warm kiss cooled on Kaylen's lips, the acrimony singeing the air like a spent gunshot shell. "*Ciao*. I'll see you tomorrow."

She scoped his descent into darkness, whipper-wills syllabic monitions in the distance, lightning bugs blinking like caution lights. Nature's harbingers, a caveat about Luke? Red flags, juju, and superstitions—ominous as thirteen steps on a staircase.

Her friendship with the men had sparked, like a balefire, melding them in sprint time. Kaylen, a girl who'd ached for friends but neutralized from acquiring them, who'd craved acceptance but didn't receive it, and finally reaping. The relationship, a rarity, like the finding of painite, or spotting a unicorn in the meadow, the procuring of one true good friendship? The odds were like glimpsing a blue moon. But in a quantity of five, curio as a view to a Leonid meteor storm. A score Kaylen couldn't discount. But it didn't mean she condoned the way Luke treated Lane, his sharp tongue, or let her dismiss her gut, flipping at the sight and tactility of him, but also signaling her spidey senses regarding him—them, even Lane. And niggled—if true and she prevailed hanging out with them anyway, what did that reflect about *her* character?

CHAPTER FIVE

The summer sizzled up, Kaylen settling into her job, assimilated into her friends' inner sanctum. She caught on in a trice on operating a campground. She excelled working with numbers, money, and the public, a multi-tasking whiz, and an eye for organization. Her initiation into the group less seamless, a shock when the men selected strip-poker as her ritual. She tamped down misgivings, wanting to fit in. Anyway, just a silly game, lounging around in undergarments and playing cards with the men (Lane not a participant). The evening marched on, and the men, fueled by smoking weed and feasting on Kaylen's near nakedness, couldn't wait until she revealed more. Their eyes glinted, and she was down to her bra and panties when she lost the next play. She hesitated a microsecond but unhooked, and the lacy bra fell. The men only got to feast a few moments before Lane stepped in. Acting as a human shield, he blocked Kaylen's bare breasts from the others, their threats at his interference. Okay, strip poker wouldn't have been Kaylen's pick for initiation, but no biggie. As a pledge, she accepted their terms. But she served them notice when the game was over; the initiation was not a prelude to something more. She wasn't their centerfold, nor their good-time girl.

A blood-pact sealed their initiation, a covenant dating back to when each boy carried out the initiation chosen by the group. And now Kaylen, a link in their chain. Their friendship a contract in flesh, slitting a finger, pressing index to index, blood-to-blood—an alliance that marked her genesis. Kaylen realized too late that it was the beginning of the end. If only she had acted differently that night, maybe she could have escaped fate's grasp. What she once thought were harmless pranks, she now knew, were a cover for something much more sinister.

The friendship, was a cohesive unit of six—what Kaylen considered the "cove." Then there were the stream offs into "straits" from the main body, the separate friendship she possessed with each man, different, authentic, close.

The men volleyed the idea of a strip poker rematch, Kaylen renting she wasn't their party doll nor their friend with benefits—even for Luke. Although she fancied him, Luke lacked in reciprocation. Oh, he cared for her—performed minor repairs around her house, offered her first choice when his mom baked brownies for the gang, massaged her cramping shoulders, and called her his "girl." But with his wandering peepers and Lane's account of Luke's rotating female inventory, Kaylen refused to budge on her virginity. Before moving to the lake, she chalked up a casual date or two—accompaniment to her dad's work functions and award dinners, sons of the secretaries. A handhold, a slow dance with open frame, a peck on the cheek, and one occasion, mouth mashing under the mistletoe at the company Christmas party with a boy coated in Clearasil and reeking of Hai Karate. Unsuccessful at snagging a boyfriend—though several guys desired to change her status, town hopping for her dad's work proved unconducive to dating, and those who braved, their phone calls and pen palling tapered off as the miles between them grew longer.

Although Kaylen came of age during the counter-culture and embraced free-thinking, she'd grown up on *Leave it to Beaver*, *Father Knows Best*, and *Ozzie and Harriet*. American television in the 50s coloring her perception of when a young woman should "lose it." The world in 1969 might be undergoing a sexual revolution, but Kaylen wasn't going to do it until she was good and ready. She hit Luke with the news, the refusal bewildering him. Unaccustomed to girls turning him down, the blow to his ego provided much fodder for his buddies.

"Luke, the Lover, strikes out," Bran simpered, rubbing it in.

"Whatsa' matter, chump? Losing the ol' Vincuzzi touch?" Tony ribbed him.

"Well, what did you expect? I told you. And even you said she was 'different.'"

Luke shot him a scathing scoff, but Lane refused to wither, his piercing blue irises unwavering.

"Luke's uberly bummed. He pictured getting cherries jubilee but instead got no dessert at all." Bran brayed at his own joke.

"I'm not worried about it." He torched a cigarette, peering out over the lake.

"Oh, sure you're not." Schaffer reclined upon the pool table.

"You know, you should have made your move that night at the initiation." Bran scooted his brother over. "I mean, when you took off your shirt, she was checking you out; she's gotta be groovin' on you."

"No duh. No doubt." He and Kaylen had cranked out a couple of great make-out sessions, and Luke primed to ascend the next summit. Now all he had to do was get her on board with his plan. "Well, it's gonna happen real soon."

Lane blinked at him. "No, it's not."

"What did you say?"

"Kaylen's not ready for that. She told me. She's my best friend." Even though Kaylen built rapport with each man, she and Lane transcended a different level of affinity.

"What else do you talk about, Lanesy? About me and Kay's business? Or about you. You ever talk about yourself, who *you* *really* are? *Hai rivelato il tuo vero sé* (you've revealed who you are?)" Luke's tone congenial, but the air pressure dipped, signaling the brewing storm.

Everyone sized him up. Lane's past. Group knowledge. Lane's not-so-secret secrets.

"Maybe Lane doesn't want to be a best friend. Maybe Lane wants better than a best friend—one in and out of the sheets." Tony, stirring the pot.

Luke's smile didn't reach his cold black eyes. "You've got a thing for her, don't you?"

"No. No. I don't."

"I think you do. You got the hots for Kaylen, don't you, Lanesy? *Si vuole andare a letto con lei* (you want to go bed with her)."

"She's my friend. That's it. Nothing more."

"You're a fake-out, Lane." Bran egged it on and didn't care. "We've seen how you eye her. No different than us."

"It's platonic. I know it's a concept that is beyond your grasp, but that's it."

"Bullcrap, Lane. If she gave you the green light, you'd totally go for it." Schaffer pushed up from where he'd been lounging.

"I repeat. She's a friend. The best friend I have ever had."

"Yeah? And what have we been all these years?" Bran sniggered. "You don't call that friendship?"

"That's a pact of survival. Of secrets. Not friendship."

"No, what we have with you, it's a *lot more* than friendship, Lanesy." Tony's black irises flashed. "We've gone *above and beyond* the call of what you would do for a friend."

"Lane, don't try to make it out like its all casual, all innocent with Kaylen. We all know what starts as being innocent is anything but in the end." Luke killed his cigarette in the ashtray stand.

"It's a crock," Tony said. "All this 'deep meaningful friendship' jazz. You don't hang around with a chick like Kaylen— that face, that body, and not think about trying to get with her."

"No, I do not think of her in that way."

"Who *do* you think of in that way, Lanesy? Oh, that's right. It was *her*. Only her. And now that relationship is done and gone."

Tony's words hit their mark, Lane's lips tugging downward.

"Maybe Lane's dry spell is over. Maybe Lanesy is ready for a real live woman. What do you say, little bro? Kaylen finally make you wanna fly the flag?"

"For the record, Luke, my friendship with Kaylen has flourished because I don't put pressure on her—unlike you. She trusts me."

"That's priceless, Lanesy." Tony glimpsed toward the two patrons sauntering out, leaving the men alone in the game room. "The fact that Kaylen trusts *you*. How long before you betray her trust, huh? Once a betrayer, always a betrayer."

"Lane's big on lecturing other people." Bran leaned over the jukebox, hypnotized as the Seeburg Selector's bar gripped the 45 into place. "But he forgets; he's no example. We're the ones who know you, Lanesy. We know the *real you*—no matter what brand of made-up story you give to Kaylen."

Luke closed the distance between him and his brother, latching his hand under Lane's chin, jacking him against the wall. "Don't get high and mighty with me, Lane. You're no better than us."

None of the others had seen it coming. "Put him in his place, Luke." Tony, a shark who smelled blood in the water. "Rough him up."

"Should we tell Kay about your true character? *Then* what's she going to think about your trustworthiness, huh?" Luke smiled as he crimped his brother's air supply.

Lane gagged, his coughing erupting. Luke unclenching his throat, propelling him away. He gasped, choking, and sputtering as he stumbled outside.

"He's gotta go nurse his wounds like a has-been boxer." Bran surveyed him.

"Want me to go and haul em' back?" Tony punched his fist against his palm.

"Naw. Done with Lane." Luke lighted a fresh cigarette.

"You think he's headed to Kaylen's?" Schaffer asked, poking his long hair under his bandana.

"No, but I am. All this talk from baby brother has inspired me. I can be sensitive. I can be social. I can be trustworthy."

"Go ahead. I know you're supposed to be working the front office this afternoon, but I'll cover it." Tony filched Luke's cigarette from his hand and copped a draft.

"Lane's got his best friend; I got mine," Luke laughed. "Thanks, man." Luke plodded down the embankment, leaping into one of the canoes.

"He forgot this." Tony waved the burning cigarette between his fingers.

"He wasn't thinking about smoking. Unless, of course, it's

the smoking hot babe waiting on the other side of the lake," Schaffer kidded.

Tony nodded, contently puffing as Luke glided across the water.

* * *

"What's shakin'?" Luke charged through the back door.

"Don't you know how to knock?" Kaylen, uprighting the container of lotion she had tumped, a victim of her startle.

"That'll teach you. You shouldn't have your doors unlocked anyway."

"Who are you? My father? Anyway, all five of you guys are always coming over, back and forth, day and night. More convenient to leave the back door unlocked." She pressed her creamy hands together. "Just you? Where are the other clowns?"

"Hanging." Luke, mesmerized by Kaylen's lotion ministrations, smoothing it up her thighs, slathering her neck and shoulders. An invite to bite that silky flesh. "What is that?"

"Rose milk. Aren't you supposed to be working?"

"I've never heard of it. Tony took my shift."

"It softens your skin."

"Let's find out."

Kaylen swatted his groping fingers. "Take my word for it. And why are you here instead of working?"

"Thought you might be interested in a little nooner."

"Right at the top of my priority list." She stood, stretching.

"Fetch me a brew while you're up."

"Anything else, Master? I live to serve you." Her sarcasm included an on-point imitation of TV's *I Dream of Jeannie*, folding her arms, nodding, and blinking.

"You could rub my bottle, Miss Genie-Jeannie."

"Bet you wouldn't talk that trash to Barbara Eden." She reached inside the fridge and then thrust the cold beer at him.

"I make it a point to nix the garbage talk around hot blondes in harem pants."

"Oh, that's all I gotta do? Put on a pair of Pepto-pink trousers?"

"You're fine like you are. I'm digging you in your short shorts. Anyway, staring at you is about all you'll let me do."

"Poor you."

"Poor you too. You're missing out."

"Most certainly. But probably a lot safer this way."

"Why? Don't you like to live dangerously?"

"No, I like safe. I like stability. I want to think our relationship is stable. I'd like to have a boyfriend who has googlies exclusively for me."

"Oh, I have eyes for you. See them looking you up and down right now?"

"Correction. I'd like to have a boyfriend who can keep his hands to himself."

"Oh, no. Not the dreaded hand-dating."

Kaylen giggled. "Double correction. I'd like to have a boyfriend who keeps his paws off other women."

"I can do that."

"Triple correction. I'd like to have a boyfriend who doesn't dip his ladle in other women's gravy."

"What's with you and the food euphemisms? And now we're calling it my 'ladle?'"

"What? You'd rather me be indelicate and say 'penis?'"

"Aaaah, I love it when you talk dirty. Do it some more, do it some more."

"Listen, Luke. I'm not jumping into bed with you."

"How about a hop and a skip?"

"Luke! I am not your easy lay Kay. I'm not doing it with you when you're sleeping with a dozen other girls!"

"Actually, it's half a dozen. Joke! You know, Bran-like joke?"

"Funny. I mean it, Luke. Either we're exclusive, or this isn't happening."

"My brother is a turd. *Stronzo!* Is he influencing this?"

"How would you figure?"

"Well, apparently, you two are besties."

"And this makes you jealous?"

"No. But I think he's swaying this."

"By *this*, you mean me not going all the way with you?"

"Yeah."

She half-snorted, half-laughed. "Luke, *you're* the only one who influences this."

"We had words this morning. Me and my brother. Fighting words."

"About us?"

"Yeah. He thinks I'm after your body."

"That would be an accurate account."

"Kay, you know that's not true."

"Liar-liar, pants on fire."

"It's no secret I wanna sleep with you. But that's not the only reason I'm interested in you."

"Name something else then. Name another reason why you like me."

"You're beautiful. You got a wicked figure."

"Physical reasons. Superficial."

"You're nice, smart, interesting, generous, caring. *Sei bella in ogni modo* (you're beautiful in every way)."

"Much better."

"I do care about you, Kay."

"I know you do, Luke. But unfortunately, not in the same way, I care about you."

"Which is...?"

Kaylen sighed. "Luke, I can't be any clearer."

"Exactly what have you been saying to Lane about the two of us?"

"If Lane is saying junk about you and me, he's simply relaying information that I have vented to him."

"So this is why my brother thinks he needs to protect you from me?"

"He does? How noble. What happened today between you and Lane?"

"Nothing. It's over. I choked him out, and now he's compliant."

"What? Are you serious?!"

"Absolutely."

"Because of me! You hurt Lane because of *me*?"

"No. Hard feelings between Lane and me run deep—long before you came along. And I didn't hurt him. Believe me; if I wanted to hurt him, I would have."

"You can't get your way by bullying, Luke."

"No? You don't think so, Kay? Yeah, actually, you can."

"Not with me. You're not gonna pressure me to put another notch on your belt."

"What do you want from me? Tell you what you wanna hear? Should I pledge a vow of love?"

"Not unless you mean it." Her chin notched up but tearing and teetering toward an ugly cry.

"Why's this gotta be complicated? Isn't it enough that everyone knows you're my girl?"

"I'm one in a long list of many."

"No, you're the main one."

"Oh, goody. I've moved to the head of the line."

"Listen, I'm not Lane; I'm not good with words. It's not easy for me to express myself and you're twisting this up." He took a swig of the beer, extending it to Kaylen, who shook her head.

"Okay. Try. Get it to me straight; leave out the lines."

"You want it straight? I care for you more than you'll ever know. I've *never* felt this way about any other girl, no bullcrap. You'd be the first to know if I no longer felt this way. But don't ever ask me if I love you. Words won't tie me down; no one will tie me down. If I'm with you, it's because I wanna be, not because there's some golden rule that says people in love have to be with each other every single minute of the day."

Well, there it was. Luke wanted things between them to be low-key. Kaylen didn't know if she could conform—especially if their relationship continued long-term.

"Can't we be satisfied at the moment? I mean, you want a commitment. But we have that with each other and the guys. Remember? We vowed it in blood."

"Ahh, yes. Blood vows. What girl wouldn't want that over an engagement ring?"

"Ease up, Kay. I'd love to show the ropes—if you'd be a willing partner."

"You mean about me being a virgin? What if I told you that I wasn't? That if we did it, you would *not* be my first?"

"Well, to begin with, I don't believe that. And second, I can't stand the idea of anyone else but me being with you."

His tender tone threw Kaylen, and she wolfed down her sarcasm. "No, you're right, Luke. I've never been with a man."

"What about with a girl?" he leered.

"What is it about guys getting turned on by chick-on-chick action? Sorry to disappoint, but no, and I don't intend to. I'm waiting for the right guy. If you play your cards right, well... you know."

"Cards? Finally going to rematch another game of strip poker?"

"I'm giving that serious thought. Not."

"My broken dreams, one after the other."

"I need time, Luke. Imagine how good it will be between us when I'm finally ready."

"I'd settle for it being kinda' lousy."

She smirked, shaking her head.

He sighed, placing the half-empty bottle on the coffee table. "Come here."

Cuddling had its place. But even as they embraced, Luke contemplated how to convince Kaylen to give in to him.

CHAPTER SIX

The summer's humidity slapped everyone around like an abusive spouse. Campers caviled the woes of triple-digit heat. Bran grumbled that campers complained. Nobody wanted to Kumbaya around a bonfire, and everyone scrambled for the lake—canoes and kayaks jamming the water and a waiting list for speedboat and airboat rides. Swimmers and floats clogged the beach. Guests crowded the food mart and game room—where the A/C was teeth-chattering and the cash register cha-chinged sales of beer, soda, and ice cream. The muggy, insect-swarming hiking trails lay abandoned, but the pavilions crawled with people, staking out picnic tables and slurping slices of juicy watermelon and engorged cherries. Ants trudged across the sticky tables, soldiers on a mission, the stuffy air droning with conversations, mosquitoes, and bumblebees.

On the national front, a different type of buzz permeated— political, the Chappaquiddick accident, the married Ted Kennedy under suspicion for both his account of what transpired and his relationship with the female aid who perished in his car. Or, as Schaffer put it: "Two assassinated brothers robbed of their presidency and a third one who killed his own presidential chances."

The six friends did everything together; worked, hung out, went places. With their workload at the campground, they juggled to get away. If they could manage it, they'd cruise to Daytona Beach to body wave in the surf and devour Cuban food in Ybor City Tampa. They'd ride the glass-bottom boats at Silver Springs, and visit cheesy, tourist attractions like Florida Wonderland in Titusville or Spongeorama Sponge Factory in Tarpon Springs. With each adventure, their friendship strengthened. Yet, Kaylen sensed the men hid things from her, subtext she failed to decipher. She strapped on her armor plate against their slights; after all, she dealt with rude, sophomoric boy-brains inside late teens-man-bodies. Still, the nagging doubt persisted—hovering like summer heat.

They forged rituals exclusive to their group. They met daily at the game room, and assembled at Kaylen's house every night. On occasion, they'd journey over to the pavilion to hang out with cool campers. Other times, they'd hold a community get-together, campground guests supplied with marshmallows, hot dogs, and the fixings for s'mores, roasting them in the central fire pit. They'd mingle with campers, exercising PR and ensuring repeat business.

Though customer-focused, Kaylen valued her downtime, friend time. A shared consensus among the men. From time to time, their inner circle shrunk, in the case if one of the guys left for a date or the on-call person taking care of evening emergencies and late-night check-ins. The absences spotlighted how one missing cog in their machine threw off their system, a chink when mended, restored them to their whole.

Kaylen's house was perfect for hanging out: convenient, private, and comfortable, with her dad away 95% of the time. However, Ross checked up almost daily on her by calling the landline. If one of the guys answered with a silly greeting, like "Bran the Man Landscaping. My specialty, giving attention to your bush, to your liking," it would rile him up. He'd bark, "Put Kaylen on the phone." Kaylen smoothed things over by explaining, "Daddy, we've had a busy day. They're just letting off steam." Ross questioned further, "But they all gotta be over there every night?" Kaylen reassured him, "They're only gonna be here for a little while. Everyone's tired, so they'll be leaving soon." Despite the guys making faces and acting stupid, Kaylen maintained a neutral tone.

Kaylen, even after a long day toiling, enjoyed making dinner. Lane cleared dishes, the other men retiring to the living room. Sprawling on the sofa and floor, they moaned, their tummies stuffed. Schaffer, self-appointed music director, riffled through Kaylen's extensive record collection. He slid the joint from his headband, firing it up.

"We seem to be doing this fairly regularly," Kaylen said.

"What? Getting high?" Schaffer asked. Jimi Hendrix shredded on guitar; the cut Purple Haze the appropriate backdrop for their activity.

"Yeah."

"So?"

"So it affects your body, your brain."

"It's only grass, Kaylen!" Schaffer exclaimed.

"Yeah, it's not like we're all slobbering incoherently in a back alley, tying off a tourniquet, needles sticking out of our arms." Tony reached for the doobie.

"Yeah, but some of you do much more than smoke weed," Kaylen pointed out.

"What are you, a narc?" Schaffer asked.

"Just saying," Kaylen said.

"No secret. I'll try anything once. Pot, pills, powder, tabs—euphoria!" Schaffer, lungs burning, releasing the smoke.

"Don't be a downer. You're not gonna go all Lane on us, are you?" Bran waggled a finger at Kaylen.

"I've seen him smoke pot before," Kaylen pointed out.

"Yeah, but usually under protest! With him, it's the exception, not the norm! Like he does it a couple of times a year! And he doesn't bona fide toke. Sorta takes these wimpy puffs like he's inexperienced," Bran said.

Accustomed to people talking about him like he wasn't even there, Lane bided his time, waiting for the subject to switch.

"Did y'all get a gander at that chick who checked in today?" Bran said, toking. "She's up at campsite J-7. Gorgeous!"

"She's a Barbie doll," Kaylen said.

"Oh, meow, honey!" Bran made a sound like a hissing feline.

"I'm not catty. Truth. She's got a 20-inch waist and a 42-inch bust," Kaylen said.

"You think her jugs are real?"

"I dunno, Bran. You wanna ask her big old boyfriend who's camping with her?"

"I didn't see him. How big?"

"Almost Tony-big. At least a 6'6"er and 200 pounds," Kaylen said.

"Too bad she's got the guy with her. She's my type," Bran lamented.

"Yeah, girls that get passed around more than Cutty Sark at the drive-in."

"Right, Tony, and you don't go for that because, unlike Bran, you have standards," Kaylen said.

"Now I do. Maybe not when I was a baby-teenager."

"When you were 15, you'd take anything, right?" Schaffer poked fun.

"How about when you're 12, 13." Luke cocked his head. "Huh, Lanesy?"

The other men were aiming snarky grins, Lane twitchy but silent.

"Why must every conversation center on this stuff?" Kaylen sighed.

"Stuff? You mean about chicks and doing it?" Bran asked.

"I have to listen to this raunch daily and the misogynistic remarks too," Kaylen complained.

"You're not gonna call us chauvinist boars again, are you?" Tony offered the joint to Kaylen.

"That term applies to at least four guys in this room," Kaylen said.

"Notice she didn't lump Lane into that distinguished circle?" Tony said.

"No, Lane's not a piggy. He's just a dog, right, bro? A breed that licks your hand then tears out your throat while you're sleeping," Luke said.

"I'm not a swine, nor a canine. But you, on the other hand, would eat your own young," Lane sniped.

Instead of getting irked, Luke's smile blossomed.

"Kaylen, you cannot accuse us of being anti-feminist. After all, we let you into the group," Schaffer pointed out, flipping the album over.

"Yeah, I'm honored to be the token female. Particularly since y'all originally hatched this position for me to service you guys."

"Not true. But we would love to promote you through the ranks." Tony walked his fingers up invisible stairs.

"You are not our token female," Schaffer corrected her. "We think of you as our indentured servant."

"Nice. I'll add it to my growing list. Co-worker, token female, nursemaid, kindergarten teacher."

"How about adding this to your list - French maid! I would love to see you in one of those little outfits."

"See what I mean? You would demean me by asking me to dress like that, Bran?"

"Absolutely. Or don't dress at all. Even better," Bran suggested.

"Naked maid. Oh, yeah!" Schaffer brightened.

"I think we should have casual Friday for all employees," Luke said. "Real casual for Kay. No clothes for Kay."

"Epiphany moment! Let's have a nudist campground!"

"That's a great idea, Brandy. Clothes get in the way anyhow," Schaffer twinkled.

"You guys really wanna run around with your dingles hanging out?"

"I got no problem with it," Luke said.

"And if memory serves, you got no problem flashing the flesh either." Tony clicked his tongue at Kaylen.

"Repeat performance, repeat performance," Bran chanted, referring to their strip poker match.

"Shut your stupid yap."

"Now she's cranky. Must be that time of the month," Bran said.

"Or it could be from hanging around you jackwads. And would you talk to a guy like that? Tony gets cranky; he's moody. You wouldn't blame that on his hormones, would you?"

"Tony gets in a crappy mood whenever Lane runs his mouth about Lane-like things," Bran pointed out.

"So much different than intelligent Bran-like chatter, right?" Kaylen smirked.

"Oh, burn me, baby," Bran said.

"Not only are y'all sexist, but you also practice selective exclusion."

"Which is...?" Tony asked.

"Picking and choosing what you want me to know. Sometimes none of you can keep your mouths shut, speaking ad nauseam about certain things until I am ready to yack, then other times; you'll get all whisper-whisper and all tight-lipped around me."

"Yeah, well, some things you can't talk about in the company of women." Schaffer searched for the roach clip.

"That's a hoot! You guys do not have a problem with discussing anything in front of me! I am privy to the last time Schaffer went number two; the last girl Bran slept with, or for that matter, even though I've never seen it, how big Tony's 'Johnson' is!"

"I'll admit my cousin's tiller is very impressive. How about telling me the name of the last girl I slept with." Bran tried to jog his memory.

"Janelle," she answered without hesitation. "Camped in B-10 two weeks ago. She wore the cut-offs that left nothing to the imagination."

"Two weeks ago? It's been that long since I've done the dirty? Time to get busy again," Bran said.

"Selective exclusion," Kaylen repeated. "Too much talking sometimes, not even enough other times. Big, big talk, but then big secrets too."

"Don't you have secrets, Kay? Things you would never tell us?" Luke asked.

"No. I think I've told y'all all my deep darks."

"I got one for you," Schaffer shared. "One time, I caught Tony studying his trouser snake with a magnifying glass."

"Were you checking for a growth spurt?" Kaylen giggled.

"I was checking for chiggers and ticks. I'd been cutting down underbrush when I felt something on my pole," Tony said.

"Ick. A tick. Nothing worse than a tick on your stick."

"Bran's rhyming, like a Dr. Seuss book." Schaffer ambled over to his brother, preparing to shotgun the blunt with him.

"Probably because that's his speed for reading," Luke wise-cracked.

As Schaffer finished blowing the smoke in his brother's mouth, Bran kissed him full on the lips, hoping to get a laugh from the others. He did but at a price. Schaffer vised his mouth and cheeks, squeezing like he was a tube of toothpaste, extracting the last dab. He didn't loosen until his brother mewed like a kitten.

"I appreciate that y'all feel comfortable enough with me to be open. I think. But I could do without the filthy talk, too much information, blah-blah-blah. I'd like the juice you've been squirreling from me," Kaylen said.

"Hear that, Lanesy? She wants the good dirt. How about we rattle those skeletons in your closet?"

"She wants you guys to tone it down, Bran," Lane said coolly.

"I do, Lane. I'd like respect."

"You want respect, equal rights, equal input, this and that." Tony ticked off the points on his fingers. "You ask for a lot, Kaylen."

"Chicks and their wants. See? And it all started with letting them vote."

"Oh, absolutely, Bran! Our whole American political system went down the toilet the minute women cast their ballots. We're to blame for all social ills. And famine. And global unrest."

"It's true. Eve messed it all up in the Garden of Eden," Tony accused.

"Let's not blame Eve. As typical in most cases with men and women, it was a guy who got under her skin and made her crazy," Kaylen said.

"She just couldn't take the ribbing." Bran slapped his thigh, cornpone. "Get it?"

"Y'all sure know how to put a spin on Genesis." Schaffer plunked Joe Cocker's With a Little Help From My Friends on the turntable.

"I don't veto you guys being yourselves. But could you dial it down? F-bombs I can take. Even hearing about girls having kitties, you boys having roosters, and all that. But using the "C-word" for kitty—Big No-No," Kaylen protested.

"You mean we have to come up with a substitute word?" Schaffer asked.

"I don't think I can do that, Kaylen."

"Why, Bran? Will it strain your brain?"

"Hate to disappoint, but don't count on me to soft play the way I talk. Tony's right, you chicks want a lot."

"Chicks? That word? There you go. That's one of your problems, Luke. You still haven't figured out yet that I'm not a fowl but a woman."

"Oh, yeah? Prove it."

Kaylen bristled, then Bran interrupting her retort. "Didn't know I had to change my whole style of talking for a girl. *Lei mi sta uccidendo* (she is killing me)."

"Lady," Kaylen corrected.

"Whatever. Next, you'll want us to give up our porn," Luke said.

"You guys look at pornography?!"

"Only on the days that contain vowels," Tony quipped.

"Baby steps," Lane told Kaylen. "They've agreed to clean up the language. But giving up the dirty magazines and blue movies might send them into seizures."

"Fine. So be it. But let's talk about one more thing. Besides the lewd language, you guys need to ixnay the bad behavior. Y'all are hopelessly crude!" Kaylen accused.

"Wait, you told us we were crass," Bran said.

"You're crass. I'm brash. Schaffer's obnoxious." Tony elbowed Bran.

"I'm talking about your usual: farting, belching, spitting, scratching. Cut it out already!"

"Kaylen, you're talking about a lifestyle here," Tony chuckled.

"Yep. It has taken many a year to perfect those disgusting habits." Schaffer bobbed his head to the music.

"If I come over here, I gotta be myself! Like if I need to scratch my *coglioni*. I might as well stay home if I can't scratch my hairy boys when I want to!"

"It's not the ball scratching I object to, Bran. It's that in tandem with hose arranging. You scratch, you move it. You scratch, you re-position it," Kaylen said.

"Fine, fine. We'll be gentlemen. Kind of," Schaffer said. "Listen, you told us what you don't like about us. Shouldn't we be able to do the same with you?"

"Kaylen's nearly perfect. There's nothing wrong with her."

She beamed. What Tony lacked in looks, he compensated for with his charm.

"Okay. Sock it to me," Kaylen said.

"Here goes. You drive us crazy with your clean freak, put-things-in-order, Lane-like superiority, lord-your-smarts-over-us, and I'm-virtuous-and-you-should-be-too attitude," Bran said.

"Gee, don't hold back."

"Look, you asked for it," Schaffer pointed out.

"Yep. That's what this group is all about now," Tony said. "Being frank."

"Frank? We have a Frank? Who's Frank?" Bran asked.

"Frank is my make-believe brother. The smart brother I always wanted but didn't get," Schaffer brayed.

"He means frank, as in honesty," Kaylen explained. "What we want in our group. Transparency, integrity."

"All good stuff, just for you, honey," Tony said.

"Pivotal moments," Kaylen said.

"And here you argued we were all beyond reform," Luke said.

"With personalities, only a mother could love." Schaffer finger-combed the tangles out of his long hair, then allowed Kaylen to do it more effectively.

"Oh, speaking of mothers, I talked to Rosa this morning."

"Okay, my mom spoke to you, or you talked to her?" Luke crushed out his cigarette. "Because there's a distinct difference. With her, it depends on who does the talking and how it ends up getting interpreted. All these years of living in America, and she still has a hard time grasping the English language."

"The same could be said for Bran."

"How's this for understanding it, huh? Screw off, Tony, and do it clockwise. *E spero che fa male* (and I hope it hurts)."

"No, we understand each other fine. She thinks y'all need monitoring. She worries about you," Kaylen said.

"Yeah. Especially since we got arrested," Luke said.

"You what?! When? See what I mean? Now, *that's* a secret! And nobody ever told me?" Kaylen cried.

"It was no big deal," Bran said. "We never expected to get caught."

"Prisons are full of law-breakers who've uttered those very words. What were the charges?"

"Shoplifting. Minor offense," Bran said.

"Purely a misdemeanor," Schaffer downplayed it. "The five-finger discount a blip on our records." He kissed the back of Kaylen's hand in thanks as she finished getting all the knots out of his hair.

"And because we were juveniles, we got community

service, and the matter was done with." Tony swiped one palm over the other.

"Where did y'all steal from?"

"A department store. In a mall." Luke lengthened his legs over Kaylen's lap as she settled upon the sofa.

"What would possess you to do such a thing?" Kaylen asked.

"It was a dare. An initiation thing," Schaffer explained.

"See? Yours wasn't that demanding. You got off easy, didn't you?"

"Says you, Bran. I beg to differ. Who was in on this?"

"All of us except pantywaist," Tony jerked a finger at Lane.

"I said from the beginning it was a bad idea. I didn't want any part of it."

"No, you don't go in for that petty nonsense. You save your involvement for the big crimes." Luke, satisfied when his brother winced.

"It should have been a breeze. You know, snatch it up and get out?" Schaffer explained.

"Hey, how was I to know she was the heat?" Bran shrugged.

"Can we start at the introductory? I love when you guys give me bits and pieces, the climax before the opening, the epilogue before the diegesis."

"I have no idea what you're talking about—epilogue, diegesis? But I do know a thing or two about climaxes." Bran bobbled his eyebrows.

"Shut your spit-hole and let Shay and me do the talking," Tony ordered. "We were supposed to go in and rip things off. Spy it and get out quick."

"Tony was on lookout; Luke was posing as a shopper; Bran and I were gonna cram our pockets with the goods, and Raymo the getaway driver, Lane sitting shotgun," Schaffer narrated.

"Bran sees this girl smiling at him. Soon he's in the rap with her." Tony picked up where Schaffer left off.

"I never could resist a beautiful face," Bran said.

"Particularly when it's your own," Luke jested.

"She did resemble Bran an awful lot." Tony said. "Great blond hair, green eyes. Genetic perfection. They would have had the most gorgeous kids if they had hooked up."

"Anyway, they flirt, and Bran tells her: 'Hey, pretty, I'd like to get to know you better. How about it?' And she grins and says: 'Yeah, darlin' let's go,' and slaps a pair of handcuffs on him! He says: 'Kinky! Alright now,' and she whips out her badge and tells him she is undercover," Tony said.

"Of course, we all watched this and were crapping our pants," Schaffer said.

"I signaled Schaffer and Luke, and we booked."

"Tony! You mean you were gonna take off without Bran?"

"That's right."

"Are you kidding me? That's not cool, bailing and letting someone else take the fall!" Kaylen cried.

"We ain't the Marines, honey," Luke snickered. "Leave no man behind is not our creed."

"It didn't matter anyway," Schaffer pointed out. "We were busted. That lady cop had pegged us all. When Raymo realized we'd gotten caught, he and Lane peeled rubber."

"I think the whole thing was all wrong. Not about Raymo ditching us. I mean about the lady cop. She got me to implicate myself under false pretenses! First, who expects a pretty cop? I wouldn't have done that, wouldn't have said those things if she'd been ugly. Second, I wouldn't have approached her had I known she was the fuzz," Bran said.

"Let me get this straight. She shouldn't have been attractive, she shouldn't have been undercover, and she shouldn't have been sneaky to catch sticky-fingered thieves? Bran, that's called a sting. And appropriately named because you got stung, baby."

He shrugged at her and blazed another joint.

"Hey, stop that bogarting," Tony said.

"Nope. Mine, all mine. Rolled by little ol' me by my little ol' self."

"I'm gonna come over there and break your little ol' hands if you don't share that," Tony said.

Bran surrendered it, his attention swiveling to Lane. "You know, you brush it off like you didn't have any responsibility for what happened. It wouldn't have killed you to help Tony on watch."

"Bran, if you gotta lay blame, go ahead. But I tried to talk you guys out of it."

"Sure, and what do you care? You never had to spend a night in jail!" Bran said.

"No one would bail y'all out?" Kaylen asked.

"When we called our folks, the consensus among the Vincuzzi and Mancuso parents was that being incarcerated overnight would teach the young folks a lesson, one that we wouldn't want to repeat. My mother told us to say our Hail Marys; my father told us to suffer it out." Luke shifted his legs off Kaylen's lap.

"Wait a minute; you were juveniles. They didn't take you to juvy jail?"

"No, the juvy house was full up. They put us in a regular jail but stuck us in the quadrant for light-weight offenders and minor crimes. That's why our folks were fine with us staying overnight." Tony plumped the couch cushion and changed position.

"All our parents were livid," Luke said.

"Your poor mother," Kaylen said.

"Their poor mother? Pity us! We spent the night in a hot,

smelly cell with a big black dude with bad breath and bowling-ball sized biceps, a wino who counted pink elephants all night, and a Vidal Sassoon wannabe who kept telling me how fab my long hair was and wanted to do something divine to it!" Schaffer exclaimed.

"Jail was a learning experience for sure. We were young and not yet privy to the ways of the hard-cold world."

"That's a lie, Tony. Rosa told me one reason they moved down here was to get you, Luke and Lane away from the older gang kids in your neighborhood. The Bronx?"

"Brooklyn. We were young and stupid. Needed to learn how not to get caught ripping off things."

"In other words, you kept on doing it but got better?" Kaylen asked.

"That is an assumption on your part."

"Right-o. What I love is that you, Luke, and Lane moved here to get away from getting into trouble but then managed to take Schaffer and Bran down with you," Kaylen said.

"You got me. I am the ringleader," Tony said.

"Are you kidding? What makes you think Schaffer and Bran got enlisted? How do you know they weren't the instigators?" Luke asked Kaylen.

"That's right. Me and Luke might have brought our street-wise ways with us, but my cousins? Those yahoos were just as bad! These boys with rebel roots? They got country gumption and do things that I would seriously think twice before doing it! They're redneck crazy," Tony said.

"Don't believe what he says," Schaffer twinkled, twisting his camo patterned bandana and tying back his hair.

"Come on. I am not capable of these things. I have the face of an angel!" Bran sunk his index fingers inside his dimples, raising his gaze to the heavens.

"And the mind of a dingbat." Luke rapped on Bran's skull.

"Y'all are all such miscreants! I can't believe this. I am hanging out with jailbirds."

"Reformed J.D.'s," Bran corrected Kaylen.

"A very informative conversation. I love our theme of openness and honesty," Kaylen said.

Lane sighed at the men's snide smiles, knowing the threat of blackmail loomed over every conversation with Kaylen.

"All this talking, it's worked up an appetite." Bran played his tummy like a bongo.

"Do you have a tapeworm? I fixed you a lovely dinner not even two hours ago."

"An eternity for me. I'm gonna rummage your fridge and cabinets." He called from the kitchen: "I can't find what I want! Specifically, Lucky Charms. Where's my magically delicious cereal?"

"I think there's a box of Frosted Flakes. That'll have to suffice," Kaylen said.

"No, no, no! I have a taste for Lucky Charms."

"I sense a Bran pout coming on," Luke muttered.

"Munchies and a temper tantrum—the worst combination," Tony said. "Right, you big baby?"

"Up yours, all of you." Bran returned, eating from a box of Fruit Loops.

"What's with you guys not using utensils, cups, bowls? And are your hands clean?" Kaylen asked.

"No. They're as filthy as my mind," Bran said.

"You better had washed your hands before you started digging around in that box of cereal," Kaylen warned.

"Even better, I spit on them first," Bran said.

"Ahh, nature's cleanser. Better than soap. A little spit, and you're good to go!" Tony laughed.

"It's totally something that numb-nuts would do." Luke poked Bran in the arm. "Remember, this is the guy who actually licked all the creme out of the inside of the Oreos—and then stuck 'em back in the bag!"

"That wasn't all that gross. The fact that you ate the cookies anyway, well, I think that's a lot worse." Bran accused Luke.

"Hey, Schaffer's passed out." Kaylen pointed.

"Get up, butt wipe." Bran jabbed him, his brother non-responsive.

"How much did he party tonight?" Luke asked.

"The usual. Maybe he's extra tired," Tony said.

"Maybe he's dead. If he is, I call dibs on his bed, which by the way, is cushier than mine. Whata' you say, Tone?" Bran asked.

"That's a plan. Okay, Shay, we're divvying up your worldly goods. I get your prized comic book collection, all of your drug stash, and the nice gold chain you got hidden in the bottom of your bureau that you think we don't know anything about," Tony said.

"Wanna give him a nut shot? If he's faking it, that'll bring him around," Luke suggested.

"In case you didn't notice, he popped a pill not too long ago," Lane informed them.

"What kind of pill?" Tony asked.

"I don't have a clue. Something white," Lane said.

"Maybe barbs?" Tony asked, Bran shrugging.

Kaylen grew troubled. "Check him."

Bran pressed a palm to his brother's chest. "Still ticking. Crap, now I don't get his bed."

"Nice. I love your concern."

"Cool out, Kaylen. I'm jiving. And don't worry about Shay. It ain't like this is the first time this has happened. He'll be fine. He always is," Bran said.

"Thing is, he's probably out for the night. Which means I'm not lugging stupid home. Passed out equal's dead weight."

"Well, you can't leave him here, Tony. I mean it. When you go, take your pet with you," Kaylen said.

"Schaffer, get your lazy hump up right now, or we're gonna put a firecracker down your pants," Tony whispered in his ear.

"We are? Awesome!" Bran clicked his Zippo.

"No. Listen, each one of you grab a leg and an arm and haul him out," Kaylen said.

"And let his head drag on the ground?"

"Of course, Bran. Because we want him stoned and have a concussion."

"We came over in the Jon boat," Tony said. "It barely has enough room to maneuver five people, much less taking four of those people to balance said idiot into the boat."

"We could tie him to an inner tube and pull him behind us," Bran suggested.

"Well, absolutely. Because we want him to either drown or be a nice little midnight alligator snack," Kaylen snorted.

"Leave him put. What's the problem?"

"Wouldn't that be like letting the fox stay in the chicken coop?" Kaylen snickered at Luke's suggestion.

"My brother is harmless," Bran said.

"Hmmm. And that's what they said about Albert Fish too. All the while, he was enjoying a tasty meal made from chopping up his victims," Kaylen said.

"Come on. What's the big whoop?" Tony asked. "Schaffer is practically comatose, much less taking a middle-of-the-night stroll up to your boudoir!"

"We'll make it like a giant slumber party," Bran said. "We'll do the usual sleepover pranks. Kaylen, if you fall asleep first, we'll take your bra and freeze it. Oh, and don't forget that other all-time sleepover favorite: the water over the hand trick. We'll stick Schaffer's hand in warm water and see if it makes him pee in his sleep!"

"No. I will not have someone whizzing on my davenport!" Kaylen grumbled.

"Kaylen, why can't we stay? We'll make ourselves at home. Throw a couple of blankets our way, and we'll sack out right here in the living room."

The others exchanged a side glance. Well, of course, Kaylen would do it for Lane.

"Oh, alright. But I better not hear the pitter-patter of feet in the dark," Kaylen said.

"We promise to be good boys." Tony brandished the Cub Scout sign.

"And eat all our vegetables," Luke added.

"And come straight home from school and do all our homework," Tony said.

"And not make ca-ca in our pants." Bran cracked up at their silliness.

"Hardy-har. I mean it, no sneaking around my house in the middle of the night."

"Accommodations?" Tony asked.

"Blankets and pillows, coming up," Kaylen said.

"Can one of us sleep in the guest room?"

"Sorry, Bran. I didn't offer it because we use it as a storeroom, and it's crowded."

"I can squeeze a pallet in, right?' I'll go for it. I love having my own space for the night. These two turds I share with? One or the other snoring all night or coughing up a lung with their smoker's hack. It's noisy, noisy all night long."

"This from the person who walks and talks in his sleep." Tony jerked a thumb at him.

Kaylen dumped pillows and blankets on a chair. "Here you go. See ya in the morning." She bussed Lane's cheek.

"How come he gets a goodnight smack? Surely I am the most kissable one here!"

"Oh, for crying out loud! Come on then."

Bran dutifully minded, his mirth muffled against Kaylen's mouth, she leaning in for a quick peck, and he instead smooching a good one.

"Am I gonna have to go through this with every one of you?" She sighed, shooing Bran away.

Tony drew Kaylen to him, showing her his skills. "I pass the torch to you, buddy."

Luke kissed her long and hard, cueing his friends that she belonged to him despite his okay with them smooching Kaylen.

"Don't leave Shay out," Bran spouted. "Give him a little night-night smackaroo."

"He won't know it nor appreciate it."

"We'll tell him when he wakes up. He'll love it," Bran said.

Kaylen pecked Schaffer's forehead. She screeched, his arms snaking around her neck, locking lips, yanking her down on top of him. He twisted, ensnaring her under his hips.

"You faker! And let me up!"

"Nice maneuvering, cuz," Tony said.

"You weren't passed out at all! You were awake all this time?!" Kaylen cried.

"No, honestly, I was out. Started coming around about the time the kiss-off began," Schaffer said.

"Figures, he'd come out of a coma to suck face with a beautiful girl," Tony said.

Lane snapped his fingers. "What about your dad? Is he due home? What if he comes in and sees all of us sleeping over here?"

"I do not even have the strength to think about that right now." Kaylen yawned.

"We'll tell him we had an orgy."

"Oh, that would be most helpful, Bran."

"Okay, take your leaks, settle down, shut up and go to sleep," Tony ordered.

Kaylen traipsed up the stairs, Bran in tow, who said, "All right, goodnight ladies and sweet dreams."

"May they all be wet ones," Tony said.

"Kaylen, you wearing your birthday suit to bed?" Schaffer propped up, peering at her.

"Nope, chastity belt." Not missing a beat.

"Hey, Kay," Luke called softly, "what are you *really* gonna wear to bed?"

"Goodnight." Killing the lights and leaving Luke to his imagination.

CHAPTER SEVEN

August melded into September, the roasting months on repeat, as if summer's reign illimitable, thwarting any chance of a cool autumn respite.

The murders of *Valley of The Dolls* celebrity Sharon Tate and her house guests jolted a nation, juxtaposed with the musical event of Woodstock, peace, and love overlapping with atrocity. Both occurrences core topics of conversation for Kaylen and her friends. But as Labor Day sidled, they focused on the bustling holiday weekend at the campground.

Kaylen couldn't determine when the detection took place— before Neil Armstrong became the first man to walk on the moon or after Rolling Stones Brian Jones' death? Or was it while watching The Brady Bunch? Perhaps it was when they snickered at Nixon's promise to withdraw U.S. troops from Vietnam by November 1970, that Kaylen's scales fell from her eyes. The rebarbative, even disturbing, characteristics of her closest friends were exposed.

She'd contended with the men's disgusting running contest

with each other—a one-up of who slept with the most girls. They'd kept track since their first sexual experience. As young teens, they chronicled exploits in a "boning book"—a journal of their partners and a page for each man and their totals. As time marched on, they ditched the book, tallying a mental spreadsheet instead. Never a shortage of females at the campground for their *una botta e via'* contest (a dirty Italian phrase for fornicating, specifically 'a bang and go'), the men bragged they'd bedded more women than a rock-star.

It wasn't purely their peacocking that bothered Kaylen. She disassembled their idiosyncrasies, plotting the points to her mental graph.

Tony. His bad-boy mien, not a front. Had a trigger in him—exacerbated when loaded with liquor. His temper under restraint around Kaylen, but Lane bowed him up. He kept it cool at the campground but mixed it up off turf. Most people steered from locking horns with Tony. Those unwise enough to provoke the nineteen-year-old, Tony's thew guaranteed him the victor.

Bran. Narcissistic and used girls. Despite being the youngest, he was the reigning "king of the contest," rumpling the most sheets out of all the guys. Not the sharpest tool in the shed, but his stunning face and charisma made it easy for him. Kaylen found it hard to imagine that Bran could be drafted into the military at just seventeen years old, given his immaturity and self-absorption. Watching Walter Cronkite on CBS news, she witnessed underage draftees being sent off to fight. The oversized soldier uniforms engulfed them, making it appear they were playing dress-up in their fathers' clothes, rather than heading off to a real war.

Schaffer. Eighteen years old and committed to the "high." Smoking pot, dropping acid, tripping on "shrooms," popping pills—goofballs, cross tops, Quaaludes, T's and blues, red devils. As a recreational user, he swore he knew when to reel it in. But... hairy moments—a bad LSD trip, a near overdose. No call for alarm, folks, he'd say. Don't worry. I'm cool. His laid-back manner had one flare-off—the Vietnam War.

A Dove, he'd rancor the baby-killers, napalm, the money pumped into the war effort. He praised Timothy Leary, Abbie Hoffman, Jane Fonda. Supported protest marches, draft-card burnings, storming R.O.T.C. buildings. He'd read Hoffman's "Revolution for the Hell of It," sang Bob Dylan, Country Joe, and Phil Ochs, played the Beatles "Revolution I"—safe from the jungles, bloodshed, and gunfire of My Lai. Schaffer's systematic study of the history and politics of the Vietnam War exceeded even the analysts, proving his drug use hadn't blunted his intellect. He was spouting off statistics and memorizing every stanza of each Beatles' hit and their position and duration on Billboard's Top 40.

Lane. Her best friend, her confidant, in tune with each other like an old married couple. He the Yang to her Yin. A man who was more befitting for her than Luke. But not in love with him. She wished he'd stand up for himself, to the bullying. Eighteen-year-old Lane invited resentment, a cerebral guy whose knowledge muddled the other men's brains. Still, it didn't warrant the degree of hostility the others barraged against him.

Luke. He captured her heart. His lack of monogamy chafed. He blamed it on Kaylen's reluctance to give up her virginity. She rejected his charge, his licentiousness, his problem. He continued working his guy's game. What man wouldn't be tempted by the steady stream of females at the campground? Nineteen-year-old Luke was like a kid in a candy store. Kaylen got it. But how did Luke have time for these girls? His nose to the grindstone or else at Kaylen's house, they carved out their alone time, but the group together 24/7. Her suspicions aroused by Luke's exaggerated yawns, complaining of not getting his full eight and exiting her house earlier than the other guys. She figured that's when he scored.

Kaylen overheard the conversation in the game room, the door wide open as she checked stock in the front office. The gossipers shot pool, the fire-and-russet maned woman aiming line with solids, her companion with sausage curls calling pocket on stripes, Virginia Slims smoldering between their lips. A breakdown of their midnight rendezvous partying and sleeping with the two hot guys who worked at the campground. Kaylen didn't require a composite sketch to figure it out. Schaffer instigated the hookup, Luke his friend in tow. Luke deemed compatible with the spare girl for their coupling. Kaylen stewed the rest of the afternoon over Luke's betrayal. When her friends arrived at her house that evening, she allowed them to settle in but plowing on before anyone produced pot, pills, or booze.

Schaffer browsed through Kaylen's albums, pondering the evening's accompaniment. "Shay, pick something quick and make it mellow."

With Kaylen's mouth puckering like she had licked a lime, Schaffer hoped to assay the sour mood, his voice solacing. "I was leaning toward acid rock. Maybe Pink Floyd. Or even The Guess Who."

"More mellow than that. Maybe Donovan? Peter, Paul, and Mary? No, wait, make it instrumental, classical—Mozart, Tchaikovsky, Chopin."

"Ooookay. I'm not grooving on it, but here goes." He cranked out Beethoven.

"Death by music! Boring me into an early grave."

Kaylen ignored Bran's bemoaning. "You two have been busy boys," she snarled at Luke and Schaffer.

Everyone on the alert, Kaylen's Prussian blue eyes were snapping, the tip-off to her wrath.

Bran attempted to diffuse. "Busy, busy is better. Idle hands are the work of the devil. We're toiling like little beavers."

"Too bad it doesn't keep your stupid mouth from being in overdrive," Kaylen grumbled.

"Whoa! Miss Grumpy needs an industrial-sized Maxi Pad, a Midol, and good drugs to make it all better," Bran grunted.

"No sense of humor today and super snotty," Tony agreed.

"Hold on, honey. I got something to lift you." Schaffer pulled a hash pipe and a baggie of dope from his pocket.

"Oh, don't waste that on me. Save that for your little sleaze-ball bed mate."

"Which one?" Like his brother, he was trying for humor.

"The one who can't even pronounce your name," Kaylen said.

"Most people can't get my brother's name right. 'Chayper,' 'Shaver,' 'Skayfer'—he's heard them all."

"I earwigged an interesting conversation today. Two girls who couldn't help but brag about their latest hookup. A guy named 'Shamer' and his friend 'Luke,'" Kaylen said.

"'Shamer,' now that's a new one, bro."

"Luke is a very common name," Luke said.

"Not at all," Kaylen said.

"Wasn't me."

"You're lying!" Kaylen cried.

"Plead the fifth, dude. It's the only way."

"Shove it, Bran."

"Calm down, Kay."

"Don't you dare tell me to calm down, Luke!"

"Kaylen, quit bugging, will you? Let's see what's on the boob tube tonight." Bran said.

"The fights are about to start," Kaylen said.

"Ordinarily, I would be all the way in on that," Tony said, "but I have to agree with my cousin. Take a load off, Kaylen. Take a hit of hash."

"So I'll relax to the max? That I'll get so super stoned, I won't notice or care that Luke will find an excuse to leave early? To split to be with a girl? Meanwhile pretending he's tired and has to go?"

"He does need his rest, Kaylen. After all, he's getting older. He's pushing 20."

"Bran, I love you. But you need to shut your mouth right now. It's not helping."

"Okay, mouth locked. Throwing away the key."

"And Schaffer. What about you? Got anything to say for yourself?" Kaylen posed for battle, hands-on-hips.

"Why are you coming down on me?" Schaffer sighed.

"Because it's like you being the driver and taking an alcoholic to a liquor store! What did you think? Was Luke going to sit there and play solitaire and wait while you did your thing? No, you knew all about your skuzzy friend's friend: no fifth wheels, only twosomes. You brought Luke along to occupy the other girl. It worked," Kaylen said.

"Sweetness, I was with that shady lady and will take full responsibility for my actions. I am a cad. My good friend Luke was not a party to these terrible indiscretions," Schaffer said.

"Never mind covering for me, dude. I'll take the heat. I've had enough. You got a beef with me, Kay? Are we gonna do this now? Telling our business? *Stiamo dicendo a tutti il nostro la faccenda?* (we're telling everyone our story)" Luke said.

"Hey, aren't we among family and friends?! Anyway, we both know that whatever we discuss will eventually be broadcast to the others! You're going to give Shay, Bran, and Tony your story, and I'm gonna talk it over with Lane on my own. We might as well save breath, energy, and time and do this right here and now!" Kaylen said.

"Can we smoke a peace pipe while all this goes on?" Schaffer asked, cornering the bowl.

"That's what you're calling it now? Fine. Who cares?" Kaylen said.

"Well, you got the floor; speak your piece," Luke said.

"You going to man up, Luke? Are you gonna 'fess up? Or are you going to make me beg you for the truth?" Kaylen asked.

"Okay. You got me. I did it. I did the deed with that chick."

"Did you think I was that stupid that I couldn't figure it out eventually?!"

"You're far from stupid, Kay. I didn't do it intentionally."

"What? The lying to me or doing the girl?!" Kaylen asked.

"Hurting you. I never meant to hurt you. I never meant for you to find out like this," Luke said.

"Like this?! Luke, you never meant for me to find out *at all*!"

"Whatever, Kay. I can apologize. That's all I can do."

"Until it happens again? How many times will I have to hear your apologies, Luke? Because you and I both know that this girl wasn't the first, and she won't be the last," Kaylen said.

"Kay, you take care of me right, and I won't need to find loving in other places."

"You take care of *me* and it'll happen. It starts with not cheating. Loving is what I give you, offer you, show you every day we're together. You'll never be cared for anywhere else but here, Luke."

"Maybe. But man doesn't live on bread alone. You're offering bread and water when I'm starving. I need supplement. I've got an appetite if you know what I mean."

"Yeah, Luke. I know what you mean. Everyone here knows what you mean."

"We're not kids, Kay. We're consenting age. I'm living life now. I'm asking you to come along for the ride. We've had a gas outside of crossing over that line. Step on over and enjoy," Luke insisted.

"Until you tire of me and move on to your next catch? See, because I realize what you don't. Part of the novelty of me is that I don't put out like all the rest. I'm a challenge to you. But what you are to me is much more. *I* want to be much more."

"Kay, you already are. Do you see me—the guys—asking other girls to work here, hang out, be a blood sister?"

"You show me that by accepting me into the group, that you care. But then you disrespect me by sleeping around?!"

"Accept it. Or change it," Luke said.

"Then what? Will you promise not to be with other girls? We'll ride off into the sunset on a great white steed?" Kaylen asked.

"Hmm. Like the ending of one of your trashy novels?" Luke said.

"Romance books," she corrected. "In my stories, the princess is saved by the knight. The handsome knight does not rescue said princess and then dilly with the other damsels."

"In my story, the princess removes the knight's sword from the sheath and palms it firmly in her hand, if you know what I mean." Bran, unable to contain himself any longer.

"If I remove your sword from the sheath, I'll probably stick it in the fire until your cutlass is melted and useless," Kaylen said.

"Ouch! Sure you wanna do that? We could play 'hide the dagger' instead!"

"Bran! Enough! Can you butt out?"

"Well, excuse me, Miss-I-am-among-family-and-friends.

Can I call your attention to the fact we're all here listening to this? We hear, and we have opinions," Bran said.

"I hate to agree with him, but we're squarely in the middle here." Tony, the last person in the rotation, passed the pipe to Schaffer.

"May I suggest the happy couple get counseling?" Schaffer took a final hit right before the cherry died. "Maybe you and Luke need a professional mediator."

"Your romance books? It's fiction. This? Us? Real drama. Real problems. It's been a vicious circle, but it doesn't have to be," Luke said.

"And the problem with a circle? It keeps coming around. It's not a path; it loops back. You can go forward, but it doesn't end," Kaylen said.

"I'm telling you it can end. Right here. Right now. Like this." Luke pulled Kaylen pelvis to pelvis before she even knew it happened. "Show me, Kay. Show me, and I won't need any other woman."

"It still wouldn't be enough for you, Luke. You love the lure too much with other girls. You love the game. I won't ever be enough for you."

"No, you're the right amount." Their kiss, molten. When they broke apart, four pairs of eyes were blinking at them.

"Did you forget we were—" Bran bubbled.

"—Not even for a second," Kaylen said.

"Don't stop on our account." Schaffer stowed his para-phernalia.

"I woulda' said 'get a room,' but I don't mean it. Let's save all the live-action for out here," Bran said.

"Oh, so you wanna watch?" Kaylen cooed.

"Oooooh, pretty please, yes, yes, yes!" Bran twinkled.

"You're a pig." Frost replaced Kaylen's teasing tone.

Bran grunted. "I know."

"Wanna continue this party elsewhere? Even better, get rid of all these bozos?"

"Luke," Kaylen's lilt cloyed, "I know you guys have tagged teamed with each other. I've heard the talk. But do you think for one minute I would have my first time be with these idiots ogling? Listening from the other room? What kind of girl do you think I am?" Her convivial disposition extinguished, pushing him away.

"Obviously the type who is ending our fun," Bran sulked.

"Come on, Kay. Don't be upset with me. I wasn't going to do you right here."

"Luke, we both know had I said 'yes,' you'd have been in me and not on me."

"Uuhh, Kaylen, you gotta stop talking like that. This is from every guy in this room and me. I know you're not trying to be hot. But that's hot talk. And it's driving us wild!" Bran said.

"Then maybe you should cut out. Maybe your brother will share what's-her-name with you. Then you won't have to worry about hot talk. You'll get the real thing," Kaylen suggested.

"A cool idea at a different place and time. But right now, I'm waiting to see how this pans out," Bran said.

"Well, it's going where it always goes. Kay wants to play hard to get while all I want to do is to play ball."

"That's what you think, Luke? That I'm playing hard to get?"

"Yeah, and there's a name for that. For chicks like that," Bran said.

"I swear to you if it starts with a 'C' and ends with 'tease,' and you dare call me that, I'll come over there and rip your lips from your face," Kaylen warned him.

"My mouth is safe. I would never dream of using that word to describe you. But don't you think you're stringing Luke along?" Bran asked.

"Brandy, you're a piece of work! If anyone wrote the book on 'stringing people along,' it would be you. You use every girl you meet and then make them think that the relationship is going somewhere. Like you actually care!"

"I can't be responsible for chicks and their assumptions."

"Oh, puh-leeze. I've heard your spiel. If I didn't know you, I'd believe your lies too. Easy to assume when the charmer flashes a winning smile and waxes poetic," Kaylen snorted.

"You really think I got a great smile and talk a good game?" Bran brightened.

"Yeah, I do. Unfortunately, you also have a cold black heart," Kaylen sniped.

"Oh, man, you got chopped, cuz," Tony said.

"How did this conversation get turned on me? We were talking about you and Luke," Bran asked.

"Because you couldn't mind your beeswax, baby." Schaffer thumped his arm. "She told you to shut your trap. But the door is wide open, and we can't close it."

"Kaylen, I have to agree with my man Luke. You need to lighten up and take off your nun's habit." Tony said.

"You're a nun, and Luke gets none. Get it?" Bran added.

"Hysterical," Kaylen said.

"Come on. Lighten up. Loosen up," Bran said.

"Loosen up, huh? Like, loosen up my morals?" Kaylen asked.

"Hey, if that's what you want to do! Don't let us stop you!" Bran said.

"Yeah, come on over with us to the dark side." Tony crooked his finger.

"Amongst the sinners and dregs of society," Schaffer said.

"And perverts. Let's not leave them out," Tony added.

"But no pedophiles. We don't diddle with babies," Bran said.

"You bad boys want to see my naughty girl side?"

"Percolate! Nix the hot talk and show us the hot action," Schaffer said.

"Wowee. Hot talk combined with action. Rover is a happy dog. He's about to wag his tail," Bran grinned.

"Rover needs to get docked," Kaylen quipped, her friends chortling. "A kiss is all you're getting from me, Bran."

"You sure?"

"Unequivocally."

"I don't know what that word means. But it sounds like a 'no' to the party in my pants," Bran said.

"That's a shame, bro. I figured it was the party that never ended," Schaffer said.

"See Kaylen? Everyone's inviting you to a pants party, but you won't RSVP," Tony japed.

"Maybe you'd rather board the Schaffer Locomotive?" His green orbs glistered.

"That's a train that already derailed," Kaylen snickered.

"We've all offered our willing bodies and been turned down flat by you, Kaylen," Bran said.

"Doing the deed. Good times for everybody," Luke said.

"It's a stress-buster," Schaffer said. "Better than pot."

"Helps you make new friends," Bran said.

"Great exercise," Tony added.

"Makes the garden bloom," Kaylen snarled.

"Not if you don't fertilize it." Bran reached into his back pocket, exhibiting a foil pack.

"You happen to have that, huh?" Kaylen eyed the condom.

"He's a skeevy opportunist, remember?" Tony said.

"We all are," Schaffer admitted, and everyone except Lane tossed a condom at Kaylen. She scooped one up like it was a turd, her mouth pursed in distaste. Luke snatched it from her and opened the drawer to the small desk beside the couch. He withdrew a Sharpie, scribbled on the condom pack. "This has your name written on it now—figuratively, literally, whatever. I'm saving this for you. For us."

He had inscribed 'K' on it. "Oh, Luke. The romantic as usual." Kaylen fluttered her eyelashes fake-adoringly.

"That's a lovely gesture. It brings tears to my eyes." Bran retrieved his treasure, cramming it back into his pocket.

"It doesn't get more special than that." Tony tapped his heart. "Monogramming your girl's initial on your condom."

"Personalized condoms. That is love." Schaffer made kissing noises.

"I'm going to leave this here. Make sure daddy doesn't see it." Luke sealed the marker and condom inside the desk drawer.

"Here's a scenario. Fast forward ten years. The condom is still there. Unopened. Gathering dust. Kaylen still refuses Luke. The both of them now have grey hair." Bran spun the tale.

"Grey hair, Bran? In ten years, I won't even be in my thirties yet! You're aging me!"

"That's the thing. A lack of nookie will age you. It'll make you older than your years," Bran said.

"Ahh. The obtainment of eternal youth is at my disposal; it's simply a zipper away," Kaylen said.

"The idea of having to wait another decade for Kaylen to come around fills me with depression." Luke pretended to slit his wrists.

"It is a horrific notion," Schaffer said, patting him on the shoulder.

"Then I remember, its Kaylen's choice, not mine. You know, I'm willing to cut you some slack here. But seriously, how long am I expected to wait around for you to open the vault?"

"I don't know. What is the magic number? In the vastness

of Luke's brain, what is the correct answer? Two days? Six months?" Kaylen asked.

"It's already been a long time," Luke said.

"Time is subjective."

"*Now*, you want to contribute to the conversation, Lanesy? Time is a vice that's been squeezing my junk. Like a pressure cooker building up and waiting to blow off steam," Luke said.

"You're as dramatic as Bran! We haven't even been together a whole year yet—which, by the way, would be a minimally appropriate time to expect a relationship to develop and for a woman to remain chaste during that period," Kaylen said.

"Chaste? Who uses words like that?" Bran shrugged.

"Intelligent women," Kaylen bristled. "Who I am sure—me being the exception—you do not fraternize with."

"I'm around my mother. My mother is smart," Bran said.

"Too bad her youngest son is an imbecile."

"You're zinging 'em out today, Kaylen." Tony made a checkmark in the air.

"Quit setting yourself up, bro," Schaffer said.

"Stick it, Rapunzel. The way I see it, my mother has at least one other idiot son."

The brothers lived to one-up each other with the cutdowns.

"Where are you getting these ideas? From your trashy novels? That's what your damsels do? Hold out for a year? That's what you want me to do?" Luke asked.

"It's a respectful amount of time. And you have not suffered at all during this courtship, Luke. Since we've been together, you've had a minimum of five hookups outside of our relationship. Do not insult my intelligence by pretending I'm paranoid and imagining it! It doesn't matter if I deny you. You're still going to get yours, aren't you?" Kaylen asked.

"Don't answer that, dude. It's going to take you deeper into the crap hole," Schaffer advised.

"You wanna be a holdout? Okay, *Io accetto, così sia* (I accept it, so be it). Not that I'm digging it. But in the meantime, you've gotta give me something; let me play the other bases with you," Luke said.

"Play the bases? It's been first base since the beginning. Now you're expecting a second? Third? Until we get to fourth?" Kaylen asked.

"Fourth is home run," Bran explained, batting the air. "Grand slam, the ultimate!"

"Luke, I'm sorry to spoil your whole baseball theme, but we're not moving around the diamond. I'm stuck at first and haven't even entertained moving to second," Kaylen said.

"Who's on first, What's on second, and I Don't Know's on third," Tony said.

"I know who's on first—Luke, but he ain't about to be on second, much less third!" Bran said.

"Dipstick. Your cousin is referring to the famous sketch by Abbott and Costello. You know them, right?" Kaylen asked.

"No. Are they like the Smothers Brothers?" Bran asked.

"Abbott and Costello? Comedians. Like in the 1940s," Kaylen said.

"That explains it. Way before my time," Bran said.

"Way before our time too, crap-for-brains," Tony muttered.

"Okay, that's it, Kay? You won't put out, and you won't let me hit the bases?" Luke asked.

"I call it not caving in to pressure."

"Simpler if you would just knuckle under," Luke said.

"Simpler if you would tether the puppy instead of letting it roam in someone else's yard," Kaylen said.

"Luke's puppy and my Rover are bad, bad dogs that need training," Bran said.

"Maybe Rover needs to be picked up by the scruff of the neck and paddled," Kaylen said.

"Ohhh, yeah! Please spank the puppy too!" Bran said, the other guys grinning at the double entendre.

"Luke, you're beyond arrogant! You mess with other girls and then act like I belong to you, don't you? Like I'm your property!"

"Well, you are my girlfriend, Kay."

"That's great for you, Luke. You get it all. And you think that's okay? What if I want a comparable deal?"

"What's that supposed to mean?" Luke frowned.

"Why should you be the only one to have their cake and eat it too? What if I want another boyfriend or two? What if I want to stay with you but also go out with other guys?"

"Yeah, well, it doesn't work that way," Luke said.

"Because you decided it? Any guy would be lucky to get me."

"Maybe lucky to get you but won't be getting lucky. Know what I mean, jelly bean?"

"Or maybe they will be, Bran." Kaylen's tone, contempt, and ice. "Maybe I'll offer the same deal I have with Luke."

"What's that, Kay? You're gonna take 'em around the bases and cut them short of sliding into home?" Luke snickered.

"You think you're the only one I can go to first, second base with?"

"Bottom line, you're my girl. So any other Tom, Dick, and Harry, you better shine them on. Understand?" Luke said.

"Yeah? What about a Tony, Schaffer, Bran? What if it wasn't some random guy? What if it was one of your own?" Kaylen asked.

"Finally," Bran sighed. "Group participation. Here, I'll start it. First, a group hug. Then we'll cop a group frisk."

"Kaylen, what do you think you're doing?" Frost in Lane's tone.

"I'm proving a point. What's wrong, Luke? Don't you think

you can taste your own medicine? What if I got with, let's say... Tony. You wouldn't object to that, would you?"

"But you said you'd never be tagged teamed."

"No, Bran, not tag-teaming. One-on-one. I'm talking about first base strictly with one guy," Kaylen said.

"With Tony? You're asking me if I care if you and Tony go at it?" Luke asked.

"Wait a minute," Bran frowned. "Why Tony? Why not me?"

"Or me."

"Schaffer, I'm not happy about you being Luke's side-kick the other night. And Bran... I don't think you can you actually shut your mouth long enough to go mouth-to-mouth with me."

"That was cruel. And untrue. I have gone mouth-to-mouth with you before, and if memory serves me right, you liked it," Bran said.

"For that matter, we've all gone mouth-to-mouth with you, Kaylen," Schaffer said.

The kissing games evolved after Kaylen informed the men how her dad's job and moving-about hindered her social life. Translocating denied her the opportunity to cultivate friend-ships or attend homecoming, proms, or parties. Her friends relayed their high school hi-jinks, playing Truth or Dare and Suck and Blow (which Bran said sounded a lot dirtier than in actuality) at boy-girl parties whenever parents slipped out of sight. They asked Kaylen if she'd like to experience what she had missed out on, introducing her to Spin the Bottle (the adult version, with taking shots). Seven Minutes in Heaven dawned after Kaylen revealed the downstairs closet served as a "panic room," installed at her dad's insistence. The guys checked out the space—messing with the mechanism that locked it from the inside—Bran concluding the area perfect for playing the party game. Kaylen's house, Kaylen's rules, she told them, modifying the game to kissing only. Each man invited into her closet to play. Seven Minutes in Heaven transformed into a shortened version renamed "Four Minutes in the Closet."

"Yeah, but y'all held back, didn't you?" Kaylen asked.

"You made us!" Schaffer said.

"Otherwise, it wouldn't be the nice, clean kissing I've sanctioned. It'd be lots of moist, slobbering tongues," Kaylen said.

Bran groaned. "In the name of everything dear to me, knock off the hot talk. My boxers are about to detonate."

"You're asking my permission to go full first base with Tony?" Luke asked.

"Oh, no, I'm not asking. I'm giving as good as I get," Kaylen said.

"In other words, you're going to be a user?" Luke asked.

"Yes."

"Kaylen, you're not the user type."

"No, Schaffer? Only you guys got it down?"

"And you want to use Tony?" Luke leaned back, crossing his arms.

"Listen, forget him. I fully volunteer. Use me, abuse me, do whatever you wanna do to me," Bran beseeched.

"I'd like to tape your mouth shut," Kaylen confessed.

"All right! And bind me too, baby."

"Tony, are you a willing partner?" Kaylen asked.

She didn't have to ask Tony twice. He orbited next to Kaylen, glancing at his best friend. Kaylen was mistaken if she anticipated Luke's protest or Tony's tentativeness. Tony kneaded Kaylen's mouth with his until she submitted, full-on first base.

And more. In one quick swoop, he tugged Kaylen under him, hip to hip, kissing like mad. But when he rubbed against her, she protested. He whispered: "Remember, this is what you wanted."

"Tony!" Lane barked.

"Sit down, Lanesy," Bran ordered.

"This is even better than Four Minutes in the Closet," Schaffer said.

Kaylen was no longer smooching Tony back. He ground his hips into hers, with nothing separating their intimacy except their Levi's; he stage-whispered: "Don't start something with me that you can't finish." As he let her up, he muttered inside her ear what no one else could hear: "Because next time I won't stop."

He yanked her from the sofa to standing. "I'm not your science project, Kaylen. I'm down with being your lover if you want to take it there. But don't ever pit me against Luke again."

"I'll be your science project, honey." Bran kneeled, cadging up at her.

"You're a science experiment gone wrong." Tony fired up a cigarette.

"It's Alive!" Schaffer cried, playing out a scene from the movie *Frankenstein*.

"Okay, you got it out of your system now?" Luke asked.

"Watching your best friend with me, did you not feel anything?" Kaylen was astounded at Luke's lack of emotion.

"Forget the both of them. I'll T.C.B. for you. Four minutes in the closet again, and I'll pick up where my cousin left off."

"Yeah, things didn't work out so well for you the last time, Bran. You earned yourself a nice healthy slap," Kaylen reminded him.

"I know, and it's unfair! Tony gets on the cusp of second base, and I get in trouble trying to advance out of first," Bran complained.

"This all settled now? We know where we stand?" Luke asked.

"Luke, you still don't get it! What Tony and I did, it didn't mean anything to me."

"Thanks, Kaylen."

"Oh, so you are a user. I am proud of you, Kaylen." Bran pumped his fist in the air.

"Oh, sorry, Tony. I didn't intend it like that. You do mean something to me—a lot. You all do. I was trying to get Luke to understand what it's like to be on the receiving end of betrayal."

"Whatever your motivation, it ends up the same. I want you to go all the way. But you deny me. Therefore, I have to go someplace else. And you don't understand it. You get yourself racked. It doesn't make me feel good. But it doesn't deter me from straying. You tried to get revenge—or whatever it was. Spite? But you did it hoping to get a reaction from me. But it's my man Tony. So it's cool. It could have been any of my guys," Luke said.

"You'd pimp me out?!" Kaylen cried.

"Nope. But you know it's always going to be my pals over gals. Get it? Bros before bimbos," Luke said.

"That's what I am now? Another one of your hootchies?!"

"No. But if you take it any further with my guys, you're going to be on the path to no redemption," Luke said.

"A road I've traveled too many times." Schaffer waxed poetic.

"You're always going to be my girl, Kay. No matter what." He wrapped his arms around her. "We got history together. We got a future together. We belong together. You belong to me. You're mine. Nothing is going to change that. No one is going to change that."

Kaylen sighed. She didn't try to read into it beyond the promise he proclaimed. It was cut, dried, typical Luke. Despite his odd way of showing it, she mattered to him.

The men resumed their activities—smoking, cutting up, snacking, the group's bog-standard. Just like their friendship, their normal, considered atypical if measured by society's yardstick. These moments, they were frozen in time, lowering Kaylen's guard and veiling the portentousness of what lurked around the corner when nothing would seem the same again.

CHAPTER EIGHT

Perfect October weather brought snowbirds back to the campground, and that month was memorable for Kaylen. She learned of the Vietnam Moratorium, a day-long protest against the war, and listened to Schaffer's new Beatles album, Abbey Road, amidst rumors of Paul McCartney's death. It was also the month when Kaylen's nightmares started, although there seemed no clear cause. She didn't overeat like Bran before bed, and there was no day trauma to blame. When she shared her problem with the guys, Dr. Schaffer suggested she avoid phenobarbitals, psilocybin mushrooms, and pure cannabis as they could induce night terrors. Kaylen was okay with "plain old marijuana," an unlikely culprit for her bad dreams. In October, she also met Raymo, but she never believed that her nightmares were premonitions, even though he would change her life forever.

Kaylen worked the front desk, counting and rolling coins, the jarring of the phone throwing off her tally. "Good afternoon, Crystal Lake Campground. How may I help you?"

"Aw, cara mia."

"Hi, Rosa."

"You page my boys? I no see them all morning and do not know schedule."

"Well, I assigned Luke to dock repair, and Lane is over at Campsite G16 by request of first-time campers, to show them how to build a pit and lay it out for a campfire."

"You get them, yes? Say to them their cousin flies to Orlando and needs ride from airport. He say he take a cab, but I no hear of it."

"Of course. I'll let them know right now."

Kaylen paged Luke, the loudspeaker peeling. He silhouetted against the warm midday sun as he labored by the shore, waving his hammer in acknowledgment.

"This better be good. I am right in the middle of something."

"I hate to take you away from your fun, but Raymo is flying in and has to be picked up from the airport in O town." Shirtless, biceps and abdominals dazzling with suntan oil, shorts slung low on his hips.

"Far out! And caught you ogling."

"Well, you are a sight for sore eyes."

"Remember, you can inspect the merchandise as long as you're gonna buy."

"Tempting, particularly when you're dirty and smelly."

"Am I?" Luke sniffed his armpit. "Why are you checking me out then?"

"Admiring you from afar. Get showered and be gone. Your cousin is waiting."

"That sneaky dirtbag. He never told us he was coming here. But that's the way he does it, likes to come in on the sly."

"The running theme for the guys in this group."

"Where's Tony?"

"I've got him rewiring lights in the laundry hutch."

"I'm gonna swing by and get him."

"Listen, your mom expects you to take your brother."

"Lane will see him soon enough. Anyway, there's no love lost between them."

"Fine. You're the one who has to deal with Mommy-wrath —if there is any. I'm passing on what she said. Don't shoot the messenger."

"Advice from Dear Abby?"

"No. Shakespeare. Possibly Mark Twain. Both cited the quote. And Oscar Wilde—"

Luke groaned. "Spare me. It's all too Lane-like. The two of you are rubbing off on each other."

"You mean we're both intelligent?"

"Yes. And annoying."

"No, that would be Bran."

"Yep. He is that." He turned on his heel.

"Can't wait to meet Raymo. Your foxy mirror image."

Luke pivoted. "Raymo and I have been known to share affection with the same chick if you know what I mean. But you and me and him, that isn't the case."

"You worried I'll go to first base with him?"

"You mean like you have with Tony, Bran, and Schaffer?"

"Remember, you approved that. So now it bothers you?"

"Should it?"

"It's messing around. Good times. Kissing games and fun. Anyway, it makes Bran happy, practically giddy."

"Yeah, well, quite a few things have that effect on him; you, a meatball sandwich, finding change in between the seat of a couch, good dope."

"He's easy to entertain. But yeah, the serious loving, I save for you."

"Like us moving from first base finally and going to second base full-on?"

"I'm still mulling that."

"Yeah. Do. But as far as Raymo goes, you're my woman."

"How about grunting 'Ug'? You're a true Neanderthal. Next, you'll be clubbing me on the head and dragging me off by my hair."

"My normal foreplay. But don't forget you belong to me."

"Yeah. Me and all your other girls."

"Kay, no matter what you think, in the end, there is no other woman for me but you. *Quando chiudo gli occhi la sera, l'ultima cosa a cui penso sei sempre tu* (when I close my eyes at night, the last thing I think about is you). You're the first and last thing on my mind. Now come here." He kissed her, rough and good. "Was that enough to keep you from being curious about my cousin?" He didn't wait for her reply.

* * *

"What's cookin', good lookin'?" Bran nabbed a Popsicle from the cooler, hopping up on the counter.

"I just cleaned there!" Kaylen said, Bran biting the treat, slivers crumbling across the countertop.

"No problem. We'll let you do it again."

"How about a Dreamsicle?" Schaffer asked, his ice cream dripping.

"Get that crap outa' here!" Kaylen said.

"So crabby when we're trying to be generous." Bran licked the sticky spot off the counter.

"Do you know how many people have put their hands on that? And like you, sticking their stinky butts up there. Layers of unsanitary yuck built up over the years," Kaylen pretended to shutter.

"Hey, his spit hole has more germs on it than this counter.

We should be more worried about where his nasty mouth has been," Schaffer said.

"It's a breeding ground for bacteria, for sure. Nibbling on skanky females and tongue-probing all their orifices," Bran said.

"No more. I'm about to throw up in my mouth." Kaylen swabbed the counter with Pine-Sol. "You think the guys are gonna get back soon?"

"I checked the flights. Luke, Tony, and Mr. Beautiful should make their entrance at any time now." Bran slurped his Popsicle.

"Oh, is that jealousy I hear? Not from the one who's better looking than any other male!" Kaylen asked.

"Of course not. We are both beautiful but in different ways. I am golden and gorgeous, and Raymo is tall-dark-and-handsome," Bran said.

"Like Luke," Kaylen said.

"Yeah. *Exactly* like Luke. It weirds me out how much they resemble each other. Some people say they can't even tell them apart. Unless you're with them for a while. Then you can see it. Raymo frowns more. He's more intense, more intimidating that Luke," Bran said.

"Like Tony," Kaylen said.

"Yeah. Like if Luke and Tony made a baby together, it would be Raymo," Bran said.

"That idea is extremely disturbing. But, hey, wouldn't that be like guy-on-guy action?" Kaylen said.

Bran shuddered. "Don't even kid about it. And don't tell 'em you said it. If a dude said it, he'd probably get punched. Machismo, baby. Tony and Luke love women. Period."

"Ditto with Raymo." Schaffer hopped up beside his brother. "He's even set his sights on the same chicks we're interested in."

"He tries to edge out you guys? And you don't like it, right?"

"Never said that. Nothing wrong with a little healthy competition. We're okay with sharing too," Schaffer said.

"I've heard. And been warned," Kaylen said.

"By Lane?" Schaffer asked.

"No, Luke. He let me know that I'm his and not a potential for Raymo's affection."

"Interesting. Sounds like Luke might be more serious than you thought," Schaffer said.

"And he's gonna put something sparkly on my left ring finger? I think not. It's no secret how I feel about him. As far as that being likewise, Luke's more about establishing ownership. Like with you guys, when it comes to me and y'all, he's marking boundaries."

"Not with Raymo, he doesn't. No chicks are off limits between them. Not before you came along," Schaffer said.

Kaylen let that sink it. She remembered Luke's confession about how she occupied his waking thoughts and right before he nodded off. Now, this. Did he care for her more than he was letting on?

"If Luke gives the okay, you gonna get friendly with Raymo like you have with us?" Bran asked.

"You mean kiss him? Pull back the reins there, Kemosabe. I worked my way up to that with you guys. I don't even know him. Anyway, that sort of loving stays within our group."

"Well, then he would qualify," Bran said, dribbling his Popsicle down Kaylen's leg as she perched on a stool.

"Could you not? And what do you mean by that?"

"He's one of us. Seriously? You think Luke's cousin wouldn't be part of us?" Bran said.

"He's in our group?" Kaylen asked.

"Naw, he's a member of the Osmond Family. Weren't you

listening? What other group would I be talking about?" Bran said.

"I dunno. Doesn't Raymo belong to a gang or something?" Kaylen asked.

"Not officially. But he does have tough friends up in New York—Mafioso-like. Very stereotyped Italians. Ones who don't take any crap and will happily break your face if you give them any trouble," Bran said.

"Charming," Kaylen said.

"Yeah. So you might wanna stay on his good side. Or else you might not like what you get." The brothers cut each other a look.

It got tiresome trying to decrypt the subtext. Not worth Kaylen straining. "Great. Another prickly one like Tony. Not to mention that I'll have another pervert to contend with."

"You're welcome." Bran dripped his Popsicle down Kaylen's arm, serving her an ear-rending slurp.

"Quit dripping that crap all over the place and knock it off with that drooling!"

"Is it bothering you?" Bran asked innocently.

"Yes, but everything you do does. You're *so* irritating."

"Then you're probably gonna get big-time bent about this." He hovered, leaking the treat down Kaylen's inner thigh. She Chihuahua yipped, Bran offering: "Don't worry, I'll clean it up."

"With a tongue bath, I bet," Schaffer encouraged.

"You try it, and I'll rip that little muscle right out of your mouth," Kaylen warned.

"Oh, that's okay. I gotta another muscle as a backup. The main muscle. Know-what-I-mean, beauty queen?" Bran winked.

Kaylen's lip curled in disgust, the men sniggering. Bran face-dove, licking the Popsicle dribble from Kaylen's adductor.

She screeched, clubbing him in the head. She then lunged, wrestling the Popsicle from his hand and cramming the sticky glop down his pants. He squawked, hopping around. "That oughta cool you off."

"Temporarily. I tried to clean up my mess; the least you could do is to clean up yours," Bran suggested.

"If I put my hands in your pants, it'll be to snap off that body part you're so proud of," Kaylen threatened.

Lane appeared, startling the trio. "Okay, they're here."

"How do you that, Lanesy?" Schaffer asked. "Come up so quiet?"

But Lane's lips were sealed, and his brother, cousin, and Tony slammed through the door, everyone yabbering at once.

Kaylen's jaw dropped. Bran's description, not an exaggeration. Raymo, nineteen-and-a-half and born from another mother, but in every respect was Luke's twin—the same 6'4" beefcake with killer good looks. Skin bronzed as a medallion, his sheening hair like a line from Henley's poem Invictus—black as the pit. When his onyx eyes lit upon her, Kaylen's mouth went dry. Visceral, like a shot of Jack Daniel's down her throat, the burn in her belly superseded with a clenched gut, attraction layered over repulsion. His eyes bore into hers—perusing her to the depth of her soul—the chill skating down Kaylen's spine.

"Shay." Raymo greeted his friend, bussing both his cheeks, a traditional Italian salutation. He glimpsed at Bran, who informed him: "Hey, dude, you missed the excitement. I got a Popsicle in my pants."

"Bran-man, I see everything is normal with you." The two cheek-kissed, laughing at something Raymo said in Italian.

"Raymo, this is Kaylen," Luke said.

"Well, my cousin's description doesn't do you justice. *Sei una donna bellissima* (you're a beautiful woman)," Raymo commented.

"She's our resident hot babe, all right," Schaffer agreed.

"Nice to meet you." Kaylen extended her hand in welcome.

"Oh, we're not gonna be that formal, now are we?" Not shaking her hand, tugging her to his chest, Kaylen's mouth forming an O. Kissing both her cheeks, wrapping his arms around her waist. "It's nice to meet you too. The pleasure is all mine."

"Excuse me if I'm not all Miss Southern hospitality, but you wanna back off, Romeo?" Kaylen spouted.

Raymo grinned and loosened his grip. "Just trying to be friendly."

"I can tell. But you're in my personal space."

"Oh, you haven't seen anything yet." His mouth quirked.

"Well, apparently, someone hasn't explained the rules about that." Icicles in her voice, Kaylen extricated herself, the initial electrified attraction to him replaced by instant dislike. "Perhaps one of you gentlemen would like to enlighten him."

"Kissing, with tongue if she gives you the go-ahead," Bran explained. "Full body-to-body vertically and fully clothed with no breast poking and no probing with your kielbasa. No below the waist exploring either, nor hands inside of clothes. Unless, of course, she wants to stick her hand in *your* pants and put a Popsicle down your underwear."

"I'm sure there's a story behind that," Tony chuckled.

"There always is," Luke said.

"When do I get in on all this affection, huh, Kaylen? Remember, I'm one of the boys. I'm family," Raymo said.

"Just because your Luke's family doesn't mean I treat you the same way," Kaylen said.

"Why not? Our blood is the same. No difference. We even

look alike. Bet you couldn't even tell us apart in the dark," Raymo said, and Kaylen shivered.

Lane, done with the whole conversation, said: "What brings you down to Florida?"

"Both business and pleasure," Raymo said.

"And here I assumed you came to see your favorite cousin," Luke kidded.

He didn't say cousins, plural. Kaylen glanced sharply at Lane, pondering if he felt the slight.

"Well, of course, came to see my best friends too." Raymo nodded at Bran, Schaffer, and Tony. "And not without a present." He fished a fat joint from his front pocket.

"Mary Jane, come to papa." Bran spread his hands.

"Freaking A!" Schaffer breathed, duly impressed.

"Can we be cool here? This is an office, not a pot party." Hot Fun in the Summertime by Sly and the Family Stone reverberated from the jukebox. "See? People are in the game room. High visibility."

"Lanesy, Lanesy. You never did like the first sign of trouble, did you? Especially your own—the ones that sent you running to your big cuz, older brother, and friends, huh? *Ci prendiamo cura della nostra* (we take care of ours)."

Kaylen gawked. Raymo and Luke mirror images and spouting similar invective toward Lane.

"I take it you got more where this came from." Schaffer settled on lighting a cigarette since he couldn't smoke that jumbo joint right then and there.

"Yeah. Word's out; your state is dry. But I've made my connections, lined up a buyer in Miami. We'll do it in a few days," Raymo informed the group.

Kaylen didn't have a clue. "What's up, guys?"

"It's cool that we're discussing all of this in front of her?" Raymo asked.

"She's one of us," Schaffer said.

"Not that she doesn't have some usefulness here, but I'm not real swift on chicks being in my business," Raymo said.

"Unless it's to get down and busy with you, right?" Kaylen popped off.

An inspection of Kaylen's body, head to toe. "What do you think?" Raymo finally said.

"Well, that ain't going to happen. But I'm part of this group; I should be in the loop."

"It's serious business, honey. Not like the pranking you've gotten used to with the guys," Raymo said.

"You mean it's heavier than scamming people? Worse than walking out on paying a bill at a restaurant?" Things Kaylen's friends did, but she disapproved highly of.

"Yeah. But with higher stakes."

"And you think that because I'm not one of the boys that I can't hang?"

The blue flame flared, Raymo, sucking on a cigarette. "You either can or you can't. You lack balls, and you get weeded out right away. It's a jungle, baby. Better to prey than to become the preyed upon."

"Kaylen's up for the task."

"Is she, Shay? She doesn't come off like she's had much street cred."

"Those of us with true Southern heritage—Bran and Schaffer and me—have backwoods six sense—much like your street smarts. Did you mention Miami? Did you know that I used to live in South Florida? Not the wealthy Key Biscayne area, but Liberty City. Known for its rough neighborhoods. How's that for your street credibility?"

Raymo exhaled, smoke floating against the popcorn ceiling. "Raised it a notch. Not what I expected. But then I bet you're full of all kinds of surprises." Kaylen remained stone-faced to his words ripe with innuendo. "Understand if you're in with us, we're invested and heavily reliant upon each other," he added.

"Not to mention we've all taken a blood vow. That means something," Tony said.

"When we go to Kaylen's house tonight after work, we'll hammer out plans," Luke told them.

"And get hammered on that doobie," Schaffer said.

"You know it, bro. But first, I got a Popsicle problem I have to take care of, thanks to a beautiful but vicious blond," Bran said.

"Dude, you still haven't cleaned that crud out of your pants?!" Schaffer blurted.

"Haven't had a chance. Conversating. And actually, I'm sorta digging the sensation."

"Eeew. I bet it's all sticky and gross down there." Kaylen crinkled her face.

"A problem that you yourself are familiar with," Bran said.

"You're a disgusting pig! You better clean up that nasty mouth when you clean up your junk. Top to bottom," Kaylen said.

"I think we should add to the goop inside his pants." Tony's devilish grin lit.

"How about a nice mix of Popsicle and dirt?" Raymo suggested.

"Popsicle, dust balls, and lots of sand. Nice gritty sand," Luke said.

"No, not sand," Schaffer countered Luke's evil proposition. "Sand *spurs*. Florida grown."

"Now that could put a smarting on." Tony mock winced. "Popsicle and sand spurs whipped together inside someone's boxers."

"No way. You guys better not even be thinking it." Bran's Adam's apple spasmed at the threat.

"What do you think, Kay? Would you like to see that?"

"Yes, Luke, that'd definitely be entertaining."

"Kaylen! You're encouraging them instead of trying to prevent them?" Bran exclaimed.

"Get the party going. But, my dear, you know that someone might finish it for you if you start something. If you cavort among the merry, then you might also wind up cavorting with the enemy."

"I don't know what you're talking about. Cavorting and all that," Bran said.

"It means prepare to protect your package," Lane warned him.

A split second of silence and pandemonium erupted. Bran, envisioning getting stuff shoved down his shorts, screeched like a monkey and sprinted away. Luke, Tony, and Schaffer bolted after him. Lane, Kaylen, and Raymo remained rooted, rubber-necking the unfolding chaos.

"Just another happy tropical day." Kaylen giggled as the trio wrestled a squalling Bran to the ground. "Nothing ever changes."

"Except you're here now." Raymo wrested his gaze away from the show, staring at her. "You're part of our family. That alters the dynamics."

Kaylen silent, pivoting back, Luke and Tony locking Bran down and Schaffer troweling up sand spurs, avoiding getting roweled as he mashed them inside his brother's underwear. The spurs grew rampantly, their burs like the spikes of a medieval flail. Bran yodeled in pain, his torturers convulsing in hilarity.

"You didn't want in on that action?" Kaylen asked.

"Holding someone down to inflict pain and carry out sadistic pleasures? No, I don't waste my energies when it's not of my own making. I save it for the right time, the right person."

Raymo's dark eyes glittered. Kaylen's gut pitchpoled like she had swallowed something greasy.

Lane shot his cousin a look. Unreadable, but Kaylen wondered if Raymo's words made him uneasy as well.

The sensation deluged Kaylen many times in the months to follow.

* * *

Raymo arranged the drug deal. Kaylen hadn't wanted any part of it. But he pushed her, telling her she'd be a model distraction for their buyers. Sit There and Be Pretty. Kaylen asked Lane: "Y'all expect me to do this every time he's here?"

"No, he usually brokers deals back home in NYC. But, listen, no one's twisting your arm. You don't have to do it."

"Neither do you." Their roles: Lane, chauffeuring; Raymo, the supplier; Tony as muscle; Luke, Bran, and Schaffer, the backup, protection. Kaylen hadn't conceptualized weapons. That guns would be flashed and cocked, double-crossing their buyers and stealing back their money and drugs.

"Don't try to analyze it. It is what it is. I have to go along with what they want," Lane said.

"Or what? What is it they have on you?" Kaylen asked.

Mute, ducking his head.

"Lane, I understand why you take their bullcrap. They're intimidating. They bully you. And Raymo. He's slimy. He gets away with a lot because of his good looks and charisma. But underneath... there's something not right there."

"And yet you're still willing to go along with all this."

"As you."

The best friends eyed each other, neither acquiescing, willing to face their onus rather than group wrath for chickening out.

CHAPTER NINE

The drug deal drained Kaylen, unable to shake off her jitters. The soon-as-her-head-hit-the pillow sleep she once relished, now invaded by nightmares. The dreams, a play out of what transpired—the buyer sampling the drugs, swiping yellowed cuticles through his long oily hair, nodding his approval to his companion. The other man, extracting a wad of cash, his stringy wheat-colored ponytail a matched hue to his scuffed cowboy boots. Raymo counted the bills, cutting his eyes to cue Tony, whipping out his weapon. The greasy-haired stranger, his sallow nails disappeared into his back pocket, silver metal suddenly gleaming under the wane lights. Yelling, scuffling, Luke snaring the stranger's gun, Bran propelling the cowboy away. Schaffer and Bran, hog-tying them, Raymo ordering Kaylen and Lane to snatch the drugs and money, fleeing the shadowed warehouse, Chucks and Keds spanking the pavement, the spray of salt in the air, the screech of seagulls diving over the marina.

"Are you okay?" Lane asked days later, helping Kaylen tally sales and close out the register.

"Right as rain." A lie. Discomposed, upended since Raymo insinuated himself there. *But, she ruminated, how did we get from doing drugs for fun to selling drugs? How did we get from pranking people to threatening people? To being armed?*

"Too much for the tough girl to handle?" Kaylen jumped, Raymo appearing from behind the canned goods and camping gear, a beer sweating against his palm. "What's up, ladies? See, Lanesy, you're not the only cousin who knows how to sneak up."

"I'm not sneaky; I'm quiet. There's a difference between stepping lightly and being a stealthy stalker."

"Whatever, Lane." Raymo dug in his pocket for a cigarette. "What's the matter, Kay? You can't hang with what's been going down lately?"

"I can hang fine, Raymo. And don't call me Kay. Luke's the only one who calls me that. So it's Kaylen to you and everybody else."

"Oh, excuse me! Too personal, too intimate for you? Too much like I'm the real boyfriend?" Raymo said.

"What's that supposed to mean?" Kaylen snapped.

"Is it his pet nickname for you? What do you call him, Kay? Your Lukey-love?"

"I don't know, *Ray*. Why don't you ask him?"

"Okay, Kay-Kay. Maybe I will." Raymo tipped his head back, swigging.

"Where did you get that beer?" Lane asked.

Raymo's tone, cold. "I took it out of inventory."

"Inventory? Like out of the back cooler? You can't take items without checking. So we keep track," Lane said.

"Lanesy, Lanesy, everything is always done by the numbers, by the rules. Except when it has to do with your own life, huh? Are you not going to answer? I didn't expect you to. But, listen, don't sweat it. Put it on my tab."

"You don't have a tab, Raymo."

"Why not? I see the other idiots taking freebies all the time, Kay."

"They work here. Employee benefits," Kaylen said.

"Then put me on the payroll, honey, if it rings your bell. Meanwhile, I'm taking whatever I want, whenever I want."

"Like stealing?" Kaylen asked.

"If I'm a thief, then call a cop." Crumbled the empty can, shooting it into the trash can behind the desk.

"Perfect. Yeah, that's what I want—piquing attention. Spotlight our criminal activities," Kaylen said.

"You think you're in the big time? That drug deal was a game compared to other stuff that's gone down around here. And that's got me to thinking," Raymo said.

"Which I am sure is a stretch."

"Good one, Kay. I'm talking about the other night, about what happened," Raymo said.

"Yes, well, I've been thinking about that myself." Images of what could have gone wrong filled Kaylen's head.

"Maybe it would be a good idea if you learned how to shoot," Raymo said.

"Shoot? A gun?" Kaylen asked.

"Yeah, what else would I mean? Although we all know you can shoot your mouth off. Now let's match that with firing action," Raymo said.

"And what do you carry? The same thing Tony had?" She quivered inside, remembering how he had leveled the gun at the cowboy.

"I got several preferences, but a Magnum is my favorite," Raymo said.

"Oooohh. Such a manly weapon. A real phallic symbol," Kaylen said.

"You're not far off. When you got a gun in your hand, it's a power trip. It gets the blood coursing, the adrenaline pumping. It's better than sex." He moored her with his hot dark eyes.

Kaylen ignored both his smoldering inspection and words. "I don't like guns."

"You don't have to like them. You have to respect them," Raymo said.

"Kaylen, I think Raymo is right. You should learn how to shoot," Lane said.

"At last, we agree on something. Anyway, everybody here but Kay knows how to fire a gun. Even Lanesy can."

Another discovery regarding her friends. Another thing hid from her.

"I'm surprised you don't know how to shoot, you being a country girl. And being left alone all the time, you'd think your dad would've suggested it," Raymo said.

"We could take her out tomorrow afternoon, do a little practice," Lane said.

"Unless you can't handle it," Raymo said.

"Name the place and time, Raymo."

His smile rifted wide like he knew all Kaylen's secrets.

* * *

The group met up in the bowels of the woods outlying the campsites, the clearing corseted by waist-high weeds, heaven-hugging oaks, and spikey vines.

"Welcome to the farmland." Schaffer waved the joint at Kaylen. "See my sweet harvest?"

Marijuana plants dipped against the breeze. "Where did these come from?" Kaylen asked.

"Mother Earth. Ain't nature great?" Schaffer said.

"Since when do we grow pot back here?" Kaylen asked.

"Since we took seeds from all the batches Raymo has

brought down this past year and last. With this right combination of soil, sunlight, and seclusion, it'll make a killer crop."

"Seclusion is right. I would have never found this place had Lane not guided me back here. I must have walked miles and miles. You got a trail started but not a well-marked path," Kaylen said.

"We don't want a well-marked path; we don't want anyone nosing around back here. Only the best redneck or trails man would be able to find it. And then they'd have to have at least a three-wheeler. As you found out, it's rough to foot it," Bran said.

"This butts up to the national forest. At one time this was the back end of the campground," Luke explained. "But a bunch of hurricanes and storms flooded it out, toppled trees, made it uninhabitable."

"It's as deep woods as you can get. Probably thousands of snakes and wildlife back here," Kaylen said.

"Then you'll need this." Tony produced a rifle.

"Wait a minute! I was under the impression I was going to shoot a little gun, a pistol maybe—not a bazooka!"

"Quit exaggerating, Kaylen. It's a .30-30," Tony said.

"You got something a little less... massive?"

Luke infixed it into Kaylen's palms. "You'll get used to it. Grip it."

"That's right, honey, put my big gun in your hand, ease it back and cock it."

"Yeah. Cock it. You wish," Kaylen snickered over at Raymo.

"Kay, Since Raymo is the best shot, we've elected him to school you," Luke said.

"All right then, let's do the dang thang," Kaylen said.

"We won't get into the particulars of how to load your weapon or anything like that. I've done that for you. Right now, you're focusing on hitting a target. Okay, put the rifle up here like this. Then get your sights." Kaylen's arm drooped, unaccustomed to the weight of the weapon. "No, you gotta lift it. I always try to keep it up," he whispered, shivers spiraling down Kaylen's spine, Raymo's suggestive words, his warm breath glancing the back of her neck. "Okay, you see that brown shrub in the middle of all the green ones? That's where you're aiming. Now it's gonna give a little recoil. I'm moving away, and you're going to squeeze the trigger. Yeah, that's it."

The explosion jarred, Kaylen screeching, hitting the ground butt first. "Holy crap!"

The men howled, Lane, helping her up.

"He told you it was gonna give a little kick, babe." Luke dusted off Kaylen's backside.

"That was not a little kick. That was a body punch. And I seriously bruised my keister!"

"Quick, check for cracks," Bran quipped.

"Hardy-har. Some friend you are, hee-hee-heeing yourself sick over my tumble."

"Sorry. It was comedy. Remember when you split your side when these idiots held me down and barbed my balls with sand spurs? So who's laughing now?" Bran asked.

"Let me show you how a real pro does it." Raymo aimed at a low-hanging branch in the distance, the shot shaving it from the tree. "Girls, that's the way you do it."

"You're so impressed with yourself," Kaylen snorted.

"You think that was easy? When you can shoot like that, then you can bust my onions about my skills."

"You're on, Raymo."

The others hooted. "She's pretty confident for someone who can't even keep her balance when she's taking a shot," Raymo told his friends and cousins.

"Well, because I hadn't expected that caliber of force, the loudness!" Kaylen explained.

"Seems like excuses to me," Raymo said.

"No. Not only am I going to be your best student, but I am also going to exceed the master," Kaylen said.

"A hot girl issuing a power challenge? It makes my pocket rocket wanna launch."

Kaylen's lips pursed in disgust, Raymo getting the reaction that he wanted. "You think you're going to outshoot me, honey? Well, no one has ever done it. But okay, bring it. But this challenge is not without a bet."

"Which is...?" Kaylen questioned.

"We'll set a goal date. Say... three months from now. You'll have to be able to match what I can do. If you can't, you'll owe me. If you're shooting skills are on par with my standards, then I'll hand over any gun in my collection that you choose," Raymo said.

"Even your big bad Magnum?" Kaylen asked.

"Oh, she's my pride and joy. But yeah. Whatever you decide. I got rifles, a Smith and Wesson, a 38 special—you name it, I got it," Raymo said.

"This might be a dumb question, but how is it you have so many guns here? I mean, you flew in. You couldn't have brought all of those with you," Kaylen said.

"Well, you gotta remember, I come down to visit at least four times a year. I don't always fly; I drive down too. Then I either bring them with me or get them here. That's how I've built up my gun collection here. I got one back home too. They get stored at my cousins' house here when I'm away. Then when I'm at the cabin, I move them over there. My Magnum, she traveled with me on the plane," Raymo admitted.

"Isn't that like concealing a weapon?" Kaylen asked.

"And?"

"Never mind. I could start digging this gun business. I might start turning into a pistol-packing mama like Annie Oakley," Kaylen said.

"Maybe we can take it on the road—a modern-day Bonnie and Clyde. You can ride shotgun with me, Kay—pun intended. Like in the movie, huh? We already look the part, like the movie cast—you as the blond and beautiful Faye Dunaway and me as the handsome dark-haired Warren Beatty," Raymo said.

"Let's keep our life of crime to a minimum. I'm fine with staying put," Kaylen said.

"What if Kaylen can't deliver when y'all have this shooting contest, then what?" Bran asked.

"Oh, then she's definitely going to owe me. How are you going to pay up, Kay?" Raymo asked.

"How about Four Minutes in the Closet?" Tony asked. "Wait. Let's make it Eight Minutes in the Closet."

"Hey, no fair, that's double what I got! That's even longer than Seven Minutes in Heaven!"

"Muffle it," Tony ordered Bran. "Eight minutes, and let's see if Raymo gets out unscathed."

"It's juvenile," Lane blurted. "The game. It's for teenybops."

"Listen, you tool. Kaylen wanted to rewind her life. She wanted to experience whatever she's missed out. She's the one who wanted to play Four Minutes with us!" Bran said.

"We don't have to kiss Kaylen in the closet; we could do it in the open. But she likes the privacy. It's like getting away with something. Am I right?" Schaffer asked.

"Lane's hacked because he can't get in on the closet action. Your fault, Lanesy, if you don't canoodle Kaylen when you're in there with her in the panic room. Sit in there then, twirling your thumbs or whatever it is you do. But quit being a drag and ruining our fun!" Bran said.

"Meanwhile, back at the ranch, kids," Tony snorted. "A lot can happen in eight minutes. Either it'll be a sweet time, or every second is going to be like an eternity."

"Like putting a cat in a box. You could get a good kitty, or you could get a hellcat with claws." Schaffer imitated a cat hissing.

"What do you think, Kay? Am I going to get my time in the closet with a tame pussy or one that scratches?" Raymo asked.

The other men grinned like idiots at the double-entendre.

"I dunno, Ray. You wanna take your chances?"

"I'll make sure I maximize every minute of my eight-minute allotment," Raymo said.

"You're wasting time. Start instructing. I gotta lot to learn in a short amount of time to take you down," Kaylen said.

Raymo re-positioned the weapon, repeating the instructions. His undertone at her neck: "I'll be a good teacher, give you the best tips. But you're a long way away from perfecting your shot. In case you can't pull it off, get your flavored lip gloss ready for our big kiss, Kay. I like my girls wearing cherry."

She concentrated on her shot, determined to hone her skills and not lose the bet.

But Raymo had no intention of letting Kaylen win his weapon. So instead, he anticipated their game, getting her alone with him. He planned to take from her what she held on tight. And she would be paralyzed to stop him.

CHAPTER TEN

Ross Sadler slumped in his Barcalounger, processing the recent events. His daughter had just defected with her friends to the movies. Reluctant to leave him, but he urged her, even though he'd arrived home only moments ago, racking up several long weeks on the road and departing again in a matter of days. Corralling his Cadillac, he sauntered in from the garage via the kitchen. A tune he hadn't expected but recognized, the choral of male voices, basses, and baritones. He rounded the corner, someone booming: "Okay, my sultry siren, you better be getting ready and wearing something that's either micro-mini short, skintight, or see-through that'll blow my mind, and whoa—" Bran jumped about a mile when he spotted Ross. The other men recovered, Luke and Tony, rising to greet him. *Sultry siren?!* And what was that reference to his daughter's clothes?! Ross cataloged the living room: several packs of cigarettes stacked on the mantle—not his brand, multiple pairs of Converse, Sperry Top-Siders, and flip flops—big as a dingy, lined up against the baseboard, and a panoply of snacks— Fiddle Faddle, Pringles, and Funyuns on the coffee table. It appeared these guys were spending scads of time there and making themselves quite comfortable.

"Evening, sir." Luke and Tony leaned in, shaking his hand. Ross cut an imposing figure, but Luke hovered above him, and Tony towered over them both. Ross found it annoying to have to crane his neck to look up at other men, which he was not used to. Comparing his daughter's petite stature to her taller friends made Kaylen's vulnerability more apparent and reminded Ross of the TV show *Land of the Giants*, where she would resemble the character Earthling Valerie Scott among the planet's giants.

"Daddy!" Kaylen galloped down the staircase to hug him. "Why didn't you call me and let me know you were coming?"

"Kitten," he addressed Kaylen with the pet name. "I wasn't sure I'd be getting home this early, but I got that deal wrapped up in Atlanta."

"Congrats. You know everyone, right?"

Ross nodded, the men mumbling salutations. The cousins posed side-by-side, Ross's eyes flicked from Luke to Raymo, their resemblance spooky—two halves of a whole.

Ross took inventory of his daughter's features, transformed during his month's absence. She no longer resembled the girl he left behind, often misidentified as a teenager of 14 or 15. A new mature polish to her looks—her long mane trimmed, a sophisticated cut that draped her shoulders like a gold evening wrap. Kaylen had spiced up her makeup: midnight mascara, smoky eyelids, winged eyeliner, like Elizabeth Taylor in *Cleopatra*. Her cheekbones rouged and contoured as a runway model, her cinnamon lips glistening like a starlet. She was not overdone; her palette was spot-on. Despite Bran's suggestion for décolleté and showing off her gams, Kaylen donned a simple pair of bell bottoms and a peasant shirt that did not accentuate her figure. Ross breathed relief.

"Dad, I hate to rush off and leave you here by yourself, but if you're sure it's okay...."

He brushed her away, not begrudging his daughter and her friends a night out. Kaylen had told him in one of their daily phone calls that she had put in many hours at the campground —an increase since her promotion; the elder Vincuzzis impressed with her organizational skills and smarts, placing her in charge of scheduling, running daily operations, and keeping the guys on track. According to his daughter, lots of grumbling from the men at first, skiving off specific jobs, but Kaylen put them in line. She told Ross she loved working there, getting to know the regulars, and meeting new people.

Ross audited his daughter as the group debated which movie to see. He was not thrilled with Kaylen's friendship, hanging out with six guys all the time. He considered it strange she associated with only the men and not even one close girl pal.

During his last visit home, Kaylen had explained to Ross, "If I were on the outside peering in, I might find it a tad weird too. But you'd have to understand the relationship, the dichotomy. I am super close to each of them, but the friendship is different with each guy. But as a group, we all mesh together. It's like I wouldn't—couldn't—have that with anyone else in the world—just them. I can't explain it. I know that it is real and that they are lifelong friends. I don't need girl pals. I don't *want* girl pals. I have everything I need with the guys."

Kaylen reassured him that she wasn't sleeping with any of the men, even though she and Luke were in a relationship. Ross had asked how Luke felt about that, and Kaylen had shrugged like her friend Bran. That was when Ross had his ah-ha moment of how much the men had rubbed off on Kaylen.

"I want you to be cautious, Kitten," he said.

"What do you mean?"

"Well, you said it. You're close to them. Sometimes when we are close to someone, we don't see things incontrovertibly. So you might have a different perspective on this friendship than they do."

"Like...?"

"Well, bottom line, they're guys, Kitten. I'm a guy. Men think differently than women. It doesn't make one gender smarter than the other, but the perspective could be poles apart. Expectations are different for males than for females. What you get from the friendship and expect from them might be entirely disparate from what they're getting, wanting, expecting."

Kaylen had squirmed internally, concealing things from her father—the initiation, Raymo's schemes, Luke's pressuring to go all the way, the kissing games in the panic room—and she hated her subterfuge.

Ross had asked what they did at his home, where they divided their time between working at the campground and hanging out. Kaylen had said they listened to music, watched TV, talked, goofed around, went swimming, boating, skiing, and fishing, and she cooked for them—just the usual stuff. She had left out that they got high, got drunk, shot stuff, and went skinny dipping.

He accepted her account, the tender-hearted father who trusted her, but guilt flooded Kaylen as she played up the men's protectiveness and joked about Bran needing babysitting. "As long as they don't try to manipulate you," Ross had said, but there was something about them that he couldn't put his finger on.

Kaylen heeded his sage warning, wondering if this perception had anything to do with her nightmares—the ones that left her drenched in sweat and jounced her from her sleep, where dark figures pushed and shoved.

"We gotta go," Tony told Kaylen. "You know we have to have plenty of time for Bran to go to the concession stand."

"Food is calling my name—Goobers, Sugar Daddy, Boston Baked Beans, Mallo Cups," Bran said.

"I swear I don't know how this guy keeps from barfing, eating all that in one sitting," Kaylen said to her dad, awing.

"Let's not even mention the tub of buttered popcorn he usually gets," Schaffer said. "A *tub*! And he doesn't even share!"

"You buy me a soda, and I'll think about letting you have popcorn!" Bran said.

"That's a scam we've heard before," Tony grunted. "He gets his drink and then goes and sits at the end of the aisle by himself. He and all his precious food."

"Actually, *we* banished him to the end of the aisle because of his gas," Luke said. "All that candy, you know."

"Chocolate farts." Bran shrugged. "How can that be bad?!"

"Guys! Enough. My dad's here, remember?"

"What movie did y'all decide on?" Ross asked.

"*Bob & Carol & Ted & Alice*," Raymo answered.

Ross aimed a sharp glimpse at his daughter. He'd heard the movie was risqué.

Seconds ticked by, no one spoke. Then, finally, Raymo's sleazy smirk got under Ross's skin.

"Dad, I'll probably be getting in late."

"It's fine. You know I sleep like the dead once I'm down." But, mused Ross, how many evenings had the men kept his daughter out late, how many other questionable movies had they taken her to?

The men filed out. "Nice seeing you again, sir." Ross nodded, but noted Luke's hand at Kaylen's lumbar, his fingers resting over the top of her buttocks as he nudged her toward the door. The gesture, both intimate and dominant. Ross's jaw tautened, his eyes narrowing.

His chest cinched. A panic attack, not a coronary, he reminded himself. His physician had diagnosed the three previous times he'd experienced the stabbing pain. The first time, a sunset come and gone, his wife was missing, a sailboat capsized and drifting. The second time, the evening a chaplain and a military officer rapped at his door, the war over for his son, and the third, the moment Kaylen's vacant stare prompted him to take her to a therapist. The incidents, and the pain, were a retrospection he'd fallen short, that life spinning beyond his control, that he had failed to protect those who mattered, his loved ones slipping away from him.

After everything he'd been through, he couldn't bear it if anything else happened.

CHAPTER ELEVEN

Christmas approached, a nip in the air— "sweater weather." Invigorating yet cloaking Kaylen with a restless, homesick-sensation, a death shroud marked the passing of summer-like days. The feeling imbued her with a melancholy she hadn't experienced since her brother died.

Raymo returned to New York for the holidays, Kaylen sighing relief. Under his guidance, her shooting skills improved. She absorbed his hours of coaching but sensed he was not to be messed with. However, a menacing energy simmered between them, like rising tidal waves, or lighted gunpowder inching down a trail toward a slow-burning fuse. Unlike her love for Luke, this was something else entirely—primal attraction tinged with trepidation. Kaylen could not catch her breath around Raymo, and the simmer of desire curled around them like smoke. Despite knowing Raymo's true essence as a dangerous man with unsavory associates, Kaylen remained fascinated by him. She knew he was like a garrote piano wire, snapping without reason, but couldn't resist the pull towards danger.

His fascination with the underbelly of the world, further

proof? The Tate-LaBianca murders and Charles Manson, the case riveting Raymo—an irony Kaylen couldn't discount. Charismatic, intimidating, manipulative, and complex Manson —not unlike Raymo. Charles Manson's photo plastered across the cover of *Life Magazine*, Raymo sometimes inflecting the same evil, wide dark-eyes, both entertaining and creeping out his cousins and friends. Kaylen's nightmares, brimming with those eyes and hunkering shadows, muffled her screams, depleting her of sleep. But none of it set her on edge like the incident with Raymo had.

On that day, they'd been shooting targets in the glade in the woods. Usually, Lane accompanied them on the outings. But just the two of them this time. Kaylen had been half-listening as Raymo went on about Charles Manson, who ordered his "family" to kill people and dump them in a California desert. But when Raymo told her how easy it would be to hide a body in a swamp or forest, the hairs on the back of Kaylen's neck stood on end. Girthy Chinkapins, Shumard oaks, and booby-trapped pockets of invisible quicksand and mucoid marsh surrounded them, perfect for a body dump site. Kaylen knew, though, that Raymo lived to spout shock-value comments. She preferred to brush him off, but it unhinged her when he effulged a casual smile—and admitted his fantasy of shooting at a live target—a human target. And then he said to her: *"If I gave you a head start, do you think you could outrun me, Kay-Kay?"*

"How very The Most Dangerous Game," she referenced the classic tale by Richard Connell. *"Shall I be thou Rainsford to your Zaroff?"* The character Rainsford, a hunter who believed the world consisted of solely predators and prey, a victim of his self-fulfilling prophecy when he becomes the hunted by a character named Zaroff.

"Exactly. Except instead of being on an island like in the story, we're in a national forest. Whata' you think, Kay-Kay?

Would your physical skills help you escape, or would you be paralyzed with fear?" Kaylen whirled around, perusing him. *If he wanted to, she mused, he could shoot me out here and call it an accident, and no one would ever know any differently.* Masking her trepidation, she said: *"It goes both ways, Ray-Ray. I have a weapon too. I could ask you the same thing."*

"Tit for tat. But don't worry, baby. I'm not going to track you down as a hound dog would. You still owe me a bet. And I'm going to collect, Kay." His finger trailed along her forearm.

He found other reasons to touch her—helping adjust her weapon, pulling her out of the way of a giant spider web, a playful squeeze at the back of her neck. But he'd also lean into her, his warm breath at her shoulders and his hard body pressing against the curve of her hip. She'd snarl, his laugh booming, giving her berth. His boldness had her rethinking the whole challenge; of conceding to Eight Minutes in the Closet if she lost the shooting match.

But not letting him see any doubts she might have, she'd told him, *"Well, Raymo, you've taught me too well. I'm not going to lose because I can nearly outshoot you. And can't wait to take your beloved Magnum."*

"You're close to matching me, Kay-Kay. But remember that close only counts in horseshoes. Although you've made great progress, you have less than two months to perfect your shot, and you're not going to make it. Victory will be mine. I'll not only keep my gun, but I'm priming up for your sexy mouth on mine. And maybe on other places too."

He had chuckled, Kaylen's lip crimped in disdain. They stuck with their practice, but Kaylen, unable to get it out of her skull, his words—using her as a live target, of kissing her.

But when Raymo left for the holidays, the group fell into place as they had been before Raymo had inserted himself into their alliance of six. After attending a Christmas Eve Mass with

Al and Rosa Vincuzzi, the guys and Kaylen congregated in her living room.

"You can't be cold," Tony said, Kaylen's teeth chattering. "It's like 50 degrees out."

"It's a matter of perspective," Schaffer said. "We natives get chilled to the bone whenever the temp drops."

"You wussies need to go up North and thicken up your blood." Luke ignited a cigarette.

"Yeah, I'm sure Raymo wouldn't have minded if you had tagged along," Bran told Kaylen.

"Right. First of all, I would have had to break Mr. Touchy-Feely's hands. Second, that would be quite a pairing up."

"Hey, stranger pairing ups have happened! What about Tiny Tim and Miss Vicky getting hitched? Now that's weird!" Bran referenced the celebrity December 17th wedding. The prim and cute Miss Vicky, and curly-haired, falsetto-voiced, kooky-looking pop singer Tiny Tim of Tiptoe-Through-the-Tulips fame, joined in holy matrimony live television on *The Tonight Show* with Johnny Carson.

"Miss Vicky and Tiny Tim are like Beauty and the Beast. You and Raymo are more like Beauty and the Beauty," Tony said. "Okay, imagine doing the deed with Tiny Tim?"

"I'm sure he's very sweet, but I'm not in the least bit attracted. But then again, thinking of being coupled with Raymo is nearly as strange," Kaylen said.

"How? Are you sure about that? After all, you're with me, and Raymo is my mirror image," Luke pointed out.

"Yeah. But as much as the two of you are the same—in appearance, in mannerisms, there are still distinct differences between the two of you in personality—most of yours that I like; most of his that I don't," Kaylen said.

"How's the shooting going?" Schaffer asked.

"Plugging along. Hopefully, the payoff involves me scarfing Raymo's best weapon."

"He'll be in tears," Bran neighed.

"Is that why you two have been spending more time together?" Tony asked. "Venturing off alone to go practice?"

"You've been going by yourselves? What happened to Lanesy coming along?"

Why Luke's crisp tone? "Not if he has to work. What's the big deal? I need all the practice I can get. Don't you wanna see me win this? Or is your allegiance to your family, your blood kin, rather than to me?"

"The point is not whether I wanna see you win it, but *do you* wanna win it?"

"Of course! Put Raymo in his place? Take away his cherished Magnum? How sweet is that?" Kaylen said.

"So, are you bonding with my cousin?"

"Well, nothing draws a guy and gal closer together than conversation and bullets." *Humor Luke since he seemed agitated for some reason.*

"You do realize that Raymo isn't motivated to do anything unless the outcome favors himself, right? He's not in this for you to develop your skills to win—although you are pumping his fantasy of chicks in bikinis toting a gun." Bran said.

"My cousin's jonesing the prize. That would be you, Kay."

"He does understand that if he wins this competition, that it's only a kiss, right?" Kaylen explained.

"Which can be a gateway to much more."

"Seriously, Luke? Then he hasn't been paying attention, has he? It's making out—that's it. We've all had a good time with that, huh?" The men served Kaylen grins and nods. "Maybe he'd like to talk to Bran about how you get clocked when kissing leads to wandering fingers."

"My hand slipped," Bran made his excuses.

"Yeah, across my breast."

"It was breaking my fall."

"Now that's a good one," Kaylen snorted.

"Eight Minutes in the Closet is the longest you'll have ever gone with any of us."

"Luke, it hasn't happened yet, and won't if I can help it."

"Who decided it was gonna be eight minutes? That it was gonna be double the time?" Bran asked.

"It was my idiot cousin, wasn't it?" Schaffer said.

"Yep, I take the credit." Tony bowed.

"What's going on between you and Raymo?"

"What? Did you take a Bran-pill? Are you losing your marbles, Luke? What do you mean by that?"

"Then you're not attracted to him?" Luke asked.

"I'm attracted to *all* of you! It's a dream life being around this many hunky men." They peacocked around. Her statement was gospel truth. She kept company with the most gorgeous guys on the planet: Luke and Raymo, tall-dark-and-handsome, stepping out of the pages of a Harlequin novel; Bran, taking her breath away with his exquisite feline-eyes and Adonis-like perfection; Tony, uncomely in a world's standard of classic Bran's, but then he grew on her, oh-so-bad-boy, muscles and masculine, and gritty; and Schaffer, chartreuse-green bedroom eyes and yards of dreamy hair. Even Lane—who downplayed his looks, couldn't conceal those impaling long-lashed peepers, a deeper blue than Paul Newman's.

"Tell us, who's the best kisser in the bunch?" Bran asked.

"You're not going to put me on the spot. It's all of you, for different reasons."

"Yeah, whatever. But seriously, if you had to choose?"

"It would be you, Bran."

"I knew it! Because I have this technique and—wait a minute, are you being sarcastic or serious?"

"She is placating you," Lane told him. "She's exercising discretion. She's not gonna kiss and tell."

"Come on; we can take it. Who's the best kisser here?" Bran pushed.

"Okay. You wanna know? It's Lane."

"*Lane?* Okay, you're mind-messing us. You've never smooched Lane!" Bran insisted.

"That you know of," Kaylen teased.

"Hold up. Lane's your best friend. You said he's like a brother. You're outright lying. We know nothing happened between you two in that Closet," Bran said.

"I've kissed Lane dozens of times."

"Yes, tiny smacks on the cheek. Little pecks on the lips. Not with an open mouth," Bran argued.

"Again, not that you know of."

"Naw, I know you didn't. You wouldn't. *Ci stai prendendo in giro* (you're screwing with us)" Bran said.

Kaylen shrugged, Bran-like. "Maybe we don't like to advertise." She looked over at Lane, who didn't move a muscle. Let's keep them guessing. Besides, it was fun to toy with them.

"If what you said about Lane is true, and then with Raymo on board, it's gonna be a real family affair," Tony said. "All the Vincuzzi boys vying for one hot chick's lips."

"But in the end, only one of us gets the girl," Luke grunted. "Me."

"She is definitely the girl you wanna have," Bran agreed, then remembering his appetite, added: "Listen, don't you have Christmas egg nog?"

"Door of the fridge."

He slurped from the carton, passing it to his cousin. Kaylen scrunched her face. "When are we gonna exchange Christmas gifts?" Bran asked.

"Tomorrow. That's if you get anything. Bad boys get a lump of coal." Tony waggled his finger at him.

"Well, right back at you."

"What about me, dear chums? Did you get your precious something nice?" Kaylen asked.

"Got you a push-up bra and crotchless underwear," Bran leered.

"Classy."

"When do you expect your dad?" Tony asked.

"Late tonight."

"Whata' you say we get into the holiday spirit and smoke a little Christmas reefer?" Schaffer pulled out a joint hidden in his bandana.

"That seems wrong."

"Lighten up, Kaylen. It's a little holiday cheer. It's not like we're blaspheming anything," Schaffer said.

"You'll like this special blend," Bran assured her. "My brother rolled it for you with love—while he was over here this afternoon."

Kaylen frowned. "What do you mean? We've been gone all day. I've been gone all day."

"No one said you had to be here for me to get into your house," Schaffer said.

"What?! Now we are adding breaking and entering to our bad-stuff-we-do-list?"

"No B & E. Me by myself coming in."

"Okay. That is very stalky, creepy behavior," Kaylen said.

"Here's the deal: He's coming over here and trying on your clothes when you're gone." Bran stretched out his hand for the joint. "He's a secret crossdresser."

"That's great. He probably wears my clothes better than I do. He already has superior hair. Long and thick, flowing, and shiny," Kaylen said.

Schaffer tossed his hip skimming-length locks. "Yeah, you have every reason to be envious. But I did not come over here and try on your clothes. However, I did smell all of your panties."

"Lovely. Now how did you get in here?" Kaylen asked.

"Hey, don't sweat it, okay? I've got a key," Schaffer said.

"You're tripping. There are two keys. One for dad, the other is mine."

"I have a duplicate. Tony lifted your house key, asked me to make copies, put the house key back on your key chain," Schaffer said.

"Perhaps I should check the silver and other valuables to see if anything is missing, seeing that I am dealing with shifty people."

"Don't be dramatic. It's no big whoop," Schaffer said.

"Yeah. You shouldn't be angry. Isn't it good to know that we can get in here in case you need us?" Bran asked.

"Known perverts, mad predators, and criminals coming in at will? And this is supposed to give me a nice warm fuzzy feeling?" Kaylen asked.

"Surely you exaggerate. We have your best interests at heart. We're home protection and security," Bran said.

Kaylen threw her head back in a fake laugh. "Ho, ho, now that's rich!"

"It's downright low. Taking that key was an invasion of privacy."

"For once, stop acting like someone's parent, Lanesy. Besides, we even made a key for you," Bran said.

"No, if I come into Kaylen's house, it'll be with her permission."

"Forget it. Take it. Everyone else has one."

"Far out! Now we each got our key to our home-away-from-home and can drop in anytime we want."

"Bullcrap, Tony. I do not want to see your happy smiling faces popping up at all hours of the day and night."

"Perhaps at your bath time," Bran suggested.

"Don't even think it."

"Aw, come on. Let's do it once a week. We'll call it 'Naked Monday.'"

"Go ahead and try it. Remember, I'm a crackerjack shot now, and if I hear anyone roaming around in here when I'm in the tub, I'm liable to fire off a couple of rounds."

"Aaahh. Nude girl with a gun. Even better than Raymo's fantasy of bikini-clad women with weapons," Tony said.

"Having a key doesn't mean we should happen in anytime we want."

"Who talks like that, Lanesy?" Tony muttered. "'Happen in'?"

Lane tuned him out. "What if you pop in and her dad is here?"

"Nobody said anything about coming in when her dad is here, you douche. Give us a little credit for brains," Tony argued.

"A little credit for little brains," Lane threw back, invective he could have gotten away with if sparring with Bran. Tony sprung to his feet, fight mode.

"A peaceful Christmas, please. Listen, about the keys? Y'all gotta be on top of it. My dad would not be cool with that."

"Tell him that you gave us an extra key in case of an emergency," Bran said.

"Let's see. I am already under scrutiny about the six guys/one girl thing. The key for an emergency angle is not going to comfort him. But, seriously, I better not hear the pitter-patter of men-feet in the middle of the night." Kaylen scrutinized all of them, her gaze on Bran a measure held.

"Why do *I* get the stink eye?"

"Because I know how your brain works."

"Then you would be the only one," Tony cracked.

"Listen, you guys didn't give Raymo a key, did you?" Kaylen asked.

"He left before we could," Schaffer said.

"Are you sure? How many keys did you make?"

"Two-hundred-forty-five, we're giving them out to every camper who passes through in the next few days," Schaffer said as he toked on the joint.

"I'm serious."

"Me too. Wait till Big Dave shows up." An older gentleman who'd camped with them for years and sweet on Kaylen.

"Big Dave is nice and harmless. Raymo is not," Kaylen said.

"Whatsa' matter? Do you think Raymo will pull a Manson and get us to come in and do his dirty work? Oh, wait a minute, those freaks didn't have a key to get in. Ah, they didn't need it anyway. They walked in like they owned the place. When you got a knife and gun and rope, you simply go on in, people move out of your way. However, they did find that one guy. Shot him in the driveway and didn't even have to walk in the house and—"

"—Bran!?"

"Yeah?"

"Shut up already! You love to hear your own jaws flap," Kaylen said.

"Cool out, Kaylen. We only made five keys, alright? It's us." Schaffer offered her the joint.

His reassurances couldn't nick Kaylen's apprehension, her heart thumping, scenarios of Raymo pilfering a key, skulking into her house. She wrestled with nightmares at bedtime, jousting like a horseman wielding a lance. Shadowy images of attack haunted her, leaving her defenseless. Each night felt like being thrown into a battle, her opponents returning to leave her bleeding.

* * *

A banging. Kaylen, stumbling from sleep into the kitchen, her friends smiling at her from the back door.

"What's going on?" she asked.

"You invited us for Christmas breakfast." Luke pecked her forehead.

"What time is it? Seems awful early."

"No more than any other day when we have to open up the office," Luke pointed out. "And thanks to my folks working it today, we don't have to."

"I'm surprised you didn't mosey on in, now that everyone's got a key," Kaylen said.

"You said you were expecting your old man." Tony filed past her. "Didn't want to take a chance running into him."

Kaylen yawned. "Well, that was wise, seeing he got home last night right after you guys left. But, listen, I don't think I can handle y'all before coffee."

"I'll make it," Lane volunteered.

"Nice attitude about your friends," Schaffer said.

"Sorry, truth, especially about you-know-who," Kaylen said.

"Are you saying you can't handle my radiant personality until you've caffeinated yourself?" Bran asked.

"Yep, that pretty much sums it up."

"Don't worry; java's on the way." The rich aroma of Folger's brewing.

"I'm deeply offended, especially since we brought you this." Bran thrust a box at Kaylen. She pored over it, skimming an index finger over the gold paper.

"She's in a trance. Nice wrap job, right?" Schaffer said.

"You can never have too much Scotch tape, huh? Hold on." She spun away, returning with five identical boxes, all topped with red bows. "Merry Christmas, darlings."

They ripped into the boxes; each bestowed a gold identification bracelet bearing his name, the underside engraved: "Love and friendship always, K."

"Cool, right?" Schaffer shimmied his wrist.

"Not to mention these things are good as a pair of brass knuckles." Tony stroked the chunky band of 14kt. gold. "A very persuasive hunk of metal against someone's puss. *Sto andando busto qualcuno* (I'm gonna bust someone)."

"Hey, don't even give it a whit. I better not see one drop of blood on those babies," Kaylen forewarned.

"Relax, honey. We wouldn't dream of messing them up," Luke said.

"I love it, Kaylen. I'll never take mine off." Lane pecked her cheek.

"Not even when it turns my wrist green," Bran said.

"Do you not know quality, dimwit? That's not a Cracker Jack prize hanging from your arm. For all of you, it cost me more than a month's pay."

"Is it okay to wear it every day? We wouldn't want to crap 'em up by doing our sweaty, manual labor jobs and getting them caught on something."

"Well, Tony, you pointed out that they're thick and strong. I think they're durable enough for every day."

"Your turn," Lane said.

"Is it safe to open it?" Kaylen rattled the box. "I mean, it ain't gonna explode, is it?"

"We shoulda' done that. Rigged it to blow up! We could have' rocked it redneck style!"

"That would have been so special, Bran. Spending my Christmas in the ER."

"Blinding light, fire, noise, excitement. Everything a girl could ever want," Tony chuckled.

"Oh, my! It's beautiful!" The gold chain adorned with a dangling bell, diamonds winking across the curvature. Two pearls peeked from beneath the bell, miniature clappers. She jiggled it, dinging soft as a patter of rain. Lane latched it, the bell resting against the dip of Kaylen's neck.

"Now you're like a cat."

"You too," Kaylen shot back, referring to Bran's feline eyes.

"Kitty-cat bell around your neck. I'm going to start calling you 'Fluffy.'"

"Maybe we should get one for Lane, too," Schaffer joshed. "That way, we can hear him coming, and he won't be able to sneak up on us anymore."

"I love this; it's perfect." Kaylen kissed each man. "I wanted a necklace like this when I was a little girl! My mother was going to buy it for me but then she... but I didn't tell y'all about this, did I?"

"No. Your dad did," Luke said.

"What?!"

"Your old man. I asked him what you wanted for Christmas. He told me about that necklace. So we ordered it, like months and months ago," Luke said.

Could have knocked Kaylen over. First of all, she couldn't imagine her friends brainstorming over her gift. Second, that Bran sat on the secret without blurting it out. But the primary whammy being Luke and her father involved in a clandestine discussion.

Kaylen thanked Lane, the steaming mug creamed and sugared to her liking.

"By the way, you didn't have to go to all that trouble dressing up for us," Tony razzed her.

Braless in a sleep tee and lounging pants. The more

familiar she grew with her friends, the more casual her clothes. "Excuse me, dahling, next time I'll wear my diamonds and furs," her Eva Gabor voice, imitating the sophisticated wife from the TV show *Green Acres*.

"I love your nighty-nights. I bet you're commando under there too. Your girls hanging free, you're just a few steps away from being topless."

"And you're a few steps away from being popped in the face, Bran. So remove your googlies from my chest."

"Then you better give me another distraction. Food. Now," Bran commanded.

"Kay, did you buy something for Raymo for Christmas?" Luke asked.

"I got him a bracelet too. I'll give it to him when he gets back from New York."

"That's good. You know he chipped in on your present," Luke said.

"Did he? Not that I'm ungrateful, but I was hoping he'd fork over his Magnum, or at least his Beretta."

"The bet is still on. That'll be up to your skills," Luke said.

"Yep. I'm sure gonna try and take him down." Kaylen hefted food from the Frigidaire. "Okay, what would y'all like besides eggs?"

"I want pancakes, bacon, hash browns, sausage, and biscuits," Bran said.

"I'd like grits, ham, and waffles," Schaffer added.

"Do I look like a short-order cook?"

"No, more like a *Penthouse Pet*. Now that's a fantasy. Naked pinup girl cooking," Bran said.

"Dream on, sweetie, because that's all it'll ever be. And what sane person cooks in the buff? Can you imagine hot oil popping? But, of course, now y'all aren't expecting me to cook all that, are you?"

"Would you? That would be epic," Tony said.

"Oh, alright. But only because it's Christmas. Lane, would you please set the table?" He retrieved plates, cups, and silverware.

"I'm going to ask my dad if he'd like to join us. Tony, man the omelets. Bran, you're on skillet watch."

"Me?! How will I know when to turn the bacon?" Bran, a failure in the cooking department.

Kaylen cobbled it into Bran-terms. "When the color is a little lighter than Sugar Babies, but not as dark as a Baby Ruth bar."

Eavesdropping, Ross Sadler tiptoed back to his bed. Whenever he'd asked Kaylen details regarding her life, she told him what he wanted to hear. The rare times he'd been home and observed her with her friends, everything appeared perfect, specious—an artist's prop to paint, like a bowl of shiny plastic fruit. And Luke and the others inquiring about that Christmas gift—beaming and being on their best behavior, hadn't snowed him. Kaylen's friends, not his favorite people; Bran, a too handsome hubris; Schaffer, all that hair, hooped earring like a pirate, and trashy tattoos; Tony, looked like a cross between a wrestler and a mobster. Lane, an okay guy, a little overstrung but polite. Luke and Raymo, odd, ringers with those black, furtive irises. Ross had observed the interaction among the group, the guys' affection for Kaylen genuine, and she devoted to them. But... something not quite right about the whole thing.

"If only my wife were still alive," Ross whispered to himself. "I miss you, Kat. And Ken." He glanced at a family photo on his bureau. Nothing had been easy, he told the smiling family. The challenge of being a single dad on the road, scrambling for sitters and keeping tabs. Then the issues—Ken falling into the wrong crowd but straightening up when he'd joined the military. And Kaylen, first damaged by family tragedy, then her beauty like a loaded gun. "I tried to keep the apex predators away from her, Kat," Ross whispered to the picture. "Now Kaylen's smack in the middle of the wolf pack. But Kaylen is a grown-up and has fended for herself for many years." Ross smiled at the photo. "What more can I do now?"

"Daddy?" Kaylen stuck her head in Ross's bedroom. "My friends are here for breakfast. Come eat with us. See what they gave me?"

She glowed. Ross, initially suppressing the memory of a little girl's yearning, a wish list scribbled in crayon, his wife thumbing through a catalog, a photo, the spangling necklace nestled against a bed of green velvet. Not until Luke and his buddies inquired: Is there anything special Kaylen wants? An evocation flooding back. Ross could have kept it to himself, but guilt accumulated over his father manqué, of not carrying out his wife's wishes, his penitence earned by revealing the coveted gift.

"Luke said you told him that I wanted this. But then how did you know?"

"Well, a father certainly knows when his little girl has outgrown dolls."

"Just last year," her eyes twinkled. "You know, Mom was going to buy this for me at one time."

"I remember. It was important to you. That's why I told your friends. A special gift from special friends."

Kaylen threw her arms around her father's waist. "Merry Christmas, Dad."

"Merry Christmas, Kitten."

"I gotta get back to the food. Leaving those guys in charge, we'll end up with burnt everything."

He nodded, figuring he'd feel alienated at his own table.

"Kitten? How about changing clothes? Something more decent?"

If he knew her friends had seen her in even less... "Of course," she murmured, backing out the door.

She failed to notice her father's wrinkled brow nor hear his ragged sigh.

CHAPTER TWELVE

R aymo returned in mid-January, the group celebrating a
belated Christmas at Kaylen's house. Raymo, surprised
but jazzed over his bracelet. Since Raymo had contributed to
buying her necklace, Kaylen wasn't expecting more gifts. But
he'd also bought her several albums—Raymo's taste, but others
collector's items, and brand new releases—Chicago's Chicago
and Simon and Garfunkel's Bridge Over Troubled Waters.
The group thanked each other, Italian fashion, kissing cheeks.
Raymo whispered: "Full-on mouth real soon, Kay. When you
lose our competition." She breathed in his ear: "No way, Ray.
Get ready to give up your Magnum."

Culminating months of practice, Kaylen and Raymo
squared off, their friends cheering them on. Then, finally, the
pair, armed with their choice of weapons, calculated their
shots. Both amazing marksmen, the competition close, but in
the end, Raymo won. "You had a great teacher, honey, but you
couldn't bring it home."

"Don't rub it in. I can lose with honor. I got to hand it to you,

Raymo. That was masterful shooting." Kaylen extended her hand in congratulations. He grabbed it, snatching her forward. "Déjà vu," he breathed, enveloping her waist in his hands. "This is how we first started, remember? The first time I ever met you?"

"Yeah, and we're still at the same place because I told you then to back off, and I'm telling you the same thing now."

"Except now I won you as the grand prize."

"You won a competition, Raymo; you didn't win me." Inches apart, Raymo's glance glittering hot, Kaylen's glacial.

"Eight Minutes in the Closet. We got a date."

"You're not my date. It's a bet. Nothing more. And when I've gone through with it, it's done."

"We'll see. Don't you think we should have a little starter now? A dry run of Eight Minutes?" Raymo said, aware of Luke's cool survey.

"Give him some mouth, Kaylen," Tony said.

"Be a sport, give him a congratulatory kiss," Bran urged. "*Dolci labbra* (sweet lips)."

"Wait till its official. But, then, why jump the gun?"

"Jump the gun! Now that's a shooting pun." Raymo ha-ha'd, then on a dime, his voice gelid. "Butt out, Lanesy."

Raymo's rapid-fire mercurial nature chilled Kaylen. "I'm not giving you anything, Raymo. You'll have to work for it. Your Eight Minutes in the Closet won't come easy."

"Well, you know I like a good challenge," he brightened, his mood toggling again. "Come on. A small kiss right now ain't going to put you out. Didn't you say you could lose with honor?"

"I tell you what, Raymo. I am a gracious loser, so I'll give you a congratulatory kiss. But it's not first base; it's not frenching like with Luke; it's not like what I share with Tony, Bran, or Schaffer. Instead, it's a Lane-like kiss."

"You lied then when you said you've made out with Lane!" Bran cried.

"No, I said I don't normally kiss Lane as I do with you guys. But, I never copped to it or denied what Lane and I have and have not done in the past."

They blinked at him—Lane's wise decision to stay mum.

"Small kiss. Nothing more, or I swear you'll regret every minute in the Closet we're going to have."

"Okay. I'll behave—at least for right now. Go for it." Raymo's hands spanning Kaylen's rib cage, the air between their bodies humming. Didn't breach the space, leaning in at the same time. Lips pressed softly as a whisper, hers mist-light, traces of Fruit Stripe gum and Sprite. His were smooth, seasoned with coffee, Altoids, cigarettes—a combination that should have turned Kaylen off; instead, exotic, like liquid smoke, galvanic, like a taste of tinfoil to the tongue. That kiss, succinct as a syllable—but a duration sufficient to judder through her. Like a dizzying roller coaster ride—her blood coursing, body vibrating, stomach fluttering, her hair tingling at the roots. The kiss—a lightning strike, zapping her from head to toe. She inched back, his hands drifting to his sides—black bolts against blue, a stunned stare. Between them, and no one else could see it, right? But then Schaffer blurted: "Whoa. Sizzle and sparks."

"Better bring a fire extinguisher to Eight Minutes. Might burn up that Closet." Bran and Tony were chortling.

But Luke and Lane didn't crack a smile.

"We done here?" Luke bit out the words.

Raymo collected his weapon and ammo. "Tomorrow, we play Eight Minutes in the Closet." The group plodded back through the woods. "Hey, Kay, my friend Bran turned me on to the idea of you playing in your bikini."

"No one is going to tell me how to dress for this."

"Oh, are we getting an attitude? Becoming a sore loser?" Bran egged it on.

"It isn't a request, Kay. It's a condition. You lost, and that's what the winner wants." Raymo pointed to himself. "Wear a bikini tomorrow unless you want to wear less. Or nothing at all."

"Fine. Got a preference about the bikini?" Big deal. The men had eyeballed her in a bathing suit dozens of times.

"Something tiny. You got several of those, don'tcha'? How about the aqua-colored one? It brings out your eyes." He purposely glanced at her chest instead of her baby blues, amused by her pucker, like she'd been chomping on a dill pickle.

The group parted at Raymo's cabin, he and Luke lugging the weapons inside, Tony, Bran, and Schaffer diverging to their house for dinner, Lane tagging along with Kaylen. "Till tomorrow then, Kay. Remember, aqua bikini. Cherry lipstick. Happy disposition." The men cracked up when Kaylen big fake grinned, accompanied with a dirty Italian hand gesticulation.

* * *

Kaylen, posing at the top of the staircase. "TA-DA!" The men, whistling, whooping, and clapping. She glided down the thirteen steps in her turquoise string bikini, her mouth stained like a juicy maraschino.

With her golden hair fluffed wild and curves in all the right places, the men's pulses ticked up.

"Wow!" Bran breathed. "I'm about to go out of my gourd here, you in those stilettos."

"It's for effect." Kaylen pranced in her towering heels. "They're coming off as soon as we start."

"So's that bathing suit."

Kaylen smiled tolerantly at Raymo.

"You're slammin'," Schaffer said. "Keep the shoes on. It's a look."

"Spoken like a true guy. You try balancing in these things a while and see if you'd wanna wear them any longer than necessary."

"Love the blood-red lips."

"Cherry," Kaylen corrected Luke.

"Same rules that apply to Four Minutes in the Closet? Applies to this too," Schaffer told Raymo. "Kaylen sets the boundaries. Hopefully, she gives you the full first-base experience, so don't mess it up by getting her mad."

"Yeah, like farting in there. Apparently, this is a turn-off to girls, and you won't get anywhere after that." Everyone cracked up at Bran.

"Cheeks puckered up and on shut down. Got it. You're okay with this, right, cuz? Me and Kay?" Raymo asked Luke.

"Why wouldn't I be?" Ice-tipped words.

"I say get your money's worth."

"I ain't a street-walker, Brandy."

"Oh, but you do have those hooker heels," Tony said.

"Shut up, the lot of you. Idiots," Kaylen breathed, unstrapping and kicking off her stilts.

"Are we doing this or what?" Tony fired up a cigarette.

"Ladies first." Raymo opened the closet door. "Or is it age before beauty?"

Kaylen snickered, brushing past him and shutting the door behind them, standing side by side in the cramped space, waiting for their optics to acclimate to the darkness. The air stirred, the plink of the door. Kaylen, her father, and the men were the sole ones aware of the closet door mechanism; if pulled on twice, would lock from the inside, preventing it from being opened from the outside.

"Why did you do that?"

"To prevent your escape. You're in the box with the beast, baby."

Kaylen's flesh prickled. "I could say the same to you. But, anyway, I'm here for a solid eight, Raymo."

"And what an eight minutes it will be. Just securing the door. Making sure we wouldn't be disturbed."

"Yeah, well, you're disturbed enough already," she spat, he guffawing beside her.

"I'm starting the timer. So y'all better be settled." Schaffer called. "Ready, set, go!"

Kaylen, intending to move away from Raymo, captured at the waist, parting her mouth with his. Not a fluke. It was the same electricity as their first time, entwining their tongues and teeth, and Kaylen unable to pretend to want to fight him off—even though she ought to. The parallel sensations racing, both repelled by and attracted to him and in her heart knew which emotion she should keen in on—not the one she surrendered to. Their kiss caught fire, back-drafting. "You feel that?" he whispered against her mouth. "What we have between us?"

"You're about forty seconds in," Schaffer called.

Raymo, backing Kaylen to the wall, burrowing into her, her breath hitching, their lips, and hips fitting together like they'd been doing it for years. The current was zipping between them. "Do you have this with *him*?" he whispered.

Ravening, his hands roaming, skimming up her leg, her inner thighs. She protesting, he purring against her lips: "Shhhh. Do you see what's happening between us? *Sai che vuoi questo* (you know you want this)." But he deferred to her objection, his hand ceasing its traverse, trammeling between her knees. Their lip-lock smoldering, unlike anything Kaylen had experienced with her other friends. Or Luke.

The guys, cat-calling outside the door, shouting out their remaining time. "Does *he* do this to you?" Raymo was kneading her lips with his. "Don't you see I'm the only one who can turn you on like this?"

Kaylen moaned; whether it was the truth of Raymo's words, the regret, and guilt, or the marvel of this passion she hadn't experienced before, she didn't know. He slid his hand from between Kaylen's knees to her warm triangle. He buttressing her; otherwise, she'd have collapsed from shock.

Her hand shot out to reprimand him, but he anticipated her slap, snaring her wrist, his tongue spun a lazy 360 inside her palm. She shivered, forgetting her outrage, mind-numb she'd intended to punish him for the infraction. Instead, he tugged the patch of aqua-colored material aside, his fingers dipping inside her before she realized it, gasping when he plied deep in a cave unexplored. He nibbled along a pulsing vein in her throat, his fingers matching rhythm to her call, a Tango pattern —slow, slow, quick, quick, slow. She balled her fist into his hair, trembling, her body fluxing, her breath fluttering, taking her higher, higher to the place she had never been before, with any man, and certainly never with Luke.

When her waves subsided, he pulled her chest-to-chest, heartbeat to heartbeat. "I get bragging rights now," he purled against her ear. "First one to get to third base with Kay."

The reality dawned, mortification and astonishment burning through her like a fever. "No! This never happened!" she wobbled, punch drunk like she had woken up out of a spell. "I didn't want this! I never permitted you to do this!"

"You didn't make me stop either."

"You will *not* tell them what happened in here! They won't believe you anyway!"

"Actually, I got the evidence right here–undeniably," he chuckled, swiping his hand under Kaylen's nose, her feminine scent ripe on his fingers.

Her red-hot fury seared the air. "You disgusting pig!"

"You didn't think I was disgusting a few minutes ago, now did you? I got all the dirt on you now, waiting to get spilled."

"You can't do this, Raymo! How did this happen? I can't believe I let this happen!"

"Kay, the heat between you and me, it had to come out. There's no stopping it. Until the next time."

"No, this will *never* happen again! Do you understand?"

"You come by my cabin by tomorrow. You'll do it, or I'll blab the second this closet door opens, *capisce?*"

"You won't blackmail me. I don't know what you have on Lane, but you're not going to manipulate me like y'all have done to him."

"You'll come to me because you can't stay away. So it won't be blackmail."

"I'm not going to bed with you! I am Luke's girl!"

"Kay, you and I both know that you're with the wrong guy."

"No! I am not in love with you!"

"What happened between us had nothing to do with love," he said. "You're going to commit; you're coming to see me by tomorrow, understand? You *will* do it. Or I'm gonna tell every one of them what really happened in here. I will tell my cousin, the poor sap who can't even get any further than first base with you. Let's see how he likes his girlfriend willingly getting a grabbling by his cousin. By the way, you are the smokinest girl I've ever known. You come and see me after your sweet spot has recuperated."

The bomb exploded in her brain. Raymo was crying out as Kaylen raked her fingernails down the side of his neck, drawing blood, welting his flesh. She was fumbling in the dark, scrabbling to release the catch. The door popping, she tumbled out, Raymo right behind her, swearing. "What the...?!" Schaffer blurted. "Y'all still got time left on the clock."

"I'm done with him!" Kaylen flounced up the staircase.

"Yeah, honey, that's right. Use me and then lose me. Proud of you, Kay. You're doing it like a guy now."

Kaylen swiveled, skewering Raymo, in a tizzy and her cheeks mantling.

"If her eyeballs were flaming arrows, you'd be dead by now," Bran muttered, Kaylen rocketing away. "What went on in there?"

"Oh, you know, a little of this, a lot of that." Hiking up his hair, revealing his neck. "And this."

Whooping and carrying on. "She did a friggin' number on you!" Bran larked around.

"You must have gone for the goods to get that claw wound," Tony said.

"Yeah, I still got my kiss, though. Hot making out."

The men capered, but Luke's lips compressed.

"We've all experienced Kaylen's expert kissing, but as you found out, it usually comes with a price." Next, Tony scrutinized Raymo's injury.

"Yep, she's a fireball. Got your hands full with that one, huh, cuz?" Raymo said.

"Definitely," Luke said.

"A sarcastic quick-tempered chick with an attitude. Want me to tame her for you?"

"I can handle my girl. Unlike you," Luke shot back, staring at Raymo's scratch marks.

"Can you? *Tu la pensi cosi'* (you think so). Better than me?"

The cousins squared off, the other men goggling with interest.

"Yeah. I can. But obviously, you can't. Seeing you did something you weren't supposed to do in there." Luke touched his cousin's neck.

Raymo slapped Luke's hand away and not kindly. "Or maybe I did everything right. Maybe this is a sign of passion."

"You're talking smack as usual. This is what always happens when Kaylen thinks things have gone too far. You made her mad, and she showed you," Tony said.

"Sometimes, you have to ignore what chicks say they want and go for it. They don't know what they want until you show them—show them a good time," Raymo smiled mysteriously.

"What did you do in there to make Kaylen go psycho?" Bran asked.

"Oh, I tried to sample it all," Raymo said.

"Oh, man." Tony cried. "And you got out of there with your Johnson intact?"

"I'm feeling spacey. I think I lost blood. You don't think she scarred me up, do you?" Raymo asked.

"Dude, I don't know. You might need plastic surgery." Schaffer tilted Raymo's head to the side, examining the gouges.

"At least she didn't mess up your face," Bran said. "That woulda' been a tragedy."

"She wouldn't want to do that. She likes my great face," Raymo said.

"Our great face," Luke corrected.

"She was unglued when she left," Bran said. "Think she'll come back down and join us?"

"I'm surprised Lanesy didn't go sniffing after her," Raymo said.

"I'm more interested in finding out what happened, what's being said," Lane told his cousin.

"Sometimes it's not what is said, but what is left unspoken, know what I mean?" Raymo said cryptically.

"Haul her back down," Luke instructed his brother.

"Tell her I got just the thing to perk her up." Schaffer waved a fat joint at him.

The men in motion, lighting cigarettes, hunting snacks, choosing music. "Gotta drain the lizard," Raymo said, heading in the direction of the downstairs bathroom but out of view, blocking Lane as he ascended the staircase. "She's not going to tell you what happened, so save your breath asking her, Lanesy."

"She's my best friend. She tells me everything."

"Not this time. Like you have your secrets that only *we* know, Kaylen and I have *our* secrets."

Lane blinked at him. "What did you do to her?!"

"Nothing that she didn't want," Raymo said.

"You made an unwelcomed advance. Obviously it wasn't what she wanted," Lane said.

"Yeah, but definitely what she needed. Lane, don't you know? I rocked Kaylen's world!"

"I don't know what you're trying to pull here, Raymo, but whatever it is, it better not harm Kaylen," Lane said.

"What's going to harm Kaylen is for her to refuse to do what she's told to do. Convince her. Tell her I said it. She'll know what it is. Tell her for her own good, Lanesy. You of all people know about *that*, don'tcha'?"

Cold blue irises braced against a black granite stare. Lane pushed past his cousin, who grinned up at him in silence—like the cat that had swallowed the canary.

CHAPTER THIRTEEN

Raymo, with one elbow under him, the other hand pinching a smoldering Marlboro, observing Kaylen from behind his mirrored sunglasses. The floating raft was the gathering spot for him and his group. It had undergone significant changes since Bran and Tony first spotted Kaylen. Now three times larger, as sturdy as a fortress, and capable of accommodating up to 20 people.

Although the seven friends spent every evening together, it was rare for them to finish work at the same time during the day. So the elder Mancusos and Al Vincuzzi agreed to man the office and assume duties, allowing for the group to swim together.

Lane masked up, snorkeled, and cleaned up the shallowest part of the lake, adding another beer can, Coca-Cola bottle, or miscellaneous—sunglasses, a single flip flop, a cleft Styrofoam cooler—to his collection of trash, depositing it in the garbage bag fastened to the ladder. A companion float bobbed beside the trash bag, their transport for towels, suntan lotion, cigarettes and lighters.

The music swelled from a camper's radio. Kaylen, sunbathing, lids battened, hummed along to Eric Burdon and War, Spill the Wine. A perfect summer tune to accompany the group's activities.

"Hey, did you hear that line? The song is talking about mountain kings. That's us! King of the Mountain." Bran, delighted, elbowing his cousin in glee as they played the game.

The vocalist warbled the tale about this guy digging on a girl. The same way Raymo hungered for Kaylen. She glistened beside him beneath the hot rays, her golden skin slathered with Hawaiian Tropic.

An invite, that sluicing oil. He fantasized slip-sliding on top of Kaylen, no friction, his hard body pressing against her soft curves. Took self-control not to carry it out, focusing on tapping the ashes from his cigarette. Kaylen, either oblivious to him or cold-shouldering. Again. She'd grown proficient at it—in public. But when he ordered her to his cabin, she paying him the attention he deserved.

"You jerk." Tony skinned his ankle, Schaffer boosting him from the raft, claiming the reign of King of the Mountain. "Medic!"

"If it's a bleeder, I'll help. Otherwise, leave me alone," Kaylen said.

"I thought you liked playing nursemaid, Kaylen." Bran paddled up beside his cousin.

"Yeah, well, I know y'all think that I'm your nurse, chef, substitute mom, whatever, but I'm off duty right now."

"You can be my wet nurse anytime you want." Tony chirked. "How about now? Guaranteed I'll forget about my boo-boo."

"Wet nurse? What is that? Wait, I have a nurse fantasy right now. Kaylen in a short white, body-hugging nurses' uniform, stockings and garters, and white heels."

"I have a nurse fantasy too, Bran. Me taking a very long needle and ramming it into your bum."

"Sadist RN! I'm down with that. I'm ready for my sponge bath any time now, Nurse Kaylen."

"You're getting a little dried out there. Let me help." Schaffer splashed Kaylen.

"Hey, knock it off!"

Schaffer and Luke gained possession of the raft as the new kings, and Tony and Bran, treading water and strategizing their next besiege.

Kaylen glopped on more oil. "Can I help with that?" Raymo volunteered, Kaylen struggling to reach the space between her shoulder blades. Hesitated, then plopped on her tummy, Raymo smearing the coconutty concoction on her rhomboids.

"You feel so good under my hands, Kay. So silky," he whispered over her. "You smell delicious." His haptic exploration of her back, fingers teasing the dip below her lumbar, nibbling at the back of her neck. "Stop it," she hissed.

Lane broke the surface, Raymo's teeth scraping Kaylen's neck. He perused the pair, Kaylen flipping over on her back. Was his vision deceiving him? He blamed his foggy mask.

Raymo eased back. Lane resubmerged. He continued his survey of Kaylen's body. She was a contradiction—acting ice cold and, in a New York minute, steamy hot. Drove him crazy. It took him to the edge. He now understood his cousin's enthrallment with her. Fascinated, he scoped the bead of sweat trickling from Kaylen's collarbone to her left breast. He mused what she would do if he licked it away. Those eyes—cobalt blue when her temper torched; aquamarine, when evincing her alarm—and he wagered which color they might convert.

She sighed, her chest arching, her knee falling open. Sexy. It tingled Raymo to the core. Kaylen hadn't done it on purpose, though. That's what got to him about her—she didn't even realize how sizzling she was, that the things she did in innocence mushroomed her provocativeness. The way she held the men off, the way she allowed them at most to kiss her—she wasn't trying to be a tease, but a titillate nevertheless.

No one knew what happened between Raymo and Kaylen that night in the Closet. The secret burned inside him, yenning to blurt it out, go Bran-like (Tell-a-graph, Tell-a-phone, Tell-a-Bran, and it will be known), but he locked it down—ammo keeping Kaylen coming back to him. Raymo, the master of manipulating, extorting.

Studying the rise and fall of her chest, her toned abdomen glossed with oil. He wanted her. She belonged to his cousin. But he had stolen before, right under Luke's nose, that third base move, pumping Raymo with gratification. Fierce competition among the Vincuzzi men. But this? To grasp that hot woman in his hands, she soaring to a place she'd never ascended before and, with no other man except him, prodded his desire. Kaylen was his possession; he plotting to go to fourth base with her. Next steps. Caught in the liminal. Luke in the equation. How to bypass that? And Kaylen, the last great holdout. Raymo recalled details he'd learned in 10th-grade shop class regarding the processing of steel, how the more substantial its cold forming, the harder it became. But metal subjected to soft annealing —the heating up, forms a pliant material. Kaylen was his alloy to craft, adapting her malleability. He reshaping her— commanding her to his cabin, necking, fitting his body against hers, she thawing out instead of freezing up, becoming more his and less Luke's. He had to strike the right balance, though. Handle Kaylen with the proper amount of blackmail, the proportionate dose to keep her in line, but not overpressure, not spurring her to blab to someone, or shut him down. Kaylen wouldn't admit to wanting him, yet she did, and they both knew it. Her response to him during Eight Minutes blew his mind.

Maybe the next time he summoned her, he'd take what he wanted. He had done it before, scoring third base. Perhaps he'd steal from her what all the men wanted. Take it further than he had already. Educate her about what takes place between a man and a woman. Teach her a lesson about teasing, where it leads. Show her what happens to girls who tease and don't follow through.

Took a drag, the smoke enveloping Kaylen, but she paid no heed. Had his choice of any woman he wanted, yet Kaylen the one he coveted. What was it about her? She wasn't that special, right? Cosmetics-free and her pigtails bouncing, she looked like a 14-year-old. When her makeup was on point, her skin glowing, a bombshell—like now. An utmost combination of woman-girl in one package—innocent, sultry. His statement that night in the Closet, no exaggeration—definitely the smoke-inist girl he'd ever encountered. And although a visual pleasure, Kaylen not flawless—her cheekbones too sharp, her breasts not the D cups+ Raymo favored. Her fixation on order and conde-scending behavior, like Lane's, annoyed him. He felt compelled to give her a reality check when she rebuffed him in front of the others. He believed correcting such behavior was necessary, and she required discipline soon. Still, she lit him up, got to him like no other woman, and drove him wild with want, every inch of her turning him on—that mane like mink to the touch, golden and shimmering as a garnet; those long lashes frilling a bloom of blue daze. Her carnation-colored lips, puckering in mid-sentence, caressing each word. A place in his mental locker emerged; when she dipped strawberries in sugar, her lids closed as she sucked the juice from each one. Like a seduction. The food play had evoked a sweet ache from the pit of his belly to his groin.

He hated the way she got to him. He fixated on her—much like and parallel to Luke's preoccupation with her. Once addicted, nothing else mattered. Obsessions required management, control. Raymo craved reign. He salivated at putting Kaylen under his check.

She stretched, her heels grinding into the deck, her knees propped wide to the sky, her inner thighs slick with oil and sweat. Raymo yearned to slide his hand between those legs—like that night in the Closet. Her gasp of indignation transmuted into a sough as he nipped her neck, the velvet of a ripe peach. His fingertips solaced his own scarred neck. The way she injured him called for him to inflict poetic justice. Not a nibble next time; nosh her like a vampire, siphoning her blood, suck out her juices. Mark her as his. Maybe constrict her silky neck like a python. Would she gasp, scream, or choke in silence? Would her eyes bulge aquamarine or cobalt blue? Dare to squeeze her of her last breath? And teach her a lesson. He held Kaylen's life in his hands. Power. Transported him higher than any drug. Drunken with the power. He had the power to shake a reaction. "You know, sometimes you look exactly like Sharon Tate." It wasn't a lie; despite that Tate's eyes had shimmered hazel-brown and Kaylen's glowed blue, she resembled the slain sex symbol.

Kaylen's aqua irises rifted like a jerked roller shade. "Yeah? And you're a maniac like the person who ordered her death." A reference to Charles Manson.

"Well, we're family, aren't we? Manson had a family, and I have mine—the cousins, my bros Bran, Shay, Tony, and you."

"I will be your family one day when I marry Luke."

"Don't hold your breath on that one, Kay. So that's what you're waiting for to give up the goodies?"

She sprang up, balanced high on her Sitz bones. "It's none of your business what I'm waiting for, for how long, or why."

"Actually, it is." He edged up his sunglasses, staring Kaylen in the eye. "The night we went in that closet, and you let me do what I did—you wanted what I did, it all became my business."

"I belong to Luke," she hissed. "My heart belongs to him."

"But your body belongs to me. And in your heart—the one you say belongs to Luke, and you know that."

She flipped over, her back to him. How did this happen? All of it—her and Raymo, the things she and her friends did, the risks they took. She reflected on what had evolved several days ago. What was supposed to have been a celebration had gone wrong in minutes. She replayed the incident...

... "I can't take too many more days like the ones we've had in the past few," Kaylen admitted to her co-workers. The last 48 hours of problems at the campground included: a black bear invading the main trash bin, a runaway campfire, a huge aggressive rattlesnake terrorizing several guests on the hiking trail, and a camper who had leaned in to pick a cluster of inviting white wildflowers discovered they were attached to a stinging nettle plant. As a result, she required treatment via ambulance for a burning rash and severe allergic reaction. "This blows too," Bran raspberried, he and Kaylen cross-legged on the floor, their backs flush to the wall. Schaffer, his feet were dangling off the rails of the pool table, Tony at his left thigh. Lane, parked with his spine against the jukebox blaring Band of Gold by Freda Payne, and Luke perched atop the air hockey table. Each cradled a life jacket, its ties twisted into a million tiny knots, the handiwork of five siblings—the group christening them: "Rosemary's Baby (ies)," a nod to the horror movie. The kiddie hellions had also hoyed rocks at campers before capsizing a couple of kayaks.

"Have any of the campers complained?" Lane asked.

"Not many. They're probably afraid the little brats will set fire to their tents while they sleep," Tony said.

"Did you mention anything to the parents?"

"No, Lane. I told them to go ahead and enjoy themselves, make sure that they tore down the pavilion and torched the woods before they left. But, of course, I warned the folks. They plan to stay another week, but I'll shut them down if we get any more incidents." Tony, playing manager (in reality, Kaylen's role), the elect in the pro tem for these types of problems at the campground. Tony, with his authoritative stature and mature face, adults tended to listen to and obey him rather than gorgeous Bran or hippie-looking Schaffer.

The men struggled to unknot the straps on the life jackets as Kaylen unraveled hers at warp speed.

"Nice to see that you're now using your nails for good instead of evil." Tony slashed the air like Zorro.

One of a hundred references the men had voiced about Eight Minutes in the Closet and Kaylen gouging Raymo's neck —which didn't require plastic surgery but left him marred, white scarred. She shook off the remark, and when Lane peered over at her, dipping her head and avoiding his eyes.

Days after playing Eight Minutes with Raymo, Kaylen had noticed Lane staring at her throat. The hickies scattered on her neck raised suspicion among her peers, especially considering she had previously deemed them skanky-looking and refused to let Luke give her one. She explained them away as bruises incurred by stumbling around in the closet in the dark. Kaylen had not told anyone what happened in the Closet. But her demeanor seemed to have changed, leading Lane to wonder if Raymo's theory held any weight—perhaps it was not what was spoken but what was left unsaid. Something had rendered Kaylen's silence.

"Speaking of evil, where is Raymo?" Bran joked.

"Probably sleeping away the day since he thinks himself above manual labor."

"You're going hard on him because you're still holding a grudge, Kaylen."

"No, Tone, you taught me well; I don't hold grudges, I get even."

"Then get your chance," Bran urged. "Rematch. Rematch on both."

He meant Eight Minutes in the Closet—and another shooting competition—a flat-out turn down by Kaylen. And if Raymo desired to rematch, he remained mum on the subject. These days, his interest more on the other game the two met up for.

The group worked on the task at hand, Lane zoning out, pondering the interplay between Kaylen and his cousin. How many times had Kaylen spouted it? She pointed out that distinct characteristics delineated Luke and Raymo's identical-ness and carbon copy actions—most of Raymo's, which Kaylen detested, and Luke's, which she liked (except that he was a cheater). The way she kept her distance reflected Kaylen's distaste for Raymo. So different from the physical bonding she had with the other men, massaging their necks, smooching them, grasping their hand, outer thighs brushing when they lounged side by side with her on her couch. Lane noticed that now when Raymo took stock of Kaylen, she no longer averted his inspection as she had in the past. And sometimes, when Raymo perceived he wasn't under the radar from the other's keeks, his arm snaked up, lingering at Kaylen's hip—the draping a mimic to how Luke embraced Kaylen.

"What?" Lane, deep in his head, his friend's murmurings calling him back. Bran pointed, the pavilion and playground wrapped in toilet paper. "*Cosa sta succedendo* (what's going on)? When did this happen?"

"Apparently, while we were working on these life jackets," Kaylen told him.

"Is there any doubt who the culprits are?" Tony said.

"Those kids are industrious and fast," Kaylen said.

"Those little peckerheads are gonna be dead meat," Luke growled.

"That's it; I quit—time out. The game called off on account of rain. I'm out of here." Bran slammed the life jacket to the floor.

"No, you're not. And pick that up," Kaylen ordered.

"You're not the boss of me."

"Actually, I am, and if you walk out, I swear I'll put you on garbage detail for a month. No one leaves—except Tony. You got a job to do, Tone. Tell those campers to pack up and go. We refuse to honor their business," Kaylen said, Tony saluting, then exiting.

"We've all got to pitch in and get that mess outside cleaned up," Lane said.

It took them a good half hour with all of them on it.

"I'm almost too exhausted to celebrate Kaylen's birthday this afternoon," Bran said.

"Oh, you did remember!" Up to that point, no one had mentioned it.

"How could we forget? Especially since you've been hinting at it for two weeks, and then you circled it in red on the calendar behind the counter in the office," Schaffer said.

"A subtle reminder," Kaylen said.

"Subtle as diarrhea in a public bathroom," Bran said.

"Lovely image," Kaylen smirked.

"Hey, Pops, thanks for taking over. Okay, now that we got relief manning the office, come with us; we got a surprise for you," Luke told Kaylen.

Kaylen waved goodbye to Al Vincuzzi. "Uh-oh. The last time someone said that to me, I ended up with a Snakebite Rug Burn."

"Hey, I gave you a choice of either that or Nuggies," Bran pointed out.

So they paddle boated the six-seater over to Kaylen's house, greeted with bright yellow balloons and a glittery birthday banner swooping from the ceiling. Their decorators Tony and Raymo offered the lit joint, cracking up when Bran untied a helium-filled balloon and sucked it down, giving a rendition of Lollipop Guild from the movie *The Wizard of Oz*.

"Now for real music. Put on the album," Raymo said.

Schaffer didn't have to ask which one. Ever since they'd learned Manson's favorite Beatles LP was the double-disk White Album, it stayed on their repeat menu. The album cover blank except for the band's name embossed. A 1968 release, Schaffer had played it dozens of times. But now, he and the others listened for subliminal messages, any cryptic utterings that might have persuaded Manson's followers to commit their horrific crimes. Lane enlightened them that these kinds of messages could either be intentional backmasking or a phenomenon related to audio pareidolia. Bran asked if there were any terms for douchy dweebs who just won't let them enjoy their creepy fun, and Lane clammed up. They'd played the record at various speeds—45, 33 ½, 78, and backwards (which Kaylen complained ruined her stereo needle). Still, they hadn't detected anything out of the ordinary. But they all agreed on songs like Revolution 9 with its trippy, manic strains, machine guns rat-tat-tat-tat-tat-tatting, and people screaming, was disturbing and could have inspired a crazy like Manson to want to kill people.

Helter Skelter blared from the stereo. "Charlie likes this one." Raymo handed off the doobie to Bran.

"How do you know?" Tony asked.

"Newscast. They said it on TV. How did you think I knew? That Charlie Manson contacted me telepathically?"

"If you think Manson's contacting you telepathically, then you're both nuts," Lane coughed, fanning the smoke away as they passed the joint back and forth around him.

"Maybe Raymo and Manson both have mental powers like those freaky psychic kids in the movie *Village of the Damned*," Luke said, toking.

"No, that would be Bran. Remember how those kids had white hair and weird colored eyes? Like Bran! Whatcha' say there, Brandy? You able to communicate telepathically?"

"I dunno about that, but I can surely predict what's gonna happen to you in the next few seconds, cuz. I see a Purple Nurple in your near future." Bran delivered the blitz, Tony wailing as his cousin latched on to one of his nipples. Tony repaid the abuse, pinching and twisting.

"Hey, watch it," Schaffer warned, the pair's scuffling jostling the stereo and the album skipping. He corrected it, crooning along with the song.

"Helter Skelter? Didn't Manson have one of his guys carve that on a victim?" Bran accomplished his mission, ending the tomfoolery with his cousin.

"Pretty sure. What's it mean?" Schaffer asked his brother.

"Dunno. Gotta be satanic."

"Actually, it has to do with amusement rides. Helter skelter are rides—slides that they have over in England," Lane informed them.

"The demonic angle is so much scarier," Bran said.

"Yeah, as if killing people at random wasn't scary enough for you," Kaylen snickered.

"Charlie's got bats in the belfry." Schaffer flapped his hands above his head.

"What does that even mean? Like his elevator doesn't go to the top?"

"Yes. You and Charlie-boy are a few bricks short of a load." Tony pointed at Bran.

"Ha! Not me, but Charlie's got a major screw loose for sure."

"Yep. He's one egg shy of a dozen," Tony said.

"He's not playing with a full deck," Schaffer said.

"Like in cards? Maybe he lost it because a hot blond wouldn't carry through during Strip Poker." Tony elbowed Kaylen.

"Enough already. No more talk about Strip Poker playing—past, present, or future. Whatever happened to bringing out the watermelon and my birthday cake?"

"Patience, darlin'," Schaffer said. They'd spiked a watermelon by cutting a plug from it, pouring a whole bottle of Smirnoff into the pulp. It chilled in the fridge, soaking up until it became "wicked potent."

"Let's dig into that cake then," Tony suggested.

They drifted into the kitchen, Raymo splashing tequila into cups. Schaffer hunkered over the cake with a knife. "Wait." Bran clamped his wrist, flicking his lighter to the candles. "The birthday girl's gotta make a wish first."

Just then, the phone rang. Before Kaylen could pick it up, Bran answered, "Hello, Gilligan's Island. Don't send help. Send more hot chicks like Mary Ann and Ginger. Or Kaylen."

Kaylen snatched the receiver out of Bran's hand. "Oh, hello, Daddy. No, that's Bran's idea of a joke. I know. Most of what he says isn't funny." Kaylen's eyes narrowed as Bran grinned, and the rest of her friends stifled their laughter. "Thank you, Dad. It's okay. I know you'd be here if you could. What? That's fine. I'll look forward to a belated birthday gift. Here? Yeah, the guys got me a cake and... stuff. Okay, I'll see you in a week or two then. Love you, Daddy. Bye."

"You moron. My dad was not amused."

"How am I to know it was him? And why would he think you'd be here instead of working?"

"He called over to the office. Al told him I had the afternoon off. You have a lot to make up for."

"I can think of one way," Bran grinned.

"You can't think at all," Tony said, shoving him out of the way. "Go ahead and make your birthday wish before the candles melt all over the place."

"Hit it," Lane said, the men singing 'Happy Birthday' off-key. Kaylen's face screwed up, fingers plugging her ears.

"Kaylen, how goes it to be an old broad?" Schaffer said as Kaylen blew out her candles.

"Not bad, Shay. Still getting around with my walker."

"She's at the end road of her teens. Two more years, and she'll be 21 and legal." Tony swigged, scrunching his face, the shot searing his throat.

"Yep, she's almost an adult." Bran raised his cup to Kaylen.

"Something you'll never be able to say." Schaffer kidded his brother.

"Hysterical. Now bite me."

"Okay, now it's time for Kaylen's birthday whacks," Bran said.

"Do not mess with my backside, or I will injure you."

"Come on. One little spanking," Bran begged.

"I take Kaylen's threat seriously, especially once she gets her gift." Tony presented her with a package, and Kaylen soon shredded its wrapping. "Holy crap! For me?" She admired the 12-gauge shotgun.

"Naw. It's for John Wayne." Bran handed her a box of shells.

"The watermelon's ready. And who wants cake?" So first, Schaffer split the alcohol-saturated melon. Then, he plated slices of cake and watermelon.

"Your mom's homemade carrot cake is to die for." Kaylen smacked her lips.

"Every time. And this loaded melon is phenomenal," Luke said.

Bran spits a few watermelon seeds at his cousin.

"Knock it off, infantile," Tony said.

Bran spit seeds at his brother. Schaffer retaliated, Bran then launching a melon missile using his fork. Seeds and pink fruit exploded across the table like an artillery round, Kaylen crying: "I am not cleaning this crap up. And you're wasting food."

The action lasted a few seconds longer, the men getting it out of their system. Then, finally, Lane wiped everything down and swept up.

"Thanks, Lanesy. Glad to see you serve some purpose in life."

"He had to. Since you're busy over there smoking weed, drinking, gorging yourself on vodka-melon, and eating all the icing off the cake," Kaylen said to Bran.

"Nice burn, birthday girl." Tony saluted.

"She's right, though. I'm stoned, booze-buzzed, *and* sugared-up." Bran crammed a forkful of cake in his mouth, washed it down with the tequila, and took a hit of pot.

"Can't beat that winning combination, bro," Schaffer said.

"When are you gonna thank us properly for your birthday gift?" Tony asked.

"How about a little kissy-poo?" Schaffer suggested.

"Not one of those Lane pecks. Give me a real grown-up snog," Bran said.

"Well, come on then," Kaylen ordered, Bran locking lips with her.

Luke encouraged the jollity, not a snippet of jealousy, even when Schaffer and Tony smooched Kaylen hard.

"She saved the best for last." Luke slipped into a familiar hold with his girlfriend.

"Nothing like a little community kiss among friends, huh?" Tony wolfed a bite of cake.

"Yep, spread the disease, if you please. Mass mono for your loved ones." Schaffer licked frosting from his fork.

"Did you forget about me?"

"Aaah, you weren't gonna leave Raymo out of the kiss-fest, were you?" Bran sing-songed.

"You gonna protest?" Raymo asked.

"Should I?" Luke's jaw tightened.

"Maybe. Should he, Kay?"

"Not at all, Ray."

"Yeah, let's see that closet action y'all had," Schaffer said.

"Yeah, Kay. Wanna repeat our Eight Minutes?" Black eyes glittered, and Kaylen fidgeted internally.

"Kaylen, don't be a party pooper at your own birthday celebration," Bran said. "Give the guy some mouth."

"Do it then. Get it over with already. Make sure it's a Lane-kiss," Kaylen said.

"Come on, Kay, we both know you can do better than that, right?" Raymo's palm pressed against the small of Kaylen's back, her arms laced around his neck. It spelled familiarity, intimacy—like two people who knew each other well.

Lane's eyes snapped toward his brother, but Luke glowered at the kissing couple.

Kaylen trembled against Raymo's body, voltaic shocks flowing between them.

They finally disentangled, their friends whooping and cutting up.

But Luke had seen it, that moment of pure passion pulsing between Kaylen and Raymo.

Luke and Raymo's identical frowns, were like a thunderstorm trundling across an ebony sky.

"We got dangerous loving here tonight, boys," Schaffer said.

"I tell you one thing; we do it up big. Sucking face, tequila, spiked watermelon, cake and cannabis, and guns, this is one birthday Kaylen will never forget," Bran said.

"Yes, but now we gotta top it. Bet you can't wait to see what we plan for next year," Tony said.

"I say it should involve clowns, pony rides, and strippers," Bran exclaimed, the others cracking up.

"How about we do it now? How about a birthday challenge like no other. You like *games*, right, Kay? Strip Poker, Truth or Dare? Eight minutes in the Closet? But this game, not for the faint of heart. We haven't played it in a while. At least not since Kaylen moved here," Raymo said.

"What is it?" Kaylen asked.

"It involves guns," Raymo said.

"Well, count me in. I got a brand new one thanks to my friends for life."

"Kaylen, no."

"Stay out of it, Lanesy," Tony ordered.

Raymo plucked a Smith & Wesson Model 29 .44 Magnum from the back of his waistband. Kaylen jerked back as if it were a taipan. Had he had it there all this time?

A single bullet wabbled inside his palm, loading it into the chamber, placing the weapon in the center of the table.

"You know what this is, Kay. The ultimate game of chance —where you don't get double or nothing. Its lady luck and the hand of fate," Raymo said.

"Raymo, this is going too far, even for you. I'm not doing this."

"Come on, Kay. You're always resisting. When you let go

instead of playing it safe, that sense of danger gets the adrenaline pumping. You know what that's like, right?"

Kaylen ignored his glittering gaze. "You're psychotic. And I can't believe any of you would be a party to this!"

"I did it for my initiation," Tony said.

"Let's do it, Tone. You, me, Luke, Kaylen."

"I'm not doing this," Kaylen protested.

"Last time you said 'no' to me, you meant 'yes.' Remember?" Raymo said.

She quivered inside, petrified he'd reveal what had happened between them. Petrified by what they were about to do.

"Who's up?" Raymo asked.

"I'll go."

"Tony, no."

"Sit, Kaylen."

She sank, quivering.

The glinting muzzle at Tony's silvery temple, his finger on the trigger, Kaylen trembling as it clicked. She shuttered her eyelids, nausea raking her belly.

He deposited the gun into Luke's palms. Kaylen rasped: "Luke, please, don't." The album continued to spin, Honey Pie piping. The noise grated, Kaylen's mind screaming, turn it off, but paralyzed. "If I don't make it, you'll wish that you had given it up to me." Luke stuck the gun to his temple. Kaylen dizzied, her lungs whooshing when the weapon clicked on the empty chamber.

Raymo caressed the Magnum. "Kay, wanna give me a little kiss again, in case this is goodbye? No? Okay then." He spun the cylinder, the spindle halting, lifting it toward his head, but in a flash, twisting it in Kaylen's direction. She stared down the bore, her pulse drumming in her ears, her breath caught in her throat.

"Bang-bang," he whispered, zeroing between her aquamarine eyes. After what felt like an eternity, Raymo lowered the gun. "You did good, Kay. You didn't even flinch. A true birthday gift, don't you see? Because the good news is, you get to live another day. Another day for you and me in paradise."

She vaulted, the chair clattering to the floor, exploding like gunfire. A race up the stairwell, and when her slamming door rattled the house, inside her bedroom in private, she shook and couldn't stop...

... The memory receded when Lane resurfaced and said: "You're going to get a stripe across your back. You don't wanna tan line, right?"

"No. Unhook my top, will ya'?"

He hoisted himself up, an awkward arm thrust around Raymo, who could have unlatched it for her. Instead, Lane loosened the strings from around Kaylen's neck, flattening her breasts against the deck as he swam away.

"Hey, Kay, I think a little stripe across your back woulda' been sexy. But, if you're concerned about tan marks, why don't you go topless?" Raymo asked.

"Yeah, that would be great, so kid-friendly for our campground."

"It'd probably blow those kids' circuits. Can you imagine? Seeing a gorgeous girl like you and your ta-tas." His finger traced her lumbar.

"Cut it out right now before you attract attention. Get away from me."

"Your mouth says no-no, but your body says yes-yes."

"Leave me alone! I mean it."

"But I don't want to leave you alone, Kay. I wanna talk about us."

"There is no 'us.' But there is Luke and Kaylen."

"You don't think there's an us? Then think about that night in the Closet."

"Raymo, I've regretted it a thousand times. I can't believe I did it, and I can't take it back. You manipulated me! I let you go further with me than I've ever let Luke. He's not the type of guy who'd ever understand. He expects me to save myself for him—in every way. I will lose him if he finds out."

"And would that be so bad? Luke breaking up with you? A guy who claims he cares for you but still cheats on you?"

"Are you serious?! Who are you to judge him? *You*, who would go behind his back and make advances at his *cousin's own girlfriend?*"

"But here's the thing, Kay. He shouldn't be your boyfriend. You might think you love him, but he's not right for you. We both know who's right for you."

"Yeah, that would be Lane," Kaylen grunted. "Except there's deep friendship and love, but no chemistry."

"Exactly. You get it. There's gotta be fire. Do you have that with Luke?"

"It's none of your business what I've got with Luke. I've been coming to you like you've asked because I don't want trouble between the two of you. I don't want to do this, but I don't want Luke to find out about what happened when we played Eight Minutes. You're enjoying this blackmail, aren't you?"

"I am. I wish you would too. Maybe you will realize what you and Luke have is like pico de gallo without the serranos. No bite. That which we do have, that spice."

"Heat is not love, Raymo. I am not in love with you, and you're not in love with me. If we're going to analyze something, let's talk about the other night. About what happened—could have happened. You pointed a gun at me! One slip of your finger and a bullet could have gone through my head! That's not loving and caring, Raymo. That's disregard for my safety, what I would expect from an enemy. Friends love, enemies hate. Do you hate me that much that you'd wanna see me gone?"

"You're wrong. What I feel for you is far from being hate. It's that thing you have with the person that'll never be with anyone else. But, Kay, you're not going to have that with Luke. Not now, not ever. You'll be with him, but you won't be able to stop thinking about me."

"Don't flatter yourself, Raymo. I hate what you're making me do. I don't love you, and I hate that you've put me in this predicament."

"I know you like Luke never will. It's okay if you want to believe that it's hate instead of fire between you and me. It's a matter of time before we've gone full-on third base and then fourth. You know the strange thing about hate and passion, Kay?" He leaned in, his tongue swiping her nape. "They both come from the same place. There's not that much difference between the two."

Before she could retort, Bran called out: "Kaylen, come on, we're gonna have chicken fights."

"No, you guys go ahead."

"What's the matter? Are you afraid you'll mess up your hair? Or are you so engrossed in your conversation with Raymo that you can't join in?"

Even self-absorbed Bran noticed Raymo and Kaylen's interaction.

"You see that? Back off, Raymo. Right now because I don't wanna have to explain this to Lane or Luke."

"Kaylen, come play." Bran spits a stream of lake water at her.

She screeched, cool liquid spritzing her baking skin.

"Hey, dude, I just peed there," Luke told Bran.

It didn't deter him, slurping up another mouthful and spraying Kaylen. "Bran!" she screeched.

"That's my name, don't wear it out."

"I bet I know what'll get her off that towel." Tony colluded with his cousin. Bran accepted the perdue, easing out of the water, his fingers arachnid-like creeping near Kaylen and yanking her top from beneath her. She screamed bloody murder, jerking up, cupping her breasts, Bran wrestling her towel away. "Whatcha gonna do now, honey?" He hooked Kaylen's top on his head like a hat, waving the towel matador style.

"Give it back right now, Bran!" Kaylen said.

"Or what? Will you cry? Will you charge me like a bull? El Torro." He wielded the towel like a cape, a mariposa. The men's laugh thundered, Lane, breaking the surface to see what the commotion was.

"Cut the crap right now. You're not funny," Kaylen cried.

"Sure I am. Raymo's laughing." Bran tossed him the top.

Raymo stretched it out of Kaylen's reach. "Go for it." Left-arm wrapped across her chest, fumbling for the top with her right hand. "Aw. Too bad. Nice try." He tossed the bathing suit top back to Bran, who tethered it between his legs, the cups of the top situated vertically between his groin and buttocks, then tying off the strings at his thighs. "There's hardly enough material here to cover my gonads, much less your boobs, Kaylen."

"Get your smelly balls off my bathing suit top."

The men cackled, Bran, snatching it from between his legs and flinging it at Raymo.

"Give it back to her."

"Or what, Lanesy? You'll do what? *Oogatz* (nothing). You know better than to mess with me."

"I like this game," Bran said, Raymo bunging the top back

to him. "This is better than chicken fights. We should play it all the time."

Kaylen tried another tactic. "Give it back, please, Bran. I'll give you a great kiss, right here, right now."

"Bare-breasted? Chest to chest?"

"Don't do it, man," Tony gave him the heads up. "It's a trap."

"You go over there, and she's gonna kick you in the privates," Schaffer told him.

"Okay, as much as I would like to take you up on that offer of a kiss, I have to listen to my wise cousin and brother. They believe my junk is in danger." He chucked the top to his cousin, who launched it to Schaffer, Luke joining in, everyone lobbing it around the circle.

"There it goes."

"Can you get it, Kay-Kay?"

"Rebound for it."

"I truly hate all of you. Give me my top! Bran, you are going to be seriously penalized. You got latrine cleaning for two months."

"You can't do that. I'll tell my mommy, and she'll talk to Luke's mommy, and we'll tell her you're an unfair manager."

"I'll talk to your mommy myself and tell her exactly what her baby boy has been up to, and then we'll see what happens."

"Uh-oh. Someone's gonna get a big time out," Tony said.

"Appropriate because you guys act like two-year-olds," Kaylen said.

"Only Bran." Schaffer japed. "The rest of us are eleven and a half!"

"Incontestably not your shoe size but your intelligence quotient," Kaylen said.

"If I'm eleven and a half, then we ain't talking about age, shoe size, or IQ, baby," Bran winked.

Kaylen's lip curled in disgust. She retrieved her towel once he discarded it, soaking wet from the drenched deck. "I'll tell you what, keep the top. So you can cover your eleven and a half. Which, of course, is a measurement found only in your dreams." The men whooped; Kaylen bound the towel around her bare chest and jumped into the water.

"Untrue and mean," Bran called to her as she swam back to shore.

"Yeah, well..." Kaylen proceeded to tongue-lash him in Italian.

"That's impressive! I didn't even know she knew that much Italian," Tony said.

"Well, she pays attention. And she's smart," Schaffer said.

The men incorporated "Itanglese" into daily conversation, quickly upskilling Kaylen. In a locale where Southern dialect and nuances ruled, and the minority language Spanish, or Maskókî and Mikisúkî—spoken by Native American Seminoles, Italians were few and far between. In New York City—with its melting pot of cultures and languages—Italians populated most boroughs. Not so once Luke, Lane, and Tony moved to rural Florida—their Italian community consisting of Bran and Schaffer's parents, the Vincuzzis, and a random camper or two versed in the language.

"Whatcha gonna do now?" Luke called, Kaylen trudged up the embankment with her soggy towel.

"Commit suicide."

"And then?" Luke asked.

"Stick needles in my little Bran voodoo doll."

"Kayleee, I'm sorrrryyy."

"Stuff it, Bran. *Che palle* (what balls)." Hurling this insult, then flaying them with Italian swear words.

"Oh, man, she seriously didn't say that about my cousins, did she?" Tony cried.

"And she put an Italian hex on your future offspring too," Luke pointed out.

"She's a riot," Schaffer said.

"She hates us," Tony said.

"With a passion," Raymo mumbled.

"What?" Bran asked.

"Nothing." Raymo smiled as he monitored Kaylen's trek down the path through the woods to her house, anticipating their rendezvous later on. Lane said nothing, but glared with hatred at his cousin.

CHAPTER FOURTEEN

Kaylen stepped out of the tub, drying off and belting out the Rolling Stones song she started in the shower. She turbaned her hair, swaddling her body with a large towel. She strolled from her bathroom and shrieked.

"You know, you're an insult to Mick Jagger." Schaffer tsk-tsked, reposing upon her bed.

"Yeah, because he's such a great singer, right?" Tony snickered.

"Jagger doesn't have to have chops like Harry Nilsson, man. Not with those stage moves and being a great front man for the Stones," Schaffer said.

"Have you ever considered voice lessons?" Bran asked, balancing a cold Budweiser on his knee, sitting beside his brother.

"Pony up. I won the bet," Tony bragged. "*Cinque un pezzo* (five apiece). I told you guys she wouldn't walk out of the bathroom naked. I knew she'd throw on a towel first."

"Would you please stop doing this?" It hadn't been the first time they'd sneaked into her house, catching her by surprise. "You're gonna give me a heart attack!"

"She's a little pale. Maybe we should give her a little heart massage," Schaffer suggested.

Bran didn't have to get asked twice, lunging for Kaylen and spilling beer on them both. Then, finally, she screeched, whirling away from Bran's groping hands. "She's healed. It's a medical miracle."

She let loose a string of Italian swear words, snatching her clothes off a chair, her towel dipping and inches from losing it. Her friends whistled at the near faux pas, and she slammed the bathroom door behind her.

"We scared her good," Luke whispered. "Did you see her face when she came out of the bathroom?"

Kaylen reappeared in denim shorts and a lilac-hued Crystal Lake Campground T-shirt, aiming a dirty look at her friends.

"Did you admire our Lane-inspired ninja skills?" Bran asked.

"It's sadistic to creep up on someone," Kaylen said.

"It's not creeping if we got a key to get in," Schaffer said.

"Oh, right. The key thing. The key I did not give you," Kaylen said.

"Oh, man. You going to harp on that again?" Bran groaned.

"Yes. By the way, you can clean up that beer you spilled."

"It was the tiniest of drops. Barely noticeable," Bran said.

"But definitely stinky. Clean up your mess. And everyone off my bed."

Instead of heeding her command, Tony tugged Kaylen down, tickling her. She shrieked, throwing him off guard when she straddled him, kittling him under the neck. He captured her wrists, eye-to-eye, her knees digging into his ribs as she perched upon his stomach.

"Slide down a little bit on that saddle, and you'll make his day." Bran's green-gold eyes twinkled.

The men tickle assaulted Kaylen, yelling bloody murder, kicking and thrashing them off the bed. Luke piano-played his fingers across her side. She twisted away, Luke clutching her, them necking, no longer interested in tickling.

Raymo and Lane entered the bedroom, Luke and Kaylen caught up in their lip-lock. Raymo's face clouded. Kaylen, his idée fixe; Luke, his rival. He smarted at the couple's open affection.

"Hey, Lanesy, you would have been proud of us," Bran said, Luke and Kaylen breaking off their embrace. "We were like shinobis, tiptoeing in, catching Kaylen getting out of the shower."

"Yeah, but unfortunately, she did not grace us with being nude." Schaffer snuggled with Kaylen's pillow.

"I don't think I ever realized it before but being stealth? That is a talent. Coming in without someone hearing you? It's hard to be that quiet." Luke said.

"Especially when all of us are clumsy oafs," Tony said. "Except you, Lane."

"I've told you before; I don't try to be quiet; I just am. I am light-footed and move softly."

"Yeah, you do. You've got it down, don't you, Lane?" Kaylen said in an unfamiliar, icy tone as she and Lane glared at each other. The other men peered on with interest, their attention sparked by the uncharacteristic tension between the best friends.

Lane had confronted Kaylen a day ago after following her to Raymo's cabin. He remained hidden, just beneath a window, but had heard and seen for himself what he had suspected for some time. When he faced off with Kaylen, she denied everything. But when Lane repeated word for word Kaylen and

Raymo's conversation, Kaylen told him, "Sometimes what you hear and see does not tell the whole story."

"Then tell me," Lane said.

"It's not what you think! He made me do those things! Otherwise, he would tell Luke what happened the night we played Eight Minutes! He would lie and tell Luke something much *worse* had happened!"

"What happened? What did Raymo do to you?"

Kaylen looked off into the distance. "He took me to a place I've never been. That Luke can't. And now I can't come back from."

Lane stared at Kaylen, who had only answered the question in a language she knew. He said, "Okay. You feel a certain way. I'm not sure I understand. But, Kaylen, one thing I do know is Raymo's talent to manipulate and blackmail."

"Yes, blackmail," Kaylen repeated the word like a sour candy that had been in her mouth for too long. "He's blackmailing me."

"Well, some blackmail is more fun than other blackmail, huh?"

Kaylen's cheeks pinked, and her eyes flashed. She said, "What are you saying? You don't believe me?!"

"I watched you! I heard you!" Lane yelled.

Kaylen jumped; Lane's patience and quiet wisdom had always been rock solid. But here he was, with his eyes like blue flames and the cords in his neck straining.

Kaylen cried, "No, it's not what you think!"

"There's no thinking to it," Lane's voice croaked, sore from his accustomed hollering. "Raymo pulled you into the cabin when he saw you at his doorstep, locking the door behind him but not locking out your voices. Y'all were making out, hot and heavy, unlike I've never seen you and my brother do. And I know you haven't done with him because you told me! But it was like you and Raymo couldn't get enough of each other, like you were in one skin. You took off your shorts and shirt, standing before him in your panties and bra."

"No! It was my white bikini. Not a bra and underwear," Kaylen corrected.

"Does it matter, Kaylen?" Lane clenched his teeth. "You undressed in front of him, and you let him look."

"No, because I had to! He's making me do this."

"Kaylen, you melted when he ran his hands down your back. He spoke to you in Italian. Words maybe you did or didn't understand. He told you that you belong to him. He told you there would be nothing left but to finalize the act, and he would have you. And you told him: Soon. Then I left," Lane said, disgusted.

"I was telling him what he wanted to hear!"

"Kaylen, Raymo's got you lit up. You might be into Luke, but Raymo's gotten to you in a way you'll never be with Luke or anybody else. And you can lie to me, Luke, Tony, Bran, and Schaffer. But you can't lie to yourself."

"If you think I'm sleeping with Raymo, I'm not!"

"No, not yet."

"Not at all! I wouldn't. I love Luke, and I'm waiting for him."

"You think letting Raymo work you and leaving the prize for Luke will make a difference? You might be saving your oh-so-precious virginity for Luke, but you have as good as given Raymo who you are," Lane said.

Kaylen's frustration boiled over as she retorted, "Don't you see? I have to do this!"

Lane shook his head. "I see you are playing a game you can't win. Raymo's in the catbird seat, and he always will be. He will use this for his purpose, and he'll reveal it himself when it suits him. Anything you've done to prevent him, anything you've gone along with, will be in vain. And when that happens, this whole thing will explode. What do you think is going to happen when Luke finds out? You have no idea what you're dealing with!" He was shouting in Kaylen's face, and she shoved him, blazing with anger at the disrespect.

Lane tottered but quickly recovered. "You're on a fine line," he said. "Raymo's on one side, and Luke's on the other. Once you cross that line, Kaylen, you can't go back. Once you make a choice, it's done. I know this in a way that I hope you never will." Lane's eyes were dull, old and wise with secrets.

"What has Raymo done to you?" Kaylen asked again. Their gazes fixed on each other, burdened and bound by secrets.

In much the same way Kaylen had done, Lane answered with unspoken words and hidden meanings. "My essentio," he finally said. "Raymo has stolen my soul."

Kaylen nodded, knowing it was true because the thief had also purloined hers.

"What's up?" Tony asked Raymo and Lane, jerking Lane from his reverie.

"I finished my shift," Lane said. "Schaffer was supposed to go in next. But Raymo asked Mario if he'd cover the office for a while."

"He asked my dad? And he agreed?" Schaffer said. The Mancusos and Luke and Lane's parents didn't object to taking on extra tasks for special events—like the afternoon the group had taken off to celebrate Kaylen's birthday. But nothing extraordinary impended this day.

The group worked staggered shifts of 4-12 hours, with two to four people working from sunup to sundown per stint. One person was always on-call for late campers and evening emergencies, with Bran and Schaffer's parents helping in this capacity. Everyone accrued time off on different days during the week, and the on-call person rotated. The campground also employed Greg, a divorced 30-year-old part-timer who lived in a single-wide near the backside of the lake. He was handy with swinging a hammer, checking campers in and out, and serving as a hiking trail guide. Greg had been with the campground before the Vincuzzis took ownership and worked part-time for the county.

"Yeah, Mario said it was no problem. I convinced him. I can be quite charming," Raymo bragged.

"You mean 'manipulative,'" Kaylen said.

"Semantics. I told him we wanted to go out in the boat. It's a beautiful day. Let's take advantage of it. Let's go water skiing," Raymo said.

"That's a brilliant idea." Tony clapped Raymo on the shoulder. "We should load a cooler too. With lots of beer."

"Don't forget weed and a bong," Schaffer said.

"And a beautiful blonde." Luke shimmied his brows at his girlfriend.

"Or two," Bran said, preening his own hair.

"The essential B's, beer-bong-and-blondes, don't leave home without them," Schaffer chuckled.

"Forget all that. Let's just ski already," Kaylen snapped.

"Well, who peed in your Frosted Flakes?" Bran snorted.

"Let's not make it into a production. Give me a sec to get my swimsuit on." She grabbed her one piece, and the men groaned in unison. "I'm not wearing a bikini, guys. If I'm skiing and hit the water, I don't want my chi-chis popping out of my top."

"I live for those moments." Bran sighed.

"Who cares? I'm still wearing my one piece."

"It's ugly." Tony's face screwed up.

"It looks like what my mother would wear," Luke muttered. "Kaylen is a *mammadel* (a young girl who dresses like an old lady)."

"Mother? It's something my *grandmother* would wear!" Bran snickered.

"Your opinion about my wardrobe doesn't matter to me."

"Fine. Go put your hideous one piece on." Tony waved her away. "We got many days ahead to see the boss lady in something sexier. Kaylen's got at least a dozen bikinis."

"And we wanna see her model every one of them, okay, Miss Jean Shrimpton?" Bran strutted like he was on the catwalk. "I declare Thursday the day you wear that orange fluorescent one."

They skated down the embankment, the campground speedboat rocking beside the dock. Bran ordered: "Pile in people."

"Wait a minute. If you guys are skiing, that's too many people in the boat."

"Says who, Lanesy?" Tony growled.

"Regulations for passenger boat safety. We wouldn't allow our campers to violate those rules."

"Well, we aren't campers, and we don't need you to police us." Luke lashed back, and everyone climbed into the boat.

"*Egli da'ordini ma non ha alcuna autorita* (he gives orders, but has no authority). I'm the captain of this ship." Raymo plopped into the driver's seat.

"Who's up?" Tony shifted the skis out of the way, uncoiling the ski rope.

"How about Kay and me?" Luke asked.

"Alright," Tony said.

"Don't get your panties in a wad, Lanesy. We'll split when it comes time for Luke and Kaylen to ski. But we're all going to take a spin first," Schaffer said, tossing a boat cushion at him.

"Full throttle, dude," Bran said, and Raymo opened it up, the spray and wind whipping their hair. After a hie around the lake, the boat bounced up in front of Kaylen's dock, and Bran, Tony, and Schaffer hopped out.

"Okay, don't take all day," Tony said to Raymo. "Give Luke and Kaylen a good run and hurry back. We're waiting to ski too."

Lane fed the rope behind the motor, Luke, and Kaylen immersing. Lane tossed Kaylen a ski belt, and she looped it around her waist. Luke refused the "wussy rig." "Gotta get out there, and if you fall, take a spill like a man."

"Oh, pardon me for my fragileness. I'm a mere female."

The pair stationed the ropes between their skis. Raymo accelerated, tugging them upright. Adjacent to Raymo, Lane posted outward to spot the skiers. Kaylen waved, Lane, signaling back. Raymo arched around the bend, approaching the alcove, an area that few boaters explored since it proved more challenging to navigate than the open water.

Lane's head whipped around. *"Che fai?"* (what are you doing?)

"Giving them a challenge." Raymo's voice rose above the hum of the speedboat. He sped up, discounting the narrow opening.

"You're going too fast."

"What's the matter, Lanesy? You scared? You don't think Luke and Kaylen can handle it?"

Both were skilled skiers, able to maneuver the choppiest of waters. But Luke had dropped a ski to slalom, his sense of balance one-footed tested by the speed and constricted waterway, fighting from crashing into Kaylen. That Raymo, goofing on them, trying to get them to fall. Kaylen wasn't as amused as Luke by the antics, gesturing a slicing motion across her neck.

"They want you to cut it out."

"What? And end this fun?" Raymo asked.

"Sick fun as usual?"

"Well, you've had your own sick fun, Lanesy. Have you forgotten that?"

"How can I when I have you and the others to throw it back in my face constantly? Blackmail. Like what you're doing to Kaylen now."

"She told you?" Raymo asked.

"I saw the two of you."

"Practicing your stalking skills again, Lane? Proud of you, cuz. Didja' get an eye full?"

"What if it had been Luke instead of me seeing the two of you together? It could have been Luke or any of the guys."

"Nobody goes slinking around but you, Lanesy. So anyway, we were in the privacy of my cabin."

"You think nobody notices? The way you gawk at Kaylen? Talk to her?" Lane said.

"I'm no different with her than the rest of the guys. I act no differently than they do."

"No, it's the way *she* acts now with *you*. I can see it. We *all* see it," Lane said.

"You mean the spark that we can't hide? That fire between us? What she'll never have with Luke?"

"She doesn't love you. And blackmailing her won't work," Lane said icily.

"We don't need love. We got much more. She might think that she loves Luke but Kaylen and me together, I'm gasoline to her fire."

"She's not going to lose her virginity to you. Even if you wear her down."

"I'm not wearing her down. On the contrary, cuz, we're building something up," Raymo said.

"This is what this is about? Are you competing with Luke? Wanting what he has?"

"But that's the thing, Lanesy. Luke doesn't have Kay. They

got no commitments. They got no chemistry between them. So, it ain't competition when I can take what is already mine. What has become mine."

"She doesn't belong to you." Lane's glacial voice trilled above the motor.

"You're wrong. She absolutely belongs to me. I own her—mind and body. I'm on her mind, not Luke. And I always will be," Raymo said.

The conversation halted, the boat entering the inlet, a congested channel requiring careful piloting. Instead of slowing, Raymo swerved and sped, Kaylen and Luke pranging skis.

"They're gonna get hurt!" Lane cried.

"Luke likes a good thrill. He'll dig it. I'm going to give Luke the ride of his lifetime. Pretty soon, I'll be doing the same for Kay, know-what-I-mean?"

Kaylen spun out, one of her skis snagging on debris. She ditched the ski, joining Luke in slalom.

Raymo glanced over his shoulder, Kaylen freeing her ensnarement. "These two are great. No obstacles can foil them, huh?"

"There are always obstacles. So, you should know, the master of eliminating life's hurdles."

"Well, Lanesy, am I the only one?" Lane's past was a daily haunt—and his bullies rapture. "Kaylen has a fighting spirit, and Luke's got the Vincuzzi perseverance. Like me. *"Niente potrà stare nel mio modo."* (Nothing will stand in my way).

Raymo swerved and twirled, Luke and Kaylen battling to stay upright. "What are you doing, Raymo?!"

"Marking a path, Lanesy. It can go smooth or be choppy. It can be wide open or choke you out with nowhere to turn. You either handle it, or you don't. Right now, Luke's gotta find his way. Otherwise, he may go down." His dark eyes glittered.

"And if Luke goes down, where does that leave Kaylen?"

"Exactly where she should be. By herself. Waiting for me," Raymo said.

"You gotta end this now before something happens." The warning had nothing to do with the speeding boat, and they both knew it.

"Can't, Lanesy. It's revved up and redlined. It's like skiing. I'm taking Kaylen to the edge of danger, out of her zone to the unknown, and yet she hasn't let go; she's holding on, waiting for my cue; she's waiting for me." Raymo jerked hard left. The hairpin swerve teetered the duo, skis clashing, like a parry between two fencers brandishing their foils. Raymo wagged, swiping Luke and Kaylen from the alcove. They skirted the outer banks—islands crawling with alligators, cottonmouths, and coral snakes. The water turned from blue to black, murky with duckweed, watermeal, and saber-sharp sawgrass. The campground's airboat—not a speedboat, made for skimming the brush and swampy terrain, and Raymo knew this.

Kaylen furled the ski rope around her hand, determined not to fall. Although an experienced skier would never consider this maneuver, she had little choice; risk ripping her flesh with the rope or plunged into the alligator and snake-infested water.

Raymo tortiled around the bend, Kaylen, and Luke skipping their skis over a submerged tree. Kaylen screeched, a protruding limb jabbing her ankle, fighting from toppling, then regaining control. Raymo glimpsed back at them, admiring their prowess.

"When is this gonna end, Raymo?" Lane cried.

"When things get finished."

Lane understood what Raymo meant: *When Kaylen and I*

take it to the next level, Kaylen no longer wants Luke, and Luke moves out of the way, and Kaylen is mine.

"You know what it's like when it's all finished. You remember what has to happen for it to get done, right, Lanesy?" His smirk, mocking him, like a rat gnashing him to the bone.

Raymo's words, much like a prodding stick poking the circus elephant over and over. The rage bubbled in Lane—years of torment by his cousin and the men. It spurred him to action.

He latched on to Raymo's back and shoulders, wrestling him from the driver's seat. Raymo whirled, wrenching Lane's arm behind his own back. He cinched his forearm across Lane's larynx, Lane clutching, trying to break his cousin's chokehold. "It's over," Lane gasped.

Raymo launched Lane port side of the boat. He skittered across the bottom, his head thudding against the well. He struggled to upright himself, crab-walking against the crush of the speed. The boat had zoomed on, locked into cruise control.

Raymo reclaimed the driver's seat. Lane's sneak attack catching him off guard, but his cousin no match for a fray with Raymo, a palooka versus a mauler in the ring. His pop-off reaction? Toss Lane from the boat. Go all Tony-like and pummel Lane to a pulp. But more critical matters demanded his attention. So he tacked toward the main part of the lake, jerking the wheel into a 180.

Lane tumbled, his spine swabbing the bottom of the boat. He churned his legs in the air, scrabbling to stand but failing to kip-up—Lane like a turtle, shell-side down. When a turtle is unable to upright itself, it is doomed to die. Raymo wondered if Lane might suffer the same fate, the notion inciting a nasty smirk.

Kaylen, balancing waves like a tightrope performer without a net, smacked the water as the boat arced, her ski stripped from her foot. The rope she'd doubled around her wrist garroted her circulation as the boat yanked her behind. Water shot into her lungs, and she clawed to loosen her binding. Luke veered, a millimeter from plowing into Kaylen's fallen body, his skis slashing the shoreline.

The trio was waiting back at the beach when the boat bounded into view, Bran muttering: "Well, it's about time—"

"—Hey, where's Lane?" Tony questioned.

Lane, getting trounced by flank speed, hidden from view at the bottom of the boat.

"Kaylen!" Schaffer cried. "Why doesn't she let go of the rope?!"

Kaylen, battered by the slamming swell, wresting the rope, she strangling, the water gushing up her nostrils.

Luke jerked to the outside, skiing parallel to the side of the boat. His arms ached from gripping the rope, his mind churning regarding the exchange between his brother and cousin, fretting, witnessing Kaylen spinning like an alligator in a death roll as she draggled behind the boat—relief when Kaylen's dock came into sight.

Kaylen untwined her restraints, flinging the rope away. She sculled against the waves, the boat hurtling away, Luke readying to ski in along the beachside. Kaylen's muscles twinged, her nose and throat stinging, a gallon of water ingested.

Luke shifted against the wake, swinging to the outside, cueing Raymo to pull him toward the shore. But, instead, the boat jerked diagonally, Luke careening toward the dock.

"What is that freaking psycho Raymo doing?!" Bran shouted.

"He's trippin'!" Schaffer cried.

Raymo mused, "One down, one to go," before charging the dock. He saw it as a hulking wooden monster. He entertained a scenario of snatching the wheel in time to dodge collision, but foredooming Luke. Luke's mind scuttled with options—let go of the rope and risk pounding waves, stay up for a fast dance, or zig or zag?

Raymo tugged the wheel, his cousin streaking toward the wooden structure. Luke hooked to his right, dipping alongside the pylon, so close he could eyeball the rotting lignin inside its splintering holes. He zipped in, his ski snagging land, hurling him face forward in shin-deep water, silt shooting up his nose and blurring his vision.

Tony, Bran, and Schaffer converged on him as he rubbed his gritty eyes.

"What was that all about?" Tony asked, relieved that Luke was okay, albeit with a bruised body.

"Dunno. Gonna find out, though." Luke spat sand.

The boat roared up beside them. Resembling a graffito—Kilroy Was Here, Lane peered over the rim. "Be back in a minute. Going to get Kay," Raymo told them.

Silence, as they espied the boat, it darting in the direction where they had last seen Kaylen.

Luke's teeth chattered. Tony delegated Schaffer to retrieve a towel from Kaylen's house. He draped it around his buddy's shoulders. Tony lighted a cigarette for Luke, poking it between his friend's scraped lips. Luke sucked it, exhaling a stream long as a kite tail.

"Dude, that was a hairy ride," Schaffer said.

"You got no idea. Actually it was pretty far out! I think Kaylen and Lanesy's take might be different, though."

"Where'd they disappear to?" Bran scouted the lake.

"You got me," Luke said.

"You think Kaylen's okay?" Schaffer asked.

"She has to be. Otherwise, they would have come straight back, right?" Tony asked.

They chain-smoked, Bran toting a six-pack of Schlitz from

Kaylen's kitchen. Each man palmed a bottle, swigging and waiting for the others to return. Then, as the sky swirled blush and plum and the sun dissolved into the tepid water, Raymo rounded the corner, wedging against the dock and Lane hopping out to tie off the boat.

"You good, cuz?" Raymo asked Luke.

"Yep. What's with the gnarly ride, man?"

"Mechanical issues," Raymo said.

"And what took so long for you guys to get back?" Luke asked.

"Hunting down the skis." *And to make sure Kaylen and Lane got their stories straight.*

Kaylen lifted one of the skis, proof.

"You okay, babe?" Luke asked.

"Yes," Kaylen reassured him, but the men had no idea about the drama that had unfolded when Raymo trekked back to retrieve her, piloting her and Lane to the swamp to guarantee they were on script.

The trio joined the others down on the beach.

Kaylen rubbed her wrist, ringed carmine and raw.

"That looks painful," Luke said.

"As does yours." She stretched up, soothing Luke's skinned eyebrow, her hand lingering upon his cheek.

No one besides Lane noticed Raymo's scowl at their display of affection.

"Don't tell me I messed up my beautiful face. Then you wouldn't love me anymore," Luke said.

"Your injuries are superficial. *I'm* not superficial. I care about other things, not just your face—handsome that it is. I care more about what's on the inside, you know," Kaylen said.

"Well, even if my cousin had messed up his face, you'd still have mine. You'd see me and still see him. So give you something to remember him by," Raymo said.

Raymo's words, a sensation stirred, like a spider had crept across Kaylen's shoulders.

"What happened out there?" Tony asked.

For a moment, Kaylen thought he meant what transpired among the three of them back at the island.

"You mean with the boat? I told you. Fluky mechanical issues." Raymo's lie, smooth as buttercream, daring Lane or Kaylen to contradict him.

"I told y'all it needed to be checked out," Bran said. "Sometimes that boat gets stuck in gear and accelerates on its own."

"Why didn't you kill the ignition?" Tony grilled. "Turn off the boat?"

"Well, you know, when I turn something on, it stays turned on, right, Kay?" Raymo said. Kaylen had to fight from squirming.

"What about the override?" Tony asked.

"Didn't work. Everything seized up. I couldn't get anything to work. Then, right after Luke skied in, that's when I was able to control everything." He aimed the cryptic message toward Kaylen and Lane.

"Yeah, but I saw you and Lane," Luke said. "What was that about?"

"Was a little misunderstanding. He accused me of doing it on purpose. But I had to show him the error of his ways, right, Lanesy?"

Lane uttered the words Raymo had instructed him to. "Yeah. After I examined the control panel, I realized it was a glitch in the system. It needs to be examined by professionals. You know, outboard marine specialists."

"Got it. Will do. But why take us all the way out to no-man's land? It's a big lake. Lots of open water," Luke said.

"That's for the ordinary folk." Raymo stroked Luke's ego.

"Didn't take you any place that you and honey-blond couldn't handle."

"Our skiing was awesome, wasn't it?" Luke boasted.

"You guys were like a water ski stunt show." Raymo continued his slick flattery. "Like the hotdogging they do over at that attraction in Cypress Gardens."

"Yeah. But it could have ended badly," Kaylen blurted.

This was not part of the script, the deviance setting Raymo's jaw tight. "No. You are the steward of your fate, right, Kay? So when you stay within the boundaries expected from you, it all goes according to plan."

"And what if it doesn't, Raymo? What if everything you planned for doesn't work out? Then what?" Kaylen asked.

"Well, then you have to take your lumps, huh? Everything you could have done to protect yourself, to assure the safety of others, might be jeopardized because you didn't do what you were supposed to do. And too late, you might find this out." Raymo a hair's breadth away from Kaylen, the heat of him tingling her skin, the air was simmering between them. "And then it is done. And like a magnifying glass that will reveal your weakness. You'll either get taken out or put through. Because in the end, only the strongest survive."

The words were like weights around Lane's ankles, dragging him down but not under. Though tethered to his weakness, he had survived—because others expected him to.

The question hovered, dark as a rain cloud: Did Kaylen have the same conviction?

CHAPTER FIFTEEN

Time flew by for Kaylen and her friends, like flipping Rolodex cards. The summer of 1970 brought seismic change, starting with the National Guardsman killing student protesters at Kent State University during a peace rally against the Vietnam War. The trial of Charles Manson, who had carved an X into his forehead, added to the unease.

Kaylen couldn't shake the fear of Raymo's possessiveness, especially after seeing what he was capable of in the boat. Rattling events were everywhere, like General Westmoreland's failed visit to Vietnam. Schaffer ranted about Nixon, calling him a hypocrite for condemning Manson's barbaric actions while ignoring the blood of thousands of soldiers. Nixon had lied about withdrawing forces from Asia while supporting a draft call for 39,000 men in 1970.

Summer's shift was subtle, warm days blending with cool nights, nipping like a tiny mean dog at its heels.

Luke and Raymo, cousins and best friends, were once inseparable, but now friction has undermined their relationship. They both had feelings for the same person, causing tension and competition between them. A snide comment between them made in front of the others, eventually led to their words rupturing their bond. The group was once close, but a schism has formed. Lane finding out about his cousin and Kaylen has deepened the fracture, and Kaylen's friendship with Lane has also suffered. The tension between Raymo and Lane had been escalating for years, especially after their incident on the boat. While there were hairline cracks between the Vincuzzis and Mancusos, Bran, Schaffer, and Tony remained loyal to their best friends, Luke and Raymo. However, now the Mancuso boys were talking behind their friends' backs.

Bran, Tony, and Schaffer snorting cocaine at Raymo's cabin, the warnings of Mama Told Me Not to Come, harmonized by Three Dog Night.

"The guy's mother was right; you shouldn't hang out with people who'll get you sloshed and drugged up," Schaffer grinned, snuffling blow, turning up the radio.

"Wait. That's what the song is about?" Bran asked.

"Plainly. Listen to the lyrics. It's a party but not the guy's scene. What did you think they were talking about?" Schaffer asked.

"Well, mama told me not to *come*. So I assumed they meant liquid love. 9cc's," Bran said.

"Behold your brain. You are thinking up teeny but interesting thoughts. I wish Raymo were still here so we could get his take on your interpretation," Schaffer said. Raymo had hung with them earlier, riding the rails. After Luke's shift finished, Raymo split, the Vincuzzi parents requesting their presence, an ancient relative passing through the area. The Mancuso boys skipped, confirming they'd rendezvous with them at Kaylen's that evening. Raymo had toted a point of coke for Luke; the incentivize to combat a dull family gathering. Doing blow at Kaylen's was not an option. She and Lane disapproved of hard drugs, so the guys met over at Raymo's. He encouraged them to hang out as long as they wanted to.

"You know what I noticed?" Tony asked, a rolled-up dollar bill embedded in his nostril, vacuuming a trail of powder. "When we first got here, didn't this place smell like Kaylen?"

"I thought the same thing." Schaffer sniffled, wiping snow from his nose. "It did smell like her perfume, which is weird. I mean, why would it smell like Kaylen unless she's been here recently?"

"Well, she and Raymo still go out and practice shooting. They're into it. They come back here to talk guns, admire his collection." Bran pretended to stifle a sneeze, posed over the mirror where cuts of coke shimmered like a grandma's best pearls. He tittered as their faces contorted.

Schaffer thumped him on the skull. "Are we sure that's all they're doing?"

"Whoa, dude. What does that mean?" Bran asked.

"The two of them getting real chummy lately," Schaffer said.

"Actually, that's not true. When we're all together, you never see Kaylen and Raymo sitting next to each other or even talking to each other that much," Bran said.

"Exactly. It's like they're showing everyone that they're trying to avoid each other," Schaffer said.

"Okay, I'm confused," Bran said.

"It's a smokescreen, baby," Schaffer explained.

"Naw. Nothing is going on between the two of them. Besides, we all know how Kaylen feels about Luke," Bran said.

"Yeah. True. But that doesn't mean that Raymo doesn't have feelings for Kaylen," Schaffer said.

"Yeah, and we know what kind those are. We've all got that for her." Done, the back of his throat numb, Tony sniffled, securing the razor blade and cramming the baggie of cocaine in Raymo's drug drawer with the rest of his varied stash.

"Yes, but the thing is, she's vibing on him as well—even if it isn't what she has for Luke," Schaffer said.

"You're off base, cuz. You must be mega stoned," Tony said.

"I'm lucid, man. And on the money. The way Raymo and Kaylen are acting with each other, around us—it's smoke and mirrors. To cover up for the real thing that's burning," Schaffer said.

"What does that mean?" Bran hummed along with the Blues Image's Ride Captain Ride.

"Luke and Kaylen might be an item. She loves him, and hey, who knows? Maybe he even loves her. But when Raymo and Kaylen are together in the same room, it's like being next to a fire pit. Man, I can feel their heat even from here," Schaffer said.

"I'm with you on that, bro. I mean, y'all tell me I don't pick up on the clues sometimes. But even I've seen, felt that thing between them. You could plug them in and get electricity," Bran said.

"That's exactly what I'm talking about, Brandy," Schaffer said.

"That doesn't mean anything is going on, though. Do we forget about Luke here? You think he's gonna let Raymo get away with messing with his girl?" Bran asked.

"Since when can Luke stop Raymo from doing anything?" Tony asked.

"Because it's family. Raymo loves Luke, listens to him," Bran said.

"Yeah, under normal circumstances. This thing with Kaylen? Our relationship with her and Raymo's with her? Nothing about this has ever been conventional," Tony pointed out.

"True. Not to mention we hadn't expected Kaylen and Raymo to click as they have—lots different than how we've clicked with her," Bran said.

"Yeah. But something is up. Lane is acting weirder than usual, and he and Kaylen are acting sketchy with each other. And with Raymo? Kaylen claims she doesn't even like him. But then why do they seem to have this thing?" Schaffer said.

"You don't have to like someone to have a thing," Bran said. "It's lust, man."

"Lust. Love. Either one of them will get you into trouble," Tony said.

"Yes, you're right. But it's more than that between Kaylen and Raymo. It's like... magnetic. Think about it. You ever hooked up with someone, don't ever see them again, and don't care? But then there's that other than happens, man. It's not love or lust, it's like mixing two chemicals and it explodes, ya' know? It's like you could meet a ton of people and never find that one that matters. But then the real deal comes along, like with Kaylen and Raymo."

"Well, isn't that special? And how do you think Luke likes that?"

"Would you want your girl to get turned on by another guy?" Schaffer asked his brother. "Especially a guy who's your doppelganger!"

"Luke and Raymo have shared before," Bran pointed out.

"This is completely different. This thing between Raymo and Kaylen? I don't think they could stop it even if they wanted to. Kaylen is the moth to Raymo's flame. She can't help it, and he won't end it. Dig?" Schaffer said.

"Tone, you're Luke's best friend. For that matter, you're Raymo's too. So neither one of them has said anything to you about this?" Bran asked.

"Man, it was supposed to be status quo. I'm trying to

remember back to when Kaylen first came into our lives. Luke specifically said that Kaylen was his—not yours, not mine, not Raymo's," Tony said.

"Yet we've all been to first base with her," Bran said.

"Yeah, but under Luke's eagle eyes," Schaffer pointed out. "Raymo isn't going to get any further with Kaylen than Luke has. And Kaylen wouldn't do that with Raymo."

"Unless he's got something on her," Tony said.

"Like what?" Schaffer asked.

"Dunno. But that would be sweet blackmail! To get Kaylen to do what Raymo wanted?" Tony asked.

"Check it. If it's blackmail, then add in this attraction between the two of them, then, of course, Kaylen would do it. Do whatever Raymo wanted her to do. She'd have to do it," Bran said.

"No, she'd want to do it, Bran. Not that she would have to. Kaylen would *want* to. That's the difference," Schaffer said.

"Maybe. Maybe not. One thing we know about blackmail is that it doesn't matter whether you use it against a person or not. What matters is that you make them *think* you're going to use it against them. And continue gouging them with it. That's what puts them in check," Tony said.

"Yeah, and it's worked for years on Lane." Bran tapped a fingernail in time to the radio.

"Who's to say that Raymo isn't doing the same thing to Kaylen?" Tony said.

"Wait a minute. We all know Kaylen. She's more likely to call Raymo out and then to buckle to any blackmail," Bran said.

"Right. But what if it was out of her control? What if Kaylen got caught up in some crazy stuff she never saw coming?" Schaffer pushed up his bandana and scratched his head.

"Well, we've already seen Lane get caught up in some wild

stuff he never expected," Bran snickered. "And we know how that went down."

"Yeah, except in Kaylen's case, let's add to the mix that she can't resist Raymo," Schaffer said.

"So then is it blackmail?" Bran helped himself to a cluster of grapes on the kitchen counter.

"That's my point," Schaffer said. "Blackmail. Desire. The need to protect someone. Any of those things will make you do what you wouldn't normally do. Act like someone you weren't before."

"When did all this start to change? I mean, when did we first start seeing that Kaylen was different?" Tony's eyebrows were kinked.

"Eight Minutes. The night Kaylen and Raymo played the game in the closet," Bran said.

"What happened in there?" Tony's mouth fashioned into an O, Bran chucking a grape in.

"He kissed her. He got to first base. It was the first time they ever sucked face full out," Schaffer said, positioning like a shortstop as Bran lobbed a couple of grapes at him.

"But then he made a move on her. And she cat-scratched him." Tony chomped on the fruit.

"How does that translate to blackmail?" Bran asked. "It wasn't Kaylen doing what Raymo wanted. It was Raymo doing something that Kaylen did not want."

"Dunno. It doesn't make sense." Schaffer chewed the morsels.

"A lot of things don't. Like that day out in the boat," Tony said.

"Yeah. What was that all about?" Schaffer asked.

"No idea. The mysteries keep piling up," Bran shrugged.

"You think Kaylen's putting on an act?" Tony asked.

"In what way?" Schaffer asked.

"She says she is not putting out. That she's holding out," Tony said.

"She's definitely holding out. For that gold band, man. For the white dress and I-dos," Bran said.

"Then we should hope she's a patient girl. Luke's not going to be skipping down the aisle anytime soon. If ever," Tony said.

"Maybe she thinks she'll have better luck with his cousin?" Bran said.

Tony cocked a brow. "Then she should know better. If they look alike, then they're gonna think alike too."

"Maybe that was before Kaylen and Raymo started getting close. Before Luke and Kaylen knew what Raymo and Kaylen would become to each other," Schaffer said.

"Wouldn't it be a trip?" Bran said, popping another grape into his mouth. "All this time us thinking Kaylen and Luke were going to end up together, but instead, Kaylen ends up with someone else!"

"You mean with Raymo?" Schaffer asked.

"Or even freakier, with Lane," Bran said.

"Lane?" Tony snorted. "Now that's out there."

"Is it?" Schaffer cambered his head. "The idea is no stranger than Kaylen being with Raymo, a guy we never figured she'd go for."

"Well, obviously, she's infatuated with the Vincuzzi charm that runs in that family. But there's one big difference among the three of them: Luke and Raymo got all their equipment working. Not Lane. He hasn't done the deed since... well, you know," Tony said.

"So he wants us to believe," Schaffer said.

"You mean with Kaylen?! A wussy like Lane could not get a girl like Kaylen. *I perdenti non ottengono bellissime ragazze* (losers don't get beautiful girls)," Tony said.

"Au contraire, cuz. He's already *got* Kaylen. She doesn't

think he's too much of a loser to be her best friend. To become her boyfriend, that's not a stretch," Schaffer said.

"Makes me wanna hurl." Bran made a gagging sound. "To think of her with Lane. Especially when she could have me."

"Or even better—me." Schaffer said.

"It's fantasy anyway. We can steal a couple of kisses from time to time, but anything more... we ain't gotta chance with Kaylen," Bran said.

"Unless something changes." Tony expanded his long legs out in front of him.

"Like what?" Schaffer asked.

"Anything. Lots of things. Like Luke and Kaylen break up. Like Raymo makes a big move for her. Like Raymo lets us in on his action," Tony said.

"You mean Luke. You mean if Luke allows it," Schaffer said.

"No. I mean Raymo. Not the conversation that Luke had with us. The one I had one time with Raymo," Tony corrected.

"When was this?" Schaffer asked.

"When Raymo first came down and met Kaylen," Tony explained.

"And you never told us?" Schaffer said.

"Cut me some slack, man. We're all stoners! Totally functional, but the fine details get slightly fuzzy at times. I'm just now fully recalling it. Anyway, I didn't mention it before because it didn't seem that big a deal at the time," Tony said.

"And now?" Schaffer asked.

"I dunno. The signs are pointing that way," Tony said.

"Well, what was said?" Bran asked.

"Me and Raymo were by ourselves shooting the breeze, smoking a doobie. It came up about Kaylen, about how me and Bran first met her, but then the relationship amped up between her and Luke. About Kaylen's initiation and what we had done.

About how this thing the group has with Kaylen isn't like us being around other girls, how we treat them as opposed to how we treat her—who we consider a super close friend and part of the group. We talked about Kaylen being cherry and Luke trying to tap that. Raymo told me he was interested in Kaylen. I told him fat chance on her reciprocating. He told me even then that he felt something for her that he hadn't felt with any other chick and that he knew she felt it too. I took it as his big ego talking, didn't think much about it, I let him ramble on. I told him that all of us except Lanesy had made out with her, but that was as far as it went and would ever go."

"Then he said, 'we could have her.' I said: 'What do you mean?' He said, 'we could have her, take her. Take her and make her pay for teasing all of us. Know what I mean?' I eyeballed him like he was nuts. I told him: 'Listen, man, you can't be talking about what I think you're talking about,' and he clammed up. I didn't know what to think. I mean, you know Raymo. He can act dead serious but be farting around. And then again, he can plaster a smile on his face but be hatching something devious," Tony added.

"Yeah. Copy that." Schaffer leaned down, slurping directly from the faucet. "Then what happened?"

"He asked me if I would be into it. I said: 'Who wouldn't be into it? If Kaylen was.' 'Not even if it was to protect us?' he said. 'From exposing us? We expect group loyalty. We expect her to honor a code of silence. About whatever we tell her. About whatever she finds out about us. If she can't, she'll have to get clued as to what a mistake that would be.'"

The men were not fronting. Raymo, a *goombah* whose milieu included people from the mean streets of New York City, ones who enforced the maxim "snitches get stitches." When the book *The Godfather* hit the bestseller list, Raymo had predicted: Wait for all the goodfella-wanna-be's it'll spawn.

Correct in his assessment, and an explosion of goofballs more like characters from the movie *The Italian Job* than Corleone's. But Raymo congregated with real mobsters, adopting their mentality—no one turns against us and punishes the recreant.

Tony's cousins blinked at him. "Listen, we've gone to extreme measures to protect our secrets. But, unfortunately, we're not above it."

"Yeah, but you're talking about Kaylen!"

"I'm with Bran. And what you and Raymo were talking about? That's a felony, man."

"Wouldn't be the first time we ever committed a felony," Tony said.

"But not that," Schaffer shot back.

"Yeah. But remember I'm not the source—this is all coming from Raymo," Tony disclaimed responsibility. "This is what *he* approached *me* with. Anyway, the conversation went on, and I said: 'We don't have to think about this now, right, bro? Forget about it.' He comes back with: 'Bet you wouldn't say that if you thought we could get away with it.' I said: 'How would that work? Luke would freakin' kill us if we laid one hand on Kaylen!' Then he said: 'Who's gonna tell him?' I said: 'She'd tell him!' And he countered: 'No, she wouldn't. Not if I had something on her.' Then I asked: 'Do you?' And he tells me: 'Not yet. But maybe I will. Something that requires her to keep her mouth shut. Like she does with her legs. Shut up tight so Luke can't get in. She blows ice cold and then hot with my cousin. And we're gonna teach her that *that* isn't cool. If by the time this goes down and she's still cherry? That's what'll keep her quiet. Shame. Shame will glue her trap shut. And she's not telling anyone—not Lane, not Luke.'"

Tony paused, giving his cousins' time to process it. "I gotta tell you. I was taken back but intrigued too."

Bran's green-gold orbs were like a scary cat cutout at

Halloween. "It's Kaylen we're talking about! We love her. Isn't our duty to protect her, as being one of our own?"

"Yes. But let's think about gang code, mobster code. She's one of us—until she isn't, understand? We got no room for anyone who turns against us. So if Kaylen did that... where is our first allegiance? It's to each other, right?" Tony argued.

"This whole thing is chancy. And Raymo's wrong. Kaylen would tell. Maybe not Luke, but to Lane. And possibly her father. The plan is flawed. Raymo's thinking is flawed," Schaffer said.

"I told him the same thing, Shay. But he insisted: 'We can put Lane under dominion like always. You get two blackmails for the price of one. Lane's going to sew his mouth shut, and so is Kaylen.' At that point, I had to know. 'How would we do this? What's the plan?' And he said, 'Once and a while, the plan magically happens. Circumstances come to light, and the plan unfolds. Think about this: If Kaylen turns against us at any time, for any reason, she'll have to get taught a lesson. About loyalty. About what we expect. Then it's going down.' And that was the end of the conversation."

"Heavy. And he hasn't brought it up since?" Schaffer asked.

"No. And even now, I don't know if he meant it," Tony said.

"And if he did?" Schaffer asked.

Tony steepled his fingers in contemplation. "Then we three would need to figure out if we're on board."

"We've gotten away with worse. The thing is, it doesn't sit right, this thinking of Kaylen in that way. Second, and most importantly—I believe things have changed since you had that conversation with Raymo, Tony. Third, things have changed between Raymo and Kaylen. Even if he had been serious then, it doesn't mean he is now. Whatever's going on between them, you can bet he doesn't want anyone homing in on his action. Not us. And not Luke," Schaffer said.

"But Luke's her boyfriend," Bran argued. "Kaylen wanted him, not us. She wanted him first."

"Well, what you might have wanted at first, might not be on second thought, dig?" Schaffer said. "Tony, if you wanna clear all this up, go to Raymo and ask if he meant what he said. See what he has to say about it now, whether he's serious or jerking our chains. And whether he's willing to carry this out. Find out."

"Okay, the first chance I will. Then, after that, I'll pick his brain and see where his head is, see how far he's willing to take this."

"Then we'll know," Bran said.

"Then we'll know." Tony studied the trajectory of his cigarette smoke.

CHAPTER SIXTEEN

Summer slid away, and autumn tiptoed in, the days cooling —much like Lane and Kaylen's friendship. Could it be blamed on what happened—is still happening between Kaylen and Raymo? Lane deplored Kaylen's relationship with Raymo —giving in to his demands and going behind Luke's back— blackmail or not. But worse, Luke's cheating on Kaylen, and despite it, Kaylen moving closer to sleeping with him. Disapprobation and stress were eroding Lane and Kaylen's relationship like the pounding of rain divoting the soil. But the true deterioration was attributed to the day of Kaylen and Luke's skiing mishap, the aftermath in the boat with Kaylen, Lane, and Raymo.

When Kaylen and Luke had their skiing misadventure, Raymo haphazardly left Luke at the beach with Tony, Bran, and Schaffer, and then zoomed back to retrieve Kaylen. She bobbed against the waves. Cradling her wrist, she sidestroked to the ladder, and Lane hefted her up. Raymo took stock of Kaylen's hollowed eyes, but neither he nor Lane said a word.

Raymo steered away from the central part of the lake and

in the direction of the outlet. The ride this time slower but not relaxed, Kaylen and Lane side-glancing each other, a shared hunch that trouble was brewing.

Raymo idled, pointing at the ski floating near a hammock of trees, and Lane plucked it from the water. With two more skis to find, Lane and Kaylen assumed Raymo would cruise with the current. The lake, fed by marsh drainage and creeks, connected to the St. John's River and emptied into the Atlantic Ocean. The river flowed north and dictated the current of its tributaries. Instead of following the natural flow, Raymo yawed in the opposite direction—where Kaylen and Luke had locked skis at the back islands, isolated and teeming with reptiles and critters. Lane and Kaylen matched silent, wary scans, the boat sidling through tannin and ebony waters.

A canopy of needle palm, pop ash, and cypresses shadowed their path, a clog of hydrilla and lily pads masticated under the Evinrude. As the trio burrowed into the murky trough, Spanish moss wreathed the boat like a silver tippet, Lane punching the swag away. "What are you doing, Raymo?"

"Reminding you, Lanesy, of who I am, what I expect." He cut the motor, tossing the anchor.

Kaylen stole a quizzical glance at Lane. Dropping anchor meant Raymo planned to linger awhile.

"Which is?"

"Complete cooperation." The trio eyed an alligator lurking in the shallows of a peninsula.

"And how do you propose I do that?"

"Like you've always done it, Lane. Quietly and on-demand."

"Is that how you get it from, Kaylen?"

Her sharp intake of air from behind him. "Actually, Lane. You're half right. She gives it on demand, but there's nothing quiet about it. She whimpers my name, right, Kay?"

"Okay, leave her out of this. We know that this is about you and me. What do you want from me? What more can I give that you haven't already taken from me?"

"Let's see if you've manned up in all these years. Maybe I'll put you to the test, Lanesy."

"Then bring it, Raymo. Just do it." The challenge tumbled out, Lane breaking into a cold sweat.

"Okay, if you insist." A blur, like a black mambo strike, Raymo was wrestling him to the side of the boat, spinning him up into a fireman's carry.

Kaylen was screaming, Raymo hoisting Lane over the hull. His left arm dangling into the umbra water, his pelvis jammed under Raymo's hip. Grappling, Lane's right hand was clutching at his cousin's forearm.

Kaylen's screams pierced the air as Lane pleaded with Raymo to stop. The lone alligator they'd spied earlier, now flanked by others, a crime of opportunity enticing them like serial killers scoping their victim.

It laid bare Lane's secret: fear of the water. Living on a lake, he compensated, making peace with his aquaphobia. A passable swimmer, a snorkeler, butterfly and dolphin kicking to the floating dock and back—but Lane unable to relay all the way across the lake like his friends. He'd ski or kayak, but a life vest buckled around him. But when Kaylen flung open the stowage lockers, the life jackets and floating cushions had mysteriously vanished from the boat. And the one Lane had tucked under him, Raymo had crammed it tightly between the motor and the transom.

Aware of Lane's fear, Raymo jubilated, intent on using Lane as bait. "Stop! Stop." Kaylen screamed.

"Maybe this is *your* test, Kay. What will you do to save him?" Raymo shoves Lane's torso, legs bicycling and hooks them over the gunwale like a circus artist on the trapeze.

Raymo's palm was grinding against Lane's jaw, smashing his face into the black water.

"Anything!" Kaylen sobbed.

"Good answer, Kay. The right answer." Raymo jerked Lane up, hurling him back into the boat. He skidded across the bottom, sputtering, swiping water from his lashes, hacking as he attempted to sit up.

"Bravo, Lanesy. I put you to the test, but you were beaten by the best. See how Kay fights for you? But would you do the same for her?"

"*What is wrong with you?* This thing between you and me, Raymo? It's making you not think straight. You've let it get to you!"

"Yeah, you have gotten to me, Kay. But I've gotten to you too. Tell Lane that. Better yet, show him." He yanked her toward him, hip to hip, heart to heart. "You like to watch, Lane? Then we'll give you a show." Raymo, plying Kaylen's mouth with his, resisting but finally giving in to his hot kiss.

Lane couldn't look away, torn between morbid curiosity and the unbreakable magnetism between Kaylen and Raymo. As Raymo hovered over Kaylen, tugging her down toward the boat cushions, he asked, 'you see what's happening here, Lanesy?'"

"Yes. But does she?"

His teeth on display. "Oh yeah, Lanesy. See how she knows what to do? Like a good blackmailee." Kaylen resigned, loathing herself for giving in, but if she didn't, he'd make good on the threat to tell Luke about them.

"Wanna know what happened during Eight Minutes, Lanesy? *This.* This is why she can't go back, why she'll never respond to Luke the way she has to me. I've had her in my hands, and her skin has burned against mine. Like I've branded her. She's mine. She belongs to me." A reenactment, the night in the closet, his mouth on Kaylen's, sinking his fingers inside her.

Glittering hot coals, Raymo staring not at Kaylen but Lane. Raymo strummed Kaylen, like a guitarist who hits all the right chords, not ceasing until the song had played its last note. He withdrew his digits from Kaylen's warm center. She straightened her bathing suit, unable to meet Lane's gaze. Raymo, sticking his fingers in his mouth like he was initiating a wolf whistle, the taste of Kaylen on his tongue. He hooked his index finger along the inside of his cheek, reverberating, like a bottle of champagne uncorking. He unfolded his hand under Lane's nose, a bud blooming, offering it up. He smirked, Lane refusing the gift and Kaylen's face crumbling, her cheeks crimson.

"Here's our story: we've searched for the skis all this time—that's why we've taken so long. And to sweeten the tale, there's a mechanical problem with the boat, got it? Good thing there's not a mechanical problem with my fingers, huh, Kay?"

Lane's gritted his teeth, fisting white knuckles, forcing his hand to unclench. He trembled with self-restraint, itching to belt Raymo.

"But no problems between you and me, right, Lanesy? Right, Kay?"

"Please, let's go back. I want to see if Luke is okay!"

"Luke will live. You're even better. You got the full Raymo treatment, and now you're good to go. But, unfortunately, Lane's the one who's not okay. I think you got traumatized, huh, Lanesy? You almost got thrown into the drink. And even worse, you saw me having a good time with the object of your affection, huh? But Lanesy knows how to live with being traumatized, right? You've done it before, and you'll do it again."

Lane hauled the anchor up, signaling the end of the conversation but not his truckling, the new secret placed in Raymo's growing arsenal against his victims. Lane jerked at the throwable life cushion Raymo had wedged under the motor, grunting when it would not budge, but after several tries, it popped out from beneath. Raymo then slid into the driver's seat. The trio, silent on the ride back, each lost in their own thoughts.

Many secrets run hot—like coursing blood and fevered flesh. But Lane, Raymo, and Kaylen's secrets blazoned cold as metal, a steel trap with teeth, tearing flesh to the bone.

CHAPTER SEVENTEEN

The smack of winter, alleviating the sear of summer the group had endured, yet offering no succor for Kaylen, caught up in the jugglery of being Luke's girlfriend and Raymo's obsession. A burden with costs—pounds were melting from her thin frame, staring into the darkness from her pillow as time ticked toward daylight. When she did slumber, nightmares assaulted her, hunkering black-eyed monsters, pinning her from escape. It didn't require Kaylen to psychoanalyze herself, endeavoring to break free, black eyes? But of course, this was her being hemmed in between Luke and Raymo.

Luke continued to pressure Kaylen to sleep with him, Raymo's demands matching his cousin. Kaylen, Luke's putative girlfriend, but he kept cheating on her (he didn't attempt to hide it anymore). Raymo, not her boyfriend, yet whose actions seemed more honorable than Luke's. Raymo had rejected all female's attentiveness toward him, hadn't pursued any women since he had met Kaylen—providing fodder for his friends and cousin Luke, Raymo's larks as well-known as Bran's. What did it mean? Besotted with her to the point it left no interest for other women?

Kaylen still doted on Luke; from day one, attracted to him— what girl wouldn't be? But that initial skip of the heart she perceived as love, chemistry... the realization dawned, the sensation for Luke, flat in the wake of her emotive for Raymo— despite an aversion to him running parallel. She hated his blackmail; she hated herself for being wiled by him. An underlying truth in Lane's assessment? That it was Raymo, who stirred her heart, not Luke.

Kaylen took umbrage at Lane's slight against Luke. "You didn't know," Lane said. "Had you never met Raymo, you wouldn't have known. You'd be with Luke the rest of your life and think it was the real thing. Not a stand-in. But then you met Raymo. And you knew. He knew. Yet you want to go on pretending."

"No! I don't want this."

"That's what you claim. The blackmail is your excuse to be with him."

"No, Lane. I care for Luke. I'm doing this for him, being with Raymo. So Raymo doesn't tell him. About what happened. About what's happening now. There is what happened, and then there are the lies that Raymo could tell him. Either will pain Luke. I'm doing this for Luke."

"You're doing it for yourself."

"No. I love Luke."

"I have no doubt that you do. Sincerely if not mildly. Still, it's going to come down to having to choose. It's either Raymo or Luke. And we both know either choice will be the end."

"Of....?"

"Everything."

In the past, this prediction would have been used as a setup for a punchline, eliciting Kaylen's response, "How apocalyptic!

Of Biblical proportions, Lane?" But now, the weight of the consequences of her actions and pending choices felt like heavy cannonballs resting upon her shoulders.

"Don't you see where this whole thing is going? You're going to try to make this work, this triangle you're in. First, you'll end up sleeping with Luke. Then sleeping with Raymo—blackmail or not, because once you've done the deed with Luke, Raymo will know, and he won't let it end there; he's not gonna let Luke have what he cannot. And then both will know about each other. Bran, Tony, Schaffer will know it. Everyone will know it. You'll be no better than any of them—just like them, sleeping with more than one person at a time. One who you think you love. The other one you don't even realize that you do. And both who'll lose it when they find out the extent of your relationship with the other one. So you'll be sleeping with two guys, involved in two relationships. Then what will that make you? Because we all know the word for a girl like that, right, *puttana* (whore)?"

Her hand, a lightning bolt, cracking across Lane's cheek, his wide cerulean eyes mirroring Kaylen's own.

"I want you to leave."

"I'm sorry," Lane blurted, even though Kaylen had been the one to lash out.

"No, you're not. You meant to hurt me. I meant to hurt you. Now we're even. Now go."

"Kaylen, I am the last person who'd harm you. But you need to hear the truth. This can't go on like this. You know it, I know it, Raymo knows it. There's still time to reel this in. But soon, it'll be too late. And believe me, Kaylen. Once it's too late, they will decide the future for you. Raymo and the others, they'll make sure of it."

"As they did with you?" she asked, aware he carried his own millstone of being blackmailed. He refused to reveal it, no matter how many times she'd begged. It ate at her; his pain packed down deep, unable to share it.

"Yes," he whispered.

Their secrets had once bound them together, but now their shattered friendship was like a fault line beneath their feet. Lane's words conjured an image in Kaylen's mind: she was gripping the edge of a cliff, the ground giving way, and falling with a thud. Lane was no longer a safe haven for her. His heart was like a stone, acting like his brother. But it was Raymo who was as hot as lava, ready to scorch anything in his way to have her. They were playing with fire, and as the saying goes, you get burned when you play with fire. Raymo and Kaylen were like an uncontrolled campfire, blistering everything in their path, like a neglected fire raging through the forest. The problem with such a fire? It causes damage, even fatalities.

CHAPTER EIGHTEEN

Kaylen pondered a way out of her mess with Raymo and Luke, coming up with only one solution—get out. Leave them both behind—a self-imposed banishment. Maybe tag along with her dad on his business trips. But after her return, the problem would remain. Unless... what if she wasn't with either one of them? Not be Luke's girlfriend, nor Raymo's victim. Not be dividing her time between the two of them, nor deciding who got what and how much. Not lose her virginity. Steer away from both of them.

Kaylen paid no heed to the man who had camped there previously Labor Day weekend.

But he noticed her. This trip determined to converse beyond the polite chit-chat about the weather she offered up last time. Kaylen was a veteran of getting hit on by male campers. Her policy, remain courteous, deflect, distract, and return to business. The difference this time, she flirted back.

His teeth shone like a new moon; his face, smooth as the lake at sunrise. Kaylen compared him to her friends, to Tony with his graveled cheeks, peppered with whiskers. The evening breeze couldn't budge the guy's cropped ash-blond hair—a contrast to Bran's glimmering white-blond bouffant, contrary to the dark maned Luke, Raymo, Lane, and Tony. His mien, his buzzed head, juxtaposed to Schaffer's hair (now sweeping below his lumbar). The guy's features, a snicker magnet for her friends, an inveigle for name-calling—"check that preppy jock." A correct assessment, a compact but chock-full conversation disclosing the athlete's status as an upperclassman. He attended the university not to avoid the draft; no, he'd gear up for combat if ever called up, but to fulfill his parent's wishes for him to excel. Is he for real? Kaylen masked her crimped lips, not because she was making fun of him, but on account of Schaffer, imagining his reaction, he with his anti-war stance— he'd freak! They would like *all* freak—the stranger not of their ilk, the novelty of him piquing Kaylen's interest.

The fantasy surfacing in Kaylen's head, of having a guy like him, a normal relationship, not enduring pressure, blackmail, brainwashing. She wouldn't go beyond kissing. She would be respected, not pressed to give up her virginity. Over time, she'd demand a ring, an engagement, and nuptials. She'd save herself for her wedding day. It waxed perfect, picturesque, like a fairy-tale. Winning her prince, the knight in shining armor she envisaged.

No matter how idyllic the story, the problem in a fairy tale is the flip side, the dark one who does evil, out to destroy the prince and take the princess for himself.

Kaylen accepted the guy's invitation to his campsite that night, her Mona Lisa smile plastered following his exit.

Lane materialized, a vapor, interrupting Kaylen's daydream. "Who was that?"

"A camper, of course."

"No, who is he?" Lane pressed.

"My next distraction."

"Seriously, Kaylen? Two guys jonesing for you is not enough? So you gonna add another man to fend off from your cookie jar?"

At one time, Lane wouldn't have dreamed of talking to Kaylen like this, and she felt an intense urge to slap him across the face, just as she had done the first time. Instead, she said: "He's a new friend, that's all."

"He's your new excuse? The guy you'll use to get out of this situation you created?"

"*I* didn't create anything, Lane! I got sandbagged into this, and you know that! Raymo is blackmailing me, and Luke is pressuring me."

"And this is your way out, huh? Making both jealous?"

"Both of them want what they can't have. Both expect too much. I'm so done. They see me with another guy, and they'll know I'm serious. If I leave them, this problem dissolves."

"And another one is created."

"Does it matter, Lane? For every problem solved, another one crops up. I'm never going to break free from this unless I do something drastic."

"You won't stop it, Kaylen. You'll make it worse."

"I'm bone-tired, Lane. I'm sick of this—Luke pressuring me to go to bed with him, Raymo wanting me to choose between him and Luke. Even you said that I had to make a choice. I choose *neither one of them.*"

"Kaylen, no one stymies Raymo or Luke."

Her smile was from the heart. She reached up, tracing Lane's pale cheek. Like old times. "It'll be okay. I promise to handle it."

Handle it. Like *he* had years ago? Despite those painstaking actions, the futility plagued him—a means to an end, necessary but tragic.

"I gotta be free from them. You understand, don't you?"

Lane had a visceral understanding of the situation that he desperately wished wasn't true. The all too familiar sensation of nausea coiled in his guts as his instincts warned him of the path ahead—a dangerous and uncertain journey like a slippery road in the dark, where brakes failed and guardrails shattered, like vehicles crumpled into scrap metal and blood flowed freely, pooling as life seeped away.

He gazed at Kaylen in silence, contemplating her belief that being free meant simply strolling away without a second glance. However, when it came to Luke and Raymo, Lane knew that walking away was not an option.

* * *

Lane departed, doing as he had been taught—to be a secret keeper when necessary and an informant when he must divulge the truth.

He tracked down Tony, disclosing the details regarding Kaylen and this guy. Tony, the best of the bunch to handle Raymo and Luke. But first, Tony consulted his cousins.

"Okay, when do we tell Luke?" Schaffer asked, twisting his hair into a bun.

"He's going to freak majorly. *Egli rischia di impazzire* (he's in danger of going mad)."

"He needs to know, Bran. Kaylen is going over to this guy's site tonight." Tony scrutinized his cigarette's nebulous above his head.

"Maybe Lane can talk sense into his best friend." Bran shrugged.

"I don't think Lane has as much influence as he once did." Schaffer pointed out. "I don't think Kaylen is gonna listen to anybody right now. She seems to have made up her mind."

"I think she's lost her mind." Bran grasped his skull, vibrating his lips, something blowing up.

"Kaylen should know better. She can't up and get with a random guy. She can't go outside the group—us—to have a relationship." Schaffer stole a puff off Tony's Marlboro resting in the ashtray.

"Exactly. Listen, I finally got a chance to talk to Raymo. About what the three of us hashed around," Tony said.

"The day we were doing coke in Raymo's cabin?"

"Yep. You were right, Shay. Raymo's got the extreme hots for Kaylen. Hung up on her to the max."

"And Luke doesn't suspect this?" Schaffer asked.

"Well, Luke thinks it's nothing more than what we have with her."

"And you're okay with letting him think that?" Schaffer asked.

"No. But this could cause problems between Luke and Raymo. I think that this new situation with Kaylen—this dude she's going to go see, might be the answer," Tony said.

"In what way?" Schaffer asked.

"Cousin won't be pitted against cousin if they're working for a united cause," Tony said.

"Which is...?" Schaffer asked.

"Eliminating any competition that gets in the way of them having Kaylen. Think about it. Luke and Raymo will work together to get rid of this guy. Luke will never know that Raymo was jonesing for Kaylen. Raymo will be his usual psychotic self but will stay focused on joining forces with Luke," Tony said.

"We stand back out of the madness and wait," Schaffer said, leaning into the wall.

"Yep. Unless they ask us to jump in," Bran said.

"Raymo has it in his demented brain that Kaylen is eventually going to break up with Luke. But now Kaylen's accepted an invite from this other guy," Tony said.

"And then what? Raymo thinks he's going to step into Luke's place?" Bran asked.

"He didn't say that per se. I got the impression that he thinks Kaylen belongs to him like he owns her and she owes him. Precisely what it is she owes him or why, that's not clear."

"You think Raymo considers Kaylen as his, and by being his means her sleeping with him?" Bran asked.

"Undoubtedly."

"And he thinks Luke is gonna be okay with that?" Bran said.

"Dunno. I got the impression Raymo's more concerned with *Kaylen* being okay with it," Tony said.

"Then this is what this all about," Bran said. "The new guy today. Either Kaylen is trying to make Luke jealous, or she's sending Raymo a message."

"You think Kaylen still intends to give it up to Luke?" Schaffer asked.

"Hasn't that been her plan all along?" Bran asked.

"That was before. Before she and Raymo got tight, long before she met this new guy today," Tony said.

"You don't think she'd be stupid and give it away to the new guy?" Bran asked.

"No, but I also don't think she's necessarily saving it for Luke anymore," Tony said.

"Are you serious? I think you're wrong on this one. She's not going to sleep with Raymo."

"Well, Bran, I'm the one who spoke to Raymo, and he said a lot of junk. It could be him blowing smoke. Other things he says, I pay attention. It's obvious that Raymo is waiting on this relationship between Kaylen and Luke to taper off. They already got that kinetic thing between them. Who do you think

Kaylen's going to turn to when things fall apart between her and Luke?"

"I think Raymo has been working this a long time. I think he intended to come between Luke and Kaylen," Schaffer said.

"You mean like sabotage?" Bran asked.

"Good a word as any," Schaffer said.

"Remember the day at Raymo's cabin when we were doing blow, and I told you guys about what he had suggested with Kaylen and us?" Tony asked. "When Raymo and I were having this new conversation the other day, I rehashed that old conversation—when it had been the two of us, and he had discussed putting Kaylen in check. So I asked him: 'Are you still on board with it?' And he didn't hesitate: 'Yeah, but with the understanding, we do this to make her compliant to us, in the case she's gonna open her mouth about things we don't want her to reveal. Provided it happens under my go-ahead, my authority, got it?' And I said: 'Sure.'" Tony stubbed out his cigarette. "We're in on this, right?"

"You mean doing the wrong thing for the right reason?" Bran asked.

"Much like pulling a Lane, huh?" Schaffer asked.

"Precisely," Tony said.

Their eyes moved between each other, thinking back to that time.

"With this new problem brewing with this guy Kaylen is gonna go see, I doubt Raymo will be thinking about any of that other stuff." Bran said.

"Right. Forget about it. Let's worry about this deal now. We gotta go tell Raymo and Luke what Kaylen is up to." Tony said. "Deliver the bad news all at once. Get them collaborating rather than working against each other. Like it should be. Like it always was before."

"Before Kaylen."

"Exactly, Bran," Tony said.

"What do you think they're gonna wanna do about it?" Bran asked.

"Oh, I got a pretty good guess. Nothing good for Kaylen or this guy." Schaffer lifted a brow.

"I told you it was dicey letting Kaylen into the group. Now see what's happened, is going to happen," Tony said.

"We love Kaylen. We hit it off with her from the get-go. How could we have *not* let her in the group? But we also have to be able to rely on her loyalty. Anyway, it's a little too late to regret letting her in. What's done is done." Bran brushed his palms together.

"Call Luke. Tell him to meet us over at Raymo's after his shift," Tony ordered Schaffer. "We'll tell them then. Before Kaylen goes over to this guy's campsite."

The crap was about to hit the fan. The problem with flying dung, it misses no one, even when you're sitting on the sidelines tending your own business.

CHAPTER NINETEEN

They broke the news—a challenge dealing with one Vincuzzi with a temper, but handling two, double the fun. Luke, cursing in Italian and slamming stuff around in Raymo's cabin. Raymo letting him. Instead of raging like his cousin, Raymo brooded, subdued, but the air frizzled like a dark storm brewing. The five men then marched over to Kaylen's to confront her. Lane solo, entering with the others as if they'd charted their ETA.

"Who's this *ciuchino* (donkey/ass) you're gonna go see tonight, Kay?" Luke asked without preamble.

Kaylen outfaced Lane. "The obedient servant sent to dog me?"

Lane's baby blue's ticced in response to Kaylen's cut. She fumed, knowing he had ratted her out.

"Then you already know all about him, right?" Kaylen asked.

"He's a preppy snob, that much we know," Schaffer said. "Probably a football jockstrap."

"No, he's a track and field athlete. And a star on the aquatic team as well," she said.

"Well, la-de-da for him," Bran snickered. "Those girly-boys on the swim team? I've heard that they shave their legs!"

"One pretty boy judging another?"

There was a time when Kaylen's insults would elicit cries of "super burn," but on this occasion, the men stared at her in silence.

"Swimmers shave their bodies to reduce drag, enabling them to glide through the water better." Lane said, educating them.

"I wouldn't care if it made me glide through putain better," Raymo snickered. "Only sissies would do that." The remark set off a bunch of bantering back and forth, the others supporting Raymo's view.

Kaylen was sick to death of their immaturity, their biases. At that instant, she couldn't stand her friends.

"And his hair," Tony snorted. "Shay, you would've fell out if you had seen him. That haircut was practically military!"

"This *cocchiume* (bunghole)? He's got a wussy name too," Luke snickered. "Anderson Sterling Stavis."

"Wait a minute. Stavis? This guy's family has bucks," Lane informed them. "You've heard of R.S. Stavis? That's the patriarch. He owns a marina in Tampa and a restaurant in Clearwater, among other things. All the sons run the old man's businesses. So Anderson's dad would have to be one of the sons."

"This what this is about? Money? Hunting for a rich boy, Kay?"

"Of course not, Luke! I didn't even know his family was wealthy."

"You date is loaded. What a bonus, Kay."

"No one said anything about a date, Raymo! He's a new friend."

"Kaylen's got all types of friends, all sorta different interpretations of what a 'friend' is." Tony drew quotation marks in the air. "There's Lane, there's us, and now there's him."

"You think it's gonna be like with us?" Schaffer tipped his head. "A few kisses, and he'll go for that?"

"That stays in the family, right, guys?" Bran said. "It stays right here. With everyone in this room."

"This isn't about money. It's about me, what *I* want," Kaylen said.

"Anything you want, you got it right here. You wanna a beautiful blond guy? You don't have to go to this Andy dude. Here I am! You got the smorgasbord of male specimens' right here," Bran bragged.

"What I got is bullcrap. I'm fed up."

"You forget about this guy, Kay."

"I can't do that, Luke. He extended an invitation. I accepted it. I have to go."

"You don't even know this guy." Bran shrugged. "He could be a werewolf, an ax murderer, a satanical madman."

"You mean he's no different than the company I've been keeping?"

"Good one, Kaylen. But seriously, you can't go," Bran said.

"I can, and I will."

The air leached from the room. "Lane, maybe you should talk to your best friend, advise her what she should or should not be doing."

"I don't need Lane to tell me what to do, Luke. Or you either, Raymo."

Luke clutched Kaylen by the wrist, jerking her forward. "You forget this Anderson guy, Kay," his icy black eyes narrowing.

"Listen to my cousin," Raymo huffed against her nape. "You forget this guy."

Raymo breathing down her neck, and Luke shackling her arm, the pair a force to be reckoned with. Both were employing different tactics, both equally tyrannizing. But she wasn't having any of it.

"No. I'm showing up at Anderson's campsite tonight. I don't know where this is going, but I am moving forward. Toward him and away from y'all. Now let me go."

Luke's fingers digging into her wrist, his jaw clenched, propelling Kaylen away, flinging her arm as he jarred aside. She stumbled, Raymo uprighting her. He whispered into her ear the cold words no one else could hear: "You walk away from me, you'll be sorry."

"I want y'all to leave. *All* of you. I don't wanna find you here when I come back down," Kaylen said, slamming her bedroom door and shaking the house.

As Lane watched Raymo's glint reflecting Luke's fury, a sour sensation permeated the space. It knotted Lane's gut and brought to mind the scent of blood in the air—suffocating and rusty.

Raymo and Luke, nodding at Tony, Schaffer, and Bran. Their wordless conversation, speaking volumes.

They swiveled toward Lane, assaying his amenability.

"Tonight?" Tony crushed out his cigarette as Luke fired his up.

"No," Luke and Raymo spoke in unison as if they were one.

"We'll give it a few days." Luke exhaled, the grey smoke unfurling around them.

"When the time is right, in a few days," Raymo said.

Nothing else needed to be said.

* * *

Kaylen's pulse ticked. It hit her, the strangeness of meeting a man—an outlier, not of her coterie. She recalled the first time she visited the Vincuzzi house, Tony and Bran introducing her to the others, how her breath had caught in her throat when she met Luke. Eons ago.

"Hi. I was beginning to think you wouldn't show."

"I'm a woman of my word," Kaylen said.

As they sat by the fire, Anderson handed Kaylen a hot dog skewered on a palmetto stick. At first, Kaylen was hesitant, but she gradually opened up about her job at the campground, playing down her close relationship with her male co-workers, as if they weren't the core of her existence. Meanwhile, Anderson talked about his solo camping and fishing trips, relishing the peace of woods and water.

Many of Kaylen's guests shared the sentiment that the forest was a haven of serenity, with its soup of scents—ginger, vanilla, earthy fungus and dank moss. Kaylen too had once found tranquility in the lake and trees, but now the thicket felt like a prison, a looming threat of blackmail and secrets waiting to be spilled. The forest seemed patulous and toxic, like poison sumac lurking in the shadows.

"What a perfect gentleman he is," Raymo snickered, vetting the duo from his hiding place. "So sensitive and caring. He puts Kaylen's hot dog on the stick for her. Type of guy who doesn't expect her to handle his wiener."

Bran, shaking with mirth, the binoculars gripped in his hands. But Luke didn't even chink a smile, cataloging his girl-friend and her companion's moves.

On the second night, they spied on them, Tony, sand-wiched between Luke and Raymo, asking: "Now?"

"No," Luke answered. Plenty of time left.

On night three, Anderson visited Kaylen's house, the men becoming unglued. A debate on whether to barge in with their key after Kaylen had drawn the drapes. Luke and Raymo's imagination ran wild. Finally, Tony convinced them to let it play out. On night four, Kaylen and Anderson hung out at his campsite. Raymo, Luke, and Schaffer observed Anderson kissing Kaylen, G-rated compared to the men's make-out sessions with Kaylen. But even watered-down displays of affection bears gravity. A tipping point that they could not dismiss.

On the last night, Kaylen assisted Anderson in breaking camp. They roosted beside the smoldering campfire, dousing it with water and waiting for it to die.

"Kaylen, I've enjoyed being with you. I'd like to see you again. But I'm not sure you're into me the same way. You haven't said, but I suspect someone else has got your heart. Who is he?"

"Nobody. He means nothing to me." They. *They mean nothing to me*. No, they meant everything. Raymo. Luke.

"Yeah? This nobody? You're still waiting for him, whoever he is."

"It doesn't matter. It's complicated. It will never work out."

"I see."

"Andy, this isn't a rebound. I like you. I need to get to know you better."

"And you can. But we can take it slow and be friends, okay? We'll see each other whenever I can get away. Maybe you can even travel to see me too. It's only an hour or so away. So we'll take our time. No pressures. Alright?"

He stood, offering his hand, hoisting her. Her 5'5 to his 5'6, Kaylen was habituated to lofting her gaze, straining her neck, her male friends sky-scraping over her, and the odd sense of displacement as she leveled practically eye-to-eye with him. She was used to the shelterbelt of her friends, their strapping bodies like laurel oaks. However, she also feared that this same safety could be a danger, as towering pines that appeared sturdy can uproot and flatten in the ravage of storms.

He pressed his lips to hers. Like with their last kiss, Kaylen waited for... sparks. Pleasant, yes. Fireworks, no. Contrary to the fun, delicious kisses she shared with Tony, Bran, and Schaffer, and Lane's innocent pecks, warm and safe; different from Luke's familiar, thorough kisses; a radical steer from Raymo's galvanizing, thermal kisses.

Anderson promised to return soon. They double-checked, the campfire extinguished, Kaylen waving him off. Then, finally, she pivoted, heading home, turning her back as he drove out of sight.

But the men scoped his complete departure. Headlights twinkled through the forest, the shoosh of sand captured in treads, the crunch of his tires hitting the pavement, the highway a black ribbon.

"I wish we coulda' heard what they were talking about." Bran piped up from their hiding place.

"I don't need to hear them," Luke growled, jockeying the binoculars. "I've seen enough."

They rose, joining the others. Luke, tapping out the last cigarette from his pack, anchoring it between his lips, his cousin igniting the tobacco, both chuffing. "Well?"

"It's been taken care of." Raymo dispatched a smoke ring into the darkness.

"Shouldn't take too long now," Tony assured them. "*Allora sara' finite* (then it'll be over)."

"Merely a matter of time," Schaffer said.

Raymo and Luke, their eyes black as crusted blood. The others, the stain of duty, loyalty, bonds, reflected in their gaze.

CHAPTER TWENTY

Kaylen arrived for her noon shift. "Hey, hey, Crystal Lake's finest all here. Is only Lane working? And Raymo's here too. See? You can rouse yourself before 2:00 in the afternoon. You get a gold star for your effort."

Lane moved from behind the register as Kaylen relieved him.

"Okay, chop-chop. The schedule is up, and everyone's got places to be, and that would not be underfoot and in my way."

"Your friend took quite a bad slam." Bran smacked his palms, appreciating the sound effect.

"What?"

"Read the afternoon edition yet, Kaylen?" Tony quizzed her.

"Real interesting articles in there." Luke jabbed a newspaper at her.

Lane intercepted it. "Listen, Kaylen. Anderson's been in an accident."

"What? Is he all right?!"

"Kaylen, he's... I don't know how to tell...."

"—Oh, spit it out, Lanesy," Raymo said. "If you can't, I will. Kay, your little mermaid-man had a car wreck and went to that permanent fish tank in the sky."

"Great diplomacy, dude," Schaffer said.

"What do you mean...?" Kaylen snatched the newspaper from Lane. "Show me."

"Sports section, of course," Bran said.

"He was more important than we imagined," Luke said. "Not only did daddy have megabucks, but Junior was Olympic material—both in track and field and in swimming. What a talent."

"No." Kaylen breathed in disbelief as she read the caption: "Star Athlete Loses Life in Auto Accident."

"They say he lost control," she whispered. "There weren't any other cars involved."

"Maybe you kept your Robert Redford up past his bedtime." Raymo's mouth twisting.

"No, Anderson was fine when he left here!"

"What a shame and right when things were starting to cook between you two," Luke grunted. "You and him coulda' lived happily ever after with your future Blue-chip kids and his daddy's money."

"Nothing was going on between us. He was nice, and my friend, and that was it!" She gaped at their tactlessness.

"Your pal was careless, that's all. Great diver, not a driver." Bran joked, Kaylen trembling with dismay.

"Maybe he should have checked his car before he left," Tony said.

"After all, anything can happen late at night," Luke said.

"Could run out of gas," Schaffer pointed out.

"Or bust a hose," Bran said.

"And leaks. Don't forget about them. Brake fluid coulda' leaked out," Luke said.

"Now that could cause a nasty accident, couldn't it?" Raymo said.

Kaylen felt her scalp hairs prickling as a rush of adjectives came to her mind: exultant, triumphant, and victorious. She saw Raymo's smug expression, the look of someone who had won.

Lane caught her as she stumbled, clammy with shock, and sat her down on a stool as the room swayed. "What have you done?!" she gasped, staring at Raymo and Luke.

"Done? Nothing," Raymo smirked. "Unlike you, who did something."

"I didn't do anything. I made a new friend." Kaylen's voice strangled.

"Good friends are hard to come by," Tony said.

"And a better friend will make you hard and come." Bran delivered an old joke among the group. But no one was laughing this time.

"Listen, it's unfortunate that Andy decided to drive home Sunday night. The Grim Reaper set his sights on him. It was his time to go," Tony said.

"Really was." Luke's black eyes glittered.

Kaylen searched Lane's face, but he evaded her gaze, unable to help her.

"Crazy, huh?" Raymo tsk-tsked. "You try to step on the brake, turn the steering wheel, and nothing happens. Next thing you know, your car is all over the road, and then it is lights out. You know how it is, Kay. Mechanical problems are tricky. In cars. In boats. Can cause such problems. And we don't like problems. So we like to get rid of our problems."

"Your buddy should have been more careful, right?" Tony asked.

"Yeah, let that be a lesson for us to all be more careful from now on." Luke's warning tugged his lips upward.

The men filed out. "I'll see you later, right? At your house?" Luke jerked his thumb. Kaylen nodded, numb.

Raymo hung back last, out of view of the others, daring a kiss. Kaylen's lips, like snow caps, quivered. "I told you that you'd be sorry. I told you that you couldn't walk away from me, from us. Come over to my cabin when you get off shift. Show me how sorry you are for causing me—and the guys--a problem. *Capisce?*"

She hated herself for planning to meet him and allowing him to control her. She realized that in doing so, she was just as twisted as he was and felt tethered to Raymo and Luke. Lane had been right all along, and she knew deep down that she would never be truly free from their grasp.

CHAPTER TWENTY-ONE

Anderson's death drove Kaylen into a tailspin. The realization her friends premeditated an act of violence, that they had set into motion a plan to end someone's life, was beyond belief. The nauseating awareness seemed exacerbated by Kaylen's ongoing juggling act of Luke and Raymo. While the cousins had marshaled closer to each other—as if conspiring together and feeding their blood lust had tightened their family ties, it did not eliminate each from wanting, demanding, obsessing over her. They kept after her about her obligations to them, her fealty, their blood pact. Kaylen felt cornered, hesitant to contact the authorities—after all, she didn't have tangible proof that her friends caused Anderson's death. Haltered. Birdlimed. Adding to her dismay, Kaylen accepted she had become like her friends, giving in to depravity.

The men had assembled at Kaylen's house earlier on in the evening, like old times. But now, different, a radical shift. Even the music Schaffer selected—a task of pleasure he'd performed countless times before, now reflected the group's somberness, morosity-weighted lyrics, and dark tonalities. The turntable like a funeral pyre, spinning Pink Floyd's Careful with That Axe, Eugene, and Golden Earring's Everyday's Torture. Then The Lollipop Shoppe's Underground Railroad, Vanilla Fudge's Season Of The Witch, and The Doors' You're Lost Little Girl. Kaylen wondered if Schaffer was sending her a message. Previously, their pauses allowed for deep contemplation, but now they only accentuated the growing chasm between them, making the conversation awkward and unsettling.

The men, begging off for an early evening. Raymo lagged behind the others and whispered to Kaylen that he'd ring her later. Whether to check up on her or to feed his monomania, Kaylen didn't care. In response, her sharp "don't bother. I'm tired and going to bed." His reluctant departure, Kaylen turning in for the night and then rapping at her back door. She sighed, expecting to see Raymo.

"I wanted to talk to you without the others being around."

"Alright."

"Kay, what's going on with us?"

"There is no 'us,' Luke."

"Since when?"

Since Raymo. "Since the onset. When you decided it was okay to sleep with every girl you wanted yet still called me your girlfriend. Since what happened to Anderson."

"None of that changes anything between us."

"It changes everything."

"No, Kay. We're moving forward. And we know where it's going."

"No! This is going nowhere. I don't wanna be with you."

"Because...?"

"You're a liar, a cheater, a deceiver. A killer."

"A killer, Kay? Where did you get that idea? All we said was that your friend Andy should have been more careful."

"I know you killed him!"

"I never laid a hand on him."

"Then *who did*, Luke?"

He gave a sly smile. "No one."

"Who did it?!"

"Your friend's car went out of control. Destiny did it."

"Who tampered with his car? Was it you? Or was it Raymo and Tony?"

"Get a grip. We gave you scenarios. We never confessed."

"And you never will, will you?"

He grinned, the cat that ate the canary.

"Tell me, Luke, what happens to me if *I* misbehave? Will you get rid of me as you did with Andy?"

"Come on, Kay. Don't pull a Bran here and give in to the drama. That's crazy talk, tripped out thinking."

"Out of all of you—Raymo and Tony would have been the most likely ones to have done this. The ones who would have had the mentality to pull it off."

"Unlike Lane, right?"

"Lane is not even in the same hemisphere as Raymo and Tony."

"You sure?" Luke sniggered, and Kaylen shivered at his veiled words.

"You're trying to deflect this whole thing. From you, from them."

"Or I could be right, huh? See, because here's the thing, Kay. People think they're a certain way, but things happen, and they find out they're not who they thought they were after all. They don't think they would ever maim, cheat, lie for, steal from, go against, cause harm to another person. But then they're thrown into life situations and forced to choose." He folded her into a kiss. All talk and pondering about Andy evaporated. But thoughts of Raymo refused to dissipate, especially when Luke challenged: "Isn't it time to make a choice, Kay?"

"I can't go all the way with you."

"Sure you can. You're waiting for the perfect time. But there's no such thing."

No, I'm waiting for the perfect man. It's not you. It's not Raymo. And yet... he's so wrong for me, but what he is to me... that fire between us that we can't match with any other. "No, you're right. But now..."

"... Now?"

But now there's what you've done to Anderson. And Raymo is asking me for the same thing that you want from me. So now there's no way out and no way to right the wrongs.

"I wanna be, am gonna be your first, Kay. I'm going to be your last. It's that simple."

No, far from simple. Kaylen sunk her forehead into Luke's chest, her head and introspection as weighted as concrete blocks. She ached to lift her burden. He massaged her neck, she winching up her crown, meeting his gaze. Finally, like a person diseased and exhausted, who has endured the battle for too long, Kaylen surrendered. She nodded, Luke, smiling, fingers interlocking with hers, tugging her up the staircase.

"He's not gonna come back here tonight, right?"

A jolt. Then a relieved sigh. He meant her dad, not Raymo. She shook her head, hoping she was correct regarding both men.

Luke was dimming the lights, the mattress creaking, he murmuring, muscles pressing silk skin. His license for the first time to go this far with Kaylen, he went flesh-crazed, ravishing her. Kaylen, an insight, the anagnorisis as Luke attended her— an ember, not a blaze. Unlike Raymo's fire. Vile, wrong, for her to react to her victimizer rather than her boyfriend, yet indisputable. Her body responded differently to him as if Raymo's heat and luster blighted Luke's dim light. Despite a pale sheen compared to a blinding power flash, she was ready to be done with this.

Those many months of resisting Luke's advances, now lost in their consummation. When he entered her, the flare of pain yielded to a strange pleasure, Kaylen instinctively synching to Luke's rhythm. Kaylen, a virgin but not innocent, schooled by Raymo, deciphered Luke's raspy sighs of satisfaction—the same tune she hummed with Raymo. But she did not purr now, the familiar ardor failing to capture her.

Then, he crested, Kaylen embracing him, skin-to-skin, their bodies as one. A question: Was it good for you? The lie: Yes. Oblivious to the ego-crushing diverted, he kissed her, slumping beside her, comatic. Sleep proved harder for Kaylen, regrets, second-guessing, and disappointment hindering her slumber. But sapped to the bone, she submitted to the sopor, a state unattained for months, her breath settling deep and long and her body as still as death, like Andy cold in the grave.

Kaylen, roused by pinpoints of gold streaming through the window, her body cooled and her loins inflamed. Luke gone. Like a vampire in the night marking his escape, at the first sign of daylight, of having to take responsibility for deflowering Kaylen. Luke's bow out like a presage, sending Kaylen a message she unequipped to decode. Luke had not been scheduled for the first shift, then why the speedy exit before sunup? If anything, she'd have predicted Luke ready to hit another round—although Kaylen uneager for a repeat. She hadn't thought beyond the consummation. Maybe Luke had. Perhaps he read Kaylen's body language, her potential rebuff, and he unwilling to risk rejection. Or maybe their night together enough for him, the hunt over and the game bagged. Their guy-talk; she understood how their brains operated.

Despite her conviction to give up her virginity to Luke instead of Raymo, her gut burned. Fix one problem with one guy, gain another with the other. Knowing Luke, probably blabbing to the men right now. She trundled out of bed, glimpsing at the raddled girl in the mirror. The morning light accentuated her flaws; her cheeks scarped, the crinkled skin beneath her eyes like an old party streamer. She laughed bitterly. Bran insisted that once Kaylen lost her virginity, her skin would glisten like a jeweled masque. Instead, her face pasty and no afterglow. Another lie of many the men had recounted. She was lying to herself, her feelings for Luke, for Raymo. When you lie down with dogs, you get fleas. Kaylen had laid with Luke, had gotten laid by Luke; what did that say about herself? She was lying with the mangy mutt, bloodsuckers consuming her. Would infestation strike her down, crawling with flesh nibblers, feasting upon her blood? Or worse, she transmuting into a vector, a parasite among parasites.

CHAPTER TWENTY-TWO

The morning after Luke deflowered Kaylen and she discovered him missing from her bed, she soldiered on, handling business, as usual, covering the front office and checking campers in and out. Perfunctory tasks, yet her thoughts of curiosity splintering, whether Luke spilled it or not to his friends, whether he'd insist on a command performance. Kaylen's stomach twisted at the thought of being the object of gossip, sleeping with Luke again, or dealing with Raymo.

Tony and Luke's day chore, chopping down underbrush in the back acres of the campground—the purpose to minimize fire hazards and drive back lurking snakes. Lane and Schaffer assigned to repair the pavilions, and Bran had the morning off. The pairing up of Tony and Luke, providing ample opportunity for Luke to brag on his rendezvous with Kaylen the previous night. It wouldn't take any time in getting back to Schaffer, Lane, and Bran—and Raymo. What was going to happen when Luke told him? Raymo, sleeping in at his cabin and expecting Kaylen to shoot on over once she got off shift. She had no intention of going there, despite his orders. That had been Before. Before she had given her virginity away to Luke, before Kaylen perceived choosing Luke meant Raymo would consider he had lost, a guaranteed detonation for his temper.

Kaylen hoped to avoid her six comrades today. The means to accomplish that, she hadn't a clue. At one time, she'd have sought advice from Lane, and he'd be in her corner. But it wasn't that way anymore. That had been Before.

Kaylen loved her job. But she couldn't wait to finish her shift, her head throbbing, her body aching, her ideations spinning. She put in a call to Greg—their standby guy to fill in. With him at the helm, Kaylen jogged away, heading straight home to take refuge. She relaxed, collapsing on the couch in the dark. A warm hand cupped her knee. She screamed, flipping on the light, Raymo's icy stare unblinking.

"How did you get in here?!"

"Don't you worry about it. What have you gone and done, Kay?"

"Nothing."

"Luke is telling the guys that you and he did the deed."

"He's lying."

"Why would he?"

"Raymo, what would you do if your girlfriend didn't put out and your friends busted your onions about it all the time?"

"You're answering questions with questions. A sign of guilt."

"I have no reason to feel guilty."

"Sure you do. You're playing Luke."

"No. You forced me into this."

"Yet there's no protest from you about it now."

"You can call blackmail by any pretty name you want; it still is what it is."

"We've both been getting what we want from each other, Kay. That's not blackmailing; that's called reciprocation."

"I can't do this anymore."

"Then don't."

Like Luke, Raymo was making it out to be simple.

"You're fighting a battle that you can't win, Kay. This thing between you and me goes beyond anything you've had or would ever have with my cousin."

Kaylen secerned he was right—now that she had lost her virginity to Luke. "It doesn't matter. You're right; I can't fight this anymore. This between you and me, it has to end."

"For you to be with Luke?"

"No. For the two of you to resurrect what you had with each other. Family. Before I came along, and before you and I started this. Before you made me do this."

"It's not blackmailing. It's us being together. I can't be without you. I *won't* be without you."

"You're gonna have to learn, Raymo. And Luke too."

"Luke says you and him got down good and dirty."

"If that was true, would I tell him to leave me alone now?"

"I don't know what you're pulling here, Kay. Somebody's lying. Is it you, or is it my cousin?"

"Well, think about this. Out of the two of us, which one is the better liar?"

"At one time, I woulda' said Luke. But then I remember how well I've taught you. You're as good a liar as Luke and me."

"No, you're still the expert."

"I am. To get what I want."

"Like getting rid of Anderson?"

"Like finally telling Luke what you and I have been doing together."

"Why would you do that?! What purpose would it serve?"

"To have you, Kay."

"Because you want what you can't have! Not because you love me, but because you want a primal thing? And you're willing to hurt your cousin for it? So you gonna get rid of all the Anderson's of the world who stand in your way?"

"Whatever you and Luke had? It ended the day I took you in that closet, Kay. We both know it."

"No, it made everything more complicated. I care for Luke, but you do too. He will not understand this; that which has happened between us and is still happening between you and me. But not one thing happens between me and you or me and Luke, that doesn't affect our guys."

"Now that is the truth."

"Even though Luke and I have history, we don't appear to have longevity. And with you... there's no future with you either, Raymo. Just the now. What do I have—what could I ever have—with a man who would blackmail me? Who only cares about promoting his own needs and wants? You're no different than Bran! And then there's this matter about Anderson. What I suspect you did, what the others did that ended his life."

"With Luke, you thought you had found love. With Anderson, you shouldn't have been searching in the first place. Regarding me, I expect you to follow my lead."

"That's not a relationship, Raymo. That's control. That's an obsession, and I don't want to be that. You're worse than Tony, Tony's temper. You're a guy wired to pop off at any second. You're dangerous and not who I wanna be with."

"No, you'd rather be with someone who doesn't make your heart race, doesn't make your blood burn hot. Guys like Anderson. Like Luke. Luke, who brags he did it with you last night but plans to sleep with another girl tonight."

"What? What do you mean?"

"Ask him."

"I'm asking you. But then you're lying again!"

"I'm not. She's camped here before. Luke slept with her before. Check the client roster. She's on it. She's here now. Lane checked her in yesterday afternoon."

Yesterday?! Before Kaylen and Luke had slept together. Before. Did Luke know *Before* he came to Kaylen's house last night? Had he been waiting for the girl to get settled? Had she been too tired and Kaylen his second choice? If Kaylen had turned him away, would he have gone to the other girl instead? Didn't it matter to him either way? Kaylen was astonished by Luke's audacity and her sudden flare-up of jealousy. Did she love Luke after all? Or was she just as obsessed as Raymo?

"Luke told me that he'd be up for a little help tonight if you know what I mean."

"No, I don't know what you mean."

"Like old times. He and this chick and me. She's the type who's in for having a three-way party. My cousin wants to break my dry spell. All the guys think it's strange I haven't been working our contest. I'd probably never catch up to Bran anyhow. Still, I'm thinking about taking Luke up on it."

Kaylen clutched herself around her middle, his words a jab in the gut. "Oh, do the both of you get the point because you're doing the same girl? Or does it count as one, and you split it halfies?"

"I wouldn't be tempted if I knew we—you and I—could change things tonight."

"Oh, I say go for the sure thing. You guys have a great time tonight." *Get with your skank. Compare notes. Talk about me. And we'll wait for the fireworks to start.*

"I want you, Kay. I want you more than I've ever wanted anyone."

Having had a disappointing experience with one Vincuzzi, Kaylen wearied taking a chance repeating anything with another Vincuzzi. "Please leave me alone."

"Then I'm splitting." But instead of forking away, he kissed her hard. "It's not settled. You know that."

"When will it be, Raymo?" Kaylen trembled.

"Don't ask questions you already know the answers to, Kay." He coasted off without a backward glance.

* * *

Raymo departed, and Lane emerged. Kaylen took inventory of his expression. "You know. Who told you?"

"No one had to tell me anything. First, you get Greg to cover for you—highly unusual. Then you don't talk to anyone all day and try to hide out like you're a felon on the run. It wasn't that hard to put it together."

"Luke shot off his mouth to Tony and the others about us going all the way. I had Raymo over here giving me the third degree. Now Luke and Raymo are headed over to see this girl. And it's not to help her set up a tent."

"And how do you feel about that?"

"Pretty much how you'd think I would. I finally give in to Luke; he gets want he wants, he moves on right away, letting me know how supremely used I've been."

"Then why did you do it? Why did you sleep with Luke?"

"Because I am tired of the fight, Lane! Luke has been my boyfriend for a long twenty months. So, of course, I'd sleep with him over Raymo! No matter how Raymo makes me feel and no matter how much Luke doesn't. I told Raymo it was a lie that I slept with Luke. Raymo thinks it's gonna be him. And he's pushing for now."

"You know that this thing with Luke, him going to another girl? It's a temporary cooling off. It's not going to take long, though, for him to decide that he wants to exercise his rights again and expects you to sleep with him again. Consistently. But now you act like that's not what you want."

"What was I supposed to do? For too long, I've been in the middle between these guys! It was Luke and me way before Raymo came into the picture. I love Luke, even if it's, well... lukewarm. And with Raymo... there's this attraction and aversion I have for him. I hate the blackmail, and I hate him for having done this to me."

"You've got to remedy this. It's all going to fall back on you. You realize there's no happy ending here. Both are gonna get crushed when the real story comes out. But you know who you wanna be with."

"I don't wanna be with either one of them."

"And yet you are."

"Not for long. I'm going away for a while."

Lane blinked. "What do you mean? Where are you going?"

"Anderson's family is having a memorial for him. I saw the announcement in the newspaper. I'm going to attend, stay over for the weekend. I've asked Greg to cover for me."

"Kaylen, you can't be serious! The guys will think you're going to shoot off your mouth about Anderson. If you leave, this will blow up. You think Raymo and Luke are just going to let you go?"

"They don't have to know where I'm going, Lane. I'm telling *you*. I'll tell them I'm joining my dad for a few days."

"You're not thinking this through."

"Actually, it's all I've been thinking of."

"And what do you think is going to happen when you get back? You're going to come back to the same problems you left behind."

"I need time to think, Lane. I can't do that with Luke and Raymo around. You'll take me to the bus terminal, right?"

"No, Kaylen, I won't. I don't think you should go right now.

In another month, Raymo will go back to NYC for a while, and that'll give you respite."

"I can't wait that long. Both guys have worn me down. And now you're refusing to help me?! Figures. This is what I would expect from you, who's been in Raymo and Luke's back pocket for so long that you don't know anything else."

The bright blue eyes twitched at the putdown. "Please understand that I'm not going to help you make things worse. I don't want you to go."

"Yeah, but I want you to go. Leave me alone. I mean it. *Get out of my house!* Right now."

He welled up, tromping off. Within a nanosecond, Kaylen regretted the order. But in the end, she did nothing.

Years after, in times of retrospection and rue, she coped with that by doing nothing; it snowballed to something. And cost her everything.

CHAPTER TWENTY-THREE

Someone pounded on Raymo's door. He swung wide, stirring a marijuana cloud. "Hi, sexy, you can interrupt our late-night all-boys poker game anytime."

"There's someone in the office! With flashlights," Kaylen cried.

At 9:00 pm, the operations were closed. Earlier that day, Greg had worked for Kaylen. After confronting Raymo and Lane earlier that same day, Kaylen finally calmed down and went to close out the evening register, which was not an unusual task for her at that time of night. While doing so, she noticed suspicious activity inside and rushed to get her friends.

"Al or my dad?" Schaffer smacked his cards face down on the table.

"No. They would've turned on the lights," Lane said. "They wouldn't be wandering around using a flashlight."

"Let's haul," Bran said.

"Grab one of your guns," Tony instructed Raymo. So he did, loading it.

"Maybe we all need one." Bran said, crushing out his

cigarette.

"This isn't redneck shoot-em-up." Kaylen ripped him. "Let's just go!"

Tony and Luke had cleared underbrush earlier in the day, stabling the work truck at the back end of the campground, meters from Raymo's cabin. Luke hopped in the driver's side; Kaylen scooted to the middle, Raymo pressing her right thigh with his. They'd sandwiched her in, with no way to escape. So much like my life, she mused. The other men leaped into the truck bed, the cold air numbing their fingers, but no one complaining.

"Slow down, Luke. If we come roaring up, it'll scare them away," Kaylen cautioned.

Luke killed the headlights, nosing up beside the building. Flashlight beams bounced around inside. The men hopped from the tailgate, huddling the truck. Schaffer said: "Is it possible that Greg forgot to lock up? That a camper got in?"

"No. I checked the side door, latched just like normal, just as Greg always does when he closes up shop. So someone had to have gotten in elsewhere. Maybe put a hole in the roof?"

"Let's storm 'em." Bran inched forward.

"No, let's see what they're gonna do." Raymo clamped him by his shirt sleeve.

"What could they steal? They couldn't get much. There's less than $100 left in the till at night, and Greg would've stashed the rest."

"Bran, for real? We got cigarettes and beer. And nutters will take your life for 20 bucks!" Tony said. "$100 would be a goldmine."

"But the cash is in the safe. Who else knows where the safe is hidden?" Kaylen asked.

"No one. Us, Greg, and our folks," Lane said.

"You sure one of you morons didn't blab it to one of your

slags during a drunken, drug rampage and between-the-sheets romp?" Kaylen sniped.

"You mean like earlier on this evening with the babe in campsite 19?" Luke smirked.

"Believe me; we were too busy for talking, right, cuz?" Raymo bragged.

"There's a difference between a quicky with a camper and serious pillow talk," Luke said. "Like with us. Right, Kay?"

Raymo stiffened against Kaylen's thigh.

"You guys work out your little love problems later," Schaffer said. "Look!"

A shift of hotspots, a flashlight's spill from office to the game room. The side door cracked, the intruders filing out. As their shadowed faces mutated into human features under the floodlight, Bran blurted: "*Roba da matti!* (crazy stuff). You recognize any of those dudes?"

"It's those two guys we ripped off during that drug deal in Miami!" Schaffer said.

"After all this time! How did they find us?" Kaylen cried.

"Dunno. Persevering pricks." Tony punched his palm.

"You said that they'd never know who we were. You said they would never come after us!" Kaylen cried.

"Yeah, well, they're here now, and they've brought rein-forcements."

The four intruders surged forward, hoisting the bags across their shoulders like Santa Claus delivering toys to the kiddies. The burglars' padded yards from their car, Luke was popping the truck lights on, the strangers blocking the glare with their elbows. Then like a typhoon, Tony stormed, slamming one of them to the pavement.

Luke slugged a second intruder, lamming him in the head until he crumbled to the ground.

Raymo hammered the butt of the gun against one of the

burglar's skull, losing count of the number of blows.

A fourth man broke away, barreling through the woods.

"Get 'em!" Luke ordered, Bran and Schaffer in hot pursuit.

Tony shot a cross hook, but his opponent returned the punch, bashing Tony in the mouth and loosening several of his teeth. He yelled and swore, the guy galloping back to his vehicle.

Bloodied, pummeled, and injured, Raymo's opponent retreated, hobbling toward the car.

"Wing 'em," Luke yelled. "Shoot them!"

"No!" Lane and Kaylen cried.

Tony's opponent loped to the car, rooting under the seat.

Raymo jammed his weapon in the guy's cheek. "Give it to me now." The man tossed his handgun. Raymo grappled with the driver for the car keys. Tony roared: "Watch out!" as the other bloodied man looped back around. Raymo whirled, yelling, clutching his side. Tony's alert, preventing him from being stabbed straight on through the back.

"You're bleeding!" Kaylen cried.

"Forget that; they're getting away!"

The bloodied man launched himself inside, the driver peeling out.

"Don't!" Kaylen shrieked as Raymo readied his enemies' enfilade. But the car catapulted through the darkness and out of his range of fire.

Tony, spitting blood, scraping his tongue over his loose teeth.

"Your mouth!" Kaylen freaked out.

Tony bared a bloody grin. "Don't worry; I'll get new solid gold ones."

Luke's pulverized opponent regained consciousness. Then, witnessing his ride fleeing, he hurried into the forest.

"He's bolting! Get him, Tony," Luke ordered. "Lane, go in

there and see what they got." Lane dashed inside the office, grabbing the bags discarded during the melee.

"Get in the truck." Luke hollered, Kaylen and Raymo piling in.

"What are you gonna do?!" Kaylen cried.

"We're going after them," Luke said.

"Let them go! Call the police."

"The police? Kay, we ripped off those guys, and now they've tried to rip us off! We can't tell the cops about that!"

"Then let it go!"

"You think this is over, Kay? It's begun. They found us, and now with what happened tonight, it's on! They hurt my cousin. And you saw what they did to Tony. They're not going to mess with us and get away with it!"

"Forget them. Raymo is bleeding; he needs to go to the hospital!"

"What I need is retribution. Got some napkins in this heap?"

"Nothing. Sorry, man," Luke said.

Kaylen shrugged off her jacket and pressed it to Raymo's wound. "I love it when you start taking your clothes off for me," he whispered, stacking his hand over hers and oddly intimate.

Trees whipped by as the truck rocketed down the highway. "Luke, slow down!" Kaylen cried out for the tenth time.

"Enough, Kay. Just let me do the driving!"

"That's them! Run 'em down," Raymo cried as they barreled toward the smaller vehicle.

The driver hit his brakes, causing the truck's back bumper to collide with a sickening thump, sending a jolt to Kaylen's C_1 like a whiplash strike.

"Ah, they wanna play chicken, huh?"

"Show 'em how the game's played, Luke," Raymo said.

"No, Luke!"

"I mean it, Kay; you better stifle it. *Chiudi il becco* (shut up)." Whizzing parallel, Luke jerked the steering wheel, smashing the driver's door.

Kaylen gasped in horror, but her friends laughed.

The car revved away, Luke stomping the gas, gaining. "If I get closer, can you do it?"

"Never miss. We gotta teach them a lesson. About who not to screw with." Raymo patted the gun.

"No. They got us back for what we did to them. Let it go! They didn't even get away with anything, nothing was taken!" Kaylen cried.

"Something was taken all right—our sense of security. Do you think this will stop? They'll keep coming back! I'm going to make sure they don't. *Noi li finire* (we finish them)," Luke said. The truck's grill, gnawing at the car's back bumper.

The frosted air rushed up, stinging Raymo's ears as he leaned out the passenger window, aiming his gun. Kaylen wrestled for the weapon, but Luke backhanded her hard. With Kaylen out of the way, Raymo fired the shot, and the stranger's rear window exploded. The vehicle skidded, flipped, struck the guardrail, and burst into flames.

Luke and Raymo blocked Kaylen from exiting the truck when she begged to get out to help. The trio watched as the orange and gold flames blazed across the black velvet sky, and Kaylen's screams rose in tandem with the howls of the twosome in the car, fracturing the night. The intense heat blasted the air, instantly bathing the trio in sweat. While they listened to the mad pounding of fists and feet against jagged metal and boiling door handles, Luke inched back the truck, keeping the burning car within view. Finally, the crackling inferno silenced the victim's wails, and only then did Luke guide the truck into a bosom of darkness, distancing them from the fetor of leaking gas and bubbling flesh.

CHAPTER TWENTY-FOUR

"I 'm here. What do you want?" Kaylen said, stamping into Raymo's cabin.

"You got Greg covering your shifts all week, and you won't answer your phone." Luke stubbed out his cigarette in the overflowing ashtray. "Tony came over a few days ago to check on you, but you were locked up tight in the closet and didn't even bother responding to him. He could've broken the door down, but he thought it wasn't worth the hassle. I don't appreciate having to send Lane over to fetch you."

"Well, it's never bothered you before to use your little slave. And you know why I've been avoiding all of you. I'm surprised you didn't barge on in my house tonight like you always do."

"This is a better place to conduct business. Someplace where your father won't suddenly pop up or where you can go stomping off. Now, let's talk," Luke said.

"See, the whole point of avoiding you and the other guys is, so I don't have to talk. I got nothing to say."

"A woman who doesn't have something to say? That's gotta be a first!" Bran humphed.

"Oh, I bet you got plenty to say, Kay. If you don't, I sure do."

"What do you have to say to me, Raymo? That you take responsibility for taking someone's life? Anderson's? And those guys the other night? We left them there, trapped and burning in their car! I have to live with that! Can you?"

"It was either them or us," Luke argued.

"Just for us to get away?" Kaylen cried.

"Doing something wrong to get the right outcome? You mean like what *you've* done, Kay?" Raymo said.

Unraveling. The dirty truth was coming out, and nothing Kaylen could do to bung it.

"At least I'm only a liar, Raymo. You! You're a liar, a deceiver, a blackmailer, a murderer! Or was what you did to those two burglars just an 'accident?'"

On the walk over, Lane told Kaylen what had happened the night the office was burglarized. She listened as he described how Bran and Schaffer had apprehended one of the men in the woods, while Tony had captured the other near a canal. When the cousins met up, Tony had taken revenge on the thieves, with Bran and Schaffer helping restrain them. Kaylen shuddered at the description of Tony's fury unleashed, his blows devastating, rupturing organs and snapping bones. She couldn't help but think of the men who had whimpered— one asking for his mother; the other guy praying for the torture to end. But Lane explained how Tony didn't stop until he got the job done.

Tony's lips peeled back, exposing his repaired teeth—new ones, not gold, but blinding pearl, glowing strong. "It got taken care of. Those guys won't be bothering us anymore. *Sono stati messi a tacere* (they were silenced)."

A chill shuttered down Kaylen's spine. "You're all reprehensible!"

"And yet you're with us. And still coming to see me on the q.t." Raymo smirked.

"Because you're *blackmailing* me." Kaylen cried, no longer able to stem the storm, a smiting anvil. "Luke, I swear to you it's not what you think!"

"You've been seeing my cousin? Have you been sleeping with him?!" Luke yelled.

"No! No. I didn't want to hurt you; I didn't want there to be problems between the two of you. He blackmailed me, Luke. He's blackmailing me!"

"Blackmail? What could he possibly blackmail you with, Kay?" Luke grunted.

"Tell him what's between us, Kay. It's not blackmailing. Tell him that you want me. And that you've known it for a long, long time," Raymo said.

"What have you been doing? How long has this been going on?" Luke bellowed.

"Since Eight Minutes in the Closet. We went to third base right away." Raymo spun the tale, half-truth, half-lie.

Luke slingshotted from his seat, upending the kitchen table. "You've been letting him get that far with you?! And making me wait?"

"No. No, he's lying! He's making it out to be something that it isn't. But, Luke, I did wait for you. You know that the other night was my *first time!*"

Raymo hovered over her. "You told me that you didn't sleep with Luke!" His anger pulsed dark and strong. But when he switched off—from hot wrath to cool nonchalance—Kaylen was more petrified at his detachment than his fury. "She told me she was going to do it with me."

"Luke, it's not true. I swear to you!"

Luke's rage drowned out Kaylen's words. "All this time, you've been lying and jerking me around?!"

Both he and his cousin stared Kaylen down.

"You could go after my girl, do this to me, my own cousin?" Luke oscillated toward Raymo.

But Tony diffused the tension, saying: "A woman should never get in between family. Your first allegiance should be to each other. To all of us. *La famiglia prima di tutto* (family comes first). The ones who were here before Kaylen ever came. She pitted you against each other. Think about *that*."

"First you say Luke's lying, then it's Raymo. Which one is it, Kaylen? Can't you get your story straight?" Bran chided.

"What difference does it make? None of you will believe me!"

"What did you do with him?" Luke yelled.

"You gave yourself to him in a way you'll never give yourself to Luke." Up until this point, Lane, a fly on the wall.

Everyone's head jerked toward him, varying degrees of slack jaws and stares. Kaylen's cheeks streaked bright scarlet. "Why are you saying this?!"

"Because you won't. You won't say how you feel," Lane said.

"I can't believe you're doing this, saying this! With everything that's happened and all we've been to each other. You know *I never* slept with Raymo! Lane, you know how he pushed me into this. This blackmail."

"Yeah? But then you went ahead and slept with my *brother* even though you wanted my *cousin* the whole time," Lane said.

"Is that true?" Luke cried. "You wanna be with *him* instead of *me*?!"

"No! What Raymo and I did, he *made me* do it."

"I never made you do anything that you didn't want, Kay."

Luke's breath chuffed hot, but his stare, cold and murderous. Kaylen reached for him, Luke batting her hand away, and she winced from the pain and rebuff. "*Puttanella!* (slut). You pretend all this time, not putting out and making me wait, while you mess around with my cousin? Then you talk about me? Talk crap about me to him behind my back! Disrespect me. *Tu mi avresti umiliarmi come questo?* (would you humiliate me like this)" Luke bellowed.

"Kaylen, you went way, way too far with this," Tony's index finger jabbed her below the jugular notch.

"Raymo is lying! I swear to you. I'm sorry, Luke. For getting involved with him. I wanted this blackmail from him to stop. I never wanted it to be this way. I never wanted to hurt you. I would never hurt you intentionally!"

"Yeah? Well, that's the difference between you and me, Kay. *I* would hurt you intentionally." Luke's fist tensed back like an archer in full draw, punching her face.

"Luke! *Basta!* (stop/enough)." Schaffer manacled his fore-arm, preventing him from smacking Kaylen again.

Kaylen stumbled, pressing her palm to her swelling eye. Luke, not one shred of violence toward her in the whole time they had known each other. Now in the short course of several days, hitting her twice.

"To strike me! —of course, this would be what I would expect from someone who could kill Andy, who could drive off and leave someone to burn up in their car!"

"You pushed me, Kay. You pushed me to this," Luke argued.

"No. There's never an excuse to do that—any of it! But if we're going to point fingers, it all goes back to Raymo. He's the one pulling strings here. He's the puppet master, and he's got us all working for him! *Don't y'all see it?*" Kaylen cried.

"You're quick with the accusations. You wouldn't put an end to yours and Raymo's tryst and then drove a wedge between cousin and cousin." Tony accused.

"It was never a tryst! It was blackmail. But now it's all out in the open. And I'm done." She sprung for the door.

"Where do you think you're going?!" Luke was blocking her, snarling like a rabid dog.

"I want y'all to leave me alone!" Kaylen wept. "I want out of here!"

"You come and dump this on me and then think you're gonna up and leave?!" Luke bellowed.

"You're part of us. Part of this group," Bran said.

"Yeah, it's great company I keep, bullies, murderers, and liars. But I don't want any part of this anymore. You're all scum!"

"Well, sweetheart, you had no trouble sleeping with one scum and leading the other scum on," Tony said.

"I'm leaving. Don't call me, don't come over, don't send Lane to get me."

"Take a few days and cool off," Schaffer said.

"This isn't a temper tantrum that I need to recover from. So I'm walking away, and I'm staying away. And if y'all don't leave me alone, I swear I won't keep this to myself."

"What does that mean?" Bran frowned.

"I'll go to the police."

"Yeah? What are you gonna tell them, Kay?" Raymo's lips were curling, unruffled.

"Everything. Starting with the drugs. The drugs you've been selling, that deal in Miami that led to those guys coming after us—the ones whose car caught on fire the other night. And those other two guys, the ones y'all trapped in the woods. I'll tell the cops about Anderson. About Luke's violence. Hitting me."

"Yeah? Did you forget you were involved in that drug deal? Did you forget that you were in the truck with Raymo and me the other night? You're an accomplice, Kay. You implicate us, sweetheart; you implicate yourself."

"I say if you're gonna go to the police, Kay, then give 'em something to *really* work with." Raymo challenged. The long-held secret begged to get out.

"Lanesy, do you think Kaylen will still go to the police if she believes she'll incriminate you?" Tony asked.

"Do you think your best friend will turn on you, turn you in, or will she protect you?" Luke asked, a hangman taking his prisoner up to the gallows.

Lane's cheeks, the hue of frost smoke rising over the lake at daybreak.

"Lane? I don't understand!" Kaylen cried.

"Explain it to her, Lanesy," Raymo said.

"You're not involved...?!"

"No, babe, don't worry your pretty head about that. Lane had nothing to do with finishing Andy-boy off. No, he didn't bloody his hands. *This* time," Raymo added with great effect.

"You wanna know, Kay? Do you want to know what happened?" Luke asked. "No, Anderson wasn't the first one we've had to get rid of. But then who would know that better than my *own brother*."

Lane blanched, his Adam's apple juddering.

"You see, we had no choice, did we, Lanesy? It was the only way, right? Tell her about your girlfriend, Lane. Tell her about—"

"*Shut up, Raymo!*" Lane hissed like a fanged viper, his vehemence causing everyone's jaws to drop. "You shut the hell up right now! *Giuro che ti metto nella tomba per questo!* (I swear I'll put you in the grave for this)." He lunged, grazing his cousin, Tony pinning his arms back before he could strike Raymo full-on.

Neither the ill-attempted punch nor Lane's words had injured Raymo in the least. "Pretty hot stuff for a kid barely into his puberty, huh, Lanesy? Pretty exciting having an affair with an *older married* woman. She was beautiful, available, and her husband away a lot. But it was purely for kicks, right? You never dreamed she'd threaten to tell her husband, did you? Poor Lane. Always such a good boy, never getting into trouble like bad Luke or Raymo. But then he found himself in deep crap. She threatened to make up a bunch of lies about him too. And who were people gonna believe? A kid or a politician's wife? Everyone knows what happens to a kid accused of sexually assaulting the wife of a prominent man—they go to J.D. jail for a long, long time. Our intelligent Lane, who always had all the answers—didn't know what to do. So, of course, he asked the only people he knew who could help him—his brother, his cousin, his friends. It had to be handled, *finished* by all of us."

"See, we didn't mean to kill her," Raymo said. "We only meant to scare her, to remedy a problem. Wanna know the funny part, Kay? When we realized how far it had gone–when we realized that she was actually dying–we could have still saved her! But Lane didn't want us to. He told us: 'No, let her go, let her die.' And so we did."

Kaylen's stomach pitch-poled. "I don't believe it. Tell me it's not true, Lane!"

He choked out a single sob. "It was an accident!"

"Sure, we all know that," Raymo said gently, but his mouth sickled and sharp as a scimitar sword. "But we still had to cover it up, right? So we got rid of the body and told you what to say and do when people started coming around canvassing. And she's never been found, has she, Lane?"

Lane shook his head, the tears crawling down his cheeks.

"And you wanna know something, Kay? Whether it's intentional or whether it's an accident, once you've killed, it only gets easier the next time," Luke said.

"No!" She staggered like when Luke thwacked her.

"Now you know the truth: That your best friend is as much a liar—as much a killer—as we are." Luke said.

"He's indebted to us and always will be," Raymo said. "If you go shooting off your mouth to the cops about the drugs and other stuff, they might start nosing around and find out things they weren't investigating in the first place. They might start taking a closer look at Lane. You wouldn't want that to happen, now would you?"

"I don't know any of you anymore! I don't think I ever did. I want out of this!"

"You're not leaving here." Luke traced Kaylen's cheekbone lightly. "You're not leaving us. Ever."

"You're all mental—certifiably ill, every one of you! With what happened with Anderson, those guys the other night, and now I hear *about this*! I'm not going to be a part of this. You leave me alone, or I'll go to the authorities. Lane, I swear I won't say anything about you. But these sick maniacs need to be dealt with!" Kaylen cried.

"Do you understand that if you stir up trouble about one thing, it all comes down?" Schaffer said.

"You turn against us, and we'll make you pay," Raymo promised.

"I already have. By being in this group!" Kaylen cried.

"Maybe she needs to learn a lesson." Raymo cut his eyes toward Tony.

"Are you sure? Because once we put it into motion, it can't—"

"—Yeah. I'm sure."

Tony then met his cousins' gaze, finally saying to Luke:

"We gotta teach her a lesson. You understand, right? What we must do? We can't let her go to the—"

"—I get it," Luke said.

"Bad enough that she's been stringing both of us along. Now we can't even rely on her loyalty. Let me show her what happens when someone turns against us." Raymo, toe-to-toe with his cousin, twins with their unforgiving black eyes. Luke finally saying: "Do it."

Raymo, jerking his head at Tony.

Tony's paws shackling Kaylen's slender wrists.

"But Luke...?!" Schaffer stammered, Luke, shaking his head, Raymo declaring: "It's the only way."

Lane's breath wheezed out, sucker-punched by what was unfolding, his pupils bursting like an oil spill seeping into an azure sea, the blue leached from his irises in that millisecond of posed horror when both he and Kaylen understood what was about to happen.

"I want to go home. I won't say anything after all. *I promise.* Just let me go." Kaylen's voice quivering, her aquamarine eyes bulging.

"No. You won't leave here until we're through with you." Tony was blocking her.

"*Luke! Luke!*" Lane was clutching at him, his brother shoving him, crashing against the wall. "It's a done deal. You won't change it, Lane!"

Lane, blanching with shock, slumping to the baseboard as the men corralled Kaylen, their strength in numbers outwitting any defense he might have attempted. He hugged his knees to his chest and quaked. Held captive by his helplessness, his complacency, by a debt that couldn't be paid, by a mistake he couldn't take back, and his attempts to protect his best friend, futile. The cold, nasty truth overwhelmed him, Lane's sobs thundering.

"No! No. Don't!" Kaylen screamed, Tony and Raymo forcing her toward the bed.

"Make it easy on yourself. Do what we want," Raymo said. "See, Kay? That's all you ever had to do. Do what we expect of you."

Bran flanked Tony's side, helping him yank Kaylen's jeans off, she kicking, bucking, pleading. "Pin her down," Raymo grunted.

"Please. Send them away, and I'll do whatever you want, Raymo, the two of us, just as you've asked me to do!"

He laughed. "You had your chance, Kay. But, unfortunately, it's too late for that. But I still get what I want. And I'm in a sharing mood."

"Tony! Bran! No. Stop, you're hurting me!"

"And you've been hurting us, Kay. You've lied to us and teased us. It goes back around. Now we're going to show you. The only kind of hurt you can understand." Raymo unzipped his trousers.

"*Lane! Luke! Schaffer!*" Kaylen's shrills pierced the air; Bran and Tony untangled her legs and arms, prying her thighs apart. "Someone stop them!"

Isolated, the cabin far from the campground's hub and buffered by sound-absorbing hickories, myrtle oaks, and white ash, Kaylen could not be heard by the outside world.

"Go ahead, scream your head off. No one's coming to help you. No one *here* is gonna help you." Raymo lowered himself upon her, crushing his mouth to hers. She clamped her teeth around his bottom lip, but he retaliated, gnashing her. She jolted, renting Bran's grasp from her arm and leg. She erupted upright, digging her fingernails into Raymo's side, knifed there days before. He bellowed, striking her. Reeling, she scrambled to the foot of the bed. Tony and Bran were ensnaring her, hoisting her up by the armpits, flattening her against the mattress.

Kaylen cursed Raymo in Italian with the worst words she knew, fitting for the evil monster before her. He grinned, unoffended and eager to take what he deserved, waited for indeterminately, and even better, with everyone watching.

Raymo licked the blood from his lips where she bit him, and ignored the stab wounds bleeding through his bandaged side. "Now you have to pay," he growled. "I'm going to get what you owe me. I'm gonna teach you a lesson."

Although the dark, ugly blackmail prevailed, no electricity between them existed anymore. Nothing left but cold abuse as he rammed himself inside her. She was racking with sobs at each horrible punishing thrust, her body convulsing.

Lane crouched, frozen, sickened at the sight, and unnerved by Kaylen's screams. He curled away, retching, the vomit trickling down his chin.

Luke's need for a smoke surged to a frenetic pitch, heightened, transfixed by his cousin sadistically sating himself between Kaylen's thighs. Unable to light his cigarette, his hands shaking, Schaffer leaned over and lit the Marlboro for him.

Kaylen, suspended, like a parachutist in free fall, like sinking underwater—the warp of light and shadow as she twisted under the rip current, thrashing beneath pummeling waves. She drifted in and out, willing her unconsciousness against the emotional and physical pain. Raymo, moaning his pleasure as he finished.

Kaylen's mind burst with enlightenment about her night terrors. Raymo was the dark-eyed figure who invaded her nightmares. The shadowed figures from her dreams, who had trussed and hushed her, manifested as Tony and Bran.

Raymo quickly kissed Kaylen as he rolled off, buckling his pants and squinting at Tony. "Hey, you want sloppy seconds?"

No one had to ask Tony twice. He inserted between Kaylen's knees, and Raymo swapped out, holding her down. When she spit in Tony's face, he slat her, as his best friends had. A tap compared to the damage Tony was capable of had he wanted to. But the blow disenabled her struggling, leaving her prey to his goring. When Bran went third, she cried and begged him to stop. He didn't. He wouldn't. Each time another man knelt between her legs, Kaylen wept and tried to wrest away. They made sure she wasn't going anywhere and that everyone got their chance with her, a lesson taught in multitude.

Kaylen understood the assaults occurred—but she couldn't wrap her brain around it, her spirit and body in denial. She pleaded for her friend to end it. "Lane? Lane, please!"

"Hey, Lanesy. I think she wants you next. How about that? Think you can finally get it up?" Raymo asked.

Years of being taunted and mentally eviscerated raced up, intersecting with guilt and rage. "*Tu sei il Diavolo*! (you are the devil). I hope you burn in Hell for this!" The spittle was spuming the corners of Lane's trembling white lips as he outfaced Raymo.

"Yeah, well, either way I'll see your dead lover, won't I? Whether in Heaven or if I pass her on my way to Purgatory," Raymo said.

After Tony had retreated from Kaylen's loins, he joined Luke and Raymo. Luke passed Tony a cigarette, their gaze locking for several beats. Tony monitored the scene, Bran finishing up with Kaylen, and he said: "Go, Lane. Shay, you're up."

"Lane?" Kaylen choked, his gentle palm brushing her tangled mane from her lashes. Bran prized her body open, Lane vising her shoulders to expedite Schaffer's turn. "Lane? How could you? *How could you!*"

"Forgive me," he whispered, his tears splashing upon Kaylen's cheek, pooling with hers. He swiped them away with a tremoring finger. *"Forgive me."*

* * *

The five men loitered outside Raymo's cabin in the chilly air, cigarettes glowing against the jet night, like lightning bugs signaling in flight.

Kaylen trailed Lane across the porch. Her vermillion sweater clumpy as a blood clot, sagging off her shoulders, the men having ripped her clothes from her body. Kaylen's hair was knotted, her face swollen, and her irises were wrung of blue, vacantly staring. Numb from her core to her marrow. But at the place the men had forced themselves into, her insides were cold and stinging—like the men's frigid indifference, betrayal, assault.

"Kay?" Raymo blasted smoke toward the ebony sky.

She halted but unable to stomach looking at him.

"You'll be keeping this to yourself, got it?"

"Like all the other secrets," Luke ordered.

"I despise you, Raymo!" Kaylen whispered, fire and venom. "I despise you, Luke! You're filthy, sociopathic demons! *I despise all of you.* All of you! You're dead to me. *Dead! Every one of you.* I won't tell anyone about what happened—none of it. But do not *ever contact me again!*

"Do you understand me? I don't ever want to see any of you again! *Never ever again!*" She plowed into the darkness, the black woods devouring her.

There was a crunch under Lane's foot. He squatted, scooping up the necklace—their Christmas gift to her, forever ago. The filigree gold chain, severed but the bell intact, tinkling like a girl's titter. Had it been broken during the assault, or did she snatch it from her neck? He carefully folded into his pocket, the others staring at him, the silence thick. The necklace represented the men's love for Kaylen, the semiotic of their friendship. Now it lay shattered, their bond ruptured, destroyed, and beyond repair—the symbolism for their sin.

The men shuffled inside, their cold, brutal crime forgotten within the warmth of the cabin.

CHAPTER TWENTY-FIVE

K aylen stared vacuously, the sun melting into the lake; the sky smeared the color of tupelo honey poured over a flame grapefruit. She sealed the drapes, tumping the empty bottle on the coffee table. Taking a cue from Bran, she hadn't bothered with a glass, swigging Southern Comfort straight from the bottle, the amber liquor scorching her throat but failing to heat her insides. Instead, the men had laid siege, their battering rams pounding her flesh raw. She imagined her innards as shredded meat, a gutted and filleted fish.

Raymo. Luke. Their names were tumbling inside the drum of her consciousness like sodden clothes on spin dry. She didn't want to but couldn't quit thinking about them. Of Raymo assaulting her, Luke signaling him the go-ahead. How Luke stared, smoking, letting the others have their way with her and not preventing them. She had thought she loved him. She had given him her virginity. And he had used her. Abused her. Betrayal. The word somersaulted in her brain over and over, the endless loop of rumination denoting her nervous breakdown. Betrayal. Betrayal. Betrayal. Betrayal. First Luke's indiscretions and now this.

Raymo. If he had gotten rid of her as he had with Anderson, her pain would have been over. But he knew that by handling her in this way, using rape as a weapon, that she would suffer the most. His warped sense of dishing out her condign. Raymo, a man who had once electrified her, now terrified her. His perspiration, blood, fluids were swilling inside her body, poisoning her. Killing her. Betrayal. Rape.

Betrayal. Tony. Bran. Schaffer. Betrayed by her friends. She had loved and trusted them, and this is what they had done to her. Ripping her clothes from her body, tearing her insides, detruding her heart from her chest, rifting her life from her, the sole one she'd forged—a life based on existing alongside them. Gone. Done. Over. Rape. Betrayal. The men leered at her, waiting their turn, licking their lips. It made her feel dirty, and no matter how many times since that night she writhed under a scalding spray, she couldn't get clean, the unscrubbable stench of their turpitude and deceit. Their sweat cladded her abraised skin, their semen festering inside her, infecting her, killing her. Betrayal. Rape.

The rape and betrayal unspool like an old black and white movie, jittering monochromatic images, a flickering projector screen firing neurons in Kaylen's head. It was as obscured as a filter over a lens; the grainy depictions mercifully blur her ordeal. But then, beam-splitting prisms of Technicolor reveal the lurid details, verisimilitude sharp and bright. Glaring like a spotlight, panging her head to see it, shattering her heart to feel it, to remember it. Reel by reel, the film plays: Tony's bracelet skittering his muscled arm, her gift to him like a burnished taunt, his iron fist rearing back and striking her, then violently jackhammering himself into her center; Bran's feral cat eyes glowing, grinding inside her and not stopping even as she had begged him; flashes of Schaffer's tattoos, KS.4Ever, inked to commemorate their friendship, Schaffer tethering his hair into a ponytail, out of his way so that he could rape her, his beautiful mane Kaylen had brushed hundreds of times, tawny strands unraveling from his scrunchie, tangling around Kaylen's blonde skeins as he impaled her.

Betrayal. Rape. Kaylen's heartache, born of her friends' betrayal, manifested as marathon vomiting, corkscrewing her guts, her raw throat slimy with foul bitterness as she convulsed over her toilet, the bowl swimming with tissuey chunks, bile, and mysterious stuff—things from her body, her life spilling out of her, her life's blood.

Women had to be the ones to bleed. It came every month, and for what? Parturition. For them to make little boys. Boys who would grow up and become men and would do to other women what her friends had done to her. And then there would be more blood: a vicious cycle, men-and-blood.

Rape. Betrayal. Lane. Lane's lies. An accomplice in a killing. Pretending to be someone he wasn't. His betrayal; he had called her out, made it out like she had wanted Raymo, had wished for his blackmail. Complicit, letting his cousin and friends rape her. Aiding Schaffer while he took his turn. Her best friend's betrayal, caustic as a jigger of battery acid.

"Kaylen? Listen, open up," the voice jolted her.

Her heart scampered, rancor tingling through her.

He banged on the door. "Let me in; I have to talk to you."

"We have absolutely nothing to discuss!"

"Kaylen, if you don't open the door, I'll let myself in with my key," Lane threatened.

"What do you want?!" she spat. He gaped at her in disbelief, her query hovering as he hesitated in the doorway. As Kaylen fled up the stairs, Lane blocked her path and gently touched her cheek, prompting an urge to slap him. However, the pained, remorseful, or bewildered expression on his face stayed her hand.

Kaylen noticed Lane's expression had changed suddenly. He seemed shocked, as if doused in cold water. She realized that he was taking in her appearance: her matted hair, brittle skin, cracked lips, and broken veins across her forehead. His eyes widened as he looked at her sunken and bloodshot eyes.

She vibrated with contempt, dark smudges beneath those fierce eyes—like a football player in eye black, suited up for a game that she couldn't win.

Lane's belly lurched. Where she had been held down, the bruises. Ringing Kaylen's wrists and forearms like indigo-colored bangles. Further evidence of the men's buffet, her cheekbone, and eye were stained eggplant and puce. The other cheek contused a nasty olive and plum.

"Kaylen, you look terrible."

"Oh, I must apologize for my appearance. Don't you like this look? So beaten down and bruised up, don't you know? It's so rape chic." She sank onto the couch, resigned he was not going to leave until he had his say.

"You lost this when... the other night." Lane dropped the object in her lap.

She dangled the broken chain between her fingers. Irony intersecting with atrocity. In two weeks, it would be Christmas. Her friends had given her that necklace last Christmas, a million years ago. "Something to remember them by, huh?"

"Kaylen, please. I'm—"

"—I don't want this!" She flung it in his face.

He winced, pocketing it. "Listen, Luke wants me to tell you something."

Her burst of laughter, rattling him. "Is he sorry he didn't take his turn the other night, or then perhaps the first time was enough for him, right?"

"He says he still cares for you."

Her stomach curdled, beyond dismayed at Luke's confession. "Oh, does he? Of course, see how he shows me? He hits me; he stands by and lets his cousin and friends rape me! You Vincuzzi boys, how you love to watch."

Lane grimaced, agonized when Kaylen added: "Well, Lane, did you get your voyeurism on? Got to see the big show with no commercial interruption, with no one stopping the fun, with no one—and I mean, *no one* was putting an end to it!"

"Kaylen, I couldn't stop them all!"

"You didn't stop any of them!"

"I tried. I couldn't; they wouldn't let me!"

"You led the lamb to the slaughter, Lane!"

"I didn't know that they were going to do *that*. I swear to you. I am so sorry!"

"Lane, you showed me who you were. You were a Vincuzzi through and through."

"No! I'm not like Luke. I'm not like Raymo."

"No? No, you're much, much worse."

"Please try to understand."

"Oh, I understand. You deceived me, betrayed me! I trusted you. And you lied to me—you turned on me!"

"No, maybe if I explain—"

"—Lane! *What is wrong with you?* After what's happened, we are *never* gonna be the same with each other again! What we had, that friendship? It's gone! *For good. Forever.*"

Lane waxen with grief, the finality more than he could bear. "There's still so much that you don't know. Things that you don't understand."

"Then perhaps it's time for you to be straight with me. After all, haven't your secrets cost us enough?"

"I'll tell you, all of it. It's true what Raymo said. *I was* involved with an older married woman. But I want to explain what happened—how it happened. The people who owned your house? Eric Tompson and his wife? Tompson was a politician, a busy man, and away a lot. He asked if any of us guys would want to help out around his place, earn a few extra bucks, so I said sure. Mrs. Tompson would have me mow, rake, whatever chores needed to get done. Sometimes she'd come outside and sunbathe or swim. She'd bring out a pitcher of sweet tea, would offer me a glass. She was older than me, but in her 20s, young enough we could relate to each other, and we'd talk about television shows, music, the news. It was all innocent at first—the talking, the interest in the same things. But soon, she was inviting me over to listen to The Beach Boys or Marvin Gaye instead of working in the yard. And then... I don't know; it just happened. She seduced me."

"Like in *The Graduate*?"

"Except this wasn't a book, or a movie, or fiction. It really happened."

"You were the Benjamin to her Mrs. Robinson."

"Yes. Exactly. Except, unlike the character Benjamin, I was underage. Considerably."

"Then she took advantage of you! She was an adult. She preyed on you."

"No. Maybe. Yes, from a legal stance. But I wanted her to. It didn't matter that she was an adult and I was a kid; it didn't matter to me that she was married. I didn't care, even though I knew right from wrong. When you mix adolescent lust, opportunity, temptation, attraction... well, there was no fighting it. You understand, don't you, Kaylen? It's like what happened between you and Raymo at the beginning of your relationship. When I saw that electricity between the two of you, I knew, I understood how it was impossible to fight it—even when it's completely wrong. Even when you know, there will be consequences."

Kaylen, stone-faced, waited for him to proceed. "Our affair went on all summer. I continued doing chores for her because it made a good cover story. No one suspected a thing. After all, she was a 22-year-old woman, and I was just a kid, a good kid who never got into trouble. Then that August, right after I had turned 13, she told me she was pregnant, and it was mine. She wanted to keep it! She said her husband couldn't have children, and she wanted a family. They'd been married about five years, and she was much younger—a May-December relationship. *We* had a May-December relationship! She had lied to me, said she went on the Pill. I panicked! Despite her originally initiating it and me giving in to it, I never meant for any of it to happen."

"I asked her what was going to happen when her husband found out. What would he think when he knew it couldn't be his. She told me she'd wait until her pregnancy had progressed, and he couldn't do anything about it. I asked her who she was going to say was the father. She wouldn't answer me! We argued, and she said that if I didn't leave her alone, she'd tell her husband that I had attacked her and threatened her life if she told. I pleaded with her, pointed out what would happen to her marriage, to my future, but she didn't care. She told me she had gotten what she wanted from me—the eager sperm donor she hoped I would be. I knew then that I had been targeted, groomed—manipulated, and used. I wasn't just heartbroken and duped; I was scared! It was all in jeopardy—my future, their marriage, her husband's career. I thought about the publicity, the legal system, jail time, the humiliation. I didn't know what to do! So I told Luke. My older brother would have the answers. Raymo was here for the summer, so of course, Luke told him and Tony, Schaffer, and Bran. They told me to do whatever they said to do, and I was too terrified to question them. I never dreamed that... it would go to the extreme that it did."

"That weekend, Mr. Tompson left. All of us went over there to see Mrs. Tompson—Tammy. Raymo and Luke told her that they knew about what had happened and what she planned to do. They told her she had to get rid of the baby. She said a bunch of nosy teenagers wasn't going to tell her what to do. She yelled for us to get out of her house, or she'd call the police. She told us she'd say that I had assaulted her. Luke argued that no one was going to make false accusations about his family. She laughed at us, and Raymo *lost it*! He said he didn't like it when someone wouldn't take him seriously and do what he told them. He told her—told us—that she'd have to pay. And so we made her."

"How Lane? Like they made *me* pay?"

"No. But just as brutal. They told Tammy that she was the one who had started the relationship with me—knowingly with a minor—and had gotten pregnant on purpose. That if anyone were going to go to authorities, it would be *us* reporting *her*. If she didn't want that to happen, she had no choice but to get rid of that baby. Had to. And then they made sure that she wouldn't have it." Lane choked on the words.

"Raymo and Luke grabbed Tammy, and Tony started punching her in the stomach! I was crying, yelling, begging for them to *stop*! But they *wouldn't*! She was screaming so loud! Bran took Schaffer's bandana and stuffed it in her mouth. She started gagging, but Tony kept on hitting her! Then Schaffer asked: 'how do we even know that this is gonna work?' and Raymo said: 'then we'll make sure.' And he and Tony pulled Tammy's shorts off."

"So they did do to her what they did to me!"

"No. To make sure that she wouldn't have the baby. To end the pregnancy."

"I don't understand. How?"

"They gave her an abortion." His voice faint, Kaylen certain she must have heard him wrong.

"What? No! But... how...?"

"They gave her an abortion! They saw Tammy's knitting needles. Do you understand, Kaylen? They held her down and took the needle and—"

"—No! No. I don't believe it! It's a myth that stuff like knitting needles and clothes hangers induces an abortion."

"It was no myth, Kaylen! This is *true*—all of it. In the old neighborhood, rumors that girls in trouble would use hangers, needles, and scissors to get it done. Abortion is illegal, and even if you did find someone who could do it—a real doctor willing to take the risk—it would cost. The guys thought they knew what they were doing. But then Tammy started hemorrhaging all over the place! Maybe because of Tony hitting her, or her jerking around, or Raymo perforating something...I don't know. But she was gushing blood, and it wouldn't *stop*! Schaffer said Greg could help her; he'd had paramedic training. We could hurry and take Tammy to him. But... I... I..."

"—wouldn't let them." Kaylen's heart was hammering, her stomach recoiling as she realized the truth.

Tears streamed down Lane's face. "Schaffer picked Tammy up, but *I* pushed her back down; *I* kept him from moving her! I told him—I told them—no. I told them not to stop the bleeding. I told them to let her go. Let her die."

When Kaylen emitted a noise, of protest, of disgust, Lane cried: "Don't you see? Because if she had lived, she would have told! I couldn't take that chance. It was the only solution."

"Yeah, well, we all know about the Vincuzzi men and their solutions. The extent that they'll resort to. Then what happened? She eventually bled to death?"

Lane nodded, his head drooping in guilt, shame, pain, regret.

Men-and-blood. Yes, Kaylen had been right.

"Raymo and Tony took Tammy's body away. Bran and Luke put everything back to order as if there had never been a struggle. Schaffer and I cleaned up the blood—*so much blood!* When Mr. Tompson returned, he told the police his wife was gone, maybe even kidnapped. They kept waiting for a ransom note. The police combed the woods, talked to campers and locals. When the cops came around digging for information, Raymo and Luke had coached me on what to say. I told the police that I hadn't seen, hadn't talked to Tammy in weeks. Other people told them the same thing."

"The cops thought that we were innocent. No one knew about Tammy and me. There was no definitive evidence. Mr. Tompson acknowledged that he and his wife had been having problems. That put him under suspicion—especially when they found out he had a girlfriend on the side—and she had unsavory relatives—ones who had spent time in jail for robbery, kidnapping, assault, and other theft. They learned that Tompson had taken out a huge insurance policy on his wife, and the girlfriend had been telling people that she wanted Tammy gone so she could be the next Mrs. Tompson. This kept the heat off us and on Eric Tompson and his mistress. Everything racked up sketchy for Tompson. The police vetted many angles: that maybe Tammy was in cahoots with her husband to collect on the policy and had faked her disappearance. Or maybe it was all a huge publicity stunt; perhaps it had been one of Tompson's political enemies intent on ruining his career, maybe Tompson's girlfriend had gotten rid of Tammy."

"Prior to going missing, Tammy withdrew ten grand from her and Tompson's joint bank account. The press, locals, and the police speculated. Rumors flew, Eric Tompson had been difficult to live with, a verbally abusive drinker and that Tammy had left him to begin a new life somewhere else. As time went on, it appeared the gossip mill might be right. Eventually, the authorities gave Tompson the green light to leave. He boarded up this house, took his girlfriend, and moved. The investigation went cold. For over five years, this house remained empty. Until you."

"Lane, the night I invited you and the others to dinner for the first time? You were nervous, but I didn't know why. Now I know it was because of what took place here."

"I liked you—loved you—right away and wanted to be friends. But having to come here for dinner that night... I didn't want to face this, this house, what had happened here. I had tried to forget it. But it can't be done with these guys always throwing it back at me."

"They wouldn't let it go."

"No, never. That's why I'm indebted to them. Don't you understand? They own me. They've expected me to pay for this all these years, but I can never pay it off! And then there's that mindset, what they perceive as being important, what is machismo. I was the first one of all the guys to lose my virginity —not Luke, Tony, or Raymo, despite that they're older. It was *me!*

You can imagine their resentment, jealousy, anger. Plus them having to get rid of Tammy—their first kill—and me causing all this, I became the target of their hostility, their blackmail."

"There's something else that happened, though. It's what it unlocked in them—especially Raymo. The thrill of having gotten away with it, the power of it. A high. A taste for blood and killing and the high of it. The high of being in control. They controlled me. Every time I'd refuse to do what the guys wanted, they'd threaten me. And then you came along. I didn't want you to hate me. Raymo got himself alibied for when all this happened with Tammy! He's got connections.

But what if he didn't do that for me? Then what would I do?"

"I can't answer that. I've been living in a house where a death occurred. But only you and the guys know about it."

"Right."

"I don't believe in ghosts. But there's some strange mojo here. Maybe that's why I began to have nightmares. Maybe that's why the nightmares came true. And why didn't our realtor mention all this about Tammy missing? That that was the reason, the house had been vacant for so long."

"Obviously, because the realtor wanted the sale! I mean, this house was for sale off and on for years, with no takers."

"Believe me, my dad and I puzzled that; a prime lakefront property, and it sat empty all that time? Of course, the house did have erosion and needed repairs and extensive cleaning, but still."

"Well, most people around here said it was an undertaking they didn't want to fool with. Tompson had asked full dollar at one time, but no one would pay that for what might have been a money pit. So they dropped the price when you and your dad came along. The realtor wouldn't have mentioned the story because most people around here speculated Tammy left on her own accord," Lane said.

"I gotta know—what room did it happen in?"

"Where Tammy died?"

"Where y'all *killed* her at!"

Lane's pained sigh, stung by Kaylen's revulsion. "Tammy crafted, you know, sewing and scrapbooking? She stored her things in this little room, off from the kitchen. The day we confronted her? She took us in there even though we had to cram in. Like we weren't good enough to be in her living room. She wasn't pleased to see me—see us. We had interrupted her; she had been knitting. She was getting stuff ready for a baby."

"The day before Eric Tompson reported Tammy missing, a storm blew through. An oak tree went down and collapsed the back room—the craft room. Tompson didn't bother restoring it. Instead, he had it demolished and walled up the back. It was like that room had never been there, had never existed."

"How convenient. No pesky crime scene left behind, huh? But it's a lot harder, though, to get rid of a person. So *where is she*, Lane? What did they do with the body?"

"I don't know. I swear to you. The guys said it was for my own good not to know those details. But I wondered: Did they throw her in the swamp, or bury her? I always suspected they took her to the back part of the campground, way past our shooting range, far in the deep woods. But the thing is, I know Tammy is not the only one they've taken out there."

Reeling from the shock of the past few days, Kaylen assumed this was where the men collared the two burglars.

"I had nothing to do with it. But I had to go along with it because of what they knew about me. Don't you get it? Raymo's gone beyond being a neighborhood bully; he's on edge, and when crossed, will get rid of a problem—that person, anyway he can."

"A few people who he had to teach a lesson?"

"Yeah."

"And everyone went along with it, just like that?" Kaylen considered easy-going Schaffer, vehemently against violence, the war in Vietnam, who opted for peace rather than strife. A guy who'd fish and hunt deer for food, but not for sport. And yet, he raped Kaylen.

"I don't have to tell you about Raymo's influence, his charisma, his talent of manipulating. And with what happened with Tammy? Well, there was no turning back. What it unhinged—for Raymo and Tony, guys who don't have a problem using violence. Raymo already had connections and getting deeper into things he shouldn't be in, with people he shouldn't be with, and it rubbed off on all of us."

"Like selling drugs?"

"Yes. More and more to cover up."

"Yet this thing with Tammy. You did that all on your own, didn't you, Lane?"

"No. Yes. I cared for her. Puppy love. Teen lust. I couldn't help myself."

"You can't help a lot of things, Lane. You couldn't help yourself, or Tammy, or me."

"I'm so sorry!"

"Your platitudes leave me cold, Lane. They're empty, as hollow as I am right now."

"You should know; Raymo said he expects to have your loyalty."

"In other words, don't go to the police."

"Exactly."

"Lane, I swear to you I won't go to the authorities. But I won't, I can't stay here. When my dad gets back, I will tell him I want to go with him on his next business trip. He won't be suspicious, maybe inquisitive, but I'll figure out an explanation."

"Luke and Raymo aren't gonna let you leave like that."

"If they wanted to prevent me from opening my mouth about everything, they've succeeded. To hit someone, to rape someone you claim to love..." the sob burst. "They knew by making it happen; I wouldn't tell—their code of silence. But if they want me to stay, then they'll have to plant me out there in the woods with the others. But, hey, maybe they will, right?"

"Don't kid like that, Kaylen. Don't push this."

"Or what, Lane? Will they do something *else* to me? What else can they do to me? They've destroyed me! I'm dead inside."

Lane wrung his hands, his two front teeth scrapping along his bottom lip.

"That's it then? So you've told me everything?"

He nodded at the lie. He intended to tell her. But now... not after discharging the bomb about Tammy. Overload. Shock. She'd modeled her tough act, but the pear-hued patina of Kaylen's skin exposed her butterfly-like fragility.

Raymo's news might push her over the precipice. Lane recently found out and was shaken to his core. Later. In a few days, after she'd processed her ordeal and the details of Lane's past.

"Then I want you to go—I want you out of my sight."

"Please don't make me leave," he implored, tears tumbling. "You're my best friend."

"*Was*," she corrected, envenoming.

"Please. I need you!"

"*Need me?* Lane, you have what you need, what you've always needed! *Them.* You have them—your little camarilla. Get out of my life! And don't come back. *Ever.*"

Then how would she ever know about what Raymo had revealed to him and the guys? Lane wavered—should I tell her right now? Should I tell her at all? Yes, but he'd have to convince her to see him again in a few days—when she could take it. She deserved to know.

"Lane? Did you hear me?"

"I don't want to go. I don't want our friendship to end."

"Well, we don't want a lot of things, but they happen. So it didn't exactly make my day to be raped by my friends, to find out my best friend is a murderer."

"What should I tell Luke and Raymo?"

"Tell them? What can you say to someone who could kill and rape and think it's justified? They're sick in the head.

You're all sick in the head. And I'm no better off being with y'all."

"They won't let this go."

"They have to. Because it is over. I'm done with them. And I'm done with you. *Now get up and get out.*"

He wiped his tears with the back of his hand, lumbering at the back door.

"Lane?"

"Yeah?" he about-faced, hopeful.

But Kaylen peered in the direction of the lake and away from him. "I wish you good things in your life. Only the good things."

"Me too. I wish you only the good things."

Ambivalence for her former best friend permeated her being. Her joints were aching with sadness, sympathy, apathy, disgust, love, abhorrence, and calcifying her soul. Luke's words were floating back to her from a time past: *There's a fine line between love and hate. And it forces you to make choices.* He'd reasoned that one of those sentiments will always win out over the other. Sometimes it just wasn't the one you expected.

"Good-bye, Kay," Lane whispered, the only time since he had known her to call her 'Kay' instead of 'Kaylen.' No one except Luke and Raymo referred to her as 'Kay.' Fitting that Lane had called her 'Kay'; he had metamorphosed into his brother and cousin.

She studied him as he stepped into the canoe. With his fear of the water, he was steeling himself. Today though, he'd submitted, revealing the truth to Kaylen—owning up to his actions. So why hadn't he take up for her in the first place? Prevented his friends and cousin from barbarizing her? She shut down the outside lights as Lane paddled away, fading against the dusking skies. Her shoulders quavering, sorrow rumbling her body, for Tammy, for the severance of a friendship, for the end of innocence of a girl named Kaylen.

* * *

He idled in the woods, ensconced behind a thicket of oaks and Spanish moss—frowsy as an old hillbilly's beard. His identity safe in the cover of darkness, he nursed his idée fixe, staring up at Kaylen's house.

He rubbed his chin, noting Lane's departure. He would hunker at his coign of vantage until the black skies ushered in the night and Kaylen peacefully slumbering. Playing the waiting game. Required patience, persistence, focus. Easy to do if he pictured the prize within reach.

He had tasted her, still craved her, like she was an exotic food. He had slid between her thighs and had to have her again. He burned for her and couldn't think of anything else. He coveted the heat of her body, her silky hair, her scent—like honeysuckle on a warm day; the lake at dawn when the mist curled up, fresh as linen. Her fragrance, like candy apples at a carnival, would linger on his skin long after she had left him, respiring it deep into his lungs, a breath of her vital as oxygen. He needed her. Like an organ. Like blood pumping in his veins.

She had not paid enough. Debts were meant to be paid high, paid until you bled dry. Bloodletting in the works, he'd see to that. She wasn't getting away with snubbing him, avoiding him, or escaping.

A cigarette gripped in his teeth; he cupped his hand over the flame, a buckler against the cold gale kicking up and Kaylen's eagle eyes. The gray plume levitated above the branches like a playful ghost. Then, eyes shining, he contemplated his next move, smoking, smiling.

CHAPTER TWENTY-SIX

K aylen jerked upright in her bed, her heart fibrillating. The nightmares had plagued her for months. But these dreams were dark figures with names—Tony, Bran, Schaffer. Shadowy stalkers, their bodies and faces were meshing into one as they took their turn between her legs and holding her down. The cold black eyes? Not the boogeyman or a Manson, but Raymo, possessing her like an incubus, smirking over his shoulder while Luke gawked.

The slip into REM lasted minutes—not the hours of sleep she required. She felt drained, Lane's revelation wiping her out, shoving her down deeper into a vortex of depression. The soul-crushing rape and betrayal had robbed Kaylen of all rest. A line from a John Donne poem tickled her memory—*sleep is pain's easiest salve*, and she willed it to come true. But, unfortunately, she didn't find its consolation at her couch, tossing and weeping there, a ratty robe adhering to her like an old Band-Aid she hadn't the nerve to rip from her flesh.

She couldn't recall her last meal but had downed every bottle of booze in the house. She longed for some of Schaffer's drugs to knock her out. She scavenged her sofa, trawling her bitten-down-to-the-quick nails across the seams and flipping cushions, hoping for a wayward pill, maybe a benzo or a Quaalude. Finally, she ceded the quest, vacating her post. She'd kept vigil from her couch, sentineling the house until her father's homecoming. Tonight though, she succumbed to her exhaustion, retreating from the sage green Kroehler to her cozy cashmere duveted double bed.

It wasn't a nightmare that roused her. Instead, the air changed—the oxygen sucked out of the room.

Her vertebrate tingled with the warning—someone was in the house. Inaudible, invisible, but the sentience pervaded, mightier than sight or sound, revving her heartbeat.

She had locked the doors. Six people besides herself had a key—and the one who didn't would find a way. She trembled, straining her ears, measuring time by the call of a mockingbird in the night; its chirps and trills meted out in melodic intervals. Days ago, a passing thought to contact a locksmith, but clarity to expedite it lost in her misery and alcohol-induced haze.

The unmistakable groan of the third step on the staircase, complaining like an arthritic old man. Relief swelled in Kaylen's chest. "Daddy?" She startled; her voice a whipcrack against the silence. Her father's two-pack-a-day baritone didn't respond. Instead, the external harmonics wafted into the house like smoke: the branches of a weeping willow tickling a windowpane; a bullfrog's Model T honk in the distance.

Barred doors couldn't forfend the men—nothing was going to stop them. She shivered inside her covers.

Closer. The rustling of feet. Their footsteps unhurried in the hallway they'd traversed countless times. The air frizzled, electrified as a power line—like when Kaylen was near *him*.

Her head zizzed like swarming locusts. She breathed *him* in, his raw scent—tobacco, vetiver, thunderstorms on a sizzling summer night. Familiar to her as her own name. She clapped her palm to her mouth to stifle the scream.

Excitement for Kaylen tattooed the man's heart. He wondered if she realized how close he was to catching her. The idea of ravishing her, biting her neck and shoulders until they welted, and riving her breasts intensified his longing. He was determined to make her pay.

Kaylen's brain clicked, the instinct of survival, flight-or-fight, fumbling for the telephone on her nightstand. She tried to call the police. No dial tone! She gasped, the receiver spilling from her trembling hand. *I have to get out.* No way to exit except through her bedroom door. The same one *he* was creeping toward.

Sinking to her knees, the immutable truth dawned: there was no place to hide that he wouldn't find her. If she could get to the panic room, she could lock herself in.

But then what? He'd trip it, trapping her. Inside the closet with him like Before. When he had done those things to her— and she let him. Now he would do to her what he wanted to, much more than when they steamed up that closet during Eight Minutes. He would do to her what he had done at the cabin the other night—that which she didn't want, powerless to prevent. But tonight, no one would hold her down for him: this time, his sole self and own brute force.

The room tilted. Her hand lunged across the shag carpet, keeling. Icy metal grazed her fingers, reviving her, jogging her memory about the stow. She yanked the gun from under her bed, cradling it in her lap like a colicky infant.

She levered up from the floor. She decided to stay put, to ignore the light switch on the opposite wall. She was waiting in the darkness for him. The same way he had entered her house —in pitch black, his aphotic eyes gleaming with blood lust, his dark mind and heart heaving with evil intent.

The gun felt slippery against her sweaty hands. She heard his body brush against the wall with a whoosh, like a whisper in the wind. It sounded to Kaylen like he was breathing her name. *Kay. Kay. Kay. Kay.*

The doorknob rattled. "I know who you are! I have a gun," she warned him.

"Liar!" he stage-whispered in a muffled voice. Everyone knew she kept her guns secured in the gun case downstairs. He knew it was locked up tight. He had checked.

Kaylen heard the bedroom door creak slowly, like a sound effect from a scary movie. It was the ominous lead-in to a night of terror he planned to inflict on her. His bulk blocked the doorway, leaving no chance of escape. She could imagine the grin on his face, and knew he was ready to make her submit. He would have her again, and this time he might do what he didn't get the chance to do before. They had all night.

Kaylen wasn't afraid of the dark, of staying alone in this house. That confidence had always excused her need for a nightlight or latching her bedroom door. But she underestimated the men's desire to possess her. She'd rationalized that once their assault complete, their lesson taught and finished with her. The assumption was both erroneous and grave. She had failed to see the magnitude of *his* obsession with her, his sadism, his depravity. She hadn't understood that *he* was not going to stop, not going to end his pursuit of her. The patency of truth reared, bone-chilling as liquid nitrogen, glaring as 1000 lumens.

"I'm telling you not to come any closer. I have a gun, and I will use it." Cold fear snatched back, replaced by searing fury. Blinding red rage spangled behind her eyeballs, for the degeneracy her friends had committed, the degradation, violating humiliation, and pain she had endured. Adrenaline and white-hot rage pumped through her. They had held her down and subjected her to the unthinkable. But now, *she* was in control.

He snailed forward. Kaylen's antennae whiffled, her skin prickling, inhaling him, the taste of him at the back of her throat—tannic and sweet as blackcurrants, the air briny with threat and perspiration. Her mind raced: What did he bring with him? Just himself, pure physical strength? Or implements to help him get the job done—duct tape, rope, instruments of torture? Maybe a combat knife, jagged-toothed as a sharks' mouth, or a Bowie, beveled for butchering, slitting flesh with precision, warm against his palm, fitting it snuggly into the hollow of her throat. Maybe he'd rake her neck, as she had his. A matching pair they'd be. Perhaps he'd shove his mistress in her face, the Magnum his other obsession besides Kaylen. Well, she could level the playing field right now, her own gun nestled in her hands. The weapon, her gift from her friends. He'd taught her to shoot. Shoot expertly. She'd cached the gun under her bed—loaded and ready. Ever since the rape. Ever since the betrayal. Rape. Betrayal.

She lied in wait, catlike, with the vision of a feline, able to track in the dark, her pupils dilated. Sweat and fear had cooled against her skin, her clothes clinging, a damp, vinegary fetor. Something she had to do. The gun didn't feel heavy. It felt right and ready in her hands. Never again, she raged. Rape. Betrayal.

Someone would pay tonight. It wouldn't be her body taking the abuse, ripped and raw as he had tamped himself inside her. Never again. Rape. Betrayal.

He tucked in and didn't lurch at her.

Kaylen didn't think beyond what was going to happen next. After. After she did it. All she could think of was what had happened. Before. Never again. Rape. Betrayal.

Kaylen felt him in front of her. She imagined his mouth twisted with lust and obsession, deciding how to take her, slowly, savoring every inch of her body, or head-on. He had mentioned not knowing which was better—her eyes aquamarine, the color of fear, or an angry dark blue. But Kaylen felt like a loaded gun, her eyes radiating like a polished weapon in fire blue. She knew what he wanted and had told her so, but he would not get it. He would never plunder every cranny of her body as desired—her mouth, between her thighs, her backside. He skulked towards her. Never again. Rape. Betrayal.

Her mind meted out the order. A ticking. Like a heartbeat. Her heart was careering, thundering. A bounding pulse rumbled her chest, a binary beat to a cacoethes amplified and unable to be ignored. Time tapping like a palpitation, a metronomic urging of *Now. Now. Now. Now.*

Never again. Rape. Betrayal. She released the gun's safety —a muted ping against the muzzled darkness.

Kaylen imagined his smile fading when he heard the sound. It was all too familiar, but would it register with him? But she knew he knew when he shifted in the dark and sensed he was backing out of the room. But he was too late.

She raised the barrel, whether by rote or proprioception and unhindered by the darkness, she drew a bead on him, to the place where it would hurt him the most. He'd be unable to use it again. Not on her. Not on any girl. Rape. Betrayal.

She squeezed the trigger, the silence shatters. Crying out, collapsing against the bed as if she'd gotten shot. A second explosion, the weapon sent clattering against the footboard. Her heart was banging like a trapped bird in a small cage. Her ears knelling, deafened. The explanation to why she hadn't heard him. Surely he had made a noise, had screamed, just as she did when he had raped her. She fumbled for the light, the switch plate wet and sticky.

His body slumped across the carpet, its fibers seeping crimson. The target hit, a meaty blowout between his thighs. A chunk of cold gold glinting. His name etched on the band, dangling from his limp wrist.

It was bubbling up slowly from her lungs, the scream rising to a crescendo. The strangled cry reminiscent of one she bellowed the night the men had raped her, much like an animal sprung in a steel-jaw trap, of an amputation sans anesthesia. Her wailing reverberated across the water and woods, haunting the lake forever.

She screamed and screamed until her raw vocal cords seized, the ululation only extinguished when she surrendered to a dead faint, and her body crumbling into the intruder's pooling blood.

CHAPTER TWENTY-SEVEN

Police car lights flared across Kaylen's lawn like Kodak flashcubes. The patrol vehicle's gumball's bounced scarlet over the mirrored lake; other's with their red and blues atop cream sedans resembled Bomb Pops melting over the roof. The night—nature had been smitten quiet as if the creatures of the woods signaled to keep their silence. Like it was a secret.

"Joe?"

"Yeah, what's up?"

"He's a goner."

The investigator sighed, the injustice of a young life lost. "Okay, well, now we get on it." The first responders had accessed the scene, radioing for detectives. First, Mac arrived. Then, his partner Joe soon after, the first phase of their formal investigation activated.

"Blood and brains all over the place," Mac relayed matter-of-factly. "I did the walk-through. I got the crime techs processing everything. The M.E. is on the way. That first shot did in the guy. Blasted his testicles right off."

Joe clucked, male sympathy.

"Yeah. But she knew what she was doing, even if she doesn't remember firing off the second round. According to her, it was all done in the dark. Unfortunately, she's got great aim." A seasoned cop. He and Mac worked homicide together for more than a decade. Joe spent most of his years as a Dade County investigator. Two thousand square miles of paradise but far from it with its crime, killings, and corruption. In his last promotion, he transferred to central Florida. The area was more laid-back than Miami but not lacking in murder and mayhem.

"Detective?" the policeman approached the pair.

"Yes?" both men answered in unison, equally ranked.

"You go, Joe. I'm going to check on the girl again. I left her with one of the uniforms. She was hysterical when I tried to talk to her before, rambling about bodies being buried all over the place and dark figures holding her down."

"We need a psych evaluation?"

"Maybe. Let me see what I can get out of her," Mac said.

"Detective? See those men over there? They work at the campground across the lake. They're the ones who reported the incident."

"What did they have to say?" Joe asked the officer.

"One of them, Mr. Lane Vincuzzi, was walking around the water. Thought the shots might be hunters but then heard the screams coming from Kaylen Sadler's house."

"Did he tell you why he was wandering around this time of night?"

"He's a little vague about that, sir. I think he's in shock—he's close to the female shooter; says he's a relative of the victim."

"Okay, thanks, officer." Joe lumbered down the embankment to the water's edge. "Which one of you is Lane Vincuzzi?"

"I am." Soft-toned, a chalky-faced man with penetrating blue eyes.

"You called it in?"

He nodded, staring up at the house, the gravelly police radio fading in and out.

"Wanna tell me about it?"

"Could you do this later?" barked a jumbo-sized man. "We're all a little shaken up right now, *capisce?* Anyway, we were already questioned."

"By a policeman. I'm homicide. I'll be taking your statements. Mister...?"

"Mancuso. Tony Mancuso."

"You're the victim's family?"

"No. They are." Tony jerked his head at two of the men standing in the circle.

"Mr. Vincuzzi?" Joe addressed Lane. "The relative?"

"He is... he was my older brother."

"I'm sorry for your loss." Joe jotted in his notepad, addressing the man at Lane's elbow. "Sir? You're related to the deceased?"

"He's not the 'deceased,' he is my family. *Dargli il rispetto* (give him respect). Got it, gumshoe? I'm Raymo Vincuzzi. Luke is my cousin."

"*Was* your cousin. He's dead, Raymo! Remember? I found him."

Raymo fell silent. For the first time in his life, he felt sorry for his cousin. Lane erupted, weeping. For once, no one called him a baby.

Joe allowed him to regain his composure, trudging back to the house. The men garrisoned along the shore, chain-smoking, monitoring the activity at Kaylen's home.

"They're bringing him out," Tony blurted, Luke's body wheeled across the front porch.

The other men barreled up the embankment.

"Whoa there." Mac blocked their way.

"I wanna see him!" Bran cried.

The Mancuso brothers and Raymo hadn't seen the crime scene. Lane rushed in after hearing the screams, discovering his brother beyond help and Kaylen garbling and dazed. He pulled her from Luke's blood-soaked body. Lane snatched up the receiver, the phone line dead. He ordered Kaylen to wait at the staircase until he returned, hurrying to Tony, Schaffer, and Bran's house, relaying the tragedy, and contacting the authorities. Schaffer and Bran sped to Raymo's cabin to break the horrible news. Lane and Tony dashed back to Kaylen's house, Tony confronting Kaylen, catatonic, and posed like a mannequin at the top of the stairs.

Tony shoved the unresponsive woman out of the way, bolting into the bedroom despite Lane yelling for him not to enter. Tough-guy Tony—who had committed the worst of atrocities—was unable to handle the sight of his best friend's skull blown away. He then bulldozed past Lane and Kaylen, fleeing from the house in time to throw up outside, the police arriving seconds later.

"You don't want to see him like that. Remember him like he was. Believe me; she iced him." Tony grasped Bran's shoulder. Schaffer blanched, overtaken by emotion as they carted Luke away, body-bagged for the morgue.

Kaylen, handcuffed and led from the house. Her face, pale as a bone. Her clothes, sopping with Luke's blood, an incendiary for Raymo's fury. "You, *puttana*! You killed him."

"No. No. No!"

"You did! But it was the *wrong one*, wasn't it? The wrong Vincuzzi." His tone cold, knowing, taunting.

"I didn't know it was Luke! I was trying to keep it from ever happening *again*." Kaylen, quavering as the officer steered her toward his police car.

"Were your parents notified yet?" Joe addressing Lane, having learned Kaylen and the men were employed by Lane's folks at the campground across the lake.

"No. Oh, no! They think we're here because someone broke into Kaylen's house. They don't know yet!"

"I'll tell them, Lane. I'm the oldest. It'll come from me," Raymo said.

"Any of you know what went on in there tonight?" Joe asked, the men shaking their heads. "No? We'll be calling each one of you down for an interview, so stick close by, okay?"

"We have a funeral to plan. I think we'll be around," Raymo sneered.

"Of course. After your cousin has been autopsied," the detective said.

Lane winced, but Raymo's icy black glower unyielding.

"One more thing. Kaylen Sadler told my partner a bunch of men raped her. Her *friends*. Who could that be?" Joe asked them.

"She's a nutcase. We don't know anything," Raymo said.

"What about Kaylen being pounded on? Her black eye. Her bruised cheekbones and wrists. Her split lip. Who did that to her?"

"Got no idea." Tony said.

"That'll be all. For now." Joe shut his notepad. *Liars.*

Luke's body, loaded into the vehicle, the men rooted as the taillights faded.

Kaylen blank-stared after it. When the familiar Cadillac came roaring up behind one of the police cruisers, she came to life. *"Daaaaddddyy!"*

Ross Sadler bounded from the car, his sugar-colored face twisted. "Kaylen! What's going on here? What happened?!"

"Mr. Sadler?"

"Yes! What's happening? Who beat her like that? Why's my daughter in handcuffs?!"

"Your precious daughter wasted my cousin!" Raymo yelled.

"What is he talking about?" Ross demanded.

Mac pointed at Raymo. "You'll get plenty of time to talk, Mr. Vincuzzi. So please don't speak unless we ask you."

"Or you'll do what?" Raymo challenged.

"Well, we can start with finding you a jail cell for the night. You know, interfering with an ongoing investigation?"

Tony leaned into him, whispering, Raymo's tense jaw relaxing. "He'll be cool."

"Good." When a murder occurred and family members and friends were on the scene, emotions ran high. But Mac noted the mercurial vibe emanating from the dark-haired pair, the type who switched off and on, who might not give a second thought to hitting and raping.

"Mr. Sadler, your daughter is under arrest for the shooting death of Luciano Vincuzzi," Mac informed him.

"No! No, she wouldn't have done that! It's her boyfriend! And she's responsible with her guns. So it had to be an accident. I don't understand!"

"Daddy, I had to, don't you see? I couldn't let it happen again! I thought *he* was coming to rape me again! *My friends raped me!*"

Ross's face contorted. "What is she talking about? What did you do to her?!" His eyes were blazing, fists clenched when he beetled toward the men, the air crepitating as Joe inserted his body, the break stick between snarling canines.

"Your daughter the killer, is a liar and a whore," Raymo said. "Everything was consensual."

"Consensual," Tony echoed.

"We're gonna get to the bottom of this," Joe assured the quaking father.

"But you're charging her?"

"Yes."

"But can Kaylen get out on bail? Bond? I don't know which is what."

"Mr. Sadler, being released depends on the charges, whether it's a first or second degree offense, premeditated, voluntary." It was murder, so Joe imagined Kaylen wouldn't be getting out.

"The charges. When will they do that? Who decides?" Ross asked.

"At the arraignment. By the judge," the detective explained.

"Can I ride with her?" Ross begged.

Joe, reflexive, genuine sympathy for Kaylen's dad, his mouth twitching, his hands trembling. "No, you can't ride with her, Mr. Sadler. But you can follow me to where we'll take her."

"It's okay, Kitten." Ross was grappling to hold his shock in check—the blood splattered across Kaylen's face and arms, her eyelid dark as acai berries, her contused green cheekbone. "It's gonna be okay."

"It will *never* be okay! *I* will never be okay again. They raped me! But I didn't know it was Luke tonight; I thought it was *him*!" Kaylen's mind splintered with the thought: Luke and Raymo were so alike in their gait, voice, and presence, but their auras were completely different. *How could she have mistaken that? How could she have gotten it wrong?!*

"But it wasn't 'him,' was it?" Raymo said. "'Him' being me. So the bullet was for me, huh? The one you wanted to be with. But now I see how it is, how you decided to take me out. But it ended up being Luke instead."

"You knew he would come here! What did you say to him to make him come?"

"You psycho *puttana!* I would have never sent my cousin into the firing zone!"

"Luke! Luke! I'm sorry, sorry!" Kaylen wailed.

"Get her in the car," Mac instructed the policeman.

Inside the cage, Kaylen, a wild-eyed, cornered lioness. "Lane! You tell them I didn't know it was Luke. Tell them what Raymo did to me!"

But Lane louvered his lashes, forsaking his best friend once more.

For the second time in Lane's life, he was responsible for a death he might have prevented.

For the second time in less than a decade, the house overlooking the beautiful lake was the scene of a bloody murder.

For the second time in his life, Lane was unable to tell anybody what had happened. First, to Tammy. Then Kaylen's rape. And the secret surrounding Raymo and Luke. And now, with Luke dead and Kaylen going to jail, Lane might lose the chance ever to tell Kaylen what his cousin and brother had revealed.

"We're not through yet, Kay. You've only begun to pay," Raymo whispered, the police cruiser sidewinding into the darkness like a coldblooded canebrake.

CHAPTER TWENTY-EIGHT

JANUARY 1971

"What are y'all doing?" Bran asked, meeting his brother and cousin on the dock.

"Checking out the new people." Tony squinted over the lake, his cigarette smoke drifting in the chilly air.

Ross Sadler owned twenty acres, selling off several lots to fund Kaylen's legal fees. Her case stirred national attention, Kaylen claiming self-dense for the murder of an unarmed man. The district attorney plowed forth, hell-bent on using Kaylen as an "example" and setting a precedent to squash similar pleas. Kaylen was denied bail for the capital offense. Ross moved out of his home and hoped to sell it in the future. Police tape streeled in tatters across the portico, and the detectives had poked around several times. The Vincuzzi and Mancuso boys didn't understand why; what were they searching for? Kaylen had killed Luke, and that was that.

"So far, there's a mom and dad and some kids," Tony said. The family, not put off by the recent violence, Ross's reduced price for the lots, the selling point.

"Frick." Bran shivered, the wind slicing through him.

Most people presuppose Florida weather abounds in an infinite loop of bright balminess. In truth, the climate is unpredictable. Winter boosts 85 degree days one week, plummeting into the 30s the next. Sunny and clear flips without warning, dumping buckets. But the rawest, strangest weather occurred after Kaylen had gone to jail. Temperatures dipped into the teens; resident's faces upturned in wonderment at the flurrying snowflakes, deliquescing on their tongue like dashed dreams. A succession of unbridled storms churned, the sky blasting electrocuting lightning and touching off several fires in the woods.

Dark brumal days followed; the frost coating the forest and burned out trees, their hulled branches resembling bones, like skeletons beckoning death. After the blistering heat returned, the skies suddenly turned cold and unleashed a barrage of pelting hail and torrential rain. Floods cratered the earth, sinkholes devouring, the lake sloshing over with crawling snakes and rambling alligators. The spawning of several tornadoes wreaked havoc on the campground. Schaffer considered the threats, seeing them as symbolic of the storms in their dark, stormy lives—the long, cold, bleak days and the embittered men struggling to come to terms with Luke's death. Had Kaylen transformed too, turning as sour as vinegar?

Lane proposed it went beyond symbolic; the cause and effect, the consequential. After Raymo raped Kaylen, Lane confronted, condemned him, cursing him to burn in Hell. Instead, Hell froze over. The idiom resonated in Lane's spirit, the hyperbolic descriptor of that which is never expected to occur. Actions Lane judged he wouldn't ever eventuate had happened. When Hell Freezes over, his cousin and friends would ever rape Kaylen, or she'd fire a gun on Luke, or Lane would have helped to kill someone. But Hell did freeze, no longer incinerating but a place of burning ice. Much like

Kaylen and Raymo together, sizzling in the inceptive of their relationship, but now arctic and scorched out. Hell had frozen over, their perdition on earth. Ever since—because of—Kaylen's rape; Luke dying; Kaylen's incarceration.

"Bona fide winter weather." Tony exhaled, the cloud of cigarette smoke swept away by the cold gust.

"It feels like it'll never be warm again." Bran hugged his arms. "Like summer is dead and gone forever."

"Like Luke. Like Kaylen and us." Lane plodded across the dock, wiping his snotty nose on a wadded Kleenex, his piercing blue eyes bloodshot.

"How'd it go?" Tony asked Raymo, trailing Lane.

"The usual BS and legalities. They're going to move her trial date," Raymo said.

"Maybe when the proceedings get going, the cops will quit nosing around here. I think we're gonna get subpoenaed." Bran took a draft from Tony's cigarette, the smoke streaming from his nostrils.

"So? We don't know anything, *siamo tutti d'accordo* (do we all agree)?" Raymo said. "We play it cool, and it'll be okay."

"Yep. We stick to our script. Come out clean, like always," Tony said.

"But it's not like always. And it never will be again. *Tutto e' cambiato* (everything has changed)," Lane mumbled.

"What's with him?" Bran asked Raymo.

"Not what but who. Kaylen."

"She said she wanted to see me to be sure." Lane's throat thick with the threat of another round of tears.

"Of what?" Tony asked Lane.

"That she hated me as much as she thought she did."

The men absorbed his words, the silence swirling against the chilled sky.

"I asked to meet with Kay too," Raymo told the men. "After

she spoke to Lane. She didn't want to talk to me at all, but I told her I had something important to tell her. Luke would have wanted her to know. Like a message from the grave. Lanesy almost stroked out right there when I said it. He could have—should have told her that night he'd spilled about Tammy. But he didn't. It had to come from me instead." Raymo paused to torch a cigarette, recollecting the conversation with Kaylen at the jail just hours ago...

... "What is it you wanna tell me?" Her glower, indurate and ice, the phone at her ear and the glass partition separating them smudged with greasy fingerprints and cough spittle. Next to Raymo, Lane slumped in the chair, his shoulders sagging. Kaylen had said her piece and done with him, her dark blue irises flicking him away, insignificant as a gnat.

"You look good in anything, Kay. Even a jail jumpsuit."

"I'm sure we can find one for you too, Raymo. It's all the rage in rapist couture."

"Glad to see that being in the Big House hasn't dampened that winning wit. I could do this with you all day, but it's my understanding we're on a time crunch here. I appreciate you doing it short and sweet with Lanesy, though, so we can have longer for our visitation." Inmates authorized up to two visitors at a time, but there would be no more talk between Kaylen and Lane.

Miserable at Kaylen's rebuff, Lane had no choice but to sit and grieve the loss of his friendship while he waited for Raymo.

"Say whatever it is you're going to say so I can get back to my luxury lodgings. Cold, dry chicken-fried steak is on the menu for lunch, and I sure don't wanna miss that."

Raymo swung sideways, liberating his long legs from the cramped space. "You know, Kay, the first time I ever met you, I wanted you. I knew you were Luke's girl, but I wanted to change that. We'd shared before, but he wasn't down for it this time. Still, I predicted I could convince him. But I wondered if I could convince *you*."

The glass between them prevented Kaylen from smacking that smarmy smile right off of him.

"You weren't like the other campground groupies and skuzz. I knew I had my work cut out for me. The way you eyed me, though, the hum between us when we were near each other, how you didn't have that with my cousin. Got my wheels turning, telling myself 'we got something here.'"

"But even though I wanted you, you had this way about you, that pretty nose up in the air like you were better than me, and I'd think, this girl needs to be humbled. Made me wanna take you down a few notches."

"Like teach me a lesson?"

"Yeah. But not then. I knew it would be later." He transferred the phone from one ear to the other. "I tried to figure you out. The more time I spent around you, I saw you really were like us. Like Lane—looks good on the outside, says all the right things—but when it came down to it, a guy who did what he had to do to prevent his girlfriend from turning on him, had a bad seed inside him."

"Oh, the pot calling the kettle black!" Kaylen cried.

Lane slunk in the chair, his chin to his chest, wishing he could disappear.

"But the thing is Kay; I recognized that in *you*. It was more than your picky ways—beyond wanting things to be orderly and clean. Those are quirks—we all got them. It was like... you were wrapping yourself up in a big beautiful sweater—but if one little thread got snagged, all it would take was one tiny pull, and it'd be full of holes."

An inch from slumping out of his seat, Lane pushed his legs

under himself to prop up. His chair screeched across the hideous, scuffed baby-barf yellow terrazzo floor. A couple of inmates and their visitors hearkened at the racket—like a tabby whose tail has gotten tramped. Lane's pale cheeks tinted cerise, and several bored guards perked up. Then, when a visual sweep proved the cat cry was not someone being shanked, everyone returned to their own business.

"I started hunting for that thread, Kay. The thread that would unravel you."

"Oh, and blackmail and rape were how you were going to do it?"

"No, those were to teach you a lesson. The unraveling? You did that on your own."

"Good offense, Ray. Blame the victim."

"You are good at it, aren't you, Kay? Playing the victim—the oh-poor-me."

"That's right," she spat, leaning into the glass. "I am the victim. Not you. Not Lane. Not even Luke!"

"What about before us, huh? Before you ever came to Crystal Lake? Were you the victim then, the little girl whose family died, and daddy was never at home, and she didn't have any friends? Or was that another one of your little stories?"

"Listen, you psycho; I told y'all everything that happened to me! I wasn't playing the victim; I was a survivor."

Raymo nestled the phone between his ear and shoulder, freeing up his hands. "Bravo," he clapped. "Good for you."

She was done, scooting back, vaulting to her feet.

"What happened at Sunnydale?" he posed the question a second before she slammed the phone down.

Her head yanked up. She wobbled, sinking into the grimy chair, pressing the receiver to her ear. "How do you...? It's a treatment center on the Suncoast."

"It's a psychiatric ward," he corrected. "Where you were sent to be institutionalized."

"What? I was never there for that!"

"You were taking in the scenery?"

"How do you know about this?"

"You said you had told us all your secrets, Kay. Did you forget about that one?"

"There was nothing to talk about. I had a therapy session there one time!"

"Yeah, only once—because your dad wouldn't commit you."

"Because I didn't need to be!"

"No? Even though you had borderline psychosis, anxiety, suicidal ideation, depression, stress, and a bunch of other psychotic symptoms. Am I leaving anything out?"

The recast of her face, the same gray tinge as when she'd figured out her friends had killed Anderson. "How did you get this information?!"

"I'm resourceful. If I can't find out something I want to know about someone? I got people who can." Raymo impersonated the mobster Vittorio Manalese from the movie *The Sicilian Clan*.

Of course, he could. "My records were confidential. You had no right! And what you said about my mental state? You're wrong. It wasn't like that."

"No? You were traumatized by your mom and brother's death, a lonely little outcast with no friends. So daddy takes you in for some good ol' psychiatric counseling. Come to find out, though; you were big time screwed up in the head."

"If anyone ever needed psychiatric counseling, it would be you."

"You know Kay; you always ragged on about how I blackmailed you, how I 'manipulated' you. But you're a skilled manipulator yourself. You got daddy twisted around your little finger, don'tcha? When you threatened your dad's new lady friend, he dropped her like a hot potato. And when he told you that you needed help, you turned on the boohooing, and he didn't make you carry through with the therapy."

Kaylen clutched the telephone, her knuckles bloodless.

"It wasn't like your mom had just died. She'd be gone for years. Your poor lonely dad wanted companionship. So he got back in the dating pool, met a nice lady. But you couldn't take it, huh, Kay? You didn't want daddy paying attention to anybody else. You wanted her gone."

"My brother passed away! I was grieving; I wanted my dad's comfort. But, instead, he turned to a woman he barely knew."

"He wasn't there for you. Again. He put his job first. Then it was his lady friend, right?"

Lane sprung from his seat, pacing, pivoting away, unable to bear the pain on Kaylen's face, sticking his nose in the corner like a child given time out.

"What did you tell daddy, huh? That you'd take a razor to your wrists if he kept seeing her? And if that didn't work, you'd slice her throat?" Raymo asked.

"I didn't mean it. It was said in anger. Everyone says stuff that they don't mean."

"True. Except you were going to make good on it, right? Isn't that how your dad found out? Your diary?"

"Journal. My musings. It didn't mean anything! Fantasies, nothing more."

"It was your manifesto."

Kaylen gave a sarcastic snort. "Sure. Along with the ciphers I included—like the Zodiac Killer, right?"

"Your dad took it seriously enough he tried to get you help."

"I never needed help. It was a ploy; I knew Dad would see the journal. I wanted him to eighty-six the girlfriend. I know now it was foolish and childish. I didn't know he'd force me to go to counseling!"

"You played it off. You got daddy to give up his new squeeze and got yourself out of therapy too."

"My dad saw right through the psychiatrist. After that, she was all about the money, the long, lengthy sessions she could milk."

"No, that's what your dad told you. He might have wanted to get you help, but he didn't want you sent away either. You were all he had left. Funny thing about that, though—in the end, it all came out the same. You did get sent away. Here you sit in jail for killing my cousin."

"All that neuropsychiatric mumbo-jumbo my therapist said I had? Not true. I was depressed. That much she got right."

"You know what else she got right, Kay-Kay? Your abandonment sensitivity. Classic borderline psychosis triggers—fear of rejection and abandonment. Your mother left you, and your brother left you; your dad rejected you for a new girlfriend."

Kaylen shook her head, her chin hitching up in denial... but Raymo spied the pulse at her neck, veracity, and anxiety like fishbones lodging in her throat.

"You wanted to belong, didn't you? To matter, to fit in. And you found it—at least for a little while, right? You found that with us, the guys."

"Until you blackmailed me. Until you—they—assaulted me!"

"All that, it came after I found out the truth about you. I got to know you and understood you were a bit off. I made it my mission to get down to the root of it. I knew you had lived over on the Florida west coast before you ever moved across from the campground. I had a few people who owed me favors. Got them to check around, see who knew you and your dad. Sunnydale? Not even on my radar. But when it surfaced, I got someone on the inside to get the lowdown, to pull your file. When I read about your abandonment issues, I used it, the thread to unravel you. It was too easy, Kay." He noted her audit of his movements—brushing invisible lint from his shoulders, yawning, cracking his neck. "You, the poor little girl who had lost everyone she loved, who wanted to belong but never asked to join, and then knowing I turned you on? It was only a matter of time before I had you where I wanted you."

"You conceited, delusional psychopath. You didn't have me at all. Your blackmail might have gotten you to the gate, but it didn't get you in! Luke was given my virginity—freely. But the same thing he got, you had to take it by force!"

His mouth widened, his nonchalance unnerving her. "How I could've ever been attracted to you, I don't know!" she said. "There was always that underlying repulsion too. Like intuitively, I knew how evil you were."

"There's degrees of evil, right, Kay? I mean, check out where you're at—a place for people like you, who've done things that are ugly, unforgivable. It's inside us, you and me—and Lane. His manifested when his girlfriend turned on him. Mine and the guys? When we had to problem-solve for Lanesy. Yours? When you had nobody left but your daddy—and then he wasn't there for you. It started with that but ended with you taking a life. You're no different than us; than anyone in here."

"You're arrogant and ignorant! You're always trying to work your angle, Raymo. You've taken my onetime therapy session and blown it up, making it seem I'm as demented as you! And this file of my supposed ailments? It's psychobabble. The doctor might have been an expert, but she knew me less than an hour, not long enough to make a comprehensive psychiatric diagnosis."

"No, she pegged it. I'm no psychiatrist, but I'm a study of people. It must have been hard for you with your fear of abandonment, Luke's tomcatting with other girls. To always be under threat that he could leave you for someone else. Am I right?"

She bit her lip, squelching the scream, incising blood.

"I let that work for me. Then, finally, Luke and I agreed we hadn't had that much fun since torturing Lanesy with the whole Tammy thing."

Her cheeks were hollowed, her mouth an oval—the same as when Luke had hit her.

"Luke and me. We had a contest," Raymo divulged.

"Yeah, the contest. I know all about the *una botta e via'* contest. You and the guys."

"No, not *that* contest. The one between Luke and me. The one *only we* knew about."

"Y'all know everything about each other, every secret. You and Luke wouldn't have kept it from Schaffer, Bran, and Tony."

"I swear we did—in the beginning. We let it develop, play out... play you. Before you and I ever went at it for Eight Minutes, Luke and I had a bet."

"About what?"

"Not what, but who. You. Who'd end up with you? How far you'd go with us."

"Luke would never agree to that! So this is what you came here to tell me? A bald-faced lie?"

"It's true. Before you and I ever had our shooting contest? Luke and I discussed what if you lost, what we would have you do. He couldn't talk you into playing strip poker again, but he could get you in that closet. When I won our shooting competition? That afternoon after Luke and I went back to my cabin, I bet him I could get you to go to third base during Eight Minutes. He said, 'you're on.'"

She flushed, burning as if she had swallowed hot pepper, tearing up. "That's a lie!"

"It's the truth. It was a *una botta e via'* contest—but a separate one from the other guys. A competition between the Vincuzzi boys for Kaylen. We were going to tell you—after you had slept with one of us, the winner of the contest. But everything went haywire, things we didn't plan on: like those guys breaking into the office, the aftermath, and that girl who came to the campground the day you gave Luke your virginity, like her wanting to get together with both Luke and me that next day, and of course having to teach you a lesson at my cabin, then you killing Luke."

"I don't believe you. It's your head games again!"

"It *was* a head game—one designed to sway Kaylen. Everything Luke and I did—orchestrated. From the time you and I played Eight Minutes—to get you to come to my cabin and see how far I could get with you—my 'blackmailing' you."

"No. Luke would have torn you apart if he thought you were trying to get his girl!"

"Luke was getting off on it! Don't you know how much he loved competing? Do you not know he flew the freak flag? What a kink he was? We even talked about filming you at my cabin so that he could play back our action. Figured you might be too smart though and notice the hidden cameras."

"It's not true!" Kaylen shot up, muzzy, the phone in one hand and her other palm splayed against the pane, steadying herself. Then, when his hand pressed to the partition to meet hers, crosshatch to heart line, she snatched back. She could swear his fire radiated through the glass, searing her.

"It was an acting job, get it? We were feeding each other lines, setting up the scene. We were wearing you down, Kay.

Both of us telling you we were going to be your first. We were comparing notes, prepping you up. When it was time to make a move? We played rock, paper, scissors—the best out of three, that's how we picked which one of us was going to push you on it. A simple harmless game to determine a serious outcome. The night Luke came to you, and you went all the way with him? Luke's rock crushed my scissors in the end game, giving him the mission. Had he had failed to make the big event happen that night, I was going to try with you the next day."

"It can't be true." Kaylen's coloring, puke-green as the peeling walls. "Lane?"

He reclaimed his seat, rocking his body, a child self-comforting. He wouldn't meet her gaze, his chin imprinting his chest. A slow nod and his shoulders collapsed when Kaylen cried out.

"It was a bet! *I* was a bet! Nothing more than your contest? Like I was a joke!"

"You were never a joke, Kay. So we took it very seriously, trying to get you to come around."

She choked one sob, smacking her palms to her mouth to stem her hysterics.

"You were a challenge, Kay. I couldn't get enough of you. Neither could my cousin. And even though you were predictable, you also went off script—the outline Luke and I were working from. I hadn't expected you to rip my neck that night in the closet, or that you'd take up with Anderson, or that you'd turn against us that night the office got broken into. We hadn't planned on telling you about Lane and his girlfriend, but that night at the cabin... We hadn't expected we'd have to carry through that night to preserve your loyalty to us. And no one could have foreseen you'd end up shooting Luke."

Kaylen's mind churned, configuring a riddle, replaying

Luke-Kaylen, Raymo-Kaylen conversations. "You and Luke planned what happened to me at the cabin!"

"No. Tony and I had discussed it—as a way to whip you in line. Then, after those guys broke into the office and we hunted them down? When a few days later, we sent Lane to bring you to my cabin? Luke and I finally told the guys about the contest between him and me. Yeah, they were annoyed at first for us not including them, but they got over it. After all, Bran, Tony, and Schaffer have their own family secrets they don't necessarily share with the Vincuzzi boys. But they agreed our contest was a stroke of genius."

"And you never told Lane about that contest?"

"No. Not then. After. After what we did to you at the cabin. Lane was *supposed to* tell you about me and Luke's secret contest on the same night he came to your house and spilled about his girlfriend."

She peered away, her mouth compressed. "It was staged? All that at your cabin?"

"Not all of it. Yeah, me and Luke were going to give you a hard time—him pretending to be mad at you for getting involved with me; me acting like I was angry you slept with him over me. But I didn't know he was going to hit you. Maybe he was mad that you were seeing me 'behind his back,' maybe he started thinking about how you hadn't been truthful, how you had hidden your visit to Sunnydale—the event that drove Luke and me to come up with the contest in the first place—or maybe he got caught up in the moment with his acting. And we hadn't planned to tell you about Lanesy's past—we just couldn't keep it under wraps any longer. But then the way you reacted... we couldn't let you go to the cops. So we had to terminate that—and we knew how to. So when I confronted Luke that night at my cabin and told him we had to make you pay—he had no idea that Tony and I had already talked about this."

"Then Luke had to go along with what you wanted that night. It wasn't that he wanted it to happen to me. He knew that you weren't going to be talked out of it."

"Does it help you to interpret it that way?"

"That my boyfriend watched me get raped and didn't stop it? No. But at least now I know he didn't instigate it."

Lane ticced, desperate to end the talk to prevent Raymo from using his sharpened dagger—the final impaling weapon in his arsenal.

"Instigate it? No, he didn't instigate—he wanted to participate. In our party."

Calling the rape a 'party,' nearly tipped Kaylen over the brink, rose striping across each cheek, her eyes blazing like a campfire. "*That's a lie!* He wouldn't have done that! He wouldn't have said that."

"No? Like he wouldn't have had a contest with me?" Raymo snickered. "You know the reason this contest was such a great feat to pull off, Kay? Because Luke realized there was zero chemistry between you and him, but plenty between you and me. He had something to prove. When you went all the way with him instead of me—what a coupe. He had won—or so he thought."

Kaylen's head thrummed with premonition; what words would Raymo say that could kill her?

"Luke and I weren't ready to reveal yet that we'd been working together on a secret contest. So we were going to keep it from you and Lanesy a little while longer. That night at my cabin? Luke was playing his part—the boyfriend whose cousin had blackmailed his girl. But when Lane said you wanted *me* instead of *him*, wanted to sleep with me over him—it did something to him. That was no acting job—he wigged out because he knew that he was never taking home the jackpot even though he had won the bet. And when Lane's little secret came out about his old lady Tammy, and you acted like you were going to snitch about us? Luke was totally freaked out about you and me—and hadn't minded that his girl needed to be taught a lesson about loyalty."

"You understand, Kay? He wanted to punish you. Wanted us to extract retribution. But he got punished himself—because what he thought he had won? Was in reality what he had lost. I had taken over the game. There were rules I hadn't told him. Until that moment at the cabin, Luke had no idea we were going to show you what happens when someone turns against us."

Kaylen's lips trembled, her skin waxy under the flickering fluorescent lights.

"You remember how Luke stared at you, Kay? When his guys were doing his girl? His nerves got to him so bad he had to have a nicotine fix. He couldn't light his cigarette, though. His hands were shaking, and Schaffer had to do it. He wasn't flipping out because he was upset at what was happening to you. It was because I was doing to you what he couldn't."

"That's not true." Blood rushed in her ears, her puke threatened to spew.

"It's true. He couldn't have a go with you unless he blew his cover. But there'd already been too many secrets and drama coming out that night. Anyway, we only had that one shot at getting you under our authority right then and there. It couldn't wait. But Luke's chance with you could. After we were finished with you at the cabin, after Luke and I had told Lane about our contest, Luke proposed one more thing to close out our bet. He'd become obsessed with our contest, with you. I understood; I felt the same way. I wanted to keep the contest rolling, the chipping away at you. Luke said he deserved what everyone else got that night at the cabin—and he was going to get it."

"You put it in his head to go to my house the night I shot him?"

"No. All Luke's idea. He never told me he planned to go over there that night—that same night Lane came to see you and told you about his lover."

"I believed it was *you* that night. You knew that! How did you get me to think it was *you* instead of Luke?"

"I didn't get you to think anything. You're demented, Kay."

"No. Your scent that night, your voice, your aura! Not Luke's."

"What difference did it make whether you thought it was him or me? You had a gun—and you used it."

"I would have *never* fired at Luke—even after what he had done, hitting me, letting you and the guys assault me!"

"I was your target. But if Lanesy had told you that night about the contest between Luke and me, would it have made a difference? Would it have mattered to you whether you killed Luke or me?"

The probe unanswered, her thoughts like a jabbing needle. "That's why you wanted Lane to tell me that night. About the contest. So I'd be in a rage—and want to destroy Luke like I wanted to destroy you for raping me. But Lane *didn't* tell me about the contest. And you didn't know that—Luke didn't know that. And came to my house that night, encouraged by you."

"He came of his own volition, never dreaming you'd kill him that night. None of us did."

"Was he wearing your cologne? Was he doing something to make me think it was you?"

"All in your head, Kay. Delusions."

When the realization crystallized, she lost her breath. "Were you in my house that night?!"

Lane's head jerked up.

"Wouldn't that have been something? An addendum to the contest. That whoever got into your house first would be the one to do it with you? It would have been a real game-changer." Raymo's mouth quirked.

"Oh my God. You *let* him win! You threw it, making him think he had beat you. But in truth, you led him there!"

"He came on his own. I had nothing to do with it. We're talking scenarios—not realities."

In her mind's eye, it uncurls like a wrinkled blueprint she's viewed numerous times but couldn't decipher until now. "He thought he had won. You might have even congratulated him. But, instead, you stepped inside my house to razz Luke, maybe even acted like you were going to go up the staircase ahead of him. You left your scent, your essence, behind. And then you left—because that was part of the fantasy, letting Luke think he would describe it all to you later about how he had raped Kaylen. Either way, you'd get what you wanted—either you getting off on the details of how he had assaulted me or me getting him out of the way for you."

"You are one flipped-out chick. I was never there. It's all in your head, Kay. I was in my own bed, sleeping like the dead when Luke decided to come to your house, and then you picked up that gun to kill him."

"You knew that I'd never let it happen again! That I would never be raped like that again. You had to have assumed I'd arm myself."

"You changed the rules. You changed the game, Kay. No one ever expected you to be waiting with a gun."

"I had a right to protect myself!"

"That's going to be your defense? The grounds for your case to justify killing Luke?" Personally, I'd go for the insanity plea. You're borderline already."

She ejected from her seat, the phone bouncing from her

hand and banging along the edge of the cubicle. Raymo had witnessed Kaylen display various emotions before, but never like this. Her trembling lips and icy blue eyes gleamed as dark as pitch, matching the intensity of Raymo's ebony eyes, a side of her he had never seen. But Raymo knew it well from his own reflection—a stone-cold killer. He didn't doubt she would have killed him on the spot if she had a gun. As his smile crooked with the epiphany, he realized the flashpoint had pushed Kaylen over the edge...

CHAPTER TWENTY-NINE

...**R**aymo completed his account of what had transpired at the corrections facility. "She started beating on the glass with her fists, then cracking the phone against it. She called me every filthy Italian word in the book. We were speaking Itanglese the whole time. You know they record your jailhouse talks, right? Those interpreters are probably freaking out, wondering if we were plotting some jailbreak or something. She got so agitated that they practically had to peel her off the ceiling. The chick schizoed out."

"Why didn't you leave her alone, Raymo? It's over. Between you and her. Between her and us. And Luke is dead."

"That's right, Lanesy. Luke is dead. It could have been me. But, no, I'm not gonna leave her alone. And I'm not going to forget it. Can you, Lane? That night, blood all over Kaylen— *Luke's* blood! The blood that runs in your veins and mine."

"Listen, we've been waiting all afternoon to tell you something. So go ahead, Shay." Tony patted his cousin's shoulder.

Schaffer had not ventilated the whole time they had been standing there. Pale, shell-shocked—much in the same way the men looked upon learning Luke had died. "I've been drafted," he choked.

Raymo and Lane, their mouths ovalling and their brows shooting up to their hairline.

"That can't be, man," Raymo argued. "They're withdrawing troops every day! President Dickey said we're getting our guys out of 'Nam."

"Yeah? Well, our guys might be coming home, but *I've* been drafted! They notified me today."

"Wait a minute. It has to be a mistake! When they had the draft lottery back in July, your number wasn't even close. How can that be?" Raymo asked.

"The Selective Service isn't perfect—the system isn't failproof," Lane said to Schaffer. "For whatever reason, your number got called up—six months after the lottery went out and eight months ahead of time of the next lottery. But being called up doesn't mean an automatic draft."

"Don't worry. We'll figure it out. We can get you to Canada," Raymo said.

"If they do send you, more than likely it won't be on the front line. Our involvement is ending. They'd probably stick you on a base, not in combat."

"Lane, we're talking about the government! It drives the military and operates in cronyism and corruption! There's no telling where they'll place me." With his extensive knowledge regarding the politics of Vietnam and American involvement, Schaffer hadn't fathomed he'd become a player in this despicable war.

Everything had altered. Everything was changing.

"Sometimes, I can't believe it. I thought we'd always be together. All seven of us. That we'd grow old together." Bran sniffled; his green-gold eyes were misty.

"But then it all fell apart," Raymo said.

Everyone thought it, but no one addressed it. *When Raymo first went after Kaylen.*

"Everything is different." Schaffer pulled his bandana over his ears. "If they need me to testify, you think it'll keep me here? At Kaylen's trial? If they need my statement, will it keep me from being sent overseas?"

Everyone rotated toward Lane, the smartest one in the group. "I don't know. Your written and videotaped statement might be enough for them. We'll have to find out."

"If you have to be here for her trial and they continue moving the date, it could drag on forever," Tony said.

"Yeah. Like Manson's trial," Raymo said.

"It's not the same," Lane snapped.

"No? He's a murderer, and so is Kaylen. He was found guilty, and Kaylen will be too."

The men's attention spoored across the lake. At the lots adjacent to the acreage surrounding Kaylen's house, a young woman rolled out from the family's Ford Econoline. Her blond ponytail swung around her waist like a hula-hoop. She sauntered the perimeter of the property with her folks and siblings.

Lane blanched. "For a moment, I thought—"

"—me too," Schaffer admitted.

"New tenderloin coming to the neighborhood." Raymo leered.

"She is too young for you! She couldn't be more than 14, 15 years old."

"Seriously, Lane? Are you concerned about her age? You were a *lot* younger than that when you took up with Tammy Tompson." Tony said. The subject matter booted Lane's nausea, and he couldn't defend himself in light of the truth.

"Lanesy, you think Tammy was attracted to you because of

your innocence, your lack of experience? That she easily manipulated you? You think that's why Luke wanted Kaylen?" Raymo said.

"Wasn't that why *you* wanted Kaylen?" Tony said, the sole one who could get away with popping off to Raymo.

"Yes. No. More than that. The thing between Kaylen and me? Pure want. Carnal. Chemical. That heat, I can't explain it. I just know it existed. And I couldn't ignore it—and neither could she."

Lane considered it, then analogized: "Let's put it this way. Did you know that campers' common mistake is instead of dousing a fire, they try to bury it? But instead of putting it out, it will have an opposite effect—it'll continue to burn. So a fire that you try to cover will go on smoldering. And when it comes to the surface, it catches fire. It's always a shock to people when they realize that the process they used to put it out instead made it ignite. They forget that even though you can't see it, it doesn't mean it's not there. That whatever can heat, can also burn."

"Yeah. I get it, Lane. That's exactly how it is between Kay and me. Or at least that's what it was."

Bran gazed across the water at the young blonde. "Remember when we first saw Kaylen, Tone?"

"Yeah. Swimming laps right over there."

"And the first time Luke saw her, he wanted her."

"We all wanted her," Bran said. "But Luke had to have her, no matter what."

"At all costs," Lane whispered, squeezing his baby blues shut.

The wind whistled around them, and Lane could have sworn he heard Luke's voice. He gulped, darting a glance at the others, but if they heard it, they didn't admit it.

"It's colder this year than any other winter we've ever had here." Bran rubbed his arms.

"Let's go back to the cabin where it's warm." The men followed single file behind Tony down the narrow dock.

Lane tarried, peering over the placid cyan lake at the girl. She resembled Kaylen a lot, but there could only be one. No one would ever take Kaylen's place.

"You with us, Lane?" Tony called over his shoulder.

"Yes. I'll be there."

A loaded answer. A promise—from his past, for his future. Lane would sway the direction the others asked him to follow. No matter what. It's what family does, what blood brothers do. But to remind him, Raymo whirled, toe to toe with Lane, black eyes gauging bright blue. Lane nodded, Raymo, smiling, satisfied. The pair fell into step, hip to hip, fitting their strapping bodies through the narrow walkway leading away from the dock. They were conjoined. Nothing could come between them, and nothing could breach the bond of flesh and blood.

They traversed toward the end of the dock where the others waited. The quintet was moving together as one, fused shoulder-to-shoulder, the outline of their bodies blending together until you couldn't tell where one started and the other ended—shadows in the night cusping the darkness. Then, when they entered the slavering woods, it sucked them down like a mythological Cronus, like cannibals swallowing their own children.

ACKNOWLEDGMENTS

Thank you to the Running Wild Press/RIZE team, especially Lisa Kastner, for their invaluable contributions in bringing 'Campfires' to fruition. I want to extend a huge thank you to Evangeline Estropia for her gracious coordination of details and for keeping me well-informed. Special gratitude goes to Emir from Pulp Art Studios for helping me find the campfire-themed design for my jacket cover. And, of course, I must express my deep appreciation to Sandra Bush, an author and editor extraordinaire, whose patience and keen eye was instrumental in creating a polished final product.

ABOUT RIZE PRESS

RIZE publishes great stories and great writing across genres written by People of Color and other underrepresented groups. Our team consists of:

Lisa Diane Kastner, Founder and Executive Editor
Cody Sisco, Acquisitions Editor, RIZE
Benjamin White, Acquisition Editor, Running Wild
Peter A. Wright, Acquisition Editor, Running Wild
Resa Alboher, Editor
Angela Andrews, Editor
Sandra Bush, Editor
Ashley Crantas, Editor
Rebecca Dimyan, Editor
Abigail Efird, Editor
Aimee Hardy, Editor
Henry L. Herz, Editor
Cecilia Kennedy, Editor
Barbara Lockwood, Editor
Scott Schultz, Editor